DEADFALL

DEADFALL

STEPHEN WALLENFELS

HYPERION

LOS ANGELES   NEW YORK

First Edition, December 2018
10 9 8 7 6 5 4 3 2 1
FAC-020093-18299

Printed in the United States of America

This book is set in 11-pt Adobe Caslon Pro, Adderville ITC Std, ITC Zapf Dingbats Std/Monotype; CoreCircus, KG All of Me/Fontspring

Designed by Maria Elias

Library of Congress Cataloging-in-Publication Data
Names: Wallenfels, Stephen, author.
Title: Deadfall / Stephen Wallenfels.
Description: First edition. • Los Angeles ; New York : Hyperion, 2018. • Summary: Twin brothers Cory and Ty Bic, seventeen, search for an escape from criminals in the Pacific Northwest wilderness.
Identifiers: LCCN 2018005405 (print) • LCCN 2017060798 (ebook) • ISBN 9781368022767 (e-book) • ISBN 9781368014267 (hardcover)
Subjects: • CYAC: Survival—Fiction. • Wilderness areas—Fiction. • Criminals—Fiction. • Kidnapping—Fiction. • Twins—Fiction. • Brothers—Fiction. • Family problems—Fiction. • Northwest, Pacific—Fiction.
Classification: LCC PZ7.W158864 (print) • LCC PZ7.W158864 De 2018 (ebook) • DDC [Fic]—dc23
LC record available at https://lccn.loc.gov/2018005405

Reinforced binding
Visit www.hyperionteens.com

SUSTAINABLE FORESTRY INITIATIVE
Certified Sourcing
www.sfiprogram.org
SFI-00993

THIS LABEL APPLIES TO TEXT STOCK

To my brother, Mike

*"Because brothers don't let each other wander
in the dark alone."* —Jolene Perry

1

Benny Bic slammed the truck into park, killed the engine, and said, "Get out."

They were stopped dead center in the middle of a one-lane bridge spanning a deep gorge. Cory figured the metal-and-wood structure was fifty feet end to end, and judging by the rusted bolt heads and sagging cables he wondered if it dated back to the Civil War. His father knew he hated bridges, especially the old forgotten ones like this. Being up so high made his stomach feel like it was lined with ants. He glanced at his twin brother, Ty, wondered if he was in on this stop. Ty just shrugged and opened the door. They climbed out and waited next to the truck for their father to drain the last of his beer while the whispered sound of distant rapids mixed with the ticking of the truck engine behind them as it cooled.

Benny began walking to the side of the bridge and motioned for them to follow him. Ty joined him and they looked down. Cory hung back a few feet, those ants in his stomach really beginning to crawl.

"Is that Tanum Creek?" Ty asked.

"The one and only," Benny said, and lit a cigarette.

"How far to the bottom?"

"A hundred feet, more or less."

"I thought it would be smaller."

"It is where we're goin'."

"Where are we going?" Cory asked.

"Stumptown."

Ty looked at Cory. Neither one of them liked the sound of that.

"What's a Stumptown?" Ty asked.

"It's a birthday secret. But you won't ever see it unless you stop bein' a pussy and git up here. I got another secret to share first." Cory forced his feet to move an inch at a time until he stood next to Ty. Benny took a long drag on his Camel, blew the smoke out soft and slow so it drifted across Cory's face. "See the big pool almost straight down, at the bottom of that waterfall?" Cory and Ty followed his hand pointing down, spotted the pool of still water looking turquoise where it wasn't shaded by a leaning tree. Cory had to will the ants in his stomach to settle. "We used to skinny-dip in there when I was your age. We'd tie a rope to that big ol' tree and swing out to the middle. Called it the swing tree." He shook his head at the memory. "Oh man, that was some fun."

"How deep is the pool?" Ty asked.

"We never touched bottom."

Ty whistled appreciatively.

Cory asked, "Who is we?"

"Me and a coupla migrant kids named Luis and Marco Esparza. I worked the orchards with them thinning cherries and apples for two summers. They were brothers just like you two, 'cept for the twins part. And the fact that you're alive and they're not."

After a respectful silence, Ty asked, "What happened?"

"Luis died in Mexico. All his mother would say is he had an accident. Marco wouldn't tell me anything. But the orchard manager told me he got stabbed by his stepfather because he brought home the wrong kinda beer."

Cory recalled a time last fall when he tripped over a can of Benny's beer and spilled it, the liquid mixing with all the other stains on the rug. Benny roused himself from his drunken haze long enough to grumble, "You're lucky I left my knife in the truck." Cory didn't know what that meant at the time, but he did now.

Ty asked, "What about Luis's brother?"

"Marco?" Benny frowned, flicked the butt out over the void. They watched it fall till the wind caught it and blew it under the bridge. "He died down there."

Cory felt a chill run through him. He knew where Benny was going and he didn't want to hear it. He wanted to get back in the truck and drive off this bridge. But Ty, unfazed, asked, "Did he drown?"

"Hold your horses. I'm gettin' there." Benny lit another Camel. "We spent half a summer tossing rocks from this bridge, figuring out the exact right place to jump, testing how far out we needed to go. We agreed we wouldn't do it till we hit the center of the pool ten times in a row. Eight was the closest we got." He ran his hand over the outside edge of the top rail, slid it back and forth a few times, as if looking for something. Then he stopped and said, "So here's another secret I promised you. I'm the only person alive that knows about it. Now I'm sharing it with the birthday boys." He stepped back to make room. "Go on, take a look."

5

Ty glanced at Cory. Cory shook his head. Whatever it was, he didn't want any part of it. Ty moved to the place where Benny had stood. Cory tried to step back, but Benny slipped behind him. "You need to see this too." He nudged Cory forward until he stood shoulder to shoulder with his brother. A crow launched from a nearby pine tree, its caws echoing sharply against the vertical rock walls as it flew over the chasm. Still behind them, Benny said, "Now, to see it properly you're gonna have to stand up on the bottom rail, get a good grip, and lean out." Ty took a breath, hooked his fingers over the edge of the top rail, grasped the top rail, and raised a leg. Benny said, "Nope. Both of you at the same time."

"Why at the same time?" Ty asked.

"Because that's the fucking way it needs to be."

Cory was shaking. Ty looked at him and said, "Don't worry. You've got this. On three?"

All Cory could do was nod. He tasted bile rising in his throat. He started to back away, then felt Benny's hand on his spine. Benny hissed, "No pussies on this bridge." Pressed him forward into the rail.

Ty said, "One. Two. Three."

They stepped up six inches onto the bottom rail. After taking a few seconds to adjust his balance, Ty bent at his waist and leaned way out. Cory did the same although half as far, trying to ignore the yawning distance below him and the slimy sweat on his palms. Trying not to think about the warm wetness spreading across the front of his pants. Trying to focus on what he was supposed to see on the back of the handrail. It would help if tears weren't blurring his eyes.

Cory felt the pressure of Benny's hand fade until it was gone. "Okay. That's it. Now let go with one hand, then the other." Ty let go with both hands, raised them over his head. Cory pried his left hand free for three seconds, then returned it to the handrail. Benny said, "Now for the last thing. But it's the most important." Cory heard him moving, walking closer. Smelled the cigarette, felt the smoke brush warm on his neck. "You gotta spit for good luck."

Cory managed to work up some saliva. It barely drizzled out of his mouth and stuck to his chin. Ty hawked up a big one and sent it flying. Benny backed away, said, "That'll work. C'mon down and tell me what you saw." They stepped off the rail. Cory's knees collapsed and he started to fall. Ty grabbed the neck of his shirt and held him up.

Benny said, "So? Speak up, boys. Whaddya see?"

Ty said, "Three letters, but they were upside down. I think one was a W, and maybe a T?"

Benny frowned, turned to Cory. "Wipe that spit off your face, son."

Cory wiped at his face with the back of his hand.

"And? What about you?"

Cory whispered, "MBL."

"What happened to your voice?"

"Nothing."

"Did it fall off the bridge?"

After a beat, "No."

Cory saw Benny's dark eyes flick to the front of his jeans. He braced himself for the comment sure to come. Benny with those eyes steady on him said, "Then speak up like a man so the dumbass standing next to you can hear."

"I saw MBL."

Benny's face split into a smile. "Fuckin' A that's what you saw. Marco, Benny, Luis!" He leaned back against the truck, regarded the brothers. Cory watched his eyes play over them, narrow for a moment, no doubt weighing the contrast between the two: Ty an inch taller than his brother, lean and wiry like his old man and a fighter to his core, and Cory with his hands crossed in front of his zipper, softer by thirty pounds, not an ounce of it muscle, with his father's black hair but his mother's full lips and dirt-brown eyes. Benny said, "I climbed over the edge one night with some braided baling twine tied around my waist. Marco held the twine and Luis held the flashlight. I carved those letters into that rail with this." Benny reached into his jeans pocket and came out with his red Swiss Army knife, the one with a broken tip he always had with him and went into a rage once when he thought Ty had lost it. "You were looking at the spot where we were supposed to jump." He took a long final pull on his cigarette, stomped it out with the toe of his hiking boot. He walked around the truck, climbed in, and cranked the engine. "Let's go, birthday boys. It's time we head on up to Stumptown!"

Cory slid into the front seat, followed by Ty. As they rattled off the bridge and Cory could finally draw a decent breath, Ty said, "I guess Marco missed the pool?"

"Nah. That weren't the problem. I heard he hit the pool just fine."

Benny popped the top to a beer, swung the truck right onto a rutted dirt road bordered on both sides by a split-rail fence. Green and gray mountains rose like a wall in the shimmering summer heat.

"So what was the problem?" Ty asked.

"He hit the swing tree first."

TANUM CREEK

NOW

2

Ty stops on the bridge even though we're way behind schedule and it's too dark to see. We step up on the rail, lean out over the void, and spit for good luck. The creek sounds louder than I remember, more like a rush than a whisper. I think about the pool, the swing tree, and am thankful for the blackness of this night. Just like we talked about, we yell, "No pussies on the bridge!" then climb back into the Volvo and leave without saying another word. He makes the right after the bridge and we head up toward the junction, this time in a heavy fog that settled in after six hours of solid rain. Icing could be a possibility higher up. We hadn't factored that into our plans.

He drives one-handed while drinking a Mountain Dew, taking the hairpins a little too fast in my opinion. Ty sees me reaching for the handle over the door. I stop and he smiles. If we'd been lucky we wouldn't be doing this part at night, but a truck fire on the interstate leaving town, a poorly stocked camping store, and piss-poor service at an IHOP (how long does it take to fill two bowls with lukewarm chili?) conspired to put us here six hours later than we wanted to be. As Benny would say, *Open a can of worms, don't be surprised when they start crawlin' out.*

The excitement of what we'd done had worn off by noon. Our agreement to not discuss it did little to stop the reality of our actions from sinking in. Just before we left pavement for the rutted gravel of the FS-101a turnoff, Ty asked me if I had any, you know, regrets? I said some, but I'd still do what we did. "Me too," he said. "It's not like we had a mountain of choices."

Although we didn't have a mountain, we did have at least two. But I didn't feel like bringing them up and he for sure didn't want to hear them. Ty found a radio station with decent country, cranked up the volume, and we drifted into our own heads to deal with whatever monsters were lurking there.

After the third hairpin, the fog gets so bad Ty has to turn on the wipers. We spin in the mud coming out of the turns and almost get stuck twice. But the Volvo is a champ and we make it through. Then on the incline just before the junction, Ty rounds a curve and something is in the middle of the road. A dark shape resolves out of the fog. It's too big to drive around on this one-lane road, the right side blocked by the forest, the left side a steep ravine leading down to Tanum Creek. The shape moves, tries to rise but can't.

"Are you shitting me?" Ty groans, rolling to a stop. He leaves the headlights on and the engine running. We put on our jackets, grab our cell phones out of the cooler, step out into the fog, and walk to the deer lying on its side in the mud. It's a buck, and a big one. He regards us with one glassy black eye leaking red. White bone sticks out from its right rear leg. Its breaths rattle out in pink foaming heaves. The eye blinks.

Ty says to the buck, "Looks like you picked the wrong night to cross the road."

Tire tracks in the mud tell us what happened. A vehicle must have come straight down from the junction on a fairly steep incline, swerving left, right, then hitting the deer and taking a sickening final swerve off the road and into the ravine just beyond us. We walk to the lip and peer down. Other than trees and rocks and tire tracks scarring the dirt, we can't see much without some light.

"You know it's down there somewhere," Ty says.

"Yeah."

"How long ago do you think this happened?"

"The tracks look pretty fresh. And the deer's still kicking. Thirty minutes?"

Ty nods. "Sounds about right. That's some steep terrain. Do you think they went all the way down to the creek?"

"Doubt it. That's a quarter mile at least. Let's turn on our phones. But don't activate location services." Once I get to the home screen I check for service, and it's exactly as I suspected. "I got nothing. You?"

"Same."

"I guess we do this old-school." Cupping my hands to my mouth, I yell, "IS ANYONE DOWN TH—"

Ty yanks my hands away, hisses, "Dude, don't do that!"

I'm stunned. "What's your problem?"

"We stole a car, remember?"

"Yeah. But that—"

"If we get involved it'll fuck up everything."

"I know. But we can't just leave. I don't see a choice here."

"I do. We drag the deer off the road and keep going. It can't be more than five miles to the trailhead."

I hesitate.

Ty says, "On a different night, yeah, we'd take a look. But not this night. We need to walk away, Cor. Stick to the plan."

The weight of his logic is crushing my resolve. I stare at the tire tracks leading down. Listen to our car idling behind us. And somewhere in the mix a deer is drawing its last rattling breaths. I hate myself for saying it, but he's right: "Let's clear the road."

We walk back to the buck. Neither one of us has the stomach to kill it, so we decide to each grab a front leg and drag it to the edge of the road on the forest side. We bend down, grab a leg. The animal struggles weakly, pain and fear registering in his eyes. "I can't do this," I say. I release the leg, walk toward the back of the Volvo.

Ty says, "Hey! What are you doing?"

"I'm going down. You can stay here, or come with. Whatever you decide is fine with me."

Ty turns off the engine but leaves the headlights on and activates the hazards. I stress about the battery draining, but Ty says we won't be gone that long 'cause there probably won't be any survivors. I hope he's right, then kick myself for thinking that way. I take my pack because it has the first aid kit, but add two water bottles, four granola bars, Ty's extra hoodie, and his sleeping bag in case there are multiple victims and I need to treat for shock. We put on our headlamps and start working our way down. The slope is too steep and slippery wet for a straight descent, so we have to do it in tight zigzags. I curse myself for not buying those trekking poles at REI. Meanwhile the fog is so thick we can't see more than fifty feet out. But the tire tracks digging into the pine needles and dirt are easy to follow. After a couple hundred yards the tracks slew sideways and end.

Ty says, "Looks like this is where it gets bad."

We keep walking, find pieces of metal and glass, big chunks of earth dug out where the vehicle landed and went airborne again. Farther down the slope our lights sweep across something big leaning against a boulder. It's a silver sedan, upside down, wheels facing out.

Ty says, "What a mess."

We run the final thirty feet. Inhale the stink of gas and oil and burning rubber. Shattered bits of glass are everywhere. I shed my pack while Ty checks out the driver's door, which is crushed inward. The window is gone. He crouches down, pokes his head inside. I run to the rear passenger window, which is also gone, and shine my headlamp inside, fully expecting to see multiple dead bodies. But the backseat is empty. I don't see anyone in the front passenger seat.

Ty says, "Nobody here. But there's plenty of blood on the airbag and the steering wheel. Oh, and there's more on the roof. Shit. There's a lot on the roof." Then, "Hey. Check it out." Ty shines his headlamp on the seat belt clip. A six-inch piece is hanging down, sliced at an angle. He says, "Looks like the driver had to cut his way out."

"Any sign of a passenger?"

"Don't see any blood. And the airbag didn't happen."

I say, "The gas smell is pretty bad back here." Then I step away from the car and throw up.

Ty knows the drill. He waits till I stop heaving, says while I'm wiping my face with my sleeve, "There's a bloody handprint outside the driver door. And a couple boot prints going that way." He points up the slope we just hiked down. "Looks to me like he didn't want to hang around here with all this gas leaking."

"I know how he feels," I say as my stomach finally settles and the surrounding trees wind down to a slow spin.

He says, "So? What're you thinking?"

"If he's bleeding as much as you say, he could be hurt pretty bad. Since we didn't see him up at the road, or on the way down, it could mean he collapsed somewhere between here and the road. With this fog it would be easy to miss him."

"Or her."

"Right. Or her."

"So? Can we go now, or do you need to search for the body?"

"Maybe we should yell first. Do you mind?"

"Go for it."

I yell, "HEY! WE'RE HERE TO HELP! WHERE ARE YOU?" We wait. Hear nothing. I yell again. Still nothing.

"Well?" Ty says.

Then I do hear something. But it's not coming from the forest. It's close by. A muffled, metallic sound. I look at Ty. "Did you hear that?"

"Hear what?"

"A sound. Kind of a clunky metal sound."

"Nope. All I heard is you yelling."

We wait a couple more seconds. The fog-drenched silence seeps in from the trees, coils in our headlamps, crawls up and over the big rock where the trunk of the car is resting. Whatever the sound was, it's gone.

"And the verdict is . . . ?"

I say, "Let's spread out. Stay about twenty feet apart and hike to the car. If we don't find the driver, then we're back to plan A."

Ty smiles. "Okay. Let's do it. But do it now. I don't want to kill the battery."

I put on my pack. Ty finds another boot print. It's about the same size as his hiking boot, so I figure the driver is our size, six foot, maybe a little more. Ty walks fifteen feet away, starts hiking up the hillside. I walk fifteen feet in the opposite direction, then head straight up, scanning the beam from my headlamp in 180-degree arcs. I walk ten steps and stop when I hear the same sound again. But this time there's no question about the source.

I call out to Ty, "Wait! I heard something."

He swings around.

I run to the car. Bang on the frame with my fist and yell while scanning the interior, "Hey! Where are you?"

By this time Ty is back. He says, "Cory. The car's empty. We checked. There's nothing—"

Then he hears it. A muffled *thump, thump.*

He looks at me, says, "Oh shit."

The sound is coming from the trunk.

3

D riving up to the junction with six miles between them and the bridge, Benny talked about hunting pheasant and chukar in those fields back in his teens and twenties before the habitat went to shit, back when he could scare up a big ol' rooster just by blinking. If he didn't have a sack of birds after an hour's time, he'd consider it a bad day. While he talked and drank and drove one-handed, Cory tried not to think about the empties clanking around in the passenger footwell every time Benny hit a bump. About how many times the truck would roll if Benny missed a hairpin and they bottomed out in Tanum Creek Canyon. But Benny kept the truck in second gear and the engine whined as they climbed out of wheat fields into scrub bushes and then pines.

At the junction Benny swung left and paralleled the canyon. He told Cory and Ty that a pheasant stew simmered in wine all day is a tasty treat, but nothing beats an elk steak grilled to perfection over a charcoal fire. He said he'd count down the days till archery season like a kid waiting on Christmas, that if you were willing to hump in some miles with a bow and be patient and endure a little suffering, then getting skunked just didn't happen. Then he slowed the truck to a near crawl, scanned the trees to his left, and said, "But there was one day in particular. One day that stands out from all the rest. It was the best hunting day of my life despite the fact that I came home empty-handed." Then he stopped, backed up twenty yards, and took a hard left through the trees onto a narrow road. The branches slapped angrily against the windshield and screeched like claws raking down both sides of the truck. Cory took this as a sure sign that where they were headed and where he wanted to be did not inhabit the same universe.

Ty said, "What's so amazing about that day?"

Benny said, "You're about to find out," and braked to a stop. They were in a circular clearing barely big enough for the truck to turn around. Straight ahead through the mud and bug smears on the windshield Cory saw two knee-high rocks and a dark gap between them hinting at a trail. What he didn't see was a bathroom, a trailhead sign, or even a garbage can.

"Where are we?" he asked.

"This here's the hunter's trailhead for Tanum Creek." Benny reached across the two of them, opened the glovebox, and pulled out his .45 with the pearl-and-bronze handle. He checked to make sure it was loaded and the safety was on, drained the beer on the dash, burped, and said, "Time for a walk in the deep, dark woods." He climbed out of the truck.

Over the sounds of Benny whistling while his bladder emptied against those rocks, Ty said to Cory, "Why do Dad's birthday presents always suck?"

After a quick snack of glazed donut holes, raisins, and Sunny Delight, Benny shrugged on his daypack and they hit the trail a few ticks shy of 9:30. Benny made a point of leaving his cell in the truck, telling them, "There's no service up here, so why carry the weight?" Before leaving, Cory asked Benny if he had a map, because on these outings he always had a map and compass and made sure they knew exactly where they were going and how to get back. But on this day Benny just took off his ball cap, tapped his forehead, and said, "It's all up here, boys. There's only me an' one other person that's seen what I'm about to show you. An' that other person, well...let's just say he's no longer a factor." He put on his cap and walked between the piss-stained rocks. "So you'd best make sure nothin' unfortunate happens to your old man."

Benny set the pace, his strong legs leading them up an overgrown trail that started out friendly enough with a slow but steady rise. They heard the creek but couldn't see it as they walked through a series of small meadows with wildflowers scenting the air and the foliage heavy with the fresh greens of early summer. While Benny pointed out mushrooms and berry bushes and named the various peaks, Cory couldn't stop thinking about what transpired at the bridge. He had hoped that since today was their sixteenth birthday and they were in the woods, Benny's favorite place to be, that the "other" Benny wouldn't show up. That he'd stay where he belonged, in the brooding shadows of their home, late at night after his shift ended at the potato-packing plant and everyone was in bed except him. But the other Benny had shown up. It wasn't for more than a minute, but that was long enough. Cory had to hike the rest of the day in wet underwear, keeping his shirt untucked so it would cover the dark spot on the front of his jeans. Benny saw that spot appear on the bridge, he was sure of it. But Benny didn't say anything. All he did was smile. And that one smile with the promise behind it worried Cory more than whatever secret Benny had lined up for them in these woods.

Ten minutes in they came to another meadow, this one larger than the other two. Benny stopped, took a hit off the silver flask he always carried with him on these outings, and pointed at a cluster of pine trees to their right. "That's where I was, in the shadow of those trees, crouched behind some bushes, bugling off and on for an hour, when it walked to the edge of the meadow right over there." Benny swung his arm 180 degrees. "The biggest bull elk I'd ever seen. Had an eight-point as wide as I am tall. Steam billowin' out of his nose like he was breathing fire. Hide all scarred, black eyes as big as my fist. I mean he was mag-*fucking*-nificient." Benny took another sip. "So I nocked an arrow and waited till he got clear of the trees. When he was a few yards beyond that blow-down he turned broadside just enough and it was like God smiled down on me. I pulled an' let 'er fly." He frowned at the memory. "Unfortunately it took a step at that very second. The arrow struck him true, but three inches left of where I intended. I knew it missed the lungs. He took off like a shot, headed north toward the creek. I waited where I was, hoping he'd lie down somewhere close and bleed out. But a warrior like that, I knew I was in for a march. After thirty minutes I set out to find him." Benny capped and pocketed his flask. "Well, let's go," and left the trail to make his way across the meadow.

"Where are you going?" Ty asked.

"Where are *we* going," Benny corrected. "We're gonna follow the blood trail."

"Blood trail? But it's been, like, *fourteen years*. It'll be gone by now."

Benny tapped his head. "Up here it's like yesterday."

"For how far?" Ty asked.

Benny stopped, turned to face them. "Don't matter how far. You boys've been yankin' my chain to take you hunting. Well, here we are. Consider this your introductory lesson." He started walking again.

Ty said to Cory, "Does he seem a little stranger than normal to you?"

Cory thought about that smile on the bridge, the hint of dark behind it. "Not so much," he said.

They stepped off the trail and waded through meadow grass, the mud sucking at their boots and bugs rising up in amorphous black clouds as they passed.

A couple hundred yards after the meadow the terrain sloped moderately down to the creek. Like Benny promised at the bridge, the flow of the water was much lighter up here. Twenty feet bank to bank, small hip-deep pools, ripples not rapids bending around big mossy rocks, and plenty of places to cross if you could jump three feet and your balance was decent. Benny turned downstream, striding along the bank, not saying a lot except to point at spots here and there where a hoofprint had been or how much blood he had seen on this rock or that leaf. It was clear to Cory, listening to him go on about the elk's determination, its power and sheer will to survive, that Benny had a profound appreciation bordering on love for this animal he shot with an arrow on a quiet meadow morning years ago. Cory wished it was that easy for him. That all he had to do was take an arrow in the ribs and he could impress Benny.

They hiked down and down, following the creek and crossing it twice, for what Cory figured was a mile at least, when Benny crossed a third time and leaned back against a big angular rock. He took a long pull off the flask, lit a cigarette, watched Ty, then Cory, hop boulders to where he stood. Cory panted like a sled dog while Ty looked like he could go for another hour or two without a rest.

Benny said, pointing downstream, "Follow it that way for twelve miles and you'll come to the bridge. I wouldn't advise it unless you have a rope and balls of steel 'cause not too far from here she drops into the canyon, gets ugly fast, and stays that way. There's a couple spots that'll make you shit your pants." He smiled at Cory. "That I know for a solid fact." Then he pointed upstream. "Follow it that way for six miles an' you'll come to the source, a little pocket puddle named Two Knives Lake."

"Have you ever been up to the lake?" Ty asked.

"Once."

"Was it nice?"

"We got snowed on. In June. But I caught some fine rainbows, though. An' they were natives too. Real fighters. Not the slack-eyed stock shit you catch these days."

"You said 'we,'" Cory said. "Who was with you?"

After a deep drag on the cigarette, Benny said, "Your mom."

Cory blinked. That was the first time Benny had mentioned their mom since she left. That was 397 consecutive days of forbidding them from talking or even thinking about her. All the belongings she left behind were either sold or burned, as was the refrigerator where she spray-painted in big black letters on the door: HAVE A NICE LIFE. Cory wondered if this was an opening he could explore. Like maybe there was a crack in the wall that would let in some air. But that crack disappeared when Benny tossed his cigarette into the stream and muttered, "May she rest in pieces." Then he capped and pocketed his flask. "See this rock I'm leanin' on?"

The boys nodded.

"I call it Anvil Rock 'cause of its distinctive shape. Burn that into your brains." Benny stepped aside and pointed to three white dots on the rock. "I scratched these here twelve years ago. Remember it well, 'cause this is one of three markers I'm gonna show you. See the notch in that ridge up through those two pines?" He pointed to a jagged mountain with a ridge on the west side separated by a deep V-shaped notch. "That's Gooseneck Mountain. You two better have some legs left. This is where the elk got pissed." Benny turned and started angling up a slope toward the notch. The pitch was so steep he had to grab trees and bushes to keep from falling backward. Rocks and pieces of dirt avalanched down and dropped into the creek.

Cory swallowed hard, said, "He can't be serious."

Ty said, "I wish this freaking elk would just die already."

4

Ty climbs the boulder, pounds three times on the trunk. The person replies with three muffled thumps. Ty yells, "Hang in there. We'll get you out!" Then he says to me, "The lid is crushed against the rock. There's no way we can open it from outside. Can you get in through the backseat?"

"I'll check."

I shine my light through the rear passenger window. There are two seams where the backseat folds down. I see a gray loop that is probably the pull for the seat release, but can't reach it from where I'm standing. I have to do it from inside. The smell of the gas was bad before; now it's worse. The thought occurs to me as I crawl in through the driver's window that this whole thing could explode and I'd be trapped inside. Can't think about that now. By the time I'm all the way in, Ty is on the ground. The thumps inside the trunk are getting louder, more desperate.

I say, "Ty, shine your light on the backseat. There's a gray loop." He finds the loop, steadies his beam. The fabric is soaked. Amber drops fall in a steady stream. I crawl through the gap in the front seats, place my feet on the dash, reach up, and grab the loop. It's oily. *So the leak is coming from the trunk.* More thumps from inside.

"We're almost there," I say. "Be ready. We have to get you out through the backseat." I pull on the loop. Nothing happens. I yank again, this time down toward the roof. There's a soft click. The seatback releases. I raise it as high as I can. Ty reaches in and holds it up while I shine my light inside—and almost yack again. There are legs in jeans, ankles exposed, feet in white canvas sneakers. Two black zip ties are clamped so tight around the ankles that they're raw and bleeding. A gas can is open with its contents dripping out, soaking the jeans to mid-thigh. The legs kick, hit the can hard.

I say, "It's okay, it's okay. Relax. We're here now. I have to open the other seat. Hang on."

Ty runs around to the other side while I back out. This window is shattered but still in place. He smashes it with a rock. I pull the loop, hear the click, lift the seat. The person's head and face are covered by a black stocking cap with a single hole to breathe. A spare tire is wedged on top of the head, pressing down. The hands are double zip-tied at the wrists and, like the ankles, they're raw and bleeding. I hear a gurgling noise. It sounds like choking. Time is running out. I grab the stocking cap but can't get it off. The tire is in the way. It's wedged too tight for me to pull it out, so I push back till it's off enough for me to remove the cap. Blond hair spills out, streaked with pink. Blue eyes rimmed with red and wide in terror blink back at me. Her mouth is covered with a six-inch strip of duct tape. Blood streams from a gash on her forehead, across her cheek, and down to her throat, soaking the neck of a green sweater.

Ty says, *"What the hell?"*

I say to her, "I'm going to pull the tape off your mouth."

She nods, urgently.

"On three. One…two…three!" I rip the tape off her mouth.

Vomit sprays out, coating my face and jacket. She gasps for breath in short, rasping spasms. Then she starts shaking.

I say, "You're all right. It's over now."

I lower her out of the trunk. Pass her through the window to Ty, making sure we support her spine. He carries her away while I crawl like a crazy man.

Out of this fucking car.

5

Fifteen minutes after leaving the creek they crested the slope and the terrain eased considerably. From there Benny zigzagged twice, once at a bent tree with an X carved in the bark, and once using another landmark, this time a bare spot in the forest on the east side of Gooseneck Mountain. Then Benny finally stopped. Cory, a good fifty yards behind Ty, was thankful because he wasn't sure if he could take another step. Benny dropped his pack next to a big, burned-out stump at the bottom of a small rise. He said, "Here we are. This is your birthday present. What d'ya think?"

Cory and Ty looked around. There were some rocks, a couple rotting blowdowns, lots of pine needles and dirt. There was nothing that Cory could see to make this place remarkable enough to drive twelve hours round-trip and hike another five. It looked and felt to him like the middle of nowhere.

Ty said, "Is this where the elk died?"

"Nah. Here's where I stopped to have a smoke and ponder my options. By this time I was thinking I'd gone too far and didn't want to carry out the meat. It would've spoiled by the time I got to the truck. But I was still gonna track him, because it was getting personal."

"So why are we here?" Cory asked.

"Take one more look around," Benny said. Cory noted a shift in his tone. He seemed happy, almost giddy. Like there was a joke being told here and they didn't get it. Ty must have noticed it as well. He shot Cory a wary glance. "Now, be thorough," Benny said. "Treat it like a crime scene and you're the detectives. Take your time." He pulled the .45 out of his pack, sighted on a rock twenty yards away, and pretended to fire. Cory and Ty spent the next minute doing 360s, looking up and down. They saw nothing but trees and rocks and dirt. A squirrel chattered somewhere high; otherwise silence reigned.

Benny, with the .45 still in his hand, said, "Give up?"

The boys said, "Yes." Ty, for once, sounded unsure of himself. Cory felt his heart pound just a little harder against his ribs.

"Well, that's what I figured," Benny said. "Now I get to show you. Take a walk down to that forked tree and stop, count to ten Mississippi, then turn around."

Cory and Ty hesitated.

"Go on," Benny said. "You're not gettin' your present till you do this one last thing."

Ty said to Cory, "Let's get it over with," and started walking. Cory's feet didn't want to move. But he didn't want Ty to do this alone. He caught up to his brother and they walked together toward the tree.

Halfway there Ty whispered to Cory, "You think we should run for it?"

"Run where?"

"I don't know. Anywhere."

Cory didn't see himself getting ten feet. "We won't get very far," he said.

"Maybe. But all I have to do is run faster than you."

"Not funny."

"Anyway, I was just kidding."

"No you weren't."

They reached the tree.

"Want me to count?" Ty said.

"Sure." Cory closed his eyes. He heard a soft click behind them. His breath caught in his throat.

Ty counted, "One Mississippi...two Mississippi...three Mississippi..."

At ten they slowly turned around. Benny was gone.

6

Ty says use Benny's knife, it's in his front pocket. I cut the zip ties while she shivers and cries softly in his arms. He says to hurry, she's not getting any lighter, but I can't get a good grip on the knife. I sliced my palm on something while crawling out of the car, slicking my fingers with a steady stream of blood. Her arms are pinned behind her back, plus the dark and the fog all make the cutting that much harder. I finally get through the second piece of plastic around her wrist. It sticks to the flesh as I pull it away. She moans in pain as her arms separate. That's when I notice a definite bump below the skin midway up her left forearm. The flesh is purpling around it. I help Ty lay her down on an almost-level spot near the boulder, telling him to watch out for her left arm, it's probably broken. We're about twenty feet from a car that could explode any second. The distance doesn't feel far enough.

Ty says, "What do you need?"

"My pack."

While he fetches my pack, I turn my attention to the girl. She's about our age, maybe a little older, wearing a green sweater covered with blood and puke, and gas-soaked jeans. The jeans have a fitted, designer look. Probably expensive. Shoulder-length hair with waves and pink streaks. Her breathing has settled some and she stopped crying. But her eyes, which are tracking me, are open wide and jittery. Other than the arm, and the gash on her head that's still leaking, I don't see any serious injuries. That's amazing considering what she went through in that trunk. It could be a different story internally. I crouch next to her and say, "I'm Cory. That's Ty, my brother. What's your name?"

She blinks, opens her mouth—but no sound comes out.

"That's all right," I say. "You can tell me later." She closes her eyes, opens them again. And in that moment I get a flash of something familiar. Her eyes, her face, maybe her hair. I'm not sure what it is and the context is all wrong, but the thought startles me. I shake it off a second later when Ty returns with my pack.

He says, "You get her name?"

"Not yet."

"Yo, trunk girl. What's your name?"

She starts to shake her head. I say, "You should probably keep your head movements to a minimum, okay?" Then to Ty, "She's not ready to talk. Don't push her." I open the top of my pack, start pulling out what I need—the first aid kit, an extra pair of sweatpants, the sleeping bag. The blood from my hand gets on everything.

Ty says, "What're you doing?"

My knowledge of first aid is limited to a mandatory two-hour course at work. Lucky I didn't bail on it like Ty did. I sort through the chaos in my head and come up with a plan. "I need to treat her for shock, give her some water, splint her arm, put a bandage on that cut, and figure out a way to get her gas-soaked jeans away from those cuts on her ankles." I start to pull my sleeping bag out of its sack.

Ty grabs my arm, pulls me away from the girl. Says to me in a hot whisper, "I don't know what's going on here, but I can guess. And my guess is you've gotten us into some seriously twisted shit."

"Me? I didn't—"

"Yeah, you did. I wasn't the one that wanted to come down here. Remember? But here we are, so let's deal with it. If the driver's still alive, he's gonna come looking for her. Right?"

"Yeah."

"So I say don't worry about her injuries."

"We're not leaving her here."

"I didn't say that. What I'm saying is either she walks up to the car with us, or we carry her, or—" Ty smacks his forehead with his hand. "Shit! I forgot about the car. The lights are on. And I'm not sure if I locked it."

"Well, she's not ready yet."

"How much time do you need?"

"Five minutes."

He takes a beat. "All right. I'll hike up to the car, turn off the lights, and lock it. When I get back, we're outta here no matter what."

"I'd rather not split up."

"Do you want a dead battery?"

"No."

"Then do what you have to do. Just do it fast." He turns to leave.

I say, "Wait. Take this," and toss him Benny's knife.

Ty smiles. "This'll be perfect. If the driver is a squirrel."

He turns and disappears in the fog.

7

"He left us," Ty said. "Just like Mom."

"This isn't just like Mom," Cory said.

"You're right. She left us in a house with a broccoli casserole. He left us in the middle of the wilderness with a bag of nuts. We don't even have a map."

"Why'd he leave his pack?"

"Who knows why he does a lot of stuff?"

They walked back to the burned-out stump where Benny had dropped his pack.

Cory said, "Maybe he just went to pee."

"Like he'd care if we saw him? You know I'm right, Cor. Benny's gone."

"He didn't leave us!" Cory said, his throat tightening. "Our backs were turned for *twenty seconds*. How far can he get?"

"Far enough to leave us."

"Stop saying that. He's . . . he's still here."

"Then where is he? Huh? Show me where he is!"

"I don't know. Maybe he's hiding. And this is some kind of test."

"Stop defending him."

"I'm not defending him. I'm just saying—"

"What you're saying is such bullshit! You're always defending him. And he treats you like crap. All the time. He's constantly calling you out on your weight, makes fun of your man boobs. He knows you hate bridges. I bet he made up that whole story about jumping just to see you pee your pants."

Cory had hoped Ty didn't notice the wet spot, but knew he would. That he would use it and so many other things as a way to blame Benny for everything bad that led up to their mother leaving, and everything that had gone wrong since. "It isn't like that," he said quietly, trying hard to believe his own words.

Ty kicked the backpack. "All he cares about is his booze."

"He . . . he wouldn't leave us." Cory choked back tears. "Not on our birthday."

"Yeah he would. That's exactly what he'd do."

Cory heard the anger building in his brother's voice. Once that fuse was lit, there was no turning back. In that way especially he was just like Benny. Cory turned from Ty, faced the forest. He cupped his hands to his mouth and yelled, "Dad! Where are you?" The echoes bounced twice, faded into silence.

Ty said, "You're wasting your breath."

"No I'm not."

"Okay. Then how's this?" Ty shouted, "Hey, asshole! If this is our birthday present, we don't want it!"

More silence. Not even the squirrel chattered.

Desperate, Cory said, "Maybe he's hiding behind that rock."

"I'll bet he isn't."

Cory ran over to the rock, then to a fallen tree, then farther up the slope to another tree. His heart sledgehammered in his chest, his breath leaked out in shorter and shorter gasps. The forest shadows were closing in. Everything was closing in. He returned to the stump.

Ty said, "We might as well see what he really left us for our birthday." He crouched down, opened Benny's pack, dumped the contents in the dirt. They stared at four sandwiches wrapped in plastic, four packs of Hostess cupcakes, two cans of Pepsi, two cans of Budweiser, one book of matches, and the old grease-stained blanket Benny used when he was working on the truck. Ty shook the pack, just to make sure there was nothing left.

He said, "Happy sixteenth, bro."

Cory said nothing. He was too busy fighting back tears.

Ty smiled after a beat, put a friendly hand on Cory's shoulder. "Hey, you can have the Pepsi. I call dibs on the beer."

A voice out of nowhere said, *"If you touch those beers, I'll kill you."*

Ty spun around. Cory searched the woods. The voice was close, yet far away. Like an echo. Almost like it was coming from his head. Ty looked at Cory, his eyes wide. "Who said that?"

They heard a scratching sound coming from the stump. Benny's head appeared, followed by the rest of his body as he crawled out of the stump, stood up, and lit a cigarette. Looking at Cory through the smoke he said, "What I told you on the bridge is all fact. But"—he picked up a Budweiser and popped the top—"your brother may have a point about this asshole an' the booze."

Before he officially revealed their birthday present, Benny explained how it came to be. He had followed the elk up from the creek and decided before he walked another step it was a good time to consider his options. The temp was dropping and clouds were gathering. He expected snow within the hour, which would complicate things. Benny was beginning to think that this elk deserved to live more than he deserved to eat it. While he sat and smoked, he noticed a chipmunk running into and out of this stump. At first he just sat and admired what nature had done, grown a big fat tree up between two boulders. He said at some point it must've been hit by lightning and burned out just enough of the trunk to create a cavity in the base that grew over the years. Eventually the tree died and snapped in a storm, leaving a ten-foot hollowed-out stump. Then he saw what looked like a pretty big hole in the back of it, and upon closer examination noticed a piece of dark fabric where the chipmunk disappeared. "So I got down on my hands and knees," Benny said, demonstrating exactly what he did, "and poked my head in to see what's what. That's when I discovered this." Benny crawled in and disappeared. It was like the stump swallowed him whole. Then his hand reappeared and waved. "C'mon in," he said, "and bring all my stuff with you."

Cory couldn't believe it. He and Ty just stared, jaws limp and hanging like flaps. Benny, flanked by three lit candles on a shelf, smiled at their stunned expressions. Someone had dug a hideout into the slope behind the stump. Cory estimated it to be about twelve feet square, four feet at the front angling up to a height in back that didn't quite accommodate Benny's six-foot frame. The boys stood in the middle, Ty hunched over just a bit. The side walls were river rock mortared into place. The roof was sheets of plastic under chicken wire supported by six parallel logs notched and bolted onto vertical posts. The back wall was exposed dirt and roots, with a dug-out floor-to-roof space in the center maybe four feet wide and two feet deep with evenly spaced shelves made of thick wood planks. The shelves were stocked with a dozen or so candles, some barely burned, some melted down to stubs, a rusty handsaw, a hammer, a broken kerosene lamp, four old books, and three unopened cans with faded labels. The left rear corner was dominated by a small cast-iron stove on a brick pad with an exhaust pipe that shot up through the roof and terminated somewhere on the slope outside. The floor was made of the same rough planking as the shelves. Cory noted that whoever did this knew how to build. The planks were nailed tightly into place and looked flat, except near the stove where they had warped loose. The opening through the stump was covered with a weatherworn piece of camouflage tarp with something heavy sewn into the bottom. There were circular openings on both sides of the door near the corners lined with two-inch diameter pipe. Cory figured they served the dual purposes of viewing the outside world and providing air. The only piece of furniture was an old wooden chest with a pillowed top ravaged by critters that left their mark with all manner of droppings. In the center of it all was the only color in the place—a yellow rug. The room was quiet, still, and smelled like dirt and dust and burning candles and Benny's cigarette.

After a minute, Benny said, "You like your present?"

Still stunned, they just nodded.

"Watch this." Benny reached up through the chicken wire, slid back a piece of metal, revealed a six-inch hole lined with aluminum. Sunlight streamed in. The smoke from his cigarette spiraled in the beam and sucked up through the hole. "Pretty cool, huh?"

"Did you do this?" Ty asked.

"Me? Nah, I'm not that ambitious."

"Then who?" Cory asked, finally able to speak.

"Don't know for sure. But I can make an educated guess when he did it." Benny opened the chest, brought out an old copy of *Playboy* magazine. A blond woman was smiling and waving on the cover. He asked, "Do you know who this is?"

Both boys shook their head.

"That's none other than Marilyn Monroe. Miss December, 1953. She was on the inaugural cover. I could sell this for a chunk of change if it weren't so banged up."

"How did he do this?" Ty asked. "All the wood, that stove—it had to weigh tons."

"Probably hauled it in by horse or mule. Do enough loads over enough time and you'll get it done. Plus, a lot of it looks handcrafted from trees harvested in the area. I figure the rocks came from the creek." Benny looked around slowly, admiration glowing in his eyes. "The exhaust pipe from the stove is hidden by cement painted to look like a rock. Whoever the builder was, he was a clever sonofabitch."

Ty asked, "Why did he do it?"

"There's the million-dollar question. I've got theories, but that's all they are. Whatever the reason, it was built with the goal of disappearing for a while."

"Aren't you ever afraid he'll come back?"

"I don't consider that event likely. One of those cans on the shelf has an expiration date of June 1956. But I have a contingency plan just in case." Benny reached behind his back. "He comes through that hole, I'll introduce his forehead to this." He pulled out the .45. Cory shut out the image of what that introduction would look like. He shifted his focus to a question that had bothered him ever since they crawled through the stump.

"You've known about this place for fourteen years?"

"Yup."

"How many times have you been here?"

"A few. Not nearly enough."

Cory thought about all the outings Benny had taken them on over the years, starting when they were eight. Trips to the North Cascades of Washington down to Mount Shasta, in California, plus just about everywhere with a trail between the Oregon coast and the mountains of Idaho. And all the while Benny kept this hideout a secret—until today. It didn't make sense. "Why are you telling us now?" Cory asked.

Benny crushed out his cigarette, put the butt in the stove. Cory noticed a small pile on top of a mound of congealed ash. Benny said, "It's a matter of trust, okay? This is a big secret, the biggest one I'll ever have. A one-in-a-million thing. I didn't trust you guys before not to tell Mom. But situations have changed. I'm trusting you now."

Ty asked, "Why didn't you want Mom to know?"

"Because I have a knack for turning a good hand to shit. Got that unfortunate trait from my dad. Hopefully I didn't pass it on to you. Anyway, you never know when a man's just gotta disappear." He took a sip from his beer. "I think that elk led me here for a reason."

Cory said, "But why now? What's different?"

"I'll get there, I'll get there. But first we have a birthday to celebrate." Benny spread the blanket on the floor, sat down, and nodded for the boys to join him. He set the pearl-and-bronze-handled .45 on the blanket like a centerpiece between them. When they were seated he passed out the sandwiches, cupcakes, sodas for them, the remaining Budweiser for him. Cory thought about the Benny on the bridge, and the Benny here. He wondered how the two could live together in the same body. Not well, he decided.

"Happy sixteenth birthday," Benny said, and raised his beer for a toast.

While they ate, Benny described his plans for "Stumptown." He said they'd stock it first, starting with food that wouldn't spoil, install a door with a lock, bring up some carpentry tools, fishing gear, plastic storage bins, sleeping pads, and blankets. Make this place a proper hideout, a kickass man cave. He vowed they'd come up here for a week, eat trout from the creek, grill venison over a fire, live like fucking robbers and kings. "Now say the solemn vow," he told them, raising his beer. "Say it with me: 'We'll live like fucking robbers and kings!'" In that cool space on the floor with a single beam of light drilling down from above, three cans clanked and they repeated the vow.

There was a moment of silence.

Then Benny said, "Starting today we're starting over. This is my last beer." He drained and crushed the can. Cory wondered silently about the flask. "I'm gonna stop being that asshole I see in the mirror every morning, turn over a new leaf." He looked at Cory. "I'm sorry about the fat jokes. You are who you are. Someday you'll figure it out. And I'm sorry about scaring you on the bridge. Believe it or not, that wasn't my intent." Cory didn't believe him. Benny looked at Ty. "And you—you need to stop being like me. Get a handle on all the shit that's pissing you off. Starting with your mom. What happened between me an' her is water under a bridge."

"You hit her," Ty said.

"Yes, I did. And that's a done thing I wish I could undo."

"Then why did you hit her again?"

Benny's eyes narrowed. "There's no excuse for what I did. None. I accept that. But the fact is she's gone, we're movin' on. There's the end of that sad fucking story. You unnerstand what I'm sayin'?"

Ty after a long beat, nodded yes.

"Good." Benny took a breath, shifted his attention to Cory. "Now's the time to address that question of yours. I said I'm trusting you guys now and you asked why, what's different?"

This is it, Cory thought. *This is when the hammer falls.*

"See, trust is like a kitchen door. It's gotta swing both ways. I need to do something and I'm calling on you guys to trust me." He paused, watched them carefully. "I quit my job yesterday. I'm giving the house back to the bank."

"The *house*?" Ty said. "But where—"

Benny held up a hand. "It's being emptied as we speak."

"*Emptied?*" Ty said, his voice rising.

"Why?" Cory said. "What are you doing?"

"I'm starting a business with a friend."

"What business? What friend?"

"What and who don't matter. What matters is we're moving to Portland."

"When?" both boys asked.

"Tonight."

TANUM CREEK

8

I turn to the girl, knowing there's a lot to do and not enough time to do it. I have to prioritize. Focus on her injuries and not on what Ty said, that whoever did this to the girl will come looking for her. Hopefully the driver was badly hurt in the wreck and crawled off somewhere to die of his injuries. But I know how luck runs in the Bic clan. Odds are he's out there somewhere, making plans of his own.

I shove those unhelpful thoughts away and kneel beside her. The bleeding on her head has slowed. Good. I can focus on splinting her arm if she needs it.... Her eyes are less jittery, focused even, which is also good. Maybe shock isn't as much of a problem as I thought, although a head injury is definitely a concern. She's shivering, and that is a problem. Plus, her pants reek of gasoline. I have an extra pair but she can address that later. I decide her arm is the place to start.

I drape my sleeping bag over her upper body and legs, but leave her left arm exposed. I offer her the water bottle. She drinks nearly half the bottle. When she's finished I say, "I'm worried about that arm. Does it hurt?"

She nods, opens her mouth to speak, but again no words. Her

eyebrows gather in concern. She points. I think she's aiming at my bloody hand.

"I'll take care of that in a minute. Can you move your fingers?"

She makes a loose fist, winces. I take a closer look at the bump. It's definitely swollen, and the color, a reddish-purple, is not a good sign. There isn't time to figure it out. "This needs a splint," I say. "Can you handle that?"

She nods. Then her eyes dart past me to the woods behind.

I spin around, scan the fog with my headlamp. Nothing but shadowy trees and shifting gray. Back to her, I say, "Did you see something?"

She points to her ear.

"You heard something?"

Three quick nods.

It can't be Ty. He's only been gone a minute. He'd need at least three to reach the car and that would be flying up steep, slippery terrain in the dark. It could be a critter. Or something else. Or nothing at all. I look for a weapon. All I see is an apple-size rock a couple feet away. I lean out, grab it, set it down beside me. We just wasted thirty seconds. I say, "Tell me if you hear or see something."

She nods. And it hits me again—a flash of recognition, like I've seen her before. But there isn't time to work through the improbability of that thought. I shake my head and return to the task at hand—the splint. I look around hoping for a sturdy stick, but there isn't one nearby and I sure don't want to go out in the woods searching for one. Then I spot my foam sleeping pad. It should be stiff enough to work. I stand. Her eyes go instantly wide and she flinches back toward the boulder. *What the hell has happened to her?*

I say, "It's all right. I'm just getting something from my pack to make your splint. No one's going to hurt you." She relaxes a little, but there's something new in her eyes. A speck of doubt, maybe fear, that wasn't there ten seconds ago. She watches me the whole time, still without saying a word. I wish she'd say something. Anything. Her silence mixed with the silence around us is unnerving.

I use tape scissors from the first aid kit to cut a strip of stiff foam wide enough to support the break on both sides, then tear off two long pieces of athletic tape and stick them to my leg. I say, "Can you lift your arm so I can wrap it?" She closes her eyes and slowly raises her arm. Her body tenses under the sleeping bag. I fold up the pad, hold it in place with the tape. Then I wrap it with a compression bandage, slip the sling around her neck under her arm, and knot it. It's far from perfect but all I need to do is get her up the hill. I figure we have two minutes left. I can clean the gas out of the wounds on her ankles. Or I can do a quick sweep for internal injuries. I don't have time for both. Shit. I'm sure I missed something important, but there isn't time to get it right. She points to my hand again, which continues to bleed. I say, "That can wait till we get to the car." She shakes her head, opens her mouth, but again no sound. I look at my palm; the cut is deep and full of dirt. It needs to be cleaned before I can put a bandage on it. I'll do that in the car. She needs to get ready to move.

I say, "We need to leave as soon as Ty gets back. Can you walk?"

She hesitates, nods slowly. I help her stand, then reach down for the sleeping bag just as Ty's voice rings out of the fog. "Cory! Where are you?"

I shine my light toward the slope. "Here!"

Silence for a moment, then the thump of footsteps approaching fast. First I see his light, then Ty appears, running down through the trees. His pants and coat are streaked with fresh dirt and mud. His cap is gone. And he has blood streaming down from a cut on his left cheek.

"What happened?" I ask.

"The inside of the Volvo was trashed. There was blood on the seat and ignition switch. I was trying to start it . . . and BAM! The window next to my head explodes."

"The driver?"

"He took a swing at me with the ice ax. I barely made it out the passenger door."

I stare at him, struggling for words.

"Dude, I bought us a couple minutes by hauling ass down here. Pick up your shit. We gotta go!"

While I cram the sleeping bag into my pack, he says to the girl, "I hope you can run 'cause we're gone in thirty seconds."

She nods. I shoulder the pack and clip in. "Gone where?"

"Down to the creek, lose him when we cross at Anvil Rock, then head up to Stumptown."

"In the dark? In this fog? We'll never find it."

"We'll wait for sunup. The fog will be gone by then. Let's do this!"

We follow Ty down into the dark.

9

Cory's uneasy feeling about Stanislaus "Tirk" Tirkutala started on the drive from Stumptown to there—there being a dive motel named the Vista View in a room with two single beds and a clear shot across the street of the Adult Emporium marquee flashing LIVE! LIVE! LIVE! Cory's unease was confirmed when he saw the big man for the first time, slouched in the only chair in the room smoking a joint next to the dresser that had two six-packs of beer and a brown paper bag with a bottle in it. Tirk had a full black beard peppered gray and round Santa glasses over faded denim eyes. The round glasses should have had a softening effect and were maybe intended to do just that. Cory hoped for a hint of softness in those eyes but didn't see it when Benny introduced his friend and future business partner to the boys.

Tirk looked Cory up and down and said, "You got more of your mother in you than your brother does. Her lips, her nose."

"Her boobs," Benny said, feet up on the bed, leaning back against the headboard smoking. He studied Cory through the haze, as if waiting to be challenged on this broken promise that lasted less than half a day. Cory clenched his stomach and swallowed the pain.

Tirk smiled. "So how'd that happen, you being twins 'n' all?"

Cory said, "We're dizygotic, not monozygotic."

"The hell's that?"

"Different eggs, different sperm."

"He got her smarts too, and I suppose that's a good thing," Benny said. "But he got her metabolism. That's a bad draw for him."

"Bella got fat?" Tirk asked.

"Among other things."

Both men laughed.

Tirk offered Benny a hit from his joint. Benny waved it off. "I promised the boys this very morning that I'm turning over a new leaf. So no more weed or demon alcohol for me."

Tirk exhaled and said slowly through the cloud, "I suppose that narrows the field." He pointed his joint at Ty, who stood arms folded next to Cory, his eyes glaring out from under a hood. "Tell me about that one."

Benny said, "Ty's a different story altogether. He's been making fists ever since Bella popped him out thirty seconds after his brother. Probably explains why he's into mixed martial arts, you know, that punch-'n'-kick shit."

Tirk said, "I know what MMA is." And to Ty: "You any good?"

Ty answered with silence.

Benny said, "My friend and business partner asked you a question."

"I'm all right," Ty said.

"What do you weigh?"

"One-forty-eight."

"I woulda guessed one-fifty-five. You want to fight in cages?"

"No."

"'Cause if you do I can hook that up."

"I don't."

"You sure? Money's gonna be a little tight in your household till this business gets on its feet."

Cory felt Ty shift his weight beside him. "I'm sure."

"So what, then? You just wanna be a total badass like your dad?"

"I don't want to be like him at all."

Benny and Tirk exchanged knowing smiles.

Tirk said, "Kid, looks to me like that train's already left the depot."

Benny slid off the bed, walked to the window, pulled back the curtain, and peered across the street. His face flashed purple with reflected light from the Adult Emporium marquee. He said, "You boys get some food at the Gas Mart a few blocks down. Me an' Tirk's gotta talk about our new enterprise."

Tirk stubbed out his joint. He stood and walked to the boys. For the first time Cory was able to appreciate the hulking size and dark menace of the man. Tirk pulled a thick wad of bills out of his pocket, peeled back hundreds down to fifties, then twenties, and handed Cory a bill. "Food's on me." Cory saw as he pulled his right hand away that he was missing half of his pinkie finger.

Benny, still looking out the window, said, "Nah. We do this straight up now or not at all. Start a tab. I can pay you back for the food soon as I get a check from the estate sale."

"You're gonna need that check for other things." Tirk left the "other things" out there to hang for a while. Then, "How about we start the tab tomorrow?"

Benny turned from the window, looked Tirk hard in the eyes. "How about we don't."

"Man, you haven't changed a bit." Tirk stroked his beard for a moment, frowned like this was a sad, sad thing. "Straight up it is."

Ty said to Benny, "It's eleven forty-eight. Would this be dinner or breakfast?"

"Depends on how fast you walk," he said and tossed him the spare key. "An' take your time coming back. We may be a while."

Tirk said, "We gonna cross the street an' see if those poles are up to code?"

"I believe an inspection is overdue."

Ty said to Cory, "Let's go," and opened the door.

Tirk pulled the bottle out of the bag. Cory recognized the black label. Jack Daniel's whiskey. He hesitated.

Benny said, "What? Twenty isn't enough? How many corn dogs you plannin' to eat?"

Cory said, "Does your new business even have a name?"

Benny looked at Tirk, got the go-ahead nod. "Yeah. It's a real classic. T&B Towing."

Tirk poured an inch of whiskey into two plastic glasses. He raised one to the boys in a toast, drained it, then poured again.

Benny said to the boys, "Why the fuck are you still here?"

They walked out into the rain.

The Gas Mart was six blocks down, with its blue-and-white logo barely visible in the misting rain. They crossed a puddled two-lane street to the sidewalk under the Adult Emporium's marquee. Cory heard pulsing blues music through the blacked-out windows. He looked back to check his bearings, saw Tirk's shiny black Toyota Tundra parked next to Benny's ancient quarter-ton Chevy. The two men were silhouetted in the window of room 115, facing each other, drinking. It was the only visible movement in an otherwise empty lot.

Ty said as they walked, "How does that asshole know Mom?"

"I'm trying to figure that out."

"Is he the guy from Fresno?"

"Which guy is that?"

"The one released from prison. He was going to stay with us for a week but Mom raised such a stink that Benny told him not to come."

"Maybe. But I think he's a different friend." Cory thought about the drive from Stumptown to Motel Hell, the drive where they went west toward Portland instead of east toward the home they no longer had. Ty hadn't talked for the first two hundred miles, and when he finally did have words to say they came out like fuel on fire. He had accused Benny of hiding them from Mom, to get back at her for what she did when really it was his fault. Ty and Benny had gone at it for another hour until that storm settled into a quiet rumble.

When they stopped for gas in The Dalles, Cory asked Benny to tell them about this new business idea and how he came up with it. Benny said an old acquaintance acquired a tow truck as payment on a debt. He had called Benny and asked to help him fix it up and then wondered if he'd like to make some quick money hauling DUIs out of ditches. One thing led to another and it turned into a tow truck business. That was the short-term plan.

The long-term plan was to open a body shop, then one business would feed the other. Benny would run the tow truck operation, maybe buy another one or two trucks at auction, while his partner ran the body shop. Ty asked him how long he'd been working on that plan. Benny said he'd gotten the call last week. At which point the storm erupted again when Ty said, "So we're leaving our home and our friends for a plan that's barely a week old?" Benny said he'd spin it different, but yeah, basically that's the nutshell of it.

They'd just entered the Portland city limits when Cory asked him for the second time who this partner was. "You know of him," Benny said. "But you'll meet him soon enough and don't fret, you'll like him jus' fine."

Well, we met your partner, Cory thought as he followed Ty into the Gas Mart, *and I don't see any good coming from it.*

They ate their corn dogs plus an order of jalapeño nachos without talking while the cashier with earbuds hummed and mopped around them.

Finished with his second corn dog, Cory said, "I think I know who he is."

"Yeah?"

"Remember where Dad met Mom?"

"At a bar in Seattle."

Cory smiled. "A bar" was how the story went, but he and Ty both knew what kind of bar it was. "Do you remember who introduced them?"

"A friend of Dad's. He worked at the bar with Mom."

"He was one of the bouncers. Mom said he got jailed for almost killing a patron that was hitting on one of the girls. Dad said that's what the manager told the police, but it was really for some other thing. He never told us what that other thing was. But he did say that this guy was the biggest baddest mofo he'd ever seen, hands down. And . . ." Cory watched Ty dip a nacho into cheese. "He said this guy cut off the tip of his finger just to prove he could do it."

Ty paused, mid-dip. "Oh shit. Now I remember. He's *that* guy?"

"Yup."

After an hour and a half the clerk told them they needed to buy something or move on. With no money left, they walked back to the motel. Tirk's truck was still there. Room 115 was dark. Ty used the spare key to open the door. The TV was on, an old Western playing black and white on the screen. In the dim light they took in all the empty cans, the whiskey bottle sideways on the floor and the air still thick with smoke from cigarettes and weed. Tirk was gone, so was Benny.

Ty found a note on the toilet seat.

Don't wait up. Stay off my bed.

Ty nodded to the other bed, said, "Rock-paper-scissors?"

Cory said, "Sure."

Ty won, scissors cut paper. He pulled the bedspread off the bed and gave it to Cory.

"Do I at least get the pillow?" Cory asked.

Ty said, "Use Benny's. He doesn't deserve it."

Cory took the pillow. Turned off the TV. Realized he hadn't brushed his teeth, that all his stuff was at the home they no longer had. "We should've bought toothpaste and brushes instead of the nachos," he said.

Ty said, "Use your finger. That's what I did."

All Cory wanted to do was sleep. To put this day behind him. He lowered himself to the floor, curled up under a bedspread that smelled like cigarette butts and old sweat. He tried not to think about the crusted stains on the carpet underneath him.

Ty said, "Yo. How is it down there?"

"I can't hear you," Cory answered. "There's a cockroach in my ear."

The brothers laughed themselves to sleep.

TANUM CREEK

NOW

10

We hike in a tight line without talking, Ty in front scanning the ground with his headlamp, then the girl, then me lighting up the ground for her. The terrain below the wreck is just as steep and cluttered as it was coming down from the road. I think how impossible this would be if I was still fat. Ty leads us around rocks and over blowdowns. I've seen him play football enough to know when he's hurt, and it looks like he's favoring his left ankle. That probably happened on his mad dash down from the car. The girl's canvas sneakers are worthless on the slick pine needles and rain-soaked mud underneath. She can't afford to fall on her bad arm, so each step is carefully placed, plus there's me with the backpack that seems to catch on every branch and twig.

Meanwhile there's this nagging drumbeat in the back of my head. I can't stop thinking that I hear the driver's footsteps behind me and that I have a big red target on my back. I wonder if the mess kit in my pack could stop a bullet.

After a few minutes Ty stops at the top of a particularly steep section strewn with deadfall. His beam doesn't reach the bottom. He turns ninety degrees and, keeping his left ankle on the uphill slope, works his way down sideways, grabbing on to branches and bushes as he goes. The girl with only one good arm seems to know this part will be a problem. She turns, looks up at me, takes two cautious steps, slips on the wet pine needles, and lands on her right side. She slides a couple feet before stopping when her foot lodges against a rock. I'm afraid she'll cry out in pain, but she keeps it in. All I hear is a soft moan—it's the first sound she's made since we cut the zip ties. I walk down to her, offer my still-bleeding hand, and help her up. It's a struggle to get her up because of the steep angle. Her hand, slick with mud and still shaking from the fall, grips mine and we descend the remaining sixty feet together. Ty is waiting for us at the bottom. The slope is gentle here, almost flat. Ty starts walking, gets about four steps. There's a massive KA-THUMP!

We stop, turn around, and stare at the source. The sky is lit up by a bright orange glow rising above the trees. It reminds me of another dark night and I fight off the chill.

Ty whispers, "Was that the wreck?"

"Probably."

"Tying up loose ends?"

"Yup."

He says to the girl, "Can you move any faster?"

A beat. She nods. But it's not very convincing.

"Good. 'Cause otherwise we were gonna leave your ass."

He flashes a smile like it was a joke.

I'm not so sure.

11

Benny pulled the T&B Towing Inc. truck into the driveway of a small two-story home set back in trees and bordered on three sides by tall, dense hedges. He switched off the engine, lit a Camel, and said, "There she is, boys. What d'ya think?"

"Think about what?" Ty asked.

"Our new address."

Cory peered out the window. After two weeks in Motel Hell and three months in a one-bedroom apartment where Benny rarely slept alone, this wasn't much of an upgrade. The exterior paint was peeling so bad it looked like the home had diseased skin. A detached one-car garage at the end of the driveway had two broken windows and the front porch was one loose nail from collapsing. Everything seemed to sag or droop or lean, like the house just wanted to die. Cory didn't have a good view of the backyard, but he could see weeds littered with garbage and two mattresses stacked against a decaying green sofa. Despite its flaws, this place was bigger than their old apartment—and the odds of catching a random bullet seemed a whole lot less likely.

Ty said, "We're moving *here*?"

"You heard me."

"What high school is it?"

"Don't know, don't matter."

"We're pretty close to Jefferson," Cory said.

"*Jefferson?*" Ty said, nearly spitting the name. "Their football team isn't even ranked in the top twenty in the state."

"So you turn 'em around."

"I have a game on Friday. You can't do this to me. Not again. Coach Nelson won't—"

"I called Coach Nelson this morning. Told him he's gonna have to find a different running back."

Ty hesitated. "What did he say?"

Benny lit his cigarette and opened the door. "He said turn in your uniform or you lose your deposit."

Benny, trailing smoke, led them to the front door. He turned the knob like he knew it would open and they walked in. The stench of rotted flesh nearly dropped Cory to his knees. There was clothing scattered on the floor and draped over furniture, at least a half dozen fist-size holes in the drywall, and two bowls of mold-covered sludge on a coffee table next to a hash pipe and a *People* magazine with half the cover burned off. He wondered about the circumstances that could bring someone to leave a house in this state.

Ty said to Benny, "You're moving us into a *crack house?*"

"I've seen worse," Benny said. "Job one is to find the source of that smell. You guys check upstairs, I'll look down here. If there's a body don't mess with it till I call Tirk."

Cory and Ty climbed the stairs, Cory dreading each step. The electricity wasn't working, so the only light came from a web-clouded window at the top of the stairs. They stood on the landing for a minute, looked down a short hall with three doors in a row, the middle one closed. The rooms with open doors had two mattresses on the floor with the crumpled bedding still on them. Each room had a small closet, which they also checked. Lots of junkie trash all around, including a couple used syringes, but nothing dead other than flies on windowsills. The middle door opened to a bathroom. It reeked, but it wasn't rotting meat. Ty was about to look behind the closed shower curtain when Benny yelled up from the foot of the stairs, "Found it. Git your asses down here. I'm gonna need some help."

Benny was in the kitchen facing the oven. "Open 'er up," he said. "Take a look at what's for dinner." At first Cory thought it was a baby with a bandana around its neck. A little baby, all gray and mushy and collapsing inward. Then he saw a pointy ear and counted four legs instead of two. He almost added his vomit to the stench.

Ty said, "Is that a pig?"

"Bingo," Benny said. "A little potbellied pig." He shook his head. "Looks like someone wanted baby backs. C'mon. Let's move 'er out so we can start enjoying our fine new home."

Cory found two shovels in the garage. They wrapped the carcass in a bedsheet from upstairs and dragged it to a distant corner of the backyard. While he and Ty dug a hole deep enough to keep the skunks out, Benny headed for a shed about twenty feet from the back porch. He used a key on his chain to open a heavy-duty padlock, and closed the door behind him. Cory heard a dead bolt slam home. Benny emerged five minutes later, relocked the door, then joined the boys as Ty kicked the pig carcass into the hole. They covered it with dirt.

Benny said, "Time to go. I got places to be."

They returned to the truck, climbed inside, and Benny cranked the engine. His phone rang as he backed out of the driveway. "Yeah," Benny said. Then after a beat, "They're right here beside me." Benny pulled a K-turn on the road, headed west, and said, "Your previous tenants dumped concrete in the toilets and we found a rotting pig carcass in the oven. How's that for problems?" He listened again. "It's all provisioned like you said. We're good to go." Cory heard Tirk's barrel-deep voice on the phone, but could only make out a couple of sentence fragments. One being *up the delivery* and the other *the client expects*. After a minute of listening, Benny frowned and said, "Man, that's a big fucking change of plans!... Yeah, yeah, yeah, I'll be at the warehouse by ten.... Don't worry about me.... You... you... you just tell him to do his part, I'll do mine!" He slammed his phone on the dash, muttered something under his breath, tapped out a cigarette, and lit it.

On I-84 headed back to the apartment, Benny outlined his renovation plans for the house starting with a new oven and three beds. He'd pick up some furniture and kitchen shit at Goodwill, find a plumber to deal with the concrete in the toilets. They'd do the drywall repair and interior painting themselves. Then come spring he'd shore up the front porch, replace the rotted wood, then scrape and paint the fucker top to bottom. "Any questions?" he said.

Cory said, "If we found a body in the house, why did you want to call Tirk first?"

"Being one of his rentals, I'd expect he'd have an opinion on the subject."

Cory decided if they did find a body, Tirk's solution would be to dig a bigger hole. He said, "Just to be clear, we're renting the house from Tirk?"

"How much clearer do I need to make it?"

"For how much?"

"An' why is that your concern?"

"I'm just wondering."

"Me too," Ty said.

"Let's jus' say we have a side arrangement."

Ty said, "What kind of side arrangement?"

"My inclination is to say it's a none-of-your-damn-business kind of side arrangement. But since we're having a sharing moment an' I'm in a generous mood—this here's a rent-to-buy situation. We do the repairs, he'll apply our labor to the purchase price."

"And you trust him?" Cory said.

"You best watch that tone, son. The less you sound like your mom the better."

"But it's a shithole," Ty said. "Even the junkies bailed on it."

"Maybe on the outside. But her bones are good. We keep at it an' she'll be fixed up by Thanksgiving. Then we'll have us a feast fit for kings!"

Ty said, "Just like Stumptown. That never happened."

"We'll get there someday. I've just been busy makin' us a life."

Silence descended on them as Benny slowed for traffic. Flares closed one lane. A quarter mile later they saw a wrecked Porsche 911 sideways next to an SUV with the front end crushed. Police and ambulance lights strobed in the dimming light.

Benny said, "See. Now, that's what I'm talkin' about. Business is pickin' up. An' boys, it's about to get a shitload better."

Ty snorted. "A *shitload*?"

"In that neighborhood."

"Why? What does Tirk have you doing now?"

As they passed the two wrecks a stretcher was being loaded into the back of the ambulance. Instead of answering Ty's question, Benny said, "Like I keep sayin', praise the Lord for California drivers an' their fancy-ass cars."

There was one feature to the house that Benny hadn't mentioned. Cory didn't know why, and he preferred to keep it that way. But two blocks from their apartment, Ty said, "Want to know what I liked best about the crack house?"

Benny popped a cigarette in his mouth and lit it. "I'm listenin'."

"The shed."

Benny blew smoke against the windshield, said nothing.

Cory willed Ty to drop it there, but he knew that wouldn't happen.

Ty smiled at Benny. "I'm thinking we could stay in the shed while you remodel the house."

After a beat, Benny said, "Only one person goes in there, an' that person's me."

"What about Tirk?" Ty said.

Benny stopped at the intersection a half block before their

apartment building. He looked at Ty. "Your finger's on a button you do not wanna push. Are we clear?" He stomped on the gas.

Ty just smiled.

Benny swung into the apartment parking lot, pulled up to their spot, and drilled Ty with both eyes firing. "I said are we *FUCKIN' CLEAR?*"

"Yeah."

"Not good enough. Exactly how clear are we?"

"As a fuckin' bell."

"That's right. An' that's how she stays." His tone softened but his eyes did not. "Now I got affairs to attend to, so don't expect me till late."

"How late?" Cory asked.

"Depends on how things go. Somewhere between midnight and sunup. Can you scrape up enough dinner money for Domino's?"

"Probably."

"All right. When I get back I want all your shit packed and the place cleaned. We need the deposit money, so don't do a half-assed job. Move-out day's tomorrow."

"Tomorrow?" Ty kicked the floorboard. "But I have a game!"

"Not no more you don't."

"This is total bullsh—"

"The whining stops now! You hear me? I already gave my notice. The new renters move in on Sunday. An' that's the final word on that subject."

They climbed out. Ty slammed the door. Benny roared away.

Watching him leave, Cory said, "What warehouse was he talking about on the phone earlier?"

Ty's focus was somewhere else. His eyes, narrowed down to slits, were on the taillights as they disappeared around a corner. Cory waited with him for a minute, then softly said, "I'll call Domino's." He climbed the stairs to their second-floor apartment, keyed the door open, sat on the couch that had been his bed for too long, and surveyed the soul-sucking mess he and Ty would have to clean tonight, figured there were three Hefty bags just in empties. Cory punched up Domino's on his phone, ordered a medium cheese since there wasn't enough change for pepperoni plus a dollar tip. He saw his chemistry book on the kitchen table and thought about doing his assignment, but didn't figure there was a point. Then he felt the urge to call his mother, couldn't push it away, and scrolled down through his contacts till he found her name. Not because he didn't know her number. Because he wanted to see the contact there, make sure it hadn't been deleted like it was from Ty's phone. He hovered his thumb over the call button, but knew the result would be no different than the last twenty times he tried. Three beeps, then a message saying, *This number is no longer in service.* He put down the phone, switched on the TV and the PS4, slipped on his headphones. He was ready for virtual reality to replace the smothering truth of here and now.

When the pizza guy arrived thirty minutes later, Ty was still outside. A soft rain was falling. Ty hadn't moved an inch. Cory watched him from the window while chewing a slice of pizza, considered bringing him a slice but decided Ty had a different kind of hunger. Instead, Cory thought of the house and Benny's plans to fix it up. Yeah, there were all kinds of disappointments lining up on that horizon. With Tirk involved it could go sideways and fast. But Benny seemed determined to make it work. The thought of having his own space, a place to get away from Ty's constant training. Away from Benny's smoking, from his stumbling in at two a.m. with some drunk woman wearing too much perfume bumping into the couch and falling on him and giggling on her way to Benny's bedroom followed by thirty minutes of moaning through the wall three feet away. He was way past ready to leave all that behind. Then maybe he'd be able to have actual friends with actual names instead of toadztool and durk_sqrtr. They'd come over to play *Bloodborne* on the sixty-inch Vizio Benny said they'd get, or just hang out watching *Walking Dead* reruns on Netflix. Just do the stuff he heard other kids talk about.

But if he told Ty any of this, he would say that it was all bullshit. Like the fat jokes Benny promised would end. Or the alcohol he wouldn't drink. Or the amazing week they'd spend living like robbers and kings. *What happened to those promises, huh?* Still, the more Cory toyed with the idea, the more he allowed himself to believe this house would transform into something good for all of them. Until he thought about the shed with its beefy locks and Benny's storm of anger when Ty brought it up. That was a rabbit hole that didn't belong in his dream. He pushed it out.

Ty still hadn't moved. Cory turned away from the window, ready to make all the good bits real. An appropriate place to start would be the empties on the floor. But first there was a scourge beast at the bottom of a hidden stairway, unaware that he was about to be shredded by Cory's weapon of choice on this level: *the saw cleaver.*

Cory slipped on the headphones, paused to savor the moment, then hit resume.

12

Cory was five steps up a ladder in the living room, his freshly dipped roller spreading paint across the wall, when a vehicle roared into the driveway and all the way up to the garage. He knew by the thumping Cajun music whose truck it was. Cory climbed down the ladder a little too fast, slipped off the bottom rung, and stepped on the edge of the roller tray, spilling thick green paint on the tarp and coating his left sneaker. He righted the tray, put the roller in it. By then the heavy steps were on the deck approaching the back door. He considered making a dash upstairs to his bedroom, locking himself in and pretending to not be here. But the paint on his shoe would leave tracks. His pulse raced as the doorknob rattled. A key slipped in, the door squeaked open and closed. Heavy boots thumped on the kitchen floor; then Tirk with his massive black coat and beard passed through the walkway between the kitchen and the living room. He was trailed by a man not quite half his size, who Cory and Ty called Tweaker Teeth. Cory had seen him a half-dozen times before, always in Tirk's presence except once a few weeks ago when school was called early due to freezing rain, and he and Ty caught Benny and this man smoking in Benny's pickup. They hadn't been expecting Benny home until the following day. He had a big scratch down the side of his face. The other man smiled at them through the passenger window as they passed, revealing varying shades of brown and yellow, hence the name Tweaker Teeth.

Tirk pointed to a closed door off the living room and said, "Check there first." Tweaker Teeth went to the door, opened and closed it behind him. A few beats later Cory heard a bump, then breaking glass. Tirk walked up to Cory, nodded at his freshly coated sneaker, and asked, "What color's that?" Cory could smell the beer on him. And weed. Familiar smells. Like Tirk and Benny shared cologne from the same bottle.

"Apple meringue, apple pie," Cory said, hoping that Tirk wouldn't notice the bump under his eye and ask how it got there. "Something with apple in it."

"Looks more like puke green to me."

"That's what we told Benny."

"What'd he say?"

Cory tried to ignore the loud sounds coming from Benny's bedroom. "Something dark would hide the spackle better."

Tirk scanned the spots where the former tenants had punched holes in the drywall. "Well, he may have to rethink that plan. When it comes to hiding shit, your dad isn't as good as he thinks he is." He turned from Cory and stalked the room, moving from the Craigslist sofa, to the Goodwill recliner, to the IKEA desk, bookshelf, and lamp. Cory imagined a bear inspecting a campsite. Meanwhile the sounds from Benny's bedroom had stopped. Tirk paused in front of the new Vizio TV.

"This a sixty-inch?" he asked.

"Sixty-five."

Tirk whistled in admiration. "I only got a fifty-inch. Where'd he get it?"

"Costco."

"How much?"

"I don't know. He had a coupon for two-fifty off."

"You and your brother watch any porn on it yet?"

"No."

"Not even Skinemax?"

"We don't have cable."

"You gonna get cable?"

"Probably. Or Dish. Benny's never home on weekends to get it installed." He thought about adding *He's at the warehouse, wherever that is,* but Tweaker Teeth emerged from the bedroom holding a shoebox.

"What you got there?" Tirk asked.

"It ain't shoes," Tweaker Teeth said.

"How much?"

"Twelve hundred."

"That's all?"

Tweaker Teeth nodded.

"Check the kitchen. Don't forget the freezer."

Tweaker Teeth left with the box.

Tirk said to Cory, "Where's your brother at?"

"Upstairs," Cory lied. "In his room." He didn't want Tirk thinking that he was alone. But that's probably exactly what Tirk was thinking.

"Yeah?" Tirk picked up the remote, looked at it, frowned. "Too many buttons for my tastes. We're not flying the space shuttle, right? It's just a fucking TV." He put down the remote. "So what's Mr. Badass doing up in his room?"

"I don't know."

"Why isn't he painting too?"

"He was." Cory heard the refrigerator door open, bottles rattling, something hard hitting the floor. He said, "Can I help you with something?"

Tirk regarded Cory for a moment, looked down at his green shoe. "No. I just came by to have a chat with your dad. I thought he'd be back by now."

Tirk knew Benny was at the warehouse. And he also knew that Benny rarely returned before midnight. Yet here he stood.

Cory said, "He's still gone."

"So I guess you and I are gonna have a chat instead. Unless you want to get your brother. Then the three of us could have a chat. Or if you'd prefer"—he nodded to the stairs—"I could just go up there and chat with him myself."

Cory swallowed. "That's all right. What do you want to talk about?"

Tirk walked to the coffee table, picked up a stack of envelopes, looked at them, and dropped them to the floor one by one. He said, "What's Benny told you about the warehouse?"

"Nothing."

"Not even where it's at?"

"No." All Cory knew was when Benny returned there were pine needles on the floor mat of the truck, and his clothes made the hamper smell like wood smoke. And there was that time with the bad scratch under his right eye. He spent a lot of time in the shed the next day.

Tirk dropped the last envelope. "What's he told you about the shed?"

"We can't go in it. Ever."

"But you did anyway?"

"No."

"Has Ty?"

"No." Cory wasn't sure if that was a lie or not.

"Not even a little peek?" Tirk moved to the bookcase.

"Benny keeps it locked. And the window has that curtain."

Tirk pulled out books. The first two were Cory's favorite cookbooks, *A Taste of Tuscany* and *The Ultimate Soup*. He riffled pages and said as he dropped them to the floor, "What about your friends? They ever ask you what's in the shed?"

"We don't have any friends." At least that wasn't a lie.

Tirk looked at Cory, his eyes as dark as space. Finished with the books, he shifted his attention to the desk. Tirk swept aside Cory's chemistry homework; his notes and textbook went flying. A half-consumed glass of orange juice shattered against the wall and mixed with the fresh paint. He pulled the drawer all the way out. Dumped the contents on the floor. Peered at the bottom, the back, then dropped it. Cory heard a crack, winced at the sound. He shifted his weight, reminded himself to breathe.

Tirk moved on to the side table with a new lamp on top. "Has he let anyone into the shed?"

"No."

"You sure?"

Cory hesitated. He wondered the same thing. Ty said a couple nights ago he was getting a glass of milk at two a.m. and he saw shadows on the fence, meaning Benny was in the shed. Ty had thought he heard voices, so he opened the kitchen door and stepped out onto the deck to hear better. After about thirty seconds the voices stopped. Cory said that Benny had probably turned off the radio. Ty said no, there were two voices and they were arguing. He checked the driveway but all he saw was Benny's truck.

Tirk turned the lamp upside down and studied the base.

Cory said, "Yes. I'm sure. No one else has been in it."

Tirk dropped the lamp. It shattered. "All right." He walked to the couch. "What about the house? Any odd birds stopping by?" Tirk picked up the cushions, gave each one a squeeze, tossed them to the floor.

"Like for a chat?" Cory asked.

Tirk turned. He walked up to Cory, stopped well within reach of his thick arms. His eyes behind those Santa glasses weren't smiling. "Wanna try answering that question again?"

Cory swallowed, said, "He's been bringing a woman over. Brenda. Brenna. Something like that."

"She got an accent?"

"Yes."

"I've seen her dance. Good on a pole, better on laps. How long's he been tappin' that?"

"A couple weeks. Ever since he bought the bed."

Tirk allowed a thin smile. "I hear your dad's a good tipper." Tirk reached into his coat pocket, pulled out a pack of cigarettes. Shook one out and lit it. Tweaker Teeth returned from the kitchen with one of Benny's beers and the shoebox under his arm. Tirk looked at him. Tweaker shook his head.

Tirk turned to Cory. "Looks like we're done here."

"Looks like it."

His eyes narrowed on the side of Cory's face. "Unless you got something to add."

"No. I'm good."

Tirk reached out, put his hand with that stubby pinkie finger on Cory's head. He turned it a few degrees. "How'd you get that bump under your eye?"

"PE."

"Doing what?"

"Dodgeball."

"They tossin' pool balls in class these days?"

Cory didn't answer. Tirk leaned in a little. "Looks pretty fresh to me. You should put some ice on it. Or a piece a cold meat." He pulled back, rubbed his beard. His eyes shifted from Cory to a spot behind him on the tarp. He said, "Give me that hammer." Cory picked up the hammer, gave it to Tirk. Wished his hand didn't shake so much.

Tirk walked over to the Vizio. He spun the hammer in his hands a couple times, looked at Cory, studied him for a long moment. Then he raised his arm—and crushed the remote.

Tweaker Teeth smiled. It was a scary thing to see.

Tirk said, "Tell your dad about our chat. Let him know that next time I'll be sure he's here."

Cory watched them walk across the room, stepping over the mess on their way out, that hammer still spinning in Tirk's hand.

He stopped by the kitchen entrance, turned, and pointed the hammer at him. "My advice to you. Stop playing dodgeball. Or learn how to duck."

By the time Ty got home, Cory had finished the painting and cleaned up the wreckage from Hurricane Tirk. He asked Ty about the dojo and if he sparred with that new guy from Kenya. Ty said, "No, but it'll happen soon. I spent most of my night on the heavy bag working on kicks and combinations." Then he held up the mangled remote and asked him what happened.

"Tirk."

"What did he do? Back his truck over it by accident?"

Cory told him all about the visit. About Tweaker Teeth and the shoebox. About what Tirk said, what he did, and his fall off the ladder, which explained the green sneaker in the sink and the bump under his eye, at least as far as Ty needed to know. When Cory was finished, Ty sat beside him for a minute watching him kill an endless string of zombies.

Ty said, "All this carnage is making me hungry."

"Want me to make you a grilled cheese-and-turkey sandwich? I found a new recipe that uses mayonnaise instead of butter."

"Nah. I'll just get something from the fridge."

Ty returned with a plate of chicken wings and a beer. He sat on the couch, pointed at Cory's eye. "You didn't fall off the ladder."

"Actually, I did."

"But that's not what happened to your face."

After a beat, "No."

"Did Tirk do it?"

Cory torched a zombie, reloaded his flamethrower, smoked two more.

Ty took a hit off the beer.

Cory said, "Benny counts those, you know."

Ty said, "Do I look concerned?"

"No."

Ty watched the on-screen mayhem. Cory's fingers were a blur on the controls. After a minute Ty said, "What aren't you telling me?"

"Nothing."

"Tirk and his minion can't come in here, toss our shit around, and unload on you 'cause our dad's a total fuckup. That's just not right. I think I need to have a little chat with our bearded friend."

"No. No chats."

Ty pulled out his phone.

Cory glanced at his brother, paused the screen. "Don't."

Ty pressed a button. "Too late." He held the phone to his ear.

Cory said, "Okay, okay. It...it wasn't him."

Ty stared at his brother.

Cory said, "Tirk didn't touch me. Hang up."

Ty disconnected, pocketed his phone. "Benny?"

"Yes."

"I knew it!"

"How?"

"'Cause if it was Tirk, you'd be dead."

"Good point."

"Was he tweaking?"

Cory nodded. It was a rhetorical question. Benny always tweaked up before going to the warehouse.

"What happened?"

"Let it go, okay?" Cory pushed play. "I'm all right."

"Well, I'm not!" Ty slammed his bottle on the table. He stood, stared down at his brother. "This shit has to stop, Cor. You know why Tirk was here. Benny's skimming. He's out of control."

"He didn't hit me because of that. It was my fault this time. I told him there's a better way to—"

"Wait a minute. *This time?* It's happened before?"

Cory switched from a flamethrower to the grenade launcher. "Once. Well, actually twice."

"Why didn't you tell me?"

"I thought you'd get all pissed. Do something stupid."

"Well, you got the pissed part right."

"Sit down. You're disturbing my game chi."

"Your *game chi?* Screw that. How can you not be totally pissed?"

"Because he's under a lot of stress. But he said it's only temporary, okay? He told us six months and he'll be off Tirk's tab. Then it'll be spring break and he'd take us to Stumptown to stock it up for our summer trip. Six months, Ty. I can live with that. You should too."

Ty's phone rang. He looked at the screen. "It's Tirk."

"Don't answer."

"I should tell him to c'mon over. Put that worthless shit out of our misery."

The phone kept ringing.

"Please," Cory said.

Ty sent the call to voice mail.

Cory said, "So you gonna play in or what? I'm up to my ass in monsters here."

Ty said, "Dude, you're such a pussy sometimes."

Cory snorted. "Tell that to the legion of zombies who fear my wrath."

Ty sat down, picked up the second controller. They blasted their way through three levels, considered switching to *Black Ops II* or *Halo* because Ty knew those games better. They decided not to risk it. The better choice was to be upstairs when Benny arrived. Especially if he was in the company of Brenna Dee or Breanna Dee or whatever-the-shit stripper name she used.

Cory heard the pickup pull up to the garage. He checked his phone for the time. 1:38 a.m. He listened for a female voice, didn't hear it. Heard Benny pissing in the toilet, then the familiar sounds of him settling in for whatever he did between then and when the sun came up. After the refrigerator opened and closed, Cory counted down from fifty. Got to six and smiled in his bed when Benny roared: "Hey, dickheads! What'd ya do ta my fuckin' remote?"

13

Cory had three herb-roasted turkey recipes picked out from Foodnetwork.com, but Benny said, "My way's cheaper an' better." So instead, Thanksgiving dinner was courtesy of Costco's kitchen. Mashed potatoes with a pool of butter, presliced turkey, mystery gravy, and green beans with soggy shaved almonds that Cory picked out and piled on the side of his plate. Benny sprang for a cherry pie, which they ate on paper plates while watching *The Expendables 2*. He didn't comment on Cory's three helpings of potatoes, his second piece of pie, or the Cool Whip he piled on top. He just smoked and sat in his recliner with the footrest up and a beer in the armhole.

As soon as the credits rolled Benny turned on the light. "Stay put, I got something to show you." He left through the kitchen door and closed it behind him. They heard him opening the lock on the shed.

Ty said, "What's he doing?"

Cory said, "Like I'd know?"

"I'll bet he comes back high."

"He wouldn't. Not on Thanksgiving."

"Want to bet that last piece of pie?"

"Sure."

They heard a sound. Benny was doing something outside the door.

Cory said, "No way he could tweak up that fast."

"He could if it was coke."

"Sorry," Cory said, reaching for the pie. "This piece of flaky Costco goodness is all mine."

Benny opened the door. "C'mon out! See what I got us. This is gonna blow your minds."

Ty returned Cory's smile. "Yeah. He's flying."

Cory put the pie on Ty's plate. He said, "Save me some crust, okay?"

The twins stared in equal parts amazement and shock. Shining under the garage spotlight was the meanest, fastest, coolest, most expensive-looking motorcycle Cory had ever seen. Black as night except where the light reflected off the wheels and mirrors. On top of the seat was a helmet, black and sleek like the bike. Benny stood next to the boys, beaming ear to ear.

Ty said, "That's . . . that's a Ninja!"

"Yup. A ZX-14R. Special e-fuckin'-dition. Fastest production bike on the road."

Cory's head was spinning.

Ty said, "Is it new?"

"Cherry top ta bottom. I drove her here straight from the showroom floor." Somehow he managed to smile a little wider. "Well, not exactly straight."

Ty walked up to the bike, checked out the gauges. Squeezed the throttle. He looked at Benny. "Can I?"

"Go on. Feel what I felt."

Ty put on the helmet, straddled the bike, stretched his toes to the pavement. He leaned down low, head tucked behind the small swept-back windshield. After a few moments he sat up, removed the helmet, climbed off the bike. He looked at Cory like *It's your turn now.* Cory stayed where he was, afraid to get close and not sure why.

He asked Benny, "How much does one of these cost?"

"Not to worry. I got that covered."

"Just tell me."

"I said I got it covered."

Cory turned to Ty. "Do you know?"

"Base? Sixteen-five. But this one's tricked out."

"Bet yer ass she is," Benny said. "I had her up to one-thirty on the way home an' she was just startin' to spread 'er legs."

Cory felt the gravy coming up. He said to Benny, "Why did you do this?"

"Wazzat's s'posed to mean?" Cory noted the rapid flicker in Benny's eyes. He was more than flying. He'd had a six-pack before dinner. Then who knows how many during the movie. Plus whatever he snorted or smoked or swallowed in the shed.

"What we need is a car. Something we can drive to school. Not a...not a..."

"Crotch rocket?" Ty said. Cory couldn't tell if he was on his side, or Benny's.

"But I'm gonna teach you how to ride 'er," Benny said, his altitude still up there. "Have some father-son time up the coast. Camp out by the dunes, dig for clams, bonfires. All that bonding shit." He picked up the helmet, looked at Cory. "Every boy needs to learn how to ride a bike. An' there's no finer way ta learn than on a beast like this." He walked toward Cory, holding out the helmet.

All Cory could think about was the money. *Sixteen thousand dollars!* And Tirk spinning that hammer. He didn't want to say it, tried not to. But he saw bad things heading Benny's way.

"You need to take it back."

Benny's altitude dropped like a shot bird. "So there you go again. Talkin' like your mother. Tellin' me what I can and cannot do."

Cory stepped back. Benny followed.

Benny shook the helmet at him and said, "Put this on."

"No," Cory said. "I don't want to."

"Just put it on."

"No." He stepped back again. Benny followed, closed the distance. He saw Ty move out from behind the motorcycle.

"Put it on, you dickless fat fuck!" He slammed the helmet into Cory's chest.

Cory took the helmet, slid it over his head. He felt tears, hot and wet, forming in his eyes. The world went dark. He could barely see the bike.

Benny said, "Now sit on 'er. Feel what it's like to have somethin' under your ass other than a damn couch."

Cory couldn't move. He could barely breathe. He felt a seed of anger rising up from below the fear. He hated his father for planting it there.

Benny stepped behind Cory. Three seconds passed. Then

something hard slammed into his back. He stumbled forward, almost fell, stood up. Benny pushed him again. He roared, "I said sit on the bike, you fuckin' faggot!"

"Don't call me that!"

"Why not? It's what you are. I know it." His eyes flicked to Ty. "He knows it." Benny moved a step closer, dropped his voice to a low hiss. "No wonder your mother ran. She could smell it in your—"

Cory saw the shadow of Ty pass him, moving fast.

"You keep outta this," Benny said.

Ty said, "Don't you ever call him that again."

"This is 'tween me an' him. You know I'm right."

"So what if you are? I mean seriously, who gives a shit? And a *motorcycle*? What were you thinking?"

"Why're you takin' his side?"

Cory turned, pulled off the helmet. His hands were slick with sweat. He accidentally dropped it. It crashed on the driveway, bounced, and spun.

Benny said, "Thass a hundred-dollar helmet!"

"I'm sorry. It slip—"

Benny lunged past Ty. He swung at Cory, sank a punch deep in his gut. Cory doubled over, gasping for breath. The gravy came up, plus the cranberries and turkey. He heard a grunt, a crunch. Looked up in time to see Ty's sneaker plant a sweeping kick in Benny's face. Benny sank to the ground, his nose and lips a mush of blood.

Ty stood over him saying, "If you touch him again—*ever*—I'm not gonna stop till you're dead. That's a promise. And unlike you,

I know how to keep a promise." He walked over to the black Kawasaki Ninja ZX-14R motorcycle and kicked it. The bike fell, snapping a side mirror when it hit the pavement. Ty helped Cory walk into the house. Just before they went inside, Cory took a look back. Benny was still on his knees, bent over, shoulders heaving, blood staining the concrete under his face.

Cory was in his bedroom, sleeping on his side because it hurt too much to sleep on his back, when he felt hands grip his arm, pull him out of his bed. A voice, Ty's voice, screamed, "Get up! Get up! The shed's on fire!" A shuddering BOOM shattered his window, blew glass and flames into the room.

Then smoke. Thick black smoke that smelled like ammonia. He coughed, couldn't stop. The fire alarm downstairs started wailing. Ty pulled him out into the hall. They ran down the stairs. Cory fell the last three. Ty picked him up. He felt searing heat. Saw flames in the kitchen blackening that new linoleum. So much smoke. They stumbled past Benny's bedroom. The door was closed.

Cory said, "Get Benny!"

Ty said, "He's not there!" and pushed him toward the front door.

There was another explosion, this one bigger than the first.

They ran barefoot out the door, crossed the street, and finally stopped to stare at their home, Ty in sweats and a T-shirt, Cory shirtless in his boxers. The sky above them was an angry mix of red and orange, rising up into the black.

Ty said, "Holy shit! Dude, that was close!"

Cory suddenly remembered what Ty had said: *The shed's on fire!* He said, "What about Benny?"

Tongues of orange shot out from the upstairs windows.

A car screeched to a stop in the street. A man got out, ran toward them, cell phone pressed to his ear.

Cory said, "Ty? Where is he? Where's Dad?"

Ty turned from Cory and stared across the street. His eyes flickered with the light of a raging inferno.

14

The fire behind us fades as the sound of flowing water builds from a whisper to a rush. We come to a short steep section with very loose dirt. At the base of it, Ty sweeps his headlamp across the water. We skid down the remaining sixty feet. The girl slips twice on the way, leaving deep gouges in the dirt, but we finally reach bottom and stop at the edge of Tanum Creek.

The creek is narrower than I remember, about twenty feet bank to bank, and a lot faster. The opposite bank is just as steep and intimidating as it was sixteen months ago. I scan the creek upstream and down, hoping to see something familiar. It all looks foreign to me, except for the narrow path we're standing on that Benny showed us when we followed the blood trail. The girl is a few feet away from me, focused on the slope behind us.

I ask Ty, "Which way do we go?"

"The water is way faster than I remember. Benny said it turned into a death canyon downstream."

"So you think we're below Anvil Rock?"

"Yeah."

"Me too."

The girl grabs my arm, points. I follow her finger with my eyes. All I see are the gouges in the dirt where she fell, and above that fog and trees. "What am I looking at?"

She puts a finger to her lips, signaling to be quiet. The terror in her eyes is a visceral thing. She points again.

A weak beam of light sweeps across the trees. It doesn't belong to any of us.

"Shit," Ty hisses. He kills his headlamp. I do the same.

Darkness closes in.

He whispers, "We should split up." I barely hear him over the creek.

"No way!" I whisper back.

"Dude, he has the ice ax, and probably a gun. We're leaving tracks everywhere. She smells like gas. I'll head downstream with my light on. You guys go upstream for a ways with your light off. He'll follow me. I'll take care of him in the canyon."

"What does 'take care of him' mean?" It's a stupid question. We both know the answer.

Ty slips something into my hand. It feels like an envelope. "What's this?"

"A letter. Take her to Stumptown. Give me two days."

"Then what?"

"Read the damn letter."

"This is crazy. There's two of us. With your skills, we can take him. Let's do it here. We're not splitting up." He doesn't respond. I wait a few more seconds, then get a feeling that something isn't right. I reach out to touch him. He isn't there. "Ty?" I'm tempted to turn on my light but it's not worth the risk. The girl tugs my arm. I look up. The driver's light flashes again. The beam is bigger and brighter. He's almost at the final steep section.

Then Ty's light switches on. He's fifty feet downstream, working his way around a rock. I hear his voice—he's talking as if in a conversation. The girl tugs my arm again, hard. I have to make a decision. Now.

"Okay," I whisper. "Let's go."

We feel our way through bushes and around boulders. It's hard work for both of us since I'm dealing with a huge pack that makes a cracking sound every time it snags on a branch, and she has the bad arm. Since I have no clue how far downstream we are, I'm constantly afraid of passing Anvil Rock, plus there's the very real danger of taking a wrong step and falling into the creek. After struggling over a blowdown, I whisper, "Let's stop here."

She stops. I look and listen for signs of the driver. After a minute of nothing but the creek and our heavy breathing, I decide the risk of passing Anvil Rock is greater than the risk of being spotted. I switch on my headlamp.

She points to it, then to her head.

"You want to wear it?" I ask.

She nods.

This makes me wonder if she thinks that I'll leave her—or if she's going to leave me. Since she has yet to say *one single word* and I can't exactly read minds, I have no idea what is going on inside her head, other than the obvious plan of putting as much distance as possible between her and the driver. I have lots of questions, but now isn't the time.

As for me, my concerns are simple. It's an endless loop of hating the fact that Ty could be in trouble and I just walked away, that Anvil Rock will be easy to miss even in broad daylight, and that maybe, *just maybe*, this plan to hide out at Stumptown is, as Benny would say, born to be stupid from the start. But if she has the headlamp, that might help her move faster and trust me more. I give it to her and say, "Keep it focused on the water. We're looking for a big rock shaped like—" She takes off. "An anvil," I mutter into empty air, pretty sure that I just made another mistake.

After a few minutes of steady climbing, the steepness eases considerably and the current slows to a whispering crawl. This fits with what I remember. The trail rounds a bend and the creek widens by ten feet with a pool of nearly still water in the center. She does a quick sweep but keeps walking. I ask her to stop and do it again, only slower. I don't see what I'm looking for, but the been-here-done-that feeling won't quit. I ask her to give me the light. She hesitates, but we make the switch. I do a slow pass, linger just long for a distinctively shaped boulder to emerge from the fog.

I say, "That's Anvil Rock. This is where we cross," and light up the rocks we need to cross to get there.

She stares at me. Her unblinking eyes say I'm full of shit.

"I did this before. It's not as hard as it looks." I leave out the part that there aren't as many rocks as I remember, that they're smaller and farther apart and the water is significantly higher, maybe waist deep instead of up to my ankles. Still I'm reasonably sure it's doable, even with my pack and her bad arm. And if we do fall in, worst case it's a short walk to the other side. I have spare clothes in my pack—as long as I keep it out of the water. I say, "Staying on this side isn't an option. If your friend didn't follow—"

She slams my chest with the heel of her hand. The impact sends me stumbling backward. It takes me two steps to recover my balance. One more and I'd be on my back in the creek. Her eyes are flaming. "Why'd you do that?" I say.

All I get is stone-faced silence.

I do a rewind of the past thirty seconds. "Is it because I called the driver your friend?"

She nods. Once.

A quick glance at her wrists reminds me that less than an hour ago she was trapped in the trunk of a car, zip-tied, duct-taped, blindfolded, and soaked in gasoline. "I'm sorry," I say. "He's definitely not your friend. But we can't wait here. Our tracks will lead him right to us." She looks past me, into the darkness on the other side. But I sense a softening in her resolve. I say, "How about if I cross first, dump my pack, then come back halfway and help you?"

After a beat, she gives me a slow nod.

"There are these things called words. They're very handy. Next time I say something stupid, try using them instead of hitting me." I add a smile to show that I'm just kidding, although actually I'm not. Her eyes narrow, but at least her hand doesn't move.

I readjust her sling, making sure it's snug against her body; then I cross, drop my pack, and return to help her. She groans with every hop, and for a moment I'm afraid she's going to faint and fall in. But she recovers, clamps down on my hand, and a minute later we're standing in the same spot Ty and I stood while Benny leaned back against the rock and told us about camping at a lake with Mom. I show her the three dots Benny scratched in the face of Anvil Rock and tell her my father drew these markers about fifteen years ago, that our destination is less than a mile from here. I think I see the flicker of what could be a smile.

What I don't tell her is that the next marker is a bald spot on the side of Gooseneck Mountain, and we won't be able to see it with just the headlamp. We'll have to do that when it gets light enough to make a sighting. I don't tell her that my brother and I have only been to this place once and that was more than a year ago. That it's hard to find even if you know exactly where to look. The odds are very high that we'll just be wandering around in the woods like two deer on the opening day of hunting season. A quick glance at my phone confirms there is still no service, and that sunup is about three, maybe four, hours away. We're on zero hours of sleep. But it looks like the fog is lifting. Thank God for that. Hopefully it stays that way because if we can't see Gooseneck Mountain, then we'll be in it up to our necks. Plus, there's the X factor, her arm. I don't know what kind of pain she's dealing with; maybe she won't even be able to handle the hike. *Fuck.* I wish I knew what happened to Ty.

What I tell her is, "You'll be safe where we're going. I guarantee it."

I shoulder my pack, shine the headlamp on the steep side of the creek, and say, "Let's do this." She doesn't move. It could be the prospect of climbing that slope, but I sense it's something else.

"C'mon," I say and reach for her hand to help her across a rock. Two quick steps and we'll be there.

She yanks it away.

"What's your problem now?" I ask.

She looks at me, her expression still clouded with doubt. Maybe it's information she needs. I decide to waste a few precious seconds to explain the plan. "I can't find where we need to go in the dark. So we'll climb that hillside a little ways, then hide out a couple hours till the sun comes up. Then we'll climb to the top of a ridge, make a sighting, and head to Stumptown—that's what we call our secret spot. But I need you to trust me. Can you do that?" Her expression goes from doubt to an icy glare. *What the hell?* I'm thinking this whole thing is a big fuckup. I have to remind myself that she's been through hell and has a good reason not to trust some random guy. I say, "Look, if you're worried about me making a move on you, don't even go there. Ty and I are twins, and, well, he's . . . he's not the one that's gay." I'm stunned. It's the first time I've ever said the g-word out loud. I couldn't even say it to Stellah. All it took was a voiceless girl and a psycho killer to pull it out of me. Yet she still looks unconvinced. I smile, hoping that it masks the fear in my voice. "You have no clue how hard it was for me to say that." After a long beat she gives a faint nod. I say, "Perfect," and shine my light on the steep hillside. "Can you handle that with your arm?"

She looks at her sling, adjusts the angle a little, and winces. Takes a breath, points to the headlamp.

I give her the lamp, reach for her hand to help her across the rocks. She pulls it away. Yup, there is definitely something different about her. She does three quick hops to the other side. Her balance is perfect. I'm afraid that she's going to start climbing without me and I'll have to cross in the dark. But she shines the light back at me. On the last jump my muddy boot slips and down I go. Luckily the water isn't deep. My right leg gets soaked up to the calf.

She frowns at my clumsiness, scans the slope, and starts climbing.

15

Ty said, "I've answered that question already, like twenty times."

Detective Ostrander leaned his bulky frame onto the metal table separating him from Ty and Cory. He leveled his gray eyes at Ty and said, "True. But you didn't answer it for me."

"Which part of *our father just died in an inferno* is confusing you?"

"The part where he was cooking meth in a shed and the door was locked. From the outside."

Cory looked at Ty, stunned. "It was?"

Ty shrugged. "Could be. I was kinda busy."

"Maybe this will get your memory juices flowing." Detective Ostrander slipped a full-page black-and-white photo out of a file folder in front of him. He pushed it midway across the table. It stopped next to a box full of donuts that a female officer named Benitez brought two hours ago along with clothes and sneakers for both of them. The T-shirt barely covered Cory's gut and smelled like it came out of someone's locker. Ty glanced at the photo, gave it to Cory. The photo had two halves. The top half showed what remained of the shed. The image sickened Cory, thinking about his father trapped in all that heat. Nothing was left except the blackened propane stove on its side and the mini fridge that was partially melted. Luckily there was no body, at least from what he could see in the charred rubble. The bottom image was a close-up of what had to be the door. Cory recognized the heavy-duty lock and latch. The lock was closed. Cory wanted to believe it was a mistake, or an accident, or some other explanation that Ty would reveal very soon and end this. He pushed the image back to Detective Ostrander.

"In case you're wondering," the detective said, "those are shingles in the background. We found this part of the door on the roof of the garage." His eyes stayed fixed on Ty.

"Okay," Ty said, shifting in his seat just a little. "So it was locked. I didn't do it."

"I'm not saying you did. But neither did your father. I'm thinking you saw more than what you're saying. So let's start from the part where . . ." Detective Ostrander pulled a sheet of paper out of the folder and read, "'Ty smelled smoke and left his upstairs bedroom to investigate.'" He returned the sheet to the folder. "What exactly did you see when you went downstairs to investigate?"

Ty leaned toward Detective Ostrander and whispered, "Is this the room where you grill the bad guys?"

"No," Detective Ostrander said, sighing. "That's a different room in a different building. There are no vending machines or magazines in that room. And these chairs are more comfortable."

Cory took exception to most of what he said. The vending machine didn't vend. The newest magazine of the bunch was a *Car and Driver* from six months ago. And these folding picnic chairs, with their creaking metal frames and thin, worn-out cushions, were uncomfortable from the moment they first sat in them, which, according to the clock on the wall, was over two hours ago.

Cory couldn't check his phone for the time because it was lost in the fire—along with everything else he owned.

Ty waved at one of two ceiling cameras. "Is this interrogation being recorded?"

"It's not an interrogation," the detective said. "And yes, it is being recorded."

Ty asked Cory, "Can he do that? Legally, I mean? Record us without our permission?"

"Probably," Cory said.

"It's for your protection," the detective said.

"Do we need protection?" Cory asked.

The detective looked at him. Then without a hint of a smile, he said, "Not from me you don't."

Ty asked, "Do we need a lawyer?" He reached for a donut, took one bite, and put it back. It joined all the other donuts with just one bite. Detective Ostrander tried to smile. Maybe this offering was intended to put them at ease, but from where Cory sat, it had the opposite effect. He looked at Ty and tried to silently convey the urgent message sparking in his brain: *Stop messing with this guy.*

Giving up on the smile, the detective said, "Look. I know you guys have had a long night. I know your lives have been turned upside down. Your dad is dead. Your house is gone. And from what I've read in your files, your mom is MIA. So far no one has stepped up to take you in, other than"—he referred to another sheet in the file—"Mr. Stanislaus Tirkutala, aka Bad Beard, aka Tirk. And there is no way in hell we're going to release you into the custody of that particular individual. It's a shitty deal. I get all that. But I have a job to do, okay? My job is to catch the bad guys. Because if I don't catch the bad guys, they get to keep being bad."

Cory thought, *Did he really just say that?*

Ty looked at Cory. "I think this is where he tells us that we can do it the easy way or the hard way."

Detective Ostrander said, "I gave up on easy after the first donut." He pulled two pictures out of the file and slid them across the table. They were grainy black-and-whites of Benny at a Kawasaki dealership parking lot shaking hands with a salesman, then sitting on the very same black Ninja motorcycle that Ty kicked over last night. Cory noted the time and date stamps on the photos were 10:35 a.m. and 10:39 a.m. yesterday. Detective Ostrander studied their stunned faces for a few seconds, then said, "See, the thing is we've had our eyes on your father's business partner for three years. So when your dad shows up, we're all over his little enterprise. We knew the tow truck business was a front to launder the drug money Tirk was taking in. Since the previous help left town in a hurry, we had several conversations with your father. He eventually came around to agreeing that the best play for him was to help us cut off the head of the snake. Four days after our conversation your dad buys this motorcycle. Not a very bright thing to do. Now this motorcycle is no longer at your residence—excuse me, *former* residence. We know it was there recently because we found one of the mirrors in the driveway. Which brings us to where we are now. Sitting at this table at seven forty-five a.m. on Black Friday. Let's get this over with so we can all watch the games on TV." He attempted another smile. It lasted two seconds. "If either of you saw or heard anything outside of your statement in this report, now is the time to tell me." He turned to Cory first.

Cory's head was still spinning from this latest revelation. Benny was working with the cops? That could explain Tirk's recent visit. But what happened to the motorcycle? And why was the shed door locked? Who did it? And why wasn't Ty surprised when the detective told them it was locked? He looked at his brother, hoped for some kind of a reaction. A gesture, a smile. Tears, rage—especially rage. But nothing shook out. Ty just stared at the picture of Benny and the motorcycle without blinking. Not even once.

Cory said to Detective Ostrander, "It all happened like I said. I was sleeping. Ty woke me up. There was an explosion. We ran out of the house. There was another explosion."

"When did you find out that your father was in the shed?"

"Ty told me on the street."

"Did you try to go back?"

Cory swallowed, looked at his hands. "No."

Detective Ostrander refocused on Ty. "So it's up to you. Let's go around this block one more time. Tell me what you saw."

Without taking his eyes off the picture, Ty said, "So Benny died trying to help you?"

After a beat, "Yes."

"That means he was your snitch?"

"The correct term is confidential informant."

Ty put the picture down. He reached into the donut box and grabbed an apple fritter. It was the last remaining donut that hadn't been touched. He took a bite, put it back. Then he looked directly at Detective Ostrander and said, "Can we have some more donuts?"

Detective Ostrander stiffened, closed his eyes, opened them. Cory expected to see anger flaring, but it wasn't there. More than anything, he just looked tired. The detective shook his head, stood, and said to the camera, "I tried. Send her in." Then, to Cory and Ty, he said, "You guys are in the eye of a Cat Five shitstorm. This thing that happened last night—that's just the wind toying with the cellar door. And Ty, your priors could be a factor here. You put a kid in the hospital with your fists and that kind of history doesn't exactly paint you as the picture of innocence. So the next time you and I have a conversation, you'd better check your attitude at the door." He pulled a business card out of his jacket pocket, tossed it onto the table. "I can help, but the next move is yours. If you get a change of heart, or find Jesus, or grow a damn conscience. Whatever it takes—call me. I'm sorry about what happened. I really am. Good luck, boys." He walked out of the room.

Cory and Ty sat in silence, neither looking at the other. Thanks to what Detective Ostrander just told them, Cory was 99 percent sure that Ty was holding out on him. What he needed to know was why. He wondered if maybe Ty wanted to tell him but the opportunity hadn't presented itself. That didn't hold up under scrutiny, though. They had a few hours alone after the ride to downtown Portland, in a police car. They attempted to sleep for a couple hours on cots in a small room under small blankets. They showered in a locker room, put on their "new" clothes, and waited in these chairs for their new reality to start forming. On several occasions during brief moments of privacy, Cory had asked Ty about the fire, if he knew what happened to Benny, why he didn't come out of the shed. All Ty said was that Benny was probably too high or passed out or whatever. He said nothing about the door being locked from the outside.

Cory looked at Ty and was about to demand that he tell him the truth, no matter how bad it was, but there were voices outside the room. One of them had the barrel-chested rumbles of Detective Ostrander. The other was female, and she wasn't happy. He couldn't understand most of the words, but she clearly said *I can't do that.* The detective rumbled something that included an expletive starting with *f.* Then the voices stopped and footsteps walked away.

A few seconds later the door banged open. A woman in jeans with short curly black hair, a name badge around her neck, an open black sweater down to her knees and high black boots, stepped in.

Ty said, "Are you another detective? Because if you are, we're running low on maple bars."

Cory hissed, "Stop being an idiot."

She walked up to them and said, "My name is Stellah Deshay. I'm a caseworker with CPS." She shook their hands; her grip was firm, her smile was wide. Then in a surprisingly decent impression of Arnold Schwarzenegger, she said, "Come with me if you want to live."

16

S he told them in the hall, "You can call me Ms. Deshay if you want, although Stellah is my preference. And that's Stellah with an *h*, but it's silent and does absolutely nothing except hang out next to the *a* and confuse people. I don't know why my parents did that to me, but they did. I guess in the scope of life, that little old *h* isn't a big deal. So let's just forget it's there, okay?"

Stellah led them to a lobby-looking room with blue vinyl chairs arranged around a coffee table, and a TV on the wall tuned to ESPN. A mustached police officer with *Crandall* on his name tag sat on a stool behind a counter, looking very unhappy to be there. But he brightened when Stellah stepped up to the counter. He said, "I thought you transferred to Bend?"

"Someone with more seniority but less brains got the job," she said. "Looks like I'll be bothering you for another year. But I'm starting to like this soggy city. The rain. The gray. The coffee. It's growing on me."

"Like a toenail fungus," he grunted.

"This is Ty and Cory Bic." She handed in her name badge. "Are there any personal effects?"

He checked his computer. "Stand by," he said, and exited through a door behind the counter. He emerged thirty seconds later with a small transparent garbage bag containing miscellaneous clothes. He handed the bag to Stellah over the counter. "Probably should've tossed these. The whole room smells like smoke."

She handed the bag to Cory. Ty was focused on a football player being interviewed by a smiling blonde on ESPN. Cory felt a searing jolt of pain in his gut where Benny punched him last night. Stellah asked, "Is this everything?"

Blinking through the pain, Cory said, "That's it. Just clothes. We didn't have time to get anything else. I . . . I don't even have my phone." He realized as he said it that his phone had his mother's number. He hadn't bothered to memorize it, and now it was gone. Ty managed to snag his own phone, but he made a big deal of erasing her number on New Year's Day. And the only pictures Cory had of her and him together were on his phone, which he had stupidly not bothered to back up to the cloud. Now it was like the final strand of an unraveling rope had just snapped. And he knew with an aching certainty that his mother's face would fade into a history that was doing its best to be forgotten.

Crandall back on his stool said, "Where are you going? Without being specific."

"Somewhere with coffee."

"Detective O said nothing too close."

"He made that abundantly clear."

"But not too far."

"Sweetie, this isn't a road trip."

"You ready to roll?"

She looked at Cory and Ty, then smiled at Crandall. "I guess."

He picked up a phone, said into the handset, "Tell O the package is ready," and hung up. Cory looked at Ty to see if he was catching any of this. To see if it made sense to him. But Ty's eyes were glued to the TV. It was a commercial for a razor.

"Is all this really necessary?" Stellah asked.

"Probably not," Officer Crandall said, "but this is O's party. Last night's event really got his blood boiling. Losing his second CI in three months. That's not the kind of streak that'll help his career."

"Or the CIs," she said.

"Yeah. That too." He nodded toward Cory and Ty. "And speaking of boiling blood, what did these kids say to O? He came outta that room like someone just peed in his coffee."

Stellah said, "One too many donut jokes."

Officer Crandall smiled. "I can see that. He picked 'em up at Voodoo himself, which he never does. Said he waited through a line out the door."

A short, compact woman in street clothes walked into the lobby. She scanned Cory and Ty, her dark eyes intense and not exactly friendly. Cory noted the Kevlar vest under her open coat and the black handle of a holstered gun. Officer Crandall said, "Detective Jenkins, this is Stellah De—what's your last name again?"

"Deshay."

"Stellah Deshay from CPS. They'll be stopping for coffee—somewhere."

"We met last year in juvie court," Stellah said, shaking her hand.

"I remember," Detective Jenkins said. "I believe you called the judge a gavel-wielding blowhard. To his face. How could I forget a moment like that?"

Stellah frowned at the memory. "I left my senses at home that day." Then nodded to Cory and Ty. "So how does this work?"

"I'll follow you to your first destination. Hang out for a couple minutes to make sure you didn't pick up any unwanted attention, then if it all looks good, I'll go. From that point on they're in the wind. Unless"—and she aimed those dark eyes at Ty and Cory—"you have something helpful for Detective O. This is your last chance."

"How many last chances do we get?" Ty asked.

Cory said, "I told him everything I know."

Ty pointed to the TV. "This dude with the dreads is fulla shit. Pittsburgh's gonna beat the spread and crush Atlanta by twenty-four. You can tell him that."

Detective Jenkins said, "Are you the one that wasted O's donuts?"

Ty smiled. "Tell him thanks for getting Voodoo. That was special."

Detective Jenkins muttered to Stellah, "Good luck placing these two," and opened the door.

17

Five minutes after leaving Anvil Rock my legs turn into twin demons of screaming pain. I can't imagine doing this in her shoes and in her state. I shamelessly grab every branch and rock I can reach to keep from falling backward. She plows ahead in grim silence. One bit of good news—for some unknowable reason the ground is a little harder on this side. We aren't leaving as many tracks as we did on the trail up to Anvil Rock. That should make us a little harder to hunt. At least something is going our way.

I say, "Let's look for a place to crash."

She shines the light in a sweeping arc. Stops on a big boulder about ten feet up and twenty feet to our left. I doubt there's anywhere flat to sit, but it's big enough to hide us both from anyone climbing up from below.

"That'll work," I say, and notice that our breath is clouding in the beam of the headlamp.

We trudge up to the boulder. I shed my pack and pull out one of two water bottles. The one I leave in my pack is full. This one is down to half, minus whatever we drink tonight. That won't be enough for Stumptown. I'll risk a hike down to the creek in the morning and refill them when my legs are fresh. Before giving her the water, I dig out my first aid kit and show her the bottle of ibuprofen. She stares in disbelief, as if I had just turned a pinecone into a brick of solid gold. She extends her hand, palm up. I open the bottle and shake out three pills. She motions for more.

"It hurts that much?"

She nods at her hand.

I shake out two more.

She scowls at me, nods at her hand.

I say, "Five is enough. I'll give you more before we leave." She's not happy with that call but swallows the pills. I give her the water bottle. She washes down the IBs with a long, hearty drink. I think about pulling it away, then remind myself that I'm going to replenish the water tomorrow morning. She returns the bottle to me with two inches in the bottom. I take three big gulps and finish it. I dig out one of the sleeping bags and lay the pack next to the rock for us to sit on. She starts to bend down and I get a whiff of the gas. I say, "Wait. Do you want to change out of those jeans? I have an extra pair of sweatpants in my pack." The fierce look she gives me has no room for interpretation. I'm fine with whatever. The sooner we turn off the headlamp, the better. But I see she's starting to shiver. That could be a problem. Rather than ask her a question and risk another icy glare, I reopen the pack and snag Ty's hoodie. I show it to her and say, "You need this. I'll help you put it on." She stares at the sweatshirt. Maybe she has an issue with the logo. I say, "It's the University of Oregon. Do you have a problem with ducks?" The answer must be no because she raises her good arm. I pull the sweatshirt over her arm, head, and down over her sling, trying hard not to bump it but failing because my breath keeps fogging the light, so I can't see. He body tenses with pain and a faint squeak leaks out. For once I'm glad she can't talk.

Five minutes after stopping here, we are finally ready to put an end to this night. We sit on the pack, lean back against the cold boulder, and cover ourselves as best we can with the unzipped sleeping bag. The headlamp is starting to fade. Shit. Hopefully the batteries aren't in Ty's pack, which of course is in the Volvo. I kill the light, relieved to be invisible again. Cold air slips in around my shoulders. This better be a predawn chill and not a change in the weather. I look up through the trees. Still no stars, but the sky seems a little less black. Dawn is coming. I stare out into the darkness, willing my eyelids to stay open while I try not to think about Ty, the driver, the envelope, and the chain of wrong decisions I've made with no end in sight.

Her body shivers beside me. I'd like to put my arm around her and offer what little warmth I have. Somehow I don't see that move playing out very well.

I say, "Go ahead and sleep if you want. I'll stay awake."

Amazingly, her head slumps against my shoulder.

"I like your perfume," I whisper into her hair. "Is that premium or unleaded?"

Her body shakes once, then settles into the steady breaths of sleep.

18

The ride from Portland to that coffee shop in Stellah's Honda Fit—which smelled like dog and had nose smudges all over the windows—was slow at first thanks to hordes of Black Friday shoppers. After she merged onto I-84 and drove a couple miles east of the downtown exits, the congestion finally thinned. Cory knew the reason why she kept checking the rearview every few seconds wasn't because of the traffic—she wanted to be sure Detective Jenkins's black Ford sedan was still behind them. Every time Cory checked it was still there, a couple cars back, blending with the flow. He doubted Stellah could lose her in this tiny car even if she wanted to.

For the first fifteen minutes Stellah tried to engage them in conversation. They covered the weather (rain followed by more rain), then music (she liked blues and some jazz but hated rap, so that conversation turned lame fast), and sports (she liked hockey because her brother played). But it was hard work talking around the unseen passenger in this car. Benny's ghost had climbed into this small car and filled all the quiet spaces in Cory's skull with whispers of *You let this happen to me, you fat fuck*, and *See how the world sucks even when I'm not there to stench it up?*

Ty sat in the seat behind Stellah, his head leaned against the nose smudges, eyes closed, not saying anything the whole way until the very end, when Stellah exited in Troutdale and turned onto a small side street four blocks north of the freeway. There was an unbusy strip mall with a coffee shop named the Perfect Pot at one end, a Goodwill store with an *O* in the sign out so it read GO DWILL at the other. Cory smiled at that. He looked for a video game store but didn't see one. Not that it mattered because he didn't have enough money to buy one, not even used for a buck ninety-nine.

Ty said as she pulled into the lot, "I'm staying here."

Stellah said, "No, it's not saf—"

Ty said, "It isn't what?" Daring her to finish what she started.

She said, "We're all going inside. It's time to talk about your future."

Cory steeled himself for some kind of protest from Ty, but he just said, "Fine. Whatever. Let's talk about how much our future blows," and unbuckled his seat belt. As they followed Stellah into the Perfect Pot, Cory realized that, for the first time in his life, he didn't know where he would be sleeping at the end of the day. Then he saw Detective Jenkins's sedan back slowly into a space a few slots down from theirs and remembered her Kevlar vest and gun. And what she said: *Good luck placing these two.* The engine switched off but the driver's door didn't open. Stellah said as they entered, "You better hope they didn't sell out of the cinnamon rolls. They're the best on the planet."

Stellah was right. The cinnamon rolls were the best Cory ever had. She said the secret was the cinnamon, which they ground themselves, and a hint of sour in the dough, which they made the day before to let it rise slowly overnight. Cory noted as she talked that she spent as much time watching the door as she did looking at them. Her phone rang three times while they were sitting there. One had to be a family member because she told the caller to eat leftovers for lunch and not to let your brother feed turkey skin to Jasper. The second call was definitely Detective O since she listened for a minute, then said sharply, "I'll tell them, now let me do my job!" and hung up. The third call she just muttered, "Shit," and let it go to voice mail. When they finished the last of the rolls and started on their hot chocolates, Stellah pulled a file folder from a shoulder bag she carried in with her, laid it on the table, and said, "Before we start, do you have any questions for me?"

Ty said, "Yeah, Stellah with an *h*. Are you gonna grill me about last night too? Because if you are, we might as well leave now."

"I'm not," she said. "But let's say I did. Where would you propose we go?"

The question stopped Ty cold. Ty, who had a wiseass comeback for every question, couldn't seem to think up one place to go. Cory was surprised Ty didn't say *the street* since that seemed like the only option left.

Stellah watched him for a moment or two longer. "How about we start over? I'm Stellah. I work for Child Protective Services. My job is to remove children from a harmful situation, and place them into a safe, stable, and, if all goes well, loving environment. I've been doing that for eighteen years, twelve of which were in San Diego, then four in San Antonio, and the last two here in this rain-soaked hell. The fact that they have good coffee here is the only saving grace. I've been told that I'm very good at what I do. That's because I care about every one of my placements. Too much, my soon-to-be ex-husband says, but that's neither here nor there. In fact, I don't know why I even brought it up, so forget what I just said. You have enough on your plate—and I'm not talking about pastries." Ty and Cory exchanged pained glances. She took a careful sip of her coffee, then said, "Back to why I'm here. So when Detective Ostrander contacted us last week about your situation, I was the—"

"Hold the fort," Cory said. "Did you say *last week*?"

"Yes. We had an anonymous tip and were prepared to intervene on Friday. That triggered a phone call from Detective Ostrander. He asked that we hold off until after the Thanksgiving weekend. But I'm not sure how much I can legally share, so we won't go down that road. I offered to let you sleep at our apartment last night, but Detective Ostrander said that given the circumstances and the players involved, the best place for you to sleep was at a secure location."

Cory looked at Ty, hoped for a crack in that wall. Ty was holding his hot chocolate but not drinking it, staring bullets at Stellah over the whipped cream.

She said, "So now for the good news. We've found a couple homes. I'm just—"

Detective Jenkins walked through the door. She passed by them on her way to the register without even a glance in their direction. She bought a coffee and a donut. As she walked past them she looked at Ty and took a bite of the donut, put it on his plate. Then she walked out.

Ty said to Stellah, "I think she likes me."

"It's nice to see that you're making friends." Then to both of them: "As I was saying, I'm just waiting to hear from the homes. It should be any minute."

"Do we get any say in this?" Ty asked.

"Not really."

Ty turned to Cory. "What are you thinking?"

Cory's first thought was *You need to tell me the truth.* He said, "I don't think we have a lot of choices."

Ty said to Stellah, "I don't care what hole you put us in. But you're not breaking us up."

"Our priority is to keep siblings together whenever possible, but frankly it's a challenge with teens, especially when one of them"— and she focused on Ty—"has a colorful history like yours."

Cory knew the history Stellah was referring to. And chances were that history would repeat itself.

Ty said, "Coach reported that, huh?"

Stellah said, "Your file is far from what I'd call...pristine. But I've seen worse. In the meantime, I need to know, guys—is your mother an option?"

"What do you mean, an option?" Ty asked.

"Do you know how to reach her? All our searches have come up empty. She seems to have fallen off the map."

"She bailed after Benny started smacking her around," Ty said. "All she left behind was a note on the refrigerator."

"What did the note say?"

"'Have a nice life.'"

She nodded. Her phone buzzed. It lit up with a text, which she frowned at, then asked, "You haven't heard from her at all?"

"No," Ty said.

"How long has it been?"

"Almost two years."

"Five hundred sixty-seven days," Cory said.

Stellah scribbled a note in the folder. "Can you reach out to her?"

Ty said, "I deleted her number from my phone."

Cory said, "My phone burned in the fire," and felt a flicker of tightness in his throat.

"But it doesn't matter," Ty said, "because she disconnected the number."

"Are there any relatives or friends that might know how to reach her?"

Ty shrugged. "She probably has some stripper friends in Seattle. Maybe you could call them?"

"We did. No one even remembered her. Are there any family members that might be helpful?"

"Her parents died before we were born," Cory said. "All she has is a brother in Memphis, but they don't get along."

"That would be Kyle Tate," Stellah said. "We contacted him this morning. He said they haven't spoken for three years. He may be lying to us, but we explained the situation with your father and his story didn't change."

"What did he say?" Ty asked.

"He said and I quote, 'Too bad the fucker didn't die before she left.'"

"Did he offer to take us?" Cory asked, knowing that he wouldn't. Kyle was a trucker. He was never home.

Stellah shook her head.

"Why does this matter?" Ty asked. "It's all bullshit. She left us. Why would we want to live with her?"

"But he was hitting her," Cory said. "She had to go."

"She could've taken us with her," Ty said. "She didn't even offer. She left us with a psycho meth dealer."

"He wasn't a meth dealer when she left," Cory said.

Ty smiled. "No. You're right. He was a drunk and a liar. And when he didn't have her to beat on, he switched to you."

Cory glared at Ty. He didn't need to bring that up. Not now. Not ever.

Stellah said to Cory, "Was he abusing you?"

He looked at his plate.

She said, "You can tell me. Or not. It won't make any difference on how we progress from here. But it would be helpful to know the truth."

After a beat, "He hit me a couple times. But only when he was high."

Ty snorted. "Which was basically all the time."

Stellah made a note. She tapped her pen on the table, sighed, and said, "It matters about your mother and here's why. With your father no longer . . . a concern . . . maybe she'd reengage with your lives."

A *concern*? *Reengage*? Cory wondered how she came up with those words.

"He stopped being our father when he slugged her," Ty said, his voice on edge. "From that day on he was just Benny, or asshole. Whatever. Just don't call him our father."

Stellah's phone buzzed. She snatched it up. "Hang on. I'll be right with you." Then to Ty and Cory, "Sorry. This is the call I've been waiting for." She dug a ten out of her purse and put it on the table. "Buy more rolls if you want. I'll be right outside. This could take a few minutes." She stood up and said into the phone as she headed for the door, "Yes. Yes. They're with me now. . . ."

The moment Stellah was out the door, Cory said to Ty, "What's going on? What happened last night?"

"Benny got toasted cooking meth."

"The shed didn't lock itself."

"Maybe it did."

"Do you know who did it?"

Ty stirred the remainder of the hot chocolate. "Yes. But I can't tell you."

"Why not?"

He licked the spoon. "Can't tell you that either."

"If we're in some kind of danger, I need to know about it too."

"Maybe you'd be in more danger if I tell you."

"What does that mean?"

"You figure it out."

"Was it Tirk?"

"Want another Cinnabon?" Ty held up the ten.

Cory was running out of options. In fact, there were only two that he could think of, and if it wasn't Tirk, that left the unthinkable. "Stop messing with me. We can't have secrets. Just tell me. Then we'll deal with it."

Ty frowned. For a second it looked like he was about to tell him. Then he slipped the bill in his pocket. "Sorry, Cor. You have your secrets. I have mine."

Cory didn't know where that came from, didn't know how to respond. Did he really know something, or was he just acting like he did? Ty watched him for a few beats, then said, "Aw, c'mon, Cor. It's all right. You seriously think I don't know?"

Cory felt the room spinning around him. The espresso machine, the murmured voices, chairs creaking, Christmas music—all the sounds blended into a giant ball of chaos that still couldn't drown out the sudden thudding of his heart. More than anything else, right now, at this moment, he wanted to slip on his headphones, feel the silence wrap warm around him, and dull the pain. Push play and dissolve into a different reality, a reality that didn't judge, that didn't care about who or what he was.

Then Ty stiffened. He leaned forward and whispered, "Shit," as his eyes tracked left to right.

Cory turned in time to see a man in a black leather jacket and leather biker pants, a heavy trunk on short legs, narrow face with a too-thin beard that didn't hide the tattoo on his neck, walk up to a display of mugs and bagged beans. He selected a mug but didn't look at it. His eyes were on them. An employee asked him if he needed help. He shook his head, set the mug back into the display, and walked to the door. Just before exiting he turned, locked eyes with them again, pointed a finger gun, and pretended to pull the trigger. Then he flashed a familiar brown-toothed smile and walked out the door.

After giving his heart enough time to settle, Cory said, "What was that about?"

Ty scanned the adjacent tables to make sure no one was listening. "Remember you said that the lock didn't lock itself?"

"Yeah."

"Tweaker Teeth was there too."

"Last night?"

Ty nodded. "He was the guy that—"

Stellah walked up to their table, beamed down at them, and said, "Good news! The home I was hoping for is going to work. You won't be split up." She studied the boys staring up at her for a long moment, then: "Why am I getting that oh-shit-the-world-is-ending look? This is great news. I was hoping for a . . . different reaction."

"Yay," Ty said. "You found the puppies a home."

"Okay. I deserved that." After a beat, her eyes narrowed. "Something happened while I was gone. What's wrong?"

"Nothing. We're locked in and good to go. Isn't that right, Cor?"

Locked in? Cory felt his lips form the word *yes*. Saw Stellah look at him as if he'd sprouted a second head. All he could think about was the bomb that Ty just dropped: *Tweaker Teeth was there last night.* Outside he heard a motorcycle roar out of the parking lot. Another puzzle piece fell into place. But Cory sensed it was far from complete.

Ty stood and smiled at Stellah. "Let's go meet our shiny new future."

TANUM CREEK

NOW

19

A sharp sound startles me. Subconsciously I think it's a bone snapping. My eyes fly open and I realize I had fallen asleep. She's beside me, her head on my right shoulder, eyes closed, breath slow and regular. *Did I hear something or was it a dream?* The sky has brightened enough to see the shadowy forest around us. But something is different. It takes a few seconds to register the change. White flakes sift down through the trees. My sleeping bag and pack are dusted with a film of snow. I hear the sound again. It's definitely not a bone. Something, or some*one*, is moving and it's close.

I nudge her with my right elbow. As she stirs I whisper, "Shhhhh. Don't move. I heard a sound in the woods." She raises her head and looks at me, her eyes still heavy with sleep. Then they widen in alarm as a sound echoes sharply in the cold air. Whatever it is, it's not moving very fast or being particularly quiet. It could be Ty, and my heart leaps at the thought. I open my mouth to call out to him—but kill that idea a second later. If it was Ty, wouldn't he be calling out for me? Not if the driver is still a problem. In my mind I see him creeping along, ice ax in hand, searching for us in the gray light. I'm hoping that the black sleeping bag, with its dusting of snow, will help conceal us. Another crack shatters the stillness. It's closer and louder and I tense at the sound. Her hand digs into my arm. Shit. We need to run. I'm a split second from telling her to *GO!* when she releases my arm, nods a few degrees to her right. At first all I see are trees through a filter of snow. Then two shapes resolve into mule deer making their way down the slope. Probably headed to the creek for a drink. We watch as they pass no more than ten feet from where we sit. One of them stops, antlers flecked with snow, ears twitching. Breath steams out its flaring nose and I swear a cloud of warmth brushes by my cheek. The moment lasts for several heartbeats. It blinks, snorts, and moves on. Their footsteps fade behind us. We are alone again, surrounded by the pillowed hush of snow falling steady through the trees. I look at their tracks, think about a different deer. The one in the road. Benny would call this deer a sign.

And then it hits me. I whisper, "We need to go. The snow will leave tracks."

She nods. Her body shifts away from mine.

I toss back the sleeping bag, exposing us to the bracing cold. I stand, offer a hand to help her up. She takes it, winces in pain as she rises to her feet. I shake the snow off the sleeping bag and jam it into my pack. I'm about to swing the load up to my shoulders and hit the trail, when she stops me. She makes a shaking motion with her hand, brings her palm to her mouth, and pretends to swallow.

I point to her arm in the sling.

She nods, points to her head, and rolls her eyes.

I assume that means she has a headache. Is it from the accident too? It makes me wonder again what else is wrong. For example, this no talking thing. That really needs to stop.

I dig out the first aid kit and the remaining water bottle, shake four brown pills into her palm. She swallows them, takes a hit from the bottle. Closes her eyes, draws two deep breaths. Her body stiffens, then relaxes. I pop a couple IBs myself and drink just enough to wash them down. I wish I'd saved a little of the other bottle from last night, but I thought I'd be getting a refill this morning. Without a pack it would take me three minutes to climb down to the creek, one minute to fill the bottles, another five to get back to here. Call it ten minutes round-trip. But this snow changes everything. And it seems to be falling harder. I look up at the north ridge of Gooseneck Mountain. The notch is visible—for now. If the snow gets worse, or the clouds drop, then the notch will disappear. If I can't see the notch, then I won't be able to find Stumptown. That's a risk I can't afford to take. Plus, there's the damn tracks. I might as well make a sign announcing *They went that way.*

I glance at her—she's watching me. I decide the best play is to get her safely hidden in Stumptown. The water bottle is slightly less than full. If we don't go crazy, that should be enough for today and tomorrow. Hopefully Ty will have joined us by then. I stuff the bottle in my pack, shoulder the load, offer her a thumbs-up sign.

She responds with something that might be a smile, gives me a thumbs-up.

I take a second to check my phone. No service, no surprise. The battery is at 68 percent. It was at 80 when we parked the Volvo. The time is 5:48. If all goes well, we'll be at Stumptown by 6:30. I pocket the phone, turn, and start walking. After ten steps I realize there are no sounds behind me. I look back. She hasn't moved. She looks at me, then down the hill, then back to me. I hold my hands out like *What's the deal?* She points to my tracks, then looks at the ground around her, searching for something. She spots a stick, picks it up, and starts scratching in the snow. I walk down to see what she's doing, my irritation growing with every step. In big bold letters she writes:

HE WONT STOP

Then:

HE WILL KILL US!

I try to act as if her words don't shake me to my core. "He'll have to find us first."

She stares at me, her eyes narrowed and surprisingly steady. It looks like she's digging in her heels. This can't be happening. Not now, with the snow piling up around us. I move in close and struggle to keep my voice low. "Look, whoever you are. Ty and I had a plan. It was a good plan. We were going to disappear. But we stopped to pull you out of that car. Now we're in some deep shit that we didn't ask for. Ty risked—I mean, is risking—his life because of you. I don't know where he is or how he's doing. He could be bleeding out in the creek for all I know. And that's what's killing me, okay? But I promised that we'd meet him at this place, so that's where I'm going." She backs a step away from me. I dial down my voice a notch. "So here we are. It's step-up time. Either you trust me now, or you don't. But I'm walking up that hill no matter what."

She blinks. After a moment she writes in the snow:

ASTRID

And points to herself.

"That's your name? Astrid?"

She nods.

Finally. Something to work with. "So, Astrid. Here's the deal. There's this great guy named Cory. He's wondering if you will go for a walk with him in the snowy woods?" I offer what I hope is a charming smile.

She takes another look down toward the creek, then turns back to me and nods. Barely.

"I'll take that as a yes. Are you ready?"

She motions with her hand: *After you.*

I start walking.

Astrid's footsteps fall in behind mine.

20

Stellah walked them to the Goodwill store, told them to get three pairs of pants, three shirts, a package of socks and underwear, a coat, a hat, and a sweater. "Make sure one of the outfits looks decent, because first impressions get one shot, and this impression needs to be off-the-charts good," she said. She talked on the phone while they shopped, her voice rising once above the annoying Christmas music to the point that other shoppers stopped and stared. Ty was done in five minutes. Cory took longer because he had problems finding three pairs of pants with a forty-two-inch waist. When they were done shopping, Stellah inspected all the clothes, rejected one of Ty's T-shirts because it had a picture of a marijuana plant with the words GO GREEN underneath. She picked out small duffel bags for both wardrobes, put $78.98 on her credit card, and they left.

Her phone rang on the way back to the car. She answered, said, "We're still in Troutdale. . . . It didn't come up. . . . You know I can't answer that. . . . I will. . . . He's right here. . . . Sure, hang on." Ty reached out, but she offered the phone to Cory. "It's Detective Ostrander."

Cory shrugged at Ty, then said brightly into the phone, "Hey, Detective O."

The voice at the other end growled, "I know Ty is there, so just listen to what I have to say. Your brother has gotten you into a very bad situation. You get that, right? If you do, say 'That sounds awesome.'"

Cory thought of Tweaker Teeth. He'd followed them here, then knew enough to wait for Officer Jenkins to leave. Maybe he was waiting somewhere in the shadows to follow them wherever they went next. On a motorcycle. He scanned the parking lot again as he spoke. "That sounds awesome."

"Good. I pegged you for a smart kid. You still have my card, right?"

"Yes."

"Has your brother told you anything I need to know? If he has, say, 'We can do that.' If he hasn't, say 'Maybe next time.'"

They were at the Honda Fit. Stellah remote-unlocked the doors. Cory thought about Ty's unfinished sentence after Tweaker Teeth left: *He's the guy that*... Cory avoided Ty's glare across the roof and said, "All right, Detective O," and climbed into the front seat. "Uh, maybe next time?"

"Okay," the detective said. "The way these things work is you give me something, I give you something. But to show you that I'm a good guy, even though you had nothing for me, I have some news for you. The autopsy finished about twenty minutes ago. The preliminary findings were interesting. Want to know what they were?"

Stellah was backing out of the parking space. Cory said, "Sure."

"Now, technically I'm not supposed to share this kind of

information at this stage, particularly with minors, but we're partners now. I do you a solid here. You do me one later. And it stays between us. Deal?"

Cory closes his eyes. "Yeah."

"There was smoke damage in your father's lungs, but it was minor, not bad enough to kill him. His nose was broken, which the coroner said could have happened by falling. The big player here was an impact fracture on the top of his skull. She said it was consistent with a focused blow from something heavy, like maybe a brick but more like a hammer. She said if it was a hammer, whoever whacked him was probably taller than Benny and put some muscle into it. Can you think of anyone that fits that description?"

Cory figured the broken nose was from Ty's sneaker. Then he thought about the last time he saw Tirk, how he had smashed the remote with their hammer, then walked out of the house with it spinning in his hand. And if Tweaker Teeth was there last night, so was Tirk. "Yes," Cory said.

"You get what this means, right?"

"Yes."

"Good. Because this shit won't flush away. Your father's partner has connections that go all the way back to Mexico. You ever heard of a town called Zacan?"

"No."

"Zacan is a place where heads and necks just can't stay connected. They show up in a garbage bags on playgrounds. A little girl found a bag. She thought it was full of coconuts. Until she opened the bag. They weren't coconuts." He paused, then said, "So I'm asking again. Do you have any news for me?"

Cory glanced back at Ty.

Ty said, "End the call."

"No news," Cory said. "But my brother says hey."

"Then we're done here."

"Wait. It's my turn. I have a question."

"Go ahead."

"Will there be a service?"

"A service? For Benny?" Cory heard a loud snort at the other end. "There was hardly enough left of him for the autopsy. And even if there was a service, who'd come? A couple strippers? You and Mr. Donut are persona non grata in Portland."

"Why?"

"Picture coconuts in a sack."

Cory fought off the image. "For how long?"

"Unless you have actionable news for me, I'm thinking, oh... like, *forever.*"

Ty said, "Dude, hang up the damn phone!"

Cory ignored him. "What happens to his remains?"

"He's eighty percent caramelized. I expect they'll cremate what isn't cremated already. If you want, I can see about getting the ashes to Stellah."

Cory considered asking Ty if he wanted Benny's ashes, but knew what the answer would be. Then he reminded himself that Benny was alive just two days ago and he had the bruised ribs to prove it. Without having a good reason for it, he said, "Stellah works."

"I'll see what I can do. Meanwhile, watch your back. Your brother is up to his chin in this, kid. Either he saw something, did something, or probably both. So call me if he talks to you, or you see someone you shouldn't be seeing."

"Okay." And thought, *You want me to snitch on my brother, just like you told Benny to do with Tirk.*

"Good luck."

The line went dead. Cory gave Stellah the phone. She slipped it into her open purse. Her eyes held his for a moment, then refocused on a red light turning green. "You all right?" she asked, stepping on the gas.

"Yeah."

"Well, I'm not," Ty said from the backseat. "What'd that dickwad want?"

"He's not a dickwad. In fact, he called to wish us luck."

"I'll bet."

"Whatever."

"What sounds so awesome?"

"He said next time we're in Portland to look him up. He'd take us to Voodoo."

"Right. Like that'll happen. What'd he say about the service?"

"There won't be one."

"Why not?"

"Let's just say it wouldn't be an open casket."

Stellah shot Cory a disapproving look. Ty said nothing. Stellah merged onto I-84 East, accelerated to highway speed. She said, "Are you guys finished? I'd like to talk about what happens next."

Ty leaned forward, put his head between the seats. "Well? Are we, bro?"

"Are we what?"

"Fucking finished?"

"Hey!" Stellah said. "Language, please. Keep it civilized."

"I don't know, *bro*," Cory said. "You tell me if we're finished."

"I guess we are."

"Works for me," Cory said. He glanced in the side-view mirror. Saw cars and trucks, but no motorcycle.

Ty leaned back, started tapping the window with a finger. Stellah said, "Are you two sure you aren't married? Because you sound a lot like me and my soon-to-be ex." Her phone rang. She glanced at the display, slammed it back into her purse. "Speaking of dickwads, I swear if he calls again I'll shove that... that, excuse me... *fucking phone* up his..." She looked at Cory. "Help a lady out. What's the word I'm searching for?"

Cory nodded at the dash and said, "Air vent?"

"Up his air vent." Stellah grinned. "That works for me."

Stellah used the remaining miles to tell them about the Wainwright family. They lived in The Dalles, a city on the Columbia River about eighty miles east of Portland. Cory had watched Ty play in a football game there and wasn't impressed with the place. He had guessed the population to be about ten thousand. He hadn't been able to find a single GameStop, and the Wi-Fi sucked everywhere they went. She started out by telling them how excited she was about this fit. One of the best she'd seen ever, especially on this short a notice. Travis Wainwright, the dad, coached high school lacrosse for five years in California before moving his family to The Dalles to manage a bank. Ty grunted that lacrosse was just a hockey wannabe without the ice. Stellah said, "It's probably best if you keep that opinion to yourself."

She said that Travis's wife, Tina, was a freelance graphic designer who also wrote background stories for video games. Cory wanted to know what games, but she didn't have that information. He asked her if they had any kids. She told them one, Channing, a son, age twelve. They were also watching their sister's son, Avery, who was special needs although she didn't know what the special needs were. What she did know was that Avery would go back to his mother in a week or two. Stellah asked if either of them had questions, which they did not, so she began explaining the handoff. Her involvement would end after today and a local caseworker named Dylan Sykes would take over. She said she talked to him on the phone that morning and he sounded like a nice guy—young, but nice. A lawyer would also be part of the support team at some point in the near future but she doubted that point would be today. She said that Dylan would line up grief counseling sessions for both of them, and Ty would start anger management therapy for his issues that—

"What anger management issues?" Ty asked.

"The kind that lead to incarceration if not addressed."

"Who told you? Coach?"

"I know how to read a file."

"Did Coach tell you I didn't start those fights?"

"I didn't talk to your coach. But I did read a police report for one individual named Francisco Alvarez. He had a concussion and needed sixteen stitches. Spent two days in the hospital. But apparently you two kissed and made up because no charges were pressed. Based on your priors, that should have resulted in some juvie time."

Cory suspected Tirk played a role in that outcome. Benny hinted along those lines, that maybe a certain someone visited Francisco in the hospital. Remembering Detective Ostrander's comment about the garbage bag full of coconuts, he asked, "Do the Wainwrights know our history?"

Stellah pulled out and passed a Walmart semi spraying their windshield. "Most of it, but not all. There are legal issues that need to be sorted out. But they've fostered before and know the kids come from stressed environments. And they are aware of Ty's…colorful past. To that point, Dylan told me this placement is contingent on him attending those sessions." She swerved back into the right lane just in time to see a sign that announced the exits for The Dalles. "We're the first exit," Stellah said. "Any more questions? We should be at their home in about ten minutes."

"Will I have my own computer?" Cory asked.

"I don't know. If not your own, I'm sure you'll have access to one."

"Worried about those zombie hordes?" Ty asked.

"You have your skills," Cory said. "I have mine."

Stellah exited, took a right and aimed at a Circle K. "We'll stop here. While I'm gassing up I want you guys to visit the restroom and change into your new outfits. Clean up as best you can. And, Cory, wear the black sweater with the tan pants. That looked good on you."

She pulled up to a pump. Ty and Cory climbed out, Goodwill duffel bags in hand.

Ten minutes later they returned in their new used clothes. As instructed, Cory wore the black sweater and tan pants. The sweater had a big hole under the right arm that he didn't notice when he bought it. And the neck choked the fat around his neck. Ty used the ten dollars that Stellah gave them at the coffee shop to buy toothpaste and toothbrushes and a fifty-cent comb. There wasn't enough left over for antiperspirant, so they used a combination of paper towels and the hand dryer to wipe their faces, stomachs, and armpits. A man walked in during this process and openly stared at the two of them. Ty said, "Yo, we're washing our balls next. You wanna take some pictures?" The man decided to pee at a later date.

Stellah was standing outside the car, under the canopy, talking on her phone and smoking a cigarette. Cory didn't know she smoked. As they approached she said into the phone, "Okay, then. I guess it is what it is. Thanks for trying. I'll see you in a few." She slipped the phone in her purse, dropped her unfinished cigarette, and stomped it out. Cory could tell by the grim set of her lips as she ground the butt into a pulp that something had changed. And in Cory's experience, changes were rarely good.

"I'm sorry about the cigarette," she said. "I only smoke when I'm mad."

"Your soon-to-be ex?" Cory asked.

She shook her head. "You guys look really good," she said, and offered a fleeting smile.

"Hey, I tucked in my shirt," Ty said. "I never tuck in my shirt."

"I noticed."

He said, "The puppies are ready to see their new home."

Stellah made no move to get in the car. Instead she lit another cigarette.

"Is something wrong?" Cory asked.

"I'm afraid so."

"What is it?" Ty said.

Stellah exhaled a gray stream. "The situation has changed."

"Changed how?"

"Do you remember I said that the Wainwrights were watching their sister's son, Avery?"

"The special-needs kid," Cory said.

"Right. Well, apparently Avery's mother is having personal issues of her own. She asked her sister this morning to watch Avery for longer than initially thought."

"How much longer?" Cory asked, pretty sure where this was headed.

"Four to six months."

"We can handle that," Ty said.

"I know. Unfortunately it's not that simple. Avery requires a lot of their time and resources. They're still adjusting. So anyway, Dylan said as much as the Wainwrights would like to help, and they really do, this new development means they just can't handle two placements at this time."

The Bic brothers were silent for a few moments. Stellah took a long drag, blew smoke up at the gray sky. Then Ty went where Cory hoped he wouldn't. "You said two placements?"

"That's right."

"As in they have room for one puppy?"

Stellah nodded.

"Did they say which one?"

"They did. But before I tell you—" A white Ford Focus turned in to the lot. Stellah watched as it drove slowly past them and parked facing the store. The driver's door remained closed. Stellah continued, "Before I tell you, I want you to know that we're working on a plan B. I'm expecting a call any minute."

"Fuck plan B," Ty said.

The edge in his voice was a tangible thing. *He's headed for Benny mode*, Cory thought. "Let's go," he said, not knowing where they'd go to. He just wanted to get in the car, pull off this five-dollar sweater that choked his neck and made it hard to breathe.

Ty said, "We're not going anywhere." He took a step toward Stellah. "They want my brother, right?"

"It's not a matter of wanting. It's what they can handle right now."

"Why Cory?"

"They . . . they think he's a better fit with Avery. But when Avery leaves, Dylan said they'd be willing to revisit fostering both of you." Her eyes, for the first time, flicked down and away. As if what she said and what she believed were different animals.

"Here's what I think," Ty said. "I think you knew they planned on taking Cory from the start. That you made up this bullshit story about this great home and these great people just to get us both in the car." He took another step. There was only one left. "You knew they'd split us up all along."

Cory pleaded, "Let it go, Ty." He felt tears rimming his eyes.

"Believe what you want," Stellah said, her voice calm and even. She stomped out her cigarette. "But I'm telling you the truth. Sometimes these things fall apart."

A car door opened and closed. Cory looked. It was the Focus. A young guy, tall, beard, jeans, plaid shirt untucked, walked toward them. He had a paper bag in one hand. Stellah held out a hand for him to stop.

Ty said, "That's Dylan, right?"

"Yes."

"He's here to take Cory."

"He's here to help."

"But he's here to take Cory."

"If that's what you two decide, yes."

Ty nodded. It was slow, barely a movement at all. His eyes narrowed on Stellah. Cory's intestines shifted in his gut. He knew this look, the same coiled-snake moment Benny had just before he struck. Cory wiped a tear from his face, wondered if he could stop Ty if it came to that. But Ty turned to him instead. "I think you should do it, Cor."

"No you don't."

"They want you. That's all that matters."

"What about not splitting us up? You said—"

"I'm damaged goods, bro. Can't you see that? I have a *history*. I'm the fucked-up puppy. The one that'll bite the baby and eat the family cat." Then he said to Stellah, "Tell your friend we're good to go."

"What about plan B?" Cory said, certain that he was sliding into a bottomless pit.

"The text said if I hadn't heard by noon, then it won't happen." She looked at her phone. "It's twelve thirty-five now. The important thing is that you have a good place to live. This home is a really good fit for you." She studied him a moment longer, then waved to Dylan.

Cory fought back the tears, wiped his nose with a sleeve. He said to Ty, "Please don't be like this."

"Like what?"

"Like...you know."

"Go ahead. Say it."

Dylan walked up to them. Stellah did the introductions.

Dylan said to Ty, "The Wainwrights are sorry about how this scenario played out. They want you to know that."

"That's all right. I expected it."

Dylan handed Stellah the paper bag.

"What's this?" she asked.

"Mrs. Wainwright made some turkey-and-stuffing sandwiches. For the road."

"Tell them thanks." Stellah took the bag.

Dylan turned to Cory. "Well, get your stuff. We need to head. The Wainwrights have some kind of barbecue thing that couldn't be changed. They want to get you settled before the gang shows up."

So this is it? Cory thought. *This is really happening?* He wanted to grab Ty and shake him. Shake the Benny out of him. "I can't do it," he said.

Ty said, "Dude, if the situation were reversed and you were the ugly puppy, you'd be telling me to take the deal, right?"

Cory knew that question was coming. There was really only one answer. "Yes."

"So there you go. Take the deal. End of story."

Cory said to Stellah, "What about Ty?"

"Returning to Portland is out. There's a new teen sheltering center in Hood River. I checked and they have a room. He'll go there until something more permanent comes along."

A teen sheltering center? "How long will that be?"

"Days. Weeks. Sometimes months. It's hard to tell, especially this close to the holidays."

Ty said, "We'll get back together, bro. Till then, make it work." They embraced. In the middle of it he whispered in Cory's ear, *"No pussies on the bridge."*

Cory whispered it back, grabbed his duffel from the Fit. He

walked in heavy silence with Dylan to the Honda. Dylan swept fast food wrappers off the passenger seat. "Sorry. I'm a slob. You'll learn that pretty quick." Cory wedged himself inside, stretched the seat belt across his stomach. Struggled to fasten the clip because his hand was shaking too much.

Dylan started the car, backed out of his space. Cory looked over his shoulder at the Honda. No Ty. Figured he must be in the car. Stellah was outside leaning back against the door, reading her phone. Dylan waved to her, drove toward the exit. A car was ahead of them, waiting to pull out. When it was Dylan's turn, he rolled forward. Then he looked in the rearview, muttered, "What the hell?" and hit the brakes.

Stellah ran up to the driver's door, phone in hand. Dylan lowered the window.

"What's up?" he asked.

"Plan B came through!"

"Both?"

"Yes."

"Sweet."

Dylan grinned at Cory. "I'll tell the Wainwrights you got a better offer." Cory stared at him, stunned. "Adios, dude. It's your lucky day!"

Cory had no trouble unclipping his seat belt this time. He walked with Stellah to the Fit, climbed into the backseat. Ty smiled at him like he knew this would happen.

As Stellah exited the Circle K and headed for I-82, Ty said, "So where's this plan B?"

"Luster, Oregon. Ever heard of it?"

"No," they both said.

"Neither have I." She swung the Fit into traffic and stomped on the gas, headed for the entrance to I-82 East. "But with a name like Luster, it has to be good."

Ty said, "And our new family knows the news about us?"

"What news is that?"

"That we're not housebroken."

"Oh, that won't be a problem."

"Why not?"

Stellah smiled into the rearview.

"One of them is a judge."

TANUM CREEK

NOW

22

There's a half inch of snow, hardly any under the trees. That's where I walk as much as possible, thinking the fewer obvious tracks we leave the better. It takes more effort and more time, which increases our exposure to watchful eyeballs from below, but I think it's worth the risk. If the snow keeps falling at this pace, our tracks will be buried in a couple hours. Or more likely it will warm up, turn to rain, and melt the snow. That would be even better, assuming we find Stumptown. If we don't find Stumptown? Well, I hate bridges and that's one bridge I'd rather not cross.

The top is closer than I thought. We crest the saddle in a couple minutes and the terrain turns to nearly flat. The wind must hit this spot pretty hard because there are a lot of blowdowns. It makes walking more difficult since we have to weave around and even climb over so many trees, but I get a good look at Gooseneck Mountain, the notch, and the frosted peaks beyond. This place feels vaguely familiar, even with the conditions as they are. That's a huge relief. Astrid sounds winded from the climb and signals with an open palm facing out that she needs to rest. We walk to a bare spot under a tree and I check my phone while she catches her breath.

I'm hoping that with the elevation gain maybe there's a signal, but there is not. The time is 5:59. I take a moment to remember that twenty-four hours ago I was waking up in a warm bed. Four hours later the Bic twins were slipping out of town in a stolen Volvo wagon full of camping gear and bags of food. Our future looked pretty damn good. Now I'm standing next to a girl named Astrid who eight hours ago was soaked in gasoline and locked in the trunk of a car. Somewhere between there and here we hit a massive karma bomb and everything blew up. I'm not sure what we did to light that fuse, but here we are. I need to find out Astrid's story. But before that happens I have to find a stump in the middle of nowhere, and that's all on me.

After a few moments, she straightens up, looks at me, and nods. I assume this means she has recovered enough to continue. I pocket the phone and consider telling her what we need to do next. *We need to find a pine tree shaped like a bent finger with an arrow carved in the bark. Oh, and by the way, I've seen this tree only once and that was like, more than a year ago.*

I say, "You ready?" She raises Ty's hoodie high enough to reveal the splint. Then touches the foam to show me how it has shifted position and is barely covering the purple bump of displaced bone.

"It's loose?" I ask.

She nods.

Which means it needs to be retaped. Which means taking off my pack, digging out the first aid kit. I ask, "Can it wait? We're almost there."

Astrid lowers the hoodie, grimaces, nods again.

I aim for the notch and start making tracks in what I hope is the right direction.

Five minutes later I know we're in trouble. The déjà vu feeling I had earlier is gone. Nothing looks familiar. In fact, we're starting to lose elevation and that feels entirely wrong. On top of all this, I think the weather is changing. The flakes aren't as big, they're coming in at an angle, and I've felt the occasional wet sting on my face of either sleet or rain. I think Astrid isn't enthusiastic about our worsening situation either. She yanks on my pack and spins me around, points to our tracks that appear to wander aimlessly through the forest.

"I know," I say.

She carves three huge letters in the snow with an icy sneaker:

WTF

I say, "I'll tell you. But don't go all crazy on me."

She gives me a careful nod. Her teeth are chattering.

"I'm looking for a tree with a bend like this." I show her an index finger with a slight bend. "My dad carved an arrow in it that points to the direction we need to go."

She shakes her head. Looks at me, her blue eyes blazing. So much for not thinking I'm crazy. "I know that tree's around here somewhere," I say. "If we find it, then it's just a five-minute walk and we're done."

This time the eyes narrow. It's another look I know. I prepare myself for an explosion of angry hand signals, one of them being a middle finger. Instead, she points to my right leg, then brings her hand to her ear, two fingers extended out like she's holding a phone.

"You want my cell?"

She nods.

"There's no signal. Plus, you don't talk. How's that going to work?"

Astrid motions again for the phone, this time with attitude.

I shrug, give her the iPhone.

She holds it out with the display facing her, then nods for me to hold it there. I do as asked. While she wipes and taps, I search the trees for slinking shadows. Half a minute later Astrid nods for me to look. She had pulled up the notepad app and written:

i think I saw it.

"The tree?" I ask.

She nods.

I have my doubts. If she's wrong that will be more time wasted that isn't ours to waste. But the alternative is to keep wandering. "Show me," I say.

Astrid retraces our steps. I don't like heading in a direction that could put us in direct contact with the driver. When we're within eyesight of our resting spot, she stops, scans the area to our left, points to a blowdown leaning against another tree. It has a distinct bend near the top, just like I described. How she remembered a thing like that is a question I'll save for later. For the moment I'm just thankful she did. I run to the tree. I have to brush away snow to find it, but the arrow is still there, carved deep into the bark, with *BB* underneath. That's all good. The bad part is it's pointing at the ground. Shit. Can't we get a fucking break? I try to imagine which way it was pointing before it fell. The best I can do is make an educated guess based on the orientation of the other blowdowns and how the ground is ripped up around it. The arrow would point more or less toward a smaller mountain to the east of Gooseneck. I look at Astrid, who is standing beside me now. She's watching me, her eyes alert and steady. But the color has drained from her face, and her lips are starting to match the blue of her eyes. She's shivering under Ty's hoodie. I point to the smaller mountain. "I'm pretty sure it's that way, through the gap between those two trees."

She motions for the phone. I pull it out and hold it for her. She taps:

what are u looking for now

"A small rise with a big tree stump at the bottom."
Her eyebrows gather. She motions for the phone.

where are u taking me

There's something about the question, the phrasing, *where are u taking me*, that sets an alarm off in my head. I decide that telling her the truth, or at least all of it, is not my best option. "Someplace safe and dry. Let's go."

She shakes her head. Motions for the phone. She taps and nods.

WHERE ARE YOU TAKING ME!!!

I guess that's her version of shouting.

I say, "To a hideout my father found when he was elk hunting. That's where my brother and I were headed before we found you. It has a wood floor, a wood-burning stove. Bookshelves. There's even some old magazines from the 1950s to read." I smile, hopefully not like a wolf. She stares at me. The shivering has spread to her entire body, almost to the point of convulsions. I hand her the iPhone. "Here. You keep it. When you have something to say, just show me." She gives me that unreadable stare for a moment longer, then slips the phone in the pocket of the hoodie. We head off into the uncertain woods, hopefully for the last time today.

LUSTER, OR.

ELEVEN MONTHS AGO

23

Stellah pulled into a rest stop and parked next to a yapping dog with its small black nose poking out the barely open passenger window of a pickup truck.

Ty had been sleeping. He peered out his window, rubbed his eyes, said, "Are we in Luster yet?"

Stellah said, "About twenty minutes away. I need to pee and make some calls. If you guys need to use the restroom, this is a good time. But don't wander off. Please. I really don't need that now."

Ty rolled down his window, growled at the dog, which stirred it up even more.

Cory said to Stellah from the backseat, "Go ahead. We're good."

She grabbed her purse, pulled the keys from the ignition, and left.

They watched her walk into the women's room, phone to ear. Ty opened the glove box and poked around.

"Ty? What the hell?" Cory said.

"Shit. She doesn't have one."

"One what?"

"A gun, dumbass. This is America. Everyone has a gun in their car."

"Why do you want a gun?"

"Oh well. This'll do." He pulled out a yellow LED flashlight, pushed a button. The bulb end lit up. He turned it off and slipped it into his coat pocket. Then he opened the door and said over the yapping dog, "It's time to go, Cor."

"Go where?"

"Brazil. France. Talla-fucking-hassee. Wherever the hell we want."

"How can we go to Brazil? We don't have passports."

"Don't be a dick. You know what I mean."

"You're serious?"

A woman walked out of the restroom. She was short and round. Not Stellah.

Ty said, "Dead serious. Because if we don't leave, that's what we'll be."

"What are you talking about?"

"C'mon, Cor. As if Detective Donut didn't draw you a picture."

"He didn't."

"Bullshit."

Ty exited the car. The dog went into a frenzy.

Cory unclipped his seat belt, climbed out. Another woman exited the restroom. She stared at the two boys, one with his face two inches from an extremely agitated dog.

Ty walked away. It looked like he was headed for the dense forest behind the rest stop. A waist-high chain-link fence marked the tree line. One man stood by the fence, baggie in hand, watching his poodle pinch a steaming one in the grass. Cory thought about running to the women's room, calling for Stellah. Ty was cutting across the grass, fifty yards from the fence. Cory decided to run after him instead. Catching up to Ty, he panted, "We can't do this to her."

"Dude, she can't stop us."

"What does that mean?"

"I've seen it on TV. These CPS people. If the fosters run, they can't touch us."

Cory didn't know if that was true or not. He decided it didn't matter. "She's found a good place for us. Let's give it a chance."

"Sorry. I've got a bad feeling about it."

"You never have a good feeling about anything."

"True. But some bad feelings are worse than others."

"You don't know anything about it."

"I know enough."

They stopped at the fence.

"Ty, the dude's a judge."

"And that's supposed to be a good thing?"

Cory had to admit that his brother's point was valid. Ty and judges were not a good fit. But agreeing with him would be counterproductive. "We don't have any money."

"But we have skills. You can kill zombies for hire. And I can do this." Ty pulled a packet of beef jerky out of his coat pocket. Then two chocolate bars and a pack of Chiclets. And a Red Bull. "I believe the basic food groups are covered."

"Where'd you score that?"

"The Circle K."

Cory had only shoplifted once. Ty had waited outside the Gas Mart while he took twenty minutes to stuff a snack bag of Cheese Nips under his shirt. He left sweating like a racehorse but amazingly undetected. Three minutes later in the alley behind a strip club, Cory yacked up most of those Cheese Nips while Ty laughed and smoked a stolen cigarette.

Cory said, "We can't do this to Stellah. It's not right."

"Not right? After she drops us off, that's the last we'll see of her. See ya, Bic bros. How right is that?"

"She's been good to us."

"She's doing her job."

Cory didn't agree with that. He believed Stellah was doing more than her job. She could've just dropped them off at that teen facility in Hood River and headed back to Portland. Instead she drove another two hours out of her way. She didn't bail on them then, and he refused to believe she'd bail on them now. He said, "Let's give this a chance, okay? Stellah said we'd be together. That's all I care about. We can always bail later."

"Remember what Benny said about later?"

"Blink yer eyes an' it turns into too late."

"Exactly. And I'm thinking we're just about there."

Ty placed his right hand on the fence, flexed his knees.

Cory grabbed his coat. "What's wrong with you?"

Ty shrugged his hand away. Swung a leg up and easily vaulted the fence. Landed ninja-style in the mud on the other side. Cory knew there was no way he could do that. He'd have to climb over. It would be a struggle. Probably tear a hole in his new used pants.

Then fall and get mud on the sweater that was too small for his gut. The fence extended for a hundred yards in both directions. He glanced at the man with the dog. He was focused on scooping up dog crap with a plastic bag. No help there. He looked back at the rest area. No Stellah.

Ty said, "Anyway, I'm the one in the shit. Not you. You'll be safer without me."

"Meaning what?"

"Call Detective Donut and ask him. You still have his card, right?"

Cory blinked.

Ty said, "See ya, bro. Gotta go." He waved and walked away.

Cory refused to believe this was happening. Ty wouldn't leave him. Not like this, not now. He shouted at Ty's back, "Hey! What do you want me to do?"

Ty stopped and turned. "Well, there is this one small thing."

"What?"

"Tell me what Detective Donut said on the phone."

"I did."

"I think you skipped some parts."

"Is that what this is about?"

"Basically."

Cory paused for a breath. "Okay. But not now."

Ty turned his back to Cory, walked two steps.

"Okay! Okay! He...he said the autopsy was done."

Ty slowed but didn't stop.

Cory said, "The fire didn't kill him."

Ty stopped and turned. Cory glanced at the guy with the poodle. He was staring at them, mouth hanging open, a baggie full of moist dog turds dangling from one hand.

"Why didn't you tell me that before?"

"I . . . I don't know."

Ty frowned, walked back to the fence. "What else did he say?"

Cory nodded to his right. "Can we do this later?"

Without taking his eyes off Cory, Ty shouted, "Yo, poodle dude! Have some fuckin' manners already! We're tryin' to have a private discussion here."

Cory felt a chill run through him. Ty, with his face hard like that, the force and cadence of the words—it was like his brother had dissolved and Benny was standing there in the trees. The man picked up his dog and hurried away.

Ty said, "Did he say how Benny died?"

"No. Just theories."

"What theories?"

"Blunt force trauma to the head. They think he fell, or something fell on him." Cory swallowed, tried not to picture Tirk bouncing a bloody hammer off Benny's skull.

After a beat, "What'd he say about me?"

"Same as at the station. You saw something, you're in shit up to your chin, blah blah blah."

Ty smiled as if that made perfect sense—or maybe no sense at all. He jumped the fence. Popped open the Red Bull, offered Cory the first hit.

Cory said, "I'm good." Thinking there was no way he'd keep it down. Ty took a long pull, walked toward the parking lot. Cory fell in beside him. Fifty feet from the lot he said, "I hate it when you do that."

"Do what?"

"Act like him."

Ty looked at his sneakers. They were covered with mud from the jump. "I hate it too, bro." A few more steps, then: "Did you seriously think I'd really leave your ass?"

Cory considered his three possible replies: yes, no, maybe.

He said, "No," and hoped more than anything that it was the truth.

Ty wrapped his arm around his brother's shoulder. "*Hell no* is a better answer."

They walked that way to the car.

The truck with the yapping dog had been replaced by a Mercedes sedan with Florida plates. Ty peered through the rear passenger window. "Hey, there's an iPhone on the seat." He tested the door; it was locked.

They didn't feel like sitting in the car, so they waited for Stellah under an eave next to a vending machine. Ty checked the coin return, pocketed thirty-five cents. When Stellah returned a few minutes later, Cory could smell the cigarette on her. He wanted to know what the problem was, but decided from her grim expression that she wasn't in a sharing mood.

They got in the car and drove away. Stellah was unusually quiet for a few miles, then said out of the blue, "So, Ty? Where'd you get that fresh mud on your sneakers?"

"We went for a chat."

"In the rain?"

"Aww, this ain't rain."

"Was it a nice chat?"

"Very nice. I learned a few things."

"Did you mend any fences?"

"Some." He looked at her and cracked a slow Benny smile. It made Cory's stomach hurt just to see the thing. "But, yo, check this out." Ty dug into his pocket, showed her a quarter and a dime. "I found it in the vending machine."

"Won't get you very far."

"True that." Ty drained the Red Bull, and after a burp, he said, "But it's a start."

LUSTER, OR.

ELEVEN MONTHS AGO

24

The sign carved into a slab of wood on two log posts welcomed them to their new home: LUSTER, OREGON, POPULATION 8,648. A painted plank under it read: MAKING DREAMS COME TRUE SINCE 1902. Cory wondered how good those dreams could be if the population was only 8,600 after a hundred-plus years of existence.

The GPS on Stellah's phone guided them to Constitution Ave, which appeared to be the main street through town. Shop windows were decorated with Christmas ornaments and fake snow, and the old-fashioned lampposts had big candy canes that glowed red and white. Shoppers prowled the sidewalks, enjoying Black Friday sales and a break in the rain. Stellah pointed to a coffee shop named the Drip 'n' Sip and said, "If the coffee's as good as the shopping looks, I just may move here myself." Other than not seeing a store specifically offering video games, Cory liked what he saw. It wasn't dead like Moro, Oregon, where they lived before Benny sold the house out from under them, and not choked with traffic and noise like downtown Portland. He hoped Ty agreed. So far he hadn't commented, one way or the other.

They took a left and drove past a big park with a duck pond, a huge gazebo strung up with blinking Christmas lights, and walking trails woven among the trees. Four blocks later was a busy restaurant named Bravo Burgers with an illuminated cow waving on the roof. The sign in its hoof-hand promised BOTTOMLESS SWEET TATER FRIES. Two blocks past Bravo Burgers, the buildings changed from retail shops and restaurants to Mott's Lumber and Landscaping, a giant fenced-in place selling Christmas trees starting at $29.99. Next came an old brick church, and then two blocks later, Luster High School. According to the flickering marquee out front, it was HOME OF THE SOARING APTORS.

Stellah's phone buzzed.

She asked Ty to check the screen because she needed to focus on the road.

Reading the display, Ty said, "It's a text from Dale. He says 'I'm taking the kids to Nanna's if you're not home by ten.'"

"Shit!" Stellah slammed the steering wheel.

"Who is Nanna?"

"The mother of my soon-to-be ex. If a cave troll and a Komodo dragon mated, she'd be the fire-breathing spawn."

"Want me to answer?"

"No. I'll do that later. Thanks."

"Dale sounds like a dick."

"Actually he's not," Stellah said, "but I won't deny that the potential is there."

The GPS told them to make a right on Chatham Road, then their destination would be a quarter mile straight ahead. They followed split-rail fences bordered by empty fields on both sides of the road. As Stellah closed in on a point of light in the distance, Cory tried to remember what she had told them about their future home. It was even less information than what she had on the Wainwrights. The last name was Mott, and they were recently licensed to foster teens, so Ty and Cory would be their first. They had two kids of their own, a boy and a girl, but neither was high school age. Harvey Mott, the dad, was a judge. His wife, Charlene, was a stay-at-home mom.

The split rail ended at an intersection with a stop sign. Across the way in the headlight beam was a mailbox and a narrow gravel road that headed up through pine trees on the side of a hill.

"This looks interesting," Stellah said.

The gravel road turned out to be a very long driveway that ended in front of a two-story log home with massive windows and a brick chimney with smoke rising into a half-moon sky. Cory counted four vehicles: a Mercedes SUV, a red truck with MOTT'S LOT painted on the driver's door, a green VW Bug, and a station-wagon–shaped car under a cover next to a mountain of split wood.

"Holy crap!" Ty said, staring at the home. "We're moving into a ski lodge."

"Says the guy that's never been skiing," Cory said.

"I've seen pictures, dumbass," Ty said.

"Hey, tone it down," Stellah warned. "Or I may decide to live in the ski lodge and drink good coffee while you guys move into my crappy condo with stinky diapers, a broken dishwasher, and no parking."

"Sign me up," Ty said.

The front door swung open, spilling warm light onto the expansive front porch. A man, woman, two kids, and a distressingly large brown dog walked out and arranged themselves into a perfect wedge, the man and woman in back, then the kids, then the dog. The formation was executed so perfectly that Cory decided it was either rehearsed or wired into their DNA like migrating geese. A movement on the floor above the porch caught his eye. A curtain pulled back far enough for a face to peer out. Backlit by interior light, the face was framed by long black hair. Older, definitely a teen. The curtain closed. The light switched off. Cory wondered why she wasn't part of the welcoming wedge. There was nothing in Stellah's report that mentioned a teenage girl.

The Fit rolled to a stop. Stellah said as she unbuckled her seat belt, "This'll have to be quick. It's a four-hour drive, not including a mandatory stop at the Drip 'n' Sip."

"Sorry if we're causing problems with Nanna," Cory said.

"My personal issues are not your fault," she said as she opened her door.

The Motts tumbled down from the porch as the Fit emptied.

Cory heard a deep voice bellow, "Welcome to Luster!" just before two muddy paws planted on his sweater and a wet tongue slobbered all over his face.

After the introductions were made and hands were shook, Stellah asked, "What happened to the local caseworker?"

Harvey said, "Tony's brother is on leave from a second tour in Afghanistan. He goes back tomorrow. I told him not to worry, we'd be fine for tonight. He'll stop by in the morning and introduce himself to the boys."

Stellah frowned, checked her phone. "The text I got was from a Lacey."

"Lacey told us about Ty and Cory. But Tony helped us with the licensing and got us lined up with the right classes, so I asked that he be assigned to this case." Harvey flashed an embarrassed smile. "Sorry. I just sounded like a judge. I asked that he work with us on this new addition to our family." He grinned at the boys. "You'll like Tony. He was the best shooting guard this county will ever see." Then to Stellah: "Is that a problem? I could call Lacey—"

"No, that's all right. Just have him text me tomorrow. Thanks for helping out on short notice."

"That's how these things work. We're happy to open our doors."

Charlene shot him a look. "And our hearts."

"Right," Harvey said. "Thanks, honey, for clarifying that point."

After a silence that threatened to turn awkward, Charlene said, "Speaking of open doors. Shall we take this gathering inside? I have a pizza ready to come out of the oven. Are you boys hungry?"

Ty said, "Pizza sounds great. Thank you."

"I'd love some pizza," Cory said.

"I'll take mine to go," Stellah said. "I need to get back to Portland. May I use a bathroom first?"

"Of course," Harvey said. He looked at the boys holding their Goodwill duffels. "Is that all your gear?"

"We travel light, sir," Ty said.

Justin, the younger of the two children, said to Cory, "We have a real pizza oven."

"That's cool," Cory said. "I like real pizza."

As they moved toward the porch, Cory saw a door open next to the garage. A girl in a long brown coat stepped out and walked to the VW. The kids yelled, "Bye, Kayla!" and waved. She stood by the driver's door and waved back. Seemed to hesitate for a moment as if she might join them, then climbed into the VW and drove away.

Ty asked, "Who was that?"

Harvey said, "The babysitter."

"Former," Charlene said. Then to Cory, as they entered a home that he thought only existed in magazines, "I bet you'd like to get out of that muddy sweater."

Later, after Charlene promised to take them clothes shopping tomorrow and they said good night and thank you a hundred times and climbed the steep squeaking stairs to the remodeled attic bedroom and crawled bone-weary into their parallel beds, after the downstairs voices stopped and the dog barked and the house settled into an unfamiliar silence that promised to put an end to this day, Ty said, "If you could have one do-over in your life, what would it be?"

Cory didn't have to think very long. All he had to do was breathe. The answer was right there, in the bruised flesh between his ribs. "I'd get on the motorcycle like Benny asked."

"How would that change things?"

"He wouldn't have punched me. You wouldn't have kicked him in the face. He wouldn't have been too busted up to stop whatever happened to him. The shed wouldn't have exploded. Our house wouldn't have burned down. We'd be in Portland instead of here."

"You know my opinion on that?"

"What?"

"Not getting on the bike was the balls-out bravest thing I have ever seen you do."

Cory waited for the sudden tightness in his throat to ease. Then he asked, "What's your do-over?"

Ty's voice said out of the black, "I wouldn't have missed."

"Missed what?"

"I wanted to crush his throat, not his nose. I should've known that he'd see it coming and duck."

"How would that have changed things?"

"He would've choked to death. I'd be in jail. And you'd be in our house instead of a ski lodge in Lusterfuck, Oregon."

Cory didn't know how to respond. Too many questions were storming in his skull. Finally, he said, "I hate Thanksgiving. Pilgrims. Overcooked turkey. Dry stuffing. All of it."

"You and me both. But it's not too late."

"Not too late for what?"

A beam of light hit the ceiling, where it settled on a spiderweb between the rafters. Cory followed the light beam to its source. Ty was holding the yellow flashlight he took from Stellah's car. He smiled at Cory and said, "Let's bail tonight."

Cory couldn't tell if he was serious. Considering how long the day had been already, and how good Charlene's fig-and-Brie pizza had tasted hot out of the oven—he hoped that Ty was just pulling his chain. He said, "All our clothes are in the wash. And what about the monster-dog?"

Ty laughed, as if that answer was exactly what he expected. "All right," he said. "But I'm gonna hang on to this flashlight. I think it still might come in handy."

The light clicked off. Ty's bed squeaked as he rolled onto his side, facing away. The unfamiliar silence returned.

Cory looked at the alarm clock on the nightstand between their beds. 11:38 p.m. He realized as the eight changed to a nine that their world had gone up in flames just twenty-four hours ago, almost to the minute. *What really happened? Who was there? Why was Benny in the shed? Why did Tweaker Teeth follow them? Did Ty really mean to kill Benny?* After a while, the storm of questions in his head settled down to one. He turned to look at Ty, waited for the pain in his ribs to fade, then whispered, "Dude, did you lock the shed?"

Silence.

Not even the sound of a breath.

Cory closed his eyes.

All he saw were those flames spiraling up and up and up.

TANUM CREEK

NOW

25

I spot it first, a large mound of rocks and trees, rising up from the ground like a bump under skin. I lead her around the bottom, looking for a big black burned-out stump on the other side. It's there, covered with wet snow but otherwise exactly the way I remembered. And not a second too soon. The snow has turned to a cold, steady rain.

I walk to the stump, unclip my pack, and drop it to the ground. I say, "This is it. Let's get inside while we're still relatively dry."

Astrid looks at me, then the stump, confusion filling her eyes.

"I know it looks weird. The hideout is actually dug into the hill. We enter through this stump. Inside it's big enough to stand. It's genius."

She shakes her head, backs away.

I say, "C'mon. Take a look."

She shakes her head again, violently.

This isn't going the way I saw it in my head. "Watch me," I say. I drop to my knees, crawl through the stump just like Benny showed us. The tarp is still there. I push it aside, smell a blast of something rank from the interior darkness, and immediately wish I had dug out the headlamp first. I retreat, stand up, take a grateful breath. Astrid backs away another step. She's about six feet from where I stand. Her eyes are wide and terror-filled, just like they were when I found her in the trunk. The rain is really coming down now. Her hair is plastered to her face, the hoodie so wet and heavy I see the outline of the sling underneath.

I walk toward her, slowly, hands out. She's shivering, her body tense and vibrating. I'm two feet away and closing, saying, "It's all right. There are candles inside. I can light them. We'll be safe and dry. . . ." She backs up another step; her eyes are jittery, her mouth frozen open. And I know, seeing her this way, that she isn't here. She's in the trunk of that car. Or maybe someplace even worse. I don't know what to do or say.

She glances over her shoulder. I think she's getting ready to run. "We have to go inside. You know that, right?"

She shakes her head. I'm not sure what that means. Does she actually think there are choices here? If she runs there's nowhere to go, nowhere to hide. If the driver doesn't kill her, the mountain will. I can't let that happen. Her best chance is in Stumptown with me.

"Astrid, whatever happened before, that's behind you now." She backs up another step. I'm afraid if I move forward she'll bolt. If she does, I'll have to run after her. That would mean more tracks leading back to this place. I stand where I am and say, "You're safe with me. It's okay—"

She turns and runs. Gets ten feet and slips and falls. She struggles to stand but can't do it fast enough with only one hand for balance.

I catch up to her, reach a hand down to help her up. "C'mon, Astrid. It doesn't have to be like this."

She kicks out at my legs, stands and is ready to run again. I can't let that happen. Can't let her die out there. Not without trying one more time. I wrap my arms around her as gently as I can. I try to avoid her arm, but she starts thrashing, kicking her legs.

I whisper, "Calm down. Please. Just calm down. It's okay. It's okay. We can figure this out."

But her fear is too deep. Everything I say comes out wrong. She struggles with renewed fury. It's hard to keep my balance and she's slippery with mud from her fall. Then, out of nowhere, she lets loose an earsplitting scream. The kind of scream that startles deer and echoes across mountain valleys. I clamp a hand over her mouth, hissing, "Shhhhhhhhh. He'll hear—" She bites my hand. I yell, pull my hand away from her mouth. She twists and is almost free. I make one desperate lunge with both arms, lock my hands across her rib cage. My right arm catches on something under the hoodie. I hear a distinct snap. She grunts, stiffens, sags in my arms, and finally is still. Her head tips forward, motionless.

"Astrid? Are you okay?" All I get from her is silence. It's hard to think straight with my heart pounding like it is. If I release her like this she'll just fall to the ground. Keeping my arms around her, I drag her back to the stump. I lay her on the ground, check for a pulse. Weak and fluttery, but there. I don't know what happened. Then I see a corner of the splint hanging out from under the hoodie with fresh blood dripping down off the foam. I remember that sickening snap, and I know exactly what I did. My stomach heaves and I throw up. Oh man, I can hear Benny now. He'd laugh and say, *Well done, son. Ya jus' turned a bucket of bad into a shitload of worse.* I wipe my mouth and consider my options as the rain falls. It's pretty simple, really. There's only one. If I leave her out here, she'll die from shock, or exposure, or from a killer that probably heard her scream. I crawl into the stump, reach out from the rank darkness, grab her by the shoulders.

And pull her in.

26

Breakfast was buttermilk biscuits with honey butter, turkey sausage, and eggs delivered this a.m. from a farm down the road. Cory couldn't get enough of the scrambled eggs, which had warm crumbled bacon, a cheese that Justin, the Motts' son, said sounded like "gray hair," and flecks of green floating in the creamy yellow that Mrs. Mott said were her secret ingredients—a tablespoon each of finely chopped fresh parsley, basil, and dill. When Cory told her that he didn't know eggs could taste this good, Mrs. Mott told him they were easy to make and she would teach him how if he wanted to learn. While savoring the last bite of those eggs, Cory risked revisiting a dream he'd had ever since his mother let him wear her apron and frost his own cake for his eighth birthday. A dream he gave up on when Benny told him, "A man's job is to kill the food, a woman's job is to cook it." Cory closed his eyes and pictured himself in a busy kitchen at his own restaurant, wearing a chef's hat and apron. He liked what he saw.

After breakfast, which Mr. Mott missed due to a phone call from Scotland, they held a family gathering in the "rock room." Chloe, their daughter, told them she gave it that name because of the huge fireplace made of rounded rocks. Mr. Mott explained how they were hauled in from a dry riverbed in Montana and sealed with a special chemical to enhance the colors. Which led to another story about the mantel over the fireplace, an oak slab milled down from a ceiling truss rescued out of a turn-of-the-century barn in Vermont that was destroyed in a flood. While Mr. Mott spoke, the kids wrestled with Pavlov, the monstrous dog, in front of the fire. Mrs. Mott split her attention between her husband's oration and *Sunset* magazine, occasionally frowning under her glasses when he seemed to be stretching a truth. Cory and Ty sat across from her on a leather sofa, facing two-story windows overlooking a trampoline with sagging springs, a pond with an upside-down canoe on the shore, pine trees beyond the fence, and snowcapped mountains beyond that. They were all waiting for the caseworker, Tony Tanaka. He was supposed to attend this gathering scheduled for ten a.m. Mr. Mott received a text from him at ten fifteen stating he'd be there closer to eleven. That apparently didn't work for Mr. Mott. He told them he had a shipment of Toyotas arriving at his dealership followed by an inventory audit at the lumberyard. "Plus," he said, eyeing the boys, "you have a shopping spree scheduled. We'll start without him."

First up on the agenda were the welcome-to-our-family gifts. Cory and Ty received Mott's Lot baseball caps and keychains from Chloe, and Mott's Lumber and Landscaping T-shirts from Justin. Unfortunately both shirts were size L, and Cory needed 2XL, but Charlene said she would trade it out at the store on Monday. Then Harvey began making his way down a list on his iPad, ticking off household rules, boundary issues (privacy was a big deal with the Motts), ways to address himself and Mrs. Mott (too soon for Mom and Dad, but Mr. and Mrs. were too formal; they decided on first names), chore assignments, homework expectations, medical concerns (Justin—contact dermatitis, Chloe—nearsightedness and anxiety), food preferences, church attendance (encouraged but optional) and, last on the list, family schedules.

Cory asked, "Will we have access to a computer?"

Harvey said, "Do either of you have decent skills?"

Ty shook his head, nodded to Cory.

Cory said, "I know my way around a motherboard."

"In that case I have a couple laptops at the dealership that should work. I will bring them home this afternoon."

Ty nudged Cory and whispered, "The zombies are waiting. . . ."

After the gathering, Harvey led Cory and Ty down a long hall decorated with dozens of framed photographs of Harvey holding up some very large fish. One of the pictures must have been taken on a jungle river because Cory could clearly see a hippopotamus on the shore in the background. Before opening the door with a key from his pocket, Harvey said, "This is my sanctuary, my man cave if you will, where I go to think and read, smoke the occasional cigar, or, in the case of this morning's call from Scotland, to pursue the passion I've had since high school—acquiring vintage fly-fishing equipment." Then he turned the knob, opened the door, and said, "Let's talk."

I dig out the headlamp and focus on what I've done. She's a mess. A cold, wet, bleeding, unconscious, broken mess. Her state is so bad I want to scream. Panic seizes me. I don't know where to start. It would help if I could breathe. Part of the problem is that stench. A quick scan of the small space locates the source. There's a dead animal stretched out behind the stove. I crawl over there and look. It's bigger than I thought. The beam sweeps across a brown snout, pointy ears, brown tail. It's a coyote. There's a black festering hole in a hind leg, probably from a bullet. I have to get this carcass out of here; otherwise I won't be able to concentrate on Astrid. I grab a rear leg and drag it out the door, then hold my breath, pick it up, and walk thirty feet to a big boulder and dump it out of sight.

On my way back to the stump I attempt to cover my tracks by hand-brushing them with snow. Then I crawl into Stumptown and find the water bottle. No way there's enough here to clean my hands, which are covered with dead coyote, clean her wounds, and have enough left for two people to survive. I'll have to hike down to the creek for more. With weather like this, when will that happen?

I splash a little water on my hands and dry them on my pants. Then I kneel next to Astrid and say, "Can you hear me?" No response. I touch her forehead. It feels cold, even to my fingers, which are approaching numb. Since shock and hypothermia are my biggest concerns, that means I need to get her dry and warm. The hoodie is stained with her blood and my vomit and she's soaked head to toe. I can't put her in the sleeping bag like that. Her clothes would soak the inside of the bag and she wouldn't be able to get warm. I could start a fire in the stove, but that idea dies a few seconds later when I think about the tracks I would make collecting wood, plus the smoke from that stove would be seen for miles. Since I'd rather not remove her jeans, I do the next best thing. I pull off her sneakers, then open the first aid kit and reach for the scissors.

I cut her jeans at mid-thigh, slide the legs down, and stuff them in my pack. No point having those gas fumes around when I light the candles. I slip my spare cargo pants on her, then move up to the hoodie. I'm careful to make sure it doesn't get hung up on the exposed half inch of bone, which could reopen the wound and make it start bleeding again. While I'm pulling the sweatshirt over her head, the sweater underneath, which is still dry, shifts up to the base of her rib cage, exposing the skin underneath. My heart rises to my throat. The right side of her stomach is covered in a patchwork of bruised flesh. Thanks to Benny I am intimately familiar with the life span of a bruise. The force of the impact. The resulting shades and stages of red, blue, purple, and black. I'd put this work in the seven- to ten-day range. I lower her sweater to hide the damage. She probably doesn't want me to see it. My hand is shaking. I choke back tears. It takes some effort to settle down.

I start on her arm. Should I clean the wound or not? I look as closely as I can without throwing up. There's dirt and mud and pine needles mixed in with the clotting blood. I look for barrier gloves in the first aid kit and of course there aren't any. I curse Ty for talking me into buying the crappiest first aid kit ever. The cleanest thing I have is a fresh sock, so that's what I use, wetting it first, then dabbing at the debris. I almost throw up twice. My breath clouds the light making it nearly impossible to see. I remove what I can, thinking that I will clean the rest later when I have more water. I briefly consider trying to move her arm so that the bone is no longer exposed, but that's way beyond what I learned in class and I would probably pass out anyway, so I leave it as is. I place three large gauze pads over the wound, watching her constantly for any signs of movement. She's so still I pause for a moment to see if her chest rises. It does, but barely. I wrap everything up with the compression bandage, resplint her arm with the pieces of foam, then use what's left of the athletic tape to hold it all together. The cuts from the zip ties on her wrists and ankles look pretty raw, so I wrap some gauze around them too. The last thing I do is open Ty's sleeping bag, slide it underneath her, and zip it closed. I put my bag on top of hers for extra warmth, fashion a pillow for her head using the stuff sack and the rest of my clean socks and underwear.

After all that is done I realize that I'm shivering too. It's probably a mixture of raw nerves and the fact that my clothes are still wet. My fingertips are now officially numb. I change into my long underwear, then use the lighter in my pack to fire up a dozen candles. The heat helps warm up my hands to the point that I can relax just a little. I sit on the old wooden chest and switch off the headlamp. Then look down at her and make a promise.

A promise I hope I get a chance to keep.

LUSTER, OR.

ELEVEN MONTHS AGO

28

Harvey's man cave was small and dark compared to the airy openness of the main house. It smelled of old cigar smoke and leather—a big change from the cigarettes, weed, and beer Cory was familiar with. Harvey raised a curtain on the main window to let in the morning light. There was a sliding glass door that opened onto the backyard patio, and another door with a dead bolt. The furniture was spare: a wooden desk with nothing on it except a closed laptop, a leather sofa with a folded blanket, a leather chair and ottoman. One wall was floor-to-ceiling books on built-in shelves. From what Cory could see they were mostly legal volumes, biographies of former presidents, and illustrated histories of fly-fishing. Mixed in throughout the room were framed displays of Harvey's passion: fly-fishing poles, waders, reels, and collections of fly-fishing flies. Cory felt his heartbeat elevating and wasn't sure why. It started as soon as Harvey closed the door behind them. Maybe the smell of leather and stale cigar smoke didn't agree with the eggs and sausage. Or maybe it was something about this room, the mix of old and new, and the absence of any pictures of people, living or dead, that made him anxious. He stood close to the door while Ty walked around, examining each relic as if it were the key to some ancient mystery. He stopped in front of a rod in its own cabinet with a glass door. Ty tested the door. It was locked.

"What's so special about this one?" he asked.

"That's a Hoagy Carmichael 212 bamboo rod. All the wrappings are original and the tip guides are custom. Mr. Carmichael only made one hundred and three rods, so this is particularly rare."

"What's it worth?"

"I'm a collector, not a seller."

"But if you did sell it?"

"I would ask for sixty-five hundred and wouldn't take a penny less."

Ty whistled, moved on to the next thing. Cory focused on breathing.

After watching them browse for another minute, Harvey said, "Rather than go through the discovery process—sorry, that's a legal term, but you'll get used to it. Rather than finding out the hard way, I'm going to tell you three things you need to know about me straight up. Number one, I'm a busy man. And I'm about to get busier. So if I come off as abrupt, that's just me getting down to the issue at hand. Number two, I seek order over chaos. Predictable outcomes over random events. Charlene loves surprises. Not me. So if you have a problem, the sooner I hear about it the better. And number three, I believe in the power of numbers. Charlene calls it my 'affliction.' The kids just call me sick. But if you look deep enough, numbers offer truths that others less afflicted do not see." He looked at his watch, then smiled at them. "That's enough about me. Do you have any questions so far?"

Ty just shook his head and kept browsing the fishing poles. Cory didn't know where to start. He wanted to know why Harvey looked so fit. Did he work out? Or was he just born with a runner's body? He wanted to know how old Harvey was. His square, tanned face was wrinkle-free except around his eyes when he smiled, which was a lot last night with Stellah. The short black hair with gray flecks at the temples put him anywhere between thirty-five and fifty. Cory was used to Benny, who always looked twenty years older than he was. Plus, that whole thing about seeking predictable outcomes didn't fit with all the equipment in this room; when it came to random events, Cory couldn't think of an activity more random than fishing.

But Cory chose Ty's approach and just shook his head.

"Good. In that case, I have a question for you. Gentlemen, what is your plan?"

Ty looked up from a glass case containing three fishing reels filled with green line. "Which plan are you talking about?" He glanced sideways at Cory, as if to say, *Hell, yeah, we have a plan but you won't like it.*

Harvey smiled. "You are currently juniors. If I remember your files correctly, something significant happens on June sixth, nominally nineteen months from now."

"Our birthday," Cory said.

"Correct. But more germane to this discussion, you turn eighteen, which means you will join the other twenty-three thousand kids in foster care who age out of the system every year. Did Ms. Deshay share that number with you?"

"Not that I remember," Ty said.

"No," Cory said.

"I didn't think so. Here are some more numbers I expect you don't know." He watched Ty reach out to touch a fishing pole on a horizontal rack and said, "Please don't touch anything on display in this room. Some of them are . . . fragile." Cory looked around him and wondered, *What isn't on display?* Harvey continued, saying, "By age twenty-one, one in seven of your fellow twenty-three thousand will be homeless. Fifty percent will be unemployed. And more germane to my profession, by age twenty-one seventy-seven percent of the males will have a criminal history." He gave Ty a measured look, as if that number was particularly relevant to him. "After four years on the bench in juvie court, I'd say that seventy percent figure is closer to eighty. So with those numbers in mind, I ask you again: What's your plan?"

Cory thought about breakfast, about those eggs. About Charlene's offer to teach him how to cook. He wanted to say he had a plan since he frosted that birthday cake. He wanted to own it, commit to it. But he couldn't get past the first part—that he and Ty would "age out of the system." A system that two days ago he barely even knew existed. But he had to answer before Ty did, because Ty's plan involved flashlights and stuffing his pockets with convenience store contraband. "We're working on it," Cory said.

Harvey nodded, checked his watch again. "Unfortunately, I've seen too many youths such as yourselves make bad decisions that led them to very dark places. That's why a plan—"

"Such as ourselves?" Ty said, his focus no longer on the fishing gear.

"That's correct."

"You don't know anything about us."

"Oh, I might know a little more than you think." Harvey took a key from his pocket and opened a drawer in his desk. He pulled out two file folders. One was much thicker than the other.

Harvey opened the thicker file, lifted a couple pages, pulled one, and read, "'Tyler Bic was the only shining light in an otherwise listless defense. His four sacks and three picks kept the Tornadoes in the game long enough to win. If it weren't for his late hit on QB Stenson with ten seconds remaining in the—'"

"Okay, big deal," Ty said. "So you know I play football."

"I also know that your father, Benjamin T. Bic, and I shared a common interest. He was imbued with the *entrepreneurial spirit*."

Ty glanced at Cory.

"Let's assume from this point on that I rarely make decisions based on gut instinct alone. As stated earlier, I'm not a fan of surprises." Harvey returned the sheet to the folder, put both files in the drawer, closed, and locked it. While he was doing this Cory wondered what Harvey had in the second file and if he would ever know.

Harvey said, "I'm sorry about your father. It's a horrible way to die. And your mother leaving you is another challenge. But this discussion isn't about your past. What I want to do is look ahead. What I'm—" His cell phone rang. Harvey answered, said, "It's about time. We'll meet you outside," and pocketed the phone. He stepped out from behind his desk. "What I'm proposing is this— let's make today day one of your new plan. A plan that elevates you above the perilous future of your fellow thirty thousand. Does that work for you?"

"Yes," Cory said. Ty waited a few seconds before nodding his head.

"Good. Are you familiar with the term 'milestones'?"

"Yeah. They live next to the Flintstones," Ty said.

Harvey laughed. It was warm and deep and filled the room. "I'm surprised someone your age is familiar with that cartoon." *So he does get surprised,* Cory thought. "*Milestones* originates from the ancient Romans. They carved blocks of granite into milestones and placed them on their roads at regular intervals to indicate a unit of distance traveled."

"Why do we care about old rocks?" Ty asked.

"Do you know how to drive?" The question was directed at both of them.

"Yes," they said.

"Follow me."

Harvey walked across the room, unlocked the dead bolt, and opened the second door. Cory blinked at the sunlight, then gratefully stepped out into cool, fresh air. It took a moment to see the porch, then recognize where they were. Harvey's man cave was next to the garage. They were standing in the upper driveway and had just exited the same door that Kayla, the former babysitter, used last night. Harvey walked to the car with the cover over it. He pulled it off, revealing a Volvo station wagon. It was black, although there was so much dust on it that the paint had a grayish tint. The front passenger tire was flat and there was a sizable dent in the front passenger door. "This is milestone number two. She doesn't look like much now, but her engine purrs and she's built like a tank. After you demonstrate safe driving skills, and perform well at milestone number one, this will be your car to drive while you're here."

"I'm liking this plan," Ty said.

Cory said, "I don't have my driver's license."

"Why not?"

"I lost it in the fire."

"That's unfortunate. But you have yours?" Harvey said, looking at Ty.

"Yes."

"Birth certificates?"

They answered with silence.

"All right. Tell Charlene. She'll get that worked out." He paused at the sound of a car with a sketchy muffler coming up the driveway. "Your escort is here. Before I go, do you have any questions for me?"

"What's milestone number one?" Cory asked.

A green car pulled into the circular drive and rolled to a stop.

"I'll leave that up to Tony. Let's get to work on that plan. Have an excellent day!" Harvey disappeared into his man cave. Cory heard the dead bolt click.

Cory looked at Ty. "Flintstones? Really?"

The horn honked.

"Shotgun," Ty said.

29

Her eyes finally open. Slow to start, just narrow slits showing blue. Then wide enough to focus on me sitting in my long underwear on the old chest staring down at her. She tries to sit up, winces, lowers herself slowly to the floor.

"Careful," I say, my breath clouding around me. "You'll need to take it slow for a while."

She looks at the gauze taped around her wrist.

"I bandaged the cuts. And I resplinted your arm."

Her eyes zero in on the sleeve of the shirt she's wearing; then she lifts the sleeping bag and peers inside, gives me a troubled look. I explain what I did. She stares at me for a beat, then closes her eyes and nods. Good. Now for the real test. "How's your arm?"

Her eyes fly open. She shakes her head.

"It hurts?"

Her eyes narrow on me, as if to say, *What kind of a dumbass question is that?*

"What's the pain like on a scale of one to ten?"

She shows me five fingers, then four.

A nine. I was hoping for a six or seven. I show her the bottle of ibuprofen. "Would you like some?"

A big nod this time.

I shake out four pills, lean forward, and give them to her. She puts the pills in her mouth while I uncap the water bottle. I hand it to her and say, "Easy on this. We need it to last." She washes the pills down with two short swallows. I take one myself then recap the bottle, feel her watching my every move. As if it's just a matter of time before I do some other thing to hurt her. I risk a quick look into those eyes. I don't see full-blown anger. But it's clearly in the neighborhood.

It's time to say what I've been avoiding.

"Do you remember what happened outside?"

She nods slowly. I think this is as hard for her as it is for me.

"Do you remember when you ran and fell and I picked you up?"

I get the narrow-eyed glare. For a second I think she's going to rise up and hit me. If that happens I won't stop her. In fact, I'd welcome it. She no doubt has a different take on what happened—that I chased her, maybe even knocked her down. She probably hates me and I can't blame her. I press on anyway. "Do you remember what happened after I picked you up?"

A pause. Astrid shakes her head, licks her lips. I give her another sip of water. Her eyes close tight from the obvious pain. "I screwed up, Astrid. I should have told you the truth about this place and let you decide."

She blinks, then nods. That could mean anything from *Yes, asshole, you did screw up* to *Don't stop now, asshole, you're on a roll.* Either way it's pretty clear what she thinks of me.

"While you were unconscious, I made a promise to myself that when you woke up I would never lie to you again. So from now on it's the truth, no matter what." I take a deep breath. "I broke your arm, Astrid. It was so bad there was bone sticking out of skin. You collapsed in my arms." I pause. "The wound got pretty messed up. I did the best I could to clean it, but we didn't have a lot of water." Tears are streaming from her eyes. I'm struggling to hold mine back. "So here's the deal now. This is all the water we have." I show her the remaining bottle, which is less than half. "It isn't enough for two people for two days, especially if I have to clean your wound again."

She shakes her head, like she really doesn't want that to happen.

"I'm worried about infection, Astrid. And...full disclosure here...there was a dead coyote behind the stove and I got some of it on my hands. That's the bad smell." Her eyes widen in surprise—or maybe alarm. "Don't worry about this being a coyote den. It had been shot. I think it just crawled in here to die." Her eyes go even wider. *Oh shit! Did I just really say that?* Words start geysering from my mouth. "Forget what I just said. That was seriously stupid. You're not going to die. It's just a broken arm. People break arms all the time. Ty's broken both of his, and he's—" I stop myself before I go down that road. "You'll be okay. And don't worry about the driver dude. He'll never find us here. It's all good, Astrid. It really is." I smile, as if I believe all the shit I just said. "So you stay here and relax. I'm going to get more water. The good news is, it's raining, so our tracks in the snow are almost gone. I'll be back in an hour." I begin to stand.

She shakes her head.

"What's wrong?"

Astrid points to the door, shakes her head again.

"You want me to stay?"

She points at me, then the wooden chest.

I sit.

She nods, her eyelids drifting down.

I may be wrong here, but my guess is it's not that she wants my company specifically—she just doesn't want to be alone. I listen to her breaths, watch the small puffs of vapor rise and fade. She settles into a wheezy but regular rhythm. I lean in for a quick look. Her skin has a pinkish color, which I hope is a good sign. That means she's warming up. After a few minutes, I'm pretty confident that she's asleep. With her situation stable I'm tempted to get water now. It's really what I should do. She would never know that I was gone—other than the fact that we would magically have more water. I shake that thought away. She asked me to stay and that's what I will do. Besides, I need to sleep. That need is like a heavy hand on my spirit pushing me down.

Before I collapse I look out both porthole windows—still gray and raining softly. Our tracks are pretty much gone. I make sure the ceiling vent is open and blow out all but one candle, slip the headlamp over my head in case the candle goes out; then I slide my sleeping bag off hers, zip myself inside, and hope that sleep comes fast and easy.

But sleep does not come fast or easy. I was afraid it would be the terror of the driver's flashlight coming down the slope, or Ty leaving, or even the gut-emptying sight of blood-tipped bone through skin that would haunt me in the almost dark.

It's none of those visions.

As I listen to the sound of her breathing and feel the steady rhythm pull me closer to my own personal oblivion, all I see are those bruises. I hope that whatever violences she endured are behind her and that this hole in the ground is what I promised it would be: a refuge and not a grave.

LUSTER, OR.

ELEVEN MONTHS AGO

30

ony Tanaka, their caseworker and self-appointed first cool friend in Luster, downshifted his Jeep to third to miss a squirrel crossing the road. As the gears shrieked on their way back to fourth, Tony growled between gritted teeth, "If that creature cost me a new transmission, I'll road-kill the next one and all its bucktoothed kin." He backfired through a blinking yellow light, crossed a two-lane without checking for traffic, and the tour of their new domain continued.

"This isn't the way we came in," Cory said from his spot behind Ty. His backseat companions were a Trail Blazers desk lamp, a mesh bag of basketballs, and a box of dusty books by Louis L'Amour and Danielle Steel. Cory wondered if Tony had just been to a garage sale, or was on his way to one.

Tony said, "This way is faster. Less traffic."

"What traffic?" Ty asked. "It's like the apocalypse here compared to Portland."

"Tractors and combines. I hate 'em. Almost as much as squirrels."

"Where are you taking us?" Cory asked.

"Harvey didn't say?"

"All he said is something about milestone one."

"And the Romans," Ty said.

Tony laughed. "I got the same talk back in the day."

"How long ago was that?" Cory asked.

"My senior year." They passed a sign welcoming them to the town of Luster. Tony slowed from fifty to twenty-five. "Harvey gave me my first job."

"What job was that?"

Tony glanced at Cory in the rearview. "One that sucked."

Two blocks later he turned left, then right into a car dealership. Tony parked two spots from the entrance in front of a sign that read T. TANAKA. He opened his door and said, "Welcome to Mott's Lot. Aka milestone one."

Tony didn't introduce them to their future coworkers because there wasn't time. They were meeting Mrs. M in an hour at Walmart for the shopping spree and he had two more stops to squeeze in before then—one of them being lunch and caffeine. He told them Harvey believed time and blood were of equal value, and to waste either was a sin in the Book of Mott. To repeat that error of being late again today would put him on the shit list, "and trust me, my new friends," he said on their way through the lobby door, "that is a deep dark place you do not want to be."

He led them past the showroom floor, past the waiting room, past a door with H. MOTT on it, past an office with a big whiteboard next to the door with lots of numbers and names, and above it all in big black letters: NOVEMBER MILESTONE 200 UNITS.

Tony led them through the service department into a noisy concrete room that smelled like steam and soap. There were three cars in stalls, two dripping wet and being wiped down by guys with big towels. One guy had gray hair and looked to be in his sixties, the other was in his teens. They waved to Tony, then returned to their task. The third car had all the doors open. A black hose ran from the ceiling to the front seat, where a guy on his knees was vacuuming the interior of the shining SUV.

Tony said over the noise, "This is the detail shop. It's where we make the old cars look new again. Don't worry. You'll get used to the smell."

Ty said, "I've smelled worse." He gave Cory a look that said *like a rotting pig in a crack house oven.*

Tony pointed at the guy with the vacuum. He was so deep into the car the only visible part of him were the bottoms of his Nikes. "That was me when I started. My skills with a crevice tool remain legendary to this day."

"A crevice tool?" Ty said. "It sounds like something in a porno movie."

Tony laughed. "Oh, they're gonna have fun with you!"

On their way back to the car, a frantic woman burst through the front door carrying a box in both arms. She yelled, "Tony! Wait! I have something for you!"

"What is it?" Tony asked.

"Harvey called. He said to give you these laptops."

Tony took the box, told Ty it would have to sit on his lap because there was no room in the backseat or trunk. As they drove away, Ty asked Tony if there were any dojos in this town while Cory looked out the window at a parking lot full of new and used cars and a big sign that promised a price to fit any budget. He knew he should be thinking about Benny and Detective O and Harvey and how the world had been spinning in one direction and now it was spinning in another. But all he had room for in his head at this moment was the amount of time he needed to accumulate enough money to buy noise-canceling headphones and whether or not the laptop had enough muscle to run *Dark Souls III* at fifty-five fps.

Their next stop was Bravo Burgers, the restaurant with the waving cow on the roof, except it wasn't waving now. Tony took them inside to meet the manager, Rebecca. Cory guessed she was maybe eighteen, definitely under twenty, and was certain that Ty was appreciative of how she looked in her tight orange Bravo Burgers T-shirt and cap. Tony introduced them and told her that they would be staying with the Motts through graduation next year. Cory noted the way Tony emphasized *staying with the Motts*. Like dropping that name was all he needed to do. He also noted that Tony did not include their last names in the introduction.

"You related to the Motts?" she asked.

Before either could answer, Tony said, "I'll explain later. We're on a schedule."

"Oh, right," she said and nodded at Tony, as if an explanation wasn't necessary. "Is he putting them to work?"

"At the lot."

"Too bad. Londa quit last night. She's moving to Bend." Rebecca gave Ty a hopeful look. "I could use another busser."

Tony said, "I'll tell Harvey."

"Since they don't need jobs, and you're not here to eat, why the visit?"

"Just showing them the highlights."

"In that case," she said and winked at Ty, "you better not sneeze or you'll miss it."

The last stop before meeting Charlene at Walmart for the shopping spree was the Drip 'n' Sip. Cory remembered that Stellah was going to stop here last night. While they stood in a line two customers deep he asked Tony if he'd heard from her today.

"Not yet."

"Like I told you," Ty said to Cory. "We're yesterday's meat."

"I can text or call her if you want," Tony said. "It's really not a problem."

"No, I'm good," Cory said. "If she calls, she calls."

With steaming beverages and bagel sandwiches in hand, they sat at a table overlooking the sidewalk shoppers and cars backed up at the light on Constitution Ave. The sky had clouded up since morning. Rain, or possibly snow, lurked in the very near future.

Tony gave them each a sheet of paper titled *Bic Support Team* with a list of contact names, numbers, and email addresses for himself and Lacey Sharp, the other caseworker in Luster. The contact info also included an attorney assigned to the team (they would meet him next week), a school psychologist, and a grief counselor that Tony said was on vacation until next Monday. In the meantime they could—

"Grief's not an issue," Ty said, "at least not with me."

"Maybe not now. But it'll hit once the newness of everything wears off. I know from personal experience." Tony gave them each a steady look over his coffee, then said to Ty, "Speaking of issues, your file stated that anger management therapy is strongly recommended. What's up with that?"

Ty shrugged. "I have an allergic reaction to assholes. My fists get all puffy."

"Are your fists getting puffy now?"

Ty flexed his right hand. "Too early to tell. Keep asking questions. We'll see what happens."

"How long have you had this . . . allergy?"

"As long as I can remember. I think I was overexposed when I was little."

Tony looked at Cory. "Do you have the same problem?"

Cory had a mouthful of bagel sandwich. Before he could answer, Ty said, "Assholes don't seem to bother him. I think he's immune."

Tony said, "Then Cory's the lucky one. Unfortunately, you had a reaction this fall that put a kid in the hospital. Criminal charges were filed."

"And dropped. This is a delicious sandwich. The sausage freakin' makes it."

Tony smiled at Ty's effort to deflect the conversation. "The Motts are aware of your past and they took you in. But it is a concern. They want you to go to therapy. Your first appointment is Wednesday at three o'clock at this address." Tony pulled a business card out of his wallet and slid it across the table to Ty. "Charlene said she'd take care of your transportation until you start driving the Volvo. The therapist's name is Erica Sanchez. You're lucky. In my opinion she's the best between here and Redmond. Very hard to get an appointment. But good ol' Harvey, he found a way."

Without looking at the card, Ty said, "What if I don't go?"

"There are two ways that can play out, and Harvey made them very clear. You won't be left alone with the kids until you complete the sessions without a miss. If you refuse to go, then your placement is terminated. I expect you'll be sent to a lockdown facility until you age out."

"What about Cory?"

"He didn't come up."

"Cory stays."

"That's the Motts' call, not mine."

Ty slid the card back to Tony. "This is bullshit."

"I'm afraid it's not."

While Ty and Tony glared across the table, Cory thought about the crunching sound he heard when Ty's foot hit Benny's face. He remembered the kid just after school started, Francisco, and the picture in the paper of him in the hospital with his face all bandaged up. Cory said, "Just go to the sessions, Ty. Just—"

"Just what? Shrink-wrap my head just to make some rich dude I don't know or care about happy?"

Ty's leg was shaking under the table. He was starting to vibrate. Cory said, "Tony, can I talk with Ty outside for a minute?"

"Sure. But keep it short. We're on a schedule."

As soon as they were out the door, Ty jumped all over Cory. "We should bail. Leave tonight. You an' me. Say screw you to milestone man with his six-thousand-dollar fishing poles. That's just sick, Cor. We don't need it."

"You need to chill, Ty."

"And you need to grow a pair."

"You're not thinking."

"Oh, I'm thinkin', bro. Clear as a fuckin' bell."

Benny mode was closing in. Cory had to act fast. "Just listen, okay? We have zero money. We don't even have something to sell. But we have jobs with—"

"With crevice tools, whatever the hell that is."

"He's letting us use a car. A *Volvo*! I say we work for a few months, save up some money. If this situation doesn't work out, then we talk about bailing."

Ty looked unconvinced.

"Plus," Cory added, "even if we left, we don't have a place to go."

"Not true."

"Where would we go?" Cory hoped Ty would say, *Find Mom*.

"Stumptown."

"Stumptown? Are you shitting me? Stumptown's a dream. And that dream died with Benny. We need something real. Something we can even *find*. Let's see if we can make this work. *Please*."

Ty looked down, kicked a cigarette butt off the sidewalk. In that moment, behind Ty, Cory saw a girl round the corner and walk toward them. She had long black hair, jeans, a black jacket with a hood—and then it hit him. She was the girl in the window at the ski lodge. Kayla. She walked a few steps in their direction, saw Cory looking at her, and froze.

Still with his back to her, Ty said, "I seriously don't want a shrink rooting around inside my skull."

The girl crossed the street in the middle of the block. A car slammed on its brakes to avoid her. She took one more glance over her shoulder in their direction, then hurried away.

Ty was saying, "...win. I'll do it for us. We stay together. That's all I really want."

He held out a fist. Cory bumped it.

"Well?" Tony asked.

Ty picked up the business card, acted like he was going to rip it up. Then shrugged and slipped it in his pocket. "I'll see the shrink. But it'll be a huge waste. Because I don't have a problem. Just so we're clear."

"Got it," Tony said. "You are a problem-free dude. I wish I could say the same about me." He dropped a five-spot on the table for a tip, turned for the door. "By the way, your friend Stellah called while you were outside. I told her you were busy, but that you would call her back."

"What'd she say?" Cory asked, relieved, but trying not to show it.

"Not a lot. She only had a minute. She wanted to confirm that you guys were doing okay. I said you already have jobs and are looking forward to school. She said to call or text her when you get phones. Oh, and, Cory—she said she has the package you requested, and that someone wants to talk to you." Tony handed him a napkin with a phone number scrawled on it with blue ink. Cory recognized the number. It matched the one on the business card in his pocket. "She said it's urgent. You can use mine." Tony offered him his phone.

"I know what this is about," Cory said and waved off the phone. "It's not that urgent. I'll call later."

Ty grabbed the napkin, read the number, and then stuffed it in his not-quite-finished mug of coffee.

Tony studied them for a moment. "Okay, then. Moving on. I also got a text from Charlene. She's on her way to Walmart." He stood. "Let the shopping begin."

While they approached Tony's car, Ty asked Cory, "What package does Stellah have?"

"I'll tell you later."

"What did the donut eater want?"

"Probably wanted to know if we'd seen any interesting donut shops."

Cory climbed into the backseat and closed the door a little harder than he meant to. He didn't want to get into it with Ty about why he asked for Benny's cremated remains. Some questions didn't have answers. As they headed for Walmart with huge white flakes drifting down and Tony tapping the steering wheel to "Grandma Got Run Over by a Reindeer" on the radio, Cory tried to think about what he would buy at Walmart, but all he could come up with were images of a little girl next to a playground slide opening a garbage bag full of severed heads.

31

The Toshiba wasn't a complete dog. The processor was fast enough to handle most of the games Cory played. But favorites like *Dark Souls* would be a stretch, and *Witcher 3* would turn the onboard Intel graphics card into a steaming puddle of mush. Upgrading the card and doubling the RAM would solve that problem. Cory didn't see it happening in his immediate future. But Cory could surf and that scratched a more immediate itch. With his brother snoring three feet away, Cory googled *Harvey Mott, Luster, Oregon.*

He scrolled through three pages of results: *Mott Accepts Luster Entrepreneur of the Year, Mott Announces Grand Opening of New Restaurant, Chairman Post on School Board Goes to Mott, Mott Turns Down Third Term on Bench.* Link after link celebrated the impressive accomplishments of Harvey Mott, hyper-successful businessman, civic leader, philanthropist, and apparently soon-to-be former judge. The *Luster Sentinel* ran nonstop front-page features about Harvey launching a new business, receiving an award, starting up a scholarship, or donating yet another big check to another worthy cause. The man was too good to be true. Cory tried to find something negative for balance. The only things that popped up were Harvey getting into a water rights dispute with the llama rancher adjacent to his home.

The videos Cory found had a similar affection for all things Harvey. One memorable clip from the local news channel showed him teaching a gymnasium full of fifth graders how to fly-fish. He donated a rod, reel, and two specialty flies from Perfectflystore.com to every kid in the class but only after promising to embrace the sacred creed of catch and release. "It's about the skill, not the kill!" he had them chant. Harvey also gave each child a T-shirt, which they proudly wore for the camera. The shirts displayed a smiling trout on the front, and the Mott's Lot logo emblazoned across the back. Cory viewed this act as a shamefully obvious plug for the business and suspected the love showered on Harvey by the local media was partially due to the huge advertising dollars he sent their way. Even if only 10 percent of that love was earned through his good deeds, the Honorable Harvey L. Mott deserved the Mayor's Award for Outstanding Service to the Community, a distinction he'd won six times in the past ten years.

Cory skimmed most of the pages, but there were three that he read carefully and bookmarked for future reference. The first, "Mott Explores Co-Op Venture," covered the story of Bennington's Hardware, a Luster business icon for over fifty years. It was on the verge of receivership after being rocked by an embezzlement scheme. Thirty-two of the forty-eight employees, some of whom had worked there for thirty-plus years, were destined to lose their jobs. Harvey swooped in, bought the property and business for an undisclosed sum, restructured the debt, added a landscaping service, and, in a stunning act of generosity, reorganized the new business as a co-op where the employees owned 35 percent of the company, with a goal of being 100 percent employee owned in five years. It was during this acquisition that Harvey announced he would not be seeking a third term on the bench. The article mentioned rumors that he could be eyeing a state senate seat, but Harvey would neither confirm nor deny the rumor, stating only that "I'm stepping down to pursue other matters of consequence." There was a picture of him cutting the ribbon in front of the newly minted Mott's Lumber and Landscaping, while all forty-eight employees, plus Mayor Patrick Tice, watched and applauded. One of the employees caught Cory's attention and he zoomed in for a closer look. It was Kayla, the elusive girl in the window. But this Kayla was smiling ear to ear. That was a stark contrast to the girl he saw this morning who almost got hit by a car while obviously working hard to avoid him. Something had dimmed the light in her, and he wondered what that was.

The second article was published eight years ago. A star player on the Luster High School boys' basketball team was involved in a garage-hopping incident that resulted in the shooting death of his friend and fellow teammate, DeShawn Hollywell. The article covered sentencing of the fifty-eight-year-old shooter and father of three (thirty-six years in prison) and the surviving teen (three weeks at a boot camp for repeat juvenile offenders and six months' probation). The teen was Anthony "Tony" Tanaka, and the county judge was the Honorable Harvey L. Mott.

The third article was the shortest and the most difficult for Cory to read. It was a single paragraph with a brief statement from a fire department spokesperson attributing the house fire on 59855 Chutney Road in West Portland, which resulted in the death of the homeowner, Benjamin Bic, to an explosion caused by the manufacture of methamphetamine. It concluded with Portland Police Bureau investigating officer Detective Bill Ostrander stating: "We are pursuing the death of Mr. Bic as a homicide. There are no leads or persons of interest at this time. Any individuals or family members with information pertaining to this case should contact me at PPB headquarters immediately."

Cory suspected the "family members" comment was a reach-out to him. Cory looked at Ty, sleeping soundly, then at Ty's phone charging on the nightstand. He was pretty sure he could get it off the charger without waking Ty, and reached out to do just that—then remembered AT&T had canceled their plan. Whatever desire he felt to call Detective O passed. Cory shut down the Toshiba and slid it under the bed. He switched off his light and closed his eyes.

After five minutes of tossing and turning he knew sleep would be impossible. He had another itch, and this one would only get worse until he did something about it. He looked at the clock: 12:48 a.m. He'd play for an hour, a couple levels, three at the most. Just enough to clear his head, then sleep till seven, which was when Charlene was making breakfast—a Spanish frittata with fresh cinnamon rolls—and had said he could help. But the problem with scratching this particular itch was the Wi-Fi signal. It wasn't strong enough up here to get the download speed he needed. Cory listened for sounds from below, heard nothing. He slipped out of bed, grabbed the laptop, headed for the door.

The downstairs was all silence and shadows. Charlene kept the range hood light on in the kitchen and that provided enough illumination for him to go to the pantry, grab an open bag of tortilla chips, and set up on the couch in the rock room. Pavlov gave him a quick glance from his bed next to the fireplace, thumped his tail once, then went back to sleep. Cory pinged the router, tried to hack in with the default passwords, but nothing worked. Then he checked the Wi-Fi signal. As he hoped, it was a solid five bars. He logged into his account on Battlenet.com and started the estimated twelve-minute download for his latest version of *World of Warcraft*.

With eight minutes remaining he heard what sounded like a muffled voice. Cory waited a few seconds, heard it again. It was coming from the hall that led to the garage; it had to be Harvey's office. Cory thought about packing everything up, but didn't want to stop the download midstream. He scanned the Wi-Fi network to see what other devices were on it at this time. The results showed his laptop plus another device, a Samsung mobile phone named HM*2745 with an IP address. Cory had seen Harvey using an iPhone the previous day, so having a second phone was worth noting. He glanced at the download status—a little over five minutes remaining. He was about to snap a screenshot of the scan when he heard a door open.

Footsteps approached from the hall. There wasn't enough time to clear the scan, and closing the laptop would stop the download. He pressed the Windows key +D to minimize the pop-up, then reached for a tortilla chip as Harvey, wearing boxers and nothing else, rounded the corner. He stopped, stared at Cory, then stormed up to him. "How long have you been here?" he demanded. The edge to his voice sent Cory's heartbeat soaring.

"I . . . I just sat down."

"That's what you did. I asked for a unit of time."

"Maybe five minutes."

"Maybe is not an answer."

Cory gulped. "Okay. Six minutes?"

Harvey flashed a smile. "Relax. I'm just giving you a hard time. That's all right with you, isn't it?"

Cory was stunned at how that smile came out of nowhere, as if Harvey had flipped a switch. "Sure," he said, certain that he wouldn't be able to relax for the rest of the night.

"Those of us in the legal profession have an overzealous appreciation for precise language. Lawyers that approached my bench learned that lesson quickly. What I really want to know is: Why aren't you in bed?"

"I couldn't sleep."

"Any reason in particular?"

"No. I just wasn't tired."

"I suffer from the same affliction." He nodded at the laptop. "What are you watching?"

"Nothing. I'm downloading a game."

"What game?"

"*World of Warcraft.*"

"Isn't that an old game?"

"Yes. But it's still awesome."

"What's wrong with the Wi-Fi in your room?"

"It's stronger down here. The download would have taken too long." Cory wondered if he was in Harvey's courtroom, waiting to be sentenced for a crime.

"I'll get it fixed tomorrow," Harvey said.

"A range extender might work," Cory said, jumping at the chance to shift the conversation away from what he was doing. "But an AP would be better."

"What's an AP?"

"Access point. Sometimes they're called repeaters depending on how your router is configured. I think APs have better range than a simple wireless extender."

"You lost me at repeater." Harvey smiled. "Those tortilla chips are good, but they're better with the mango salsa."

"I'm sorry. The bag was open. I didn't—"

"No. You're part of the family now. I've been known to enjoy the occasional midnight snack."

Cory doubted that. Even in the shadows, he could see the man was nearly as cut as Ty. He also noticed a three-inch horizontal scar on the right side of his chest.

Harvey asked, "How close is your download to being done?"

Cory glanced at the screen. "It has three minutes left."

"Perfect. I have something for you and Ty. Stay here. I'll be right back."

Harvey left for his office. As soon as he was out of sight, Cory screen-shot the scan, dragged it to the games folder, then wiped his browsing history. The Battlenet.com download finished seconds before Harvey, thankfully wearing a T-shirt now, returned.

He was carrying two white boxes, each about the size of a thick paperback book. Cory closed the laptop and stood, anxious to return to the attic.

Harvey said, "All the salespeople at the Lot get these." He handed the boxes to Cory. They were iPhones. The wrappers were unbroken.

"Thank you," Cory said, stunned.

"You're welcome. I'll add you to the business account on Monday."

"But me and Ty, we're not salespeople."

"Lesson number one," Harvey said, "no matter what you do in life, you're always selling."

While they were on the subject of the Lot, Cory wondered if now was the time to bring up an idea he had mentioned to Charlene when they were shopping at Walmart. Charlene had thought it sounded wonderful. Cory decided to go for it. "I was wondering if I could work somewhere other than the Lot."

"Is there a problem with the Lot?"

"Because of my size . . . it would be hard for me to handle the vacuuming."

"Fair enough. But if you're thinking about the hardware store, I'm afraid that is not an option." He gave Cory a steady look, as if to nail that coffin closed. Cory wondered what it was about that particular business that took it off the table, but he didn't want to risk derailing what he really wanted with that question.

"Actually I was thinking Bravo Burgers. The manager said she needs a busser."

"Are you sure? The pay is better at the Lot. And logistically it's more convenient for you and your brother to work at the same place. I could tell Manny that you need to do exterior washing only."

It sounded like Harvey was working up to a no. Cory decided to take another risk. "I want to learn how to cook."

That raised an eyebrow. "Is this Charlene's idea, or yours?"

"Mine. It's something I've always wanted to do. I like to read cookbooks and imagine how I would change the recipes."

"Bravo Burgers would hardly qualify as fine dining."

"It's fine enough for me."

Harvey rubbed his chin. Benny would have said something like *Are you sure someone fat as you should be working around all those fries? You'd eat up all the profits!* Cory steeled himself for the worst. Instead Harvey nodded and said, "Here's what I'll do. Charlene gets her worry on when I can't sleep. She thinks it's bad for my heart, and she's probably right." He tapped the place where Cory had seen the scar. "I had a pacemaker installed last year. If you promise to keep this encounter between us I'll tell Rebecca that she has a new busser."

It seemed like an odd request in what was turning out to be an odd conversation. But if keeping a secret from Charlene was what it took to trade a crevice tool in for a spatula, Cory was all over it. *I've been keeping secrets my entire life. What's another year?* "Sure," he said. "Not a problem. Thank you, sir."

"Please. Call me Harvey. You've had a rough couple of days. Go back to bed. I shall do the same." He started to walk away.

Cory said, "Since I won't be working at the Lot, do you want the iPhone back?"

"No. But if it gets lost, stolen, or damaged you'll owe the company eight hundred dollars."

"Thank you, sir. I mean, Harvey."

He disappeared into the shadows on the other side of the house. Cory watched Pavlov twitch in his horse-size bed by the fireplace. After a few minutes the butterflies in his stomach had calmed enough for him to put away the chips, then climb the stairs to the attic. He had a laptop, an iPhone, new clothes, and a new job. He and Ty were living together in a ski lodge. Despite a far-off voice in his head whispering, *All is not right in the house of Mott,* Cory allowed himself a smile of his own as he rolled back into bed.

Chaos was finally giving way to order.

STUMPTOWN

NOW

32

When I wake she is still sleeping. Her color looks good, but her breathing sounds a little more labored, like the rattle has moved from her throat to deep in her chest. The candle is still lit although it's barely more than a stub in a puddle of wax. I wonder how long it took to burn down that far. One hour? Three? Five? Then I look at the door and realize the crack of light is gone.

Is it night already?

I peer out one of the portholes. Total black. I have no idea what time it is. The thought disorients me. Frightens me. I need more light. With my heart pounding, I use the burning stub to light three more candles. That's better. The tightness in my chest subsides. I take two deep breaths.

Astrid stirs beside me and opens her eyes.

"How are you feeling?" I ask.

She shakes her head, motions for the phone.

Why didn't I think of that? The last time I saw it was when I gave it to her at the top of the ridge. "You put it in the hoodie pocket, right?"

She nods.

The hoodie is hanging on a nail behind the stove. I check the pockets. No phone. Although I'm 99 percent sure it's a waste of time, I open my pack and check her jeans. Empty. A sickening feeling creeps over me. Desperate, I check my pants and jacket. All I find are bandage wrappers and the alarm key for the back door at Bravo.

"Is it in your sleeping bag?"

She shakes her head.

"It has to be here. Help me look."

Astrid glares at me. It's a ridiculous request. And there's really nowhere to look. Bizarrely, I think about asking her to call my phone.

She points at the door.

"You think it's out there?"

One grim nod.

Shit. Although the phone could be anywhere between here and the top of the ridge, I'm thinking it probably fell out when we struggled (aka I broke her arm). That means I'd have to search an area of about fifty square feet.

I say, "I'd rather not look for it now. The headlamp might call attention to us. I'll take a quick look first thing tomorrow morning before I go for water. But speaking of the phone, I have a question for you. Actually, it's one question with a follow-up."

Her eyebrows gather together. I assume that means she has a question of her own.

I say, "Is there something you want to ask me?"

She nods.

"Would you like to go first?"

She shakes her head, points to me.

"Okay. Question one." I show her the clearly defined imprint of her teeth on the meaty part of my right thumb. "Do you remember how this happened?" She blinks and nods. "Right before you did that you let out a scream that could probably be heard all the way to Portland." I pause. She waits. I wonder if she knows where I'm headed with this. "At that moment I realized two things. For one, I scared the shit out of you. I'm sorry about that. So thank you for going Wolverine on my thumb. I deserved it." She nods. There's maybe the faintest hint of a smile. That's a relief. I need some encouragement for what comes next. "The other thing I realized was that your vocal cords work. Which brings me to my follow-up question." I pause again. Her eyes narrow. Yeah, she knows where I'm headed. Maybe I should stop here. If she wants to talk, she will. On the other hand, she needs to know that I know—so I blurt it out: "Did you know you have an accent when you talk in your sleep?"

Her eyes go wide. Let's call this her deer-in-the-headlights look. Again I wonder if I should stop. But I'm too far down this road to turn around. Even if it means I'm likely to crash and burn. "I think it's Australian. Or maybe British. I'm not sure because it was mostly mumbles, mixed with some *no*'s and something about a *boot*." I try to keep it light, like it's no big deal. In truth what I heard was anything but light. There is some scary shit going on in this girl's head.

Her eyes close. I wait for them to open. They do not. It looks like pain is involved. I'm not sure of my next move. *Did I go too far? Was I too insensitive? Should I have kept this information to myself?* Honestly, I thought this revelation would be good news. With her secret out, we could move past it. Wrong again. As Benny would say, *Chalk up another win for team stupid.* Her silence has gone beyond awkward. It's time for damage control. I say, "On the other hand, talking is overrated. We talk and talk and what do we really say? And given our current situation, I think hand signals and head shaking are the way to go. I'll stop talking now. After you ask your question."

Her eyes open. I don't see the spark of anger I saw before. But the lighting isn't very good, so I could be wrong. It's been known to happen. She motions with a finger for me to come closer.

I lean in.

She motions again.

I lean so close that I feel the heat radiating off her cheek. Now I'm starting to worry. "Astrid, if you're thinking about biting my ear, let's just—"

She puts her hand over my mouth.

Our little room falls silent. The candles flicker. She pulls her hand away.

Then with her fevered breath brushing my ear she whispers, "Where's the loo?"

LUSTER, OR.

33

On Saturday mornings when Charlene taught yoga at the YMCA and Harvey went on his 6.2-mile trail run with Pavlov, Cory would make breakfast for Justin and Chloe. Ty would join in when he wasn't at the dojo or at work. It was the one meal he cooked without any guidance from Charlene and he planned for it all week.

On this particular Saturday he started with a buckwheat pancake recipe he found in an old *Bon Appétit* magazine. Cory made some tweaks of his own, using 2 percent milk mixed with plain yogurt to replace the buttermilk, two egg whites folded into the batter for extra lift, one cup of shredded apples, and a half teaspoon of nutmeg instead of cinnamon. Judging by the empty plates and requests for seconds, Cory was confident that his tweaks were keepers. While Ty changed for his shift at the Lot, and Justin and Chloe loaded the dishwasher, Cory checked his phone to see if he had any texts, hoping to hear from Stellah. It had been over two weeks. The only text was from Rebecca, the gossip-in-chief at Bravo, reminding him of the mandatory CPR recert today at 1:00. Cory was replying when Harvey returned all sweaty from his run. He snagged the last slice of bacon and said to Cory, "You and your brother in my office in fifteen minutes."

They watched cartoons with Justin until the fifteen minutes were up, then walked down the hall past the fishing pictures to Harvey's office. The door was closed as usual. Ty knocked three times. A voice from inside barked, "Enter."

Harvey was seated behind his desk, laptop open and phone to his ear. He said into the phone, "We'll talk later," and hung up. Cory noticed that it was a black Samsung, not the silver iPhone he used for business. Harvey had already showered, but instead of the tan slacks and blue button-down shirt he wore to the Lot every day, he wore a dark blue suit with a cream-colored shirt and a red tie. Cory could smell the faint scent of his cologne. It mixed well with the leather and oiled wood.

Ty headed straight for the couch. Harvey said, "Don't bother sitting. The business we have to conduct here won't take long. Let's get started, shall we?" Ty glanced at Cory, his eyes saying, *WTF?* Cory shrugged. He wasn't aware of anything they had done wrong.

Harvey leveled his gaze at the two of them. "Three months and a day have passed since your arrival. You performed your duties at work without issues, and adjusted to the tone and tenor of our family." He aimed his gray eyes at Cory. "Charlene tells me that Chloe's anxiety has improved. Her anxious behaviors, particularly the nail biting, are nearly gone. I understand your math tutoring has played a role."

Cory relaxed enough to allow a smile. "She got a one hundred on her last test."

"I know. Chloe emailed me a picture of the test." Harvey smiled just a little. "While on the subject of the internet, is the wireless signal in the attic meeting your video game requirements?"

"Yes. It's perfect."

"And you're happy with the arrangement at Bravo?"

Cory understood the juxtaposition of *wireless* and *arrangement*. "Yes," Cory said, trying not to picture Harvey towering over him at two a.m. "The arrangement works for me."

"Excellent." He focused on Ty. "I spoke with Dr. Sanchez. She said you attended all your anger management sessions. She is confident that you recognize your triggers and have developed an effective anger management plan. Do you agree with her assessment?"

"Yup."

"That's good. And on another encouraging note, Tony said you are trying out for baseball. Is this true?"

"Tryouts were last Wednesday. I made varsity."

"Congratulations. What position will you play?"

"Pitcher."

Cory glanced at Ty. He did his best to convince Ty not to try out, that he could potentially have his name in the paper and that might not be helpful considering their *history*. Ty popped a Swedish Fish in his mouth and said, "Relax, dude. No one's gonna find us in Lusterfuck, Oregon." But yesterday afternoon the coach posted his varsity roster on the school website, and highlighted their newest addition to the starting rotation, a transfer from Portland named Tyler "the Steamer" Bic with a "lights-out fastball that'll make the batters cry for their mommas."

Harvey said, "Between the fastball and the curve, which pitch is your preference?"

"I don't throw curves. I just throw hard and harder."

"Why does that not surprise me?" Harvey smiled, then looked at Cory, as if he just told a joke.

"Excuse me?" Ty asked.

Harvey said, "A fastball uses brute force to intimidate the batter. There is nothing subtle about that pitch. But a curveball? That's a different animal. It uses deception to trick the batter into swinging at what often turns out to be a bad pitch." He paused, then said to Cory, "You look more like a curveballer to me."

Cory said after a careful beat, "I don't play baseball."

Harvey shrugged. "Neither do I. However, that doesn't preclude me from appreciating the game." He closed his laptop. "But I didn't call you boys in here to discuss America's pastime. You need to get on with your day, and I"—he checked his watch—"have a press conference in thirty-five minutes."

"A press conference?" Cory asked. *That explains the tie.*

"Things are about to get a little crazy around here. A state senate seat opened up and I'm announcing my intention to run." Harvey slipped the Samsung into his top middle drawer and locked it, then stepped out from behind the desk. He led them out of the office and down to the door that leads to the garage. "Do you recall our discussion about milestones?"

"Yes," the brothers said.

"Since you satisfied the requirements for milestone one..." Harvey opened the door and switched on the overhead lights and said, "Behold milestone two!"

There was a car in the first stall, but it wasn't Harvey's white Lexus. Cory had to blink twice, just to be sure that what he was looking at was real. It was the old Volvo wagon. But it wasn't old anymore. The black paint glistened, the tires shone. In this spotless four-car garage, it looked like a new car on a showroom floor. Cory had noticed that it went missing a couple weeks ago and asked Charlene about it. She said Harvey had grown tired of the eyesore and called to have it towed. "But don't worry," she said with a wink. "When the time is right you'll have a car to drive."

"I thought you junked it," Cory said.

"I'm afraid Charlene is complicit in this ruse. In fact it was her idea, seeing as I am not a fan of surprises. I had it refurbished top to bottom at a specialty shop in Redmond. The engine is rebuilt. The tires and suspension are new. The leather seating has been replaced, along with new carpeting and hood liner. I even had them install an integrated stereo, nav system, and back-up camera."

"It's...it's incredible," Ty said, circling the car, peering in windows.

"This vehicle has sentimental value for me," Harvey said. "It was the first unit I purchased for the dealership, and the first car we sold." He brushed his fingers along the driver's door as if he were caressing the fur of an exotic animal. "The owner, a local guy named Daryl Summers, was transferred to Milwaukee ten years ago. I thought I would never see this car again. But he retired and moved back to town last year, and amazingly was still driving it. I convinced him to trade it in for a new Dakota. I kept it here, thinking that I would fix it up and give it to Justin—but didn't have a reason to start the project. Then you two entered the picture, and it seemed like the right thing to do." He tossed the keys to Ty. "It's yours to drive while you're here. All I ask in return is that you help transport the kids to their various activities. Kayla used to perform that—" Harvey stopped, closed his eyes. Cory thought, *That's the first time I've ever heard him say her name.* Harvey opened his eyes. "We will pay for one tank of gas a month and cover the insurance." He pushed a button on the wall. As the garage door rumbled up, he said to them over the noise, "Go on, take her for a spin."

Cory was confused. He and Ty were allowed to drive the Motts' cars, but never without Harvey or Charlene in the vehicle. "Just me and Ty?" he asked.

Harvey grinned wide and white. "Treat her like she's my first-born child."

It was at times like this that Cory could see why the Luster-folk loved him so much. And why statewide politics seemed like the logical next step. Harvey had the kind of smile that screamed, *Vote for me and your life will be so freaking awesome!* Cory opened the passenger door, could smell the new leather. He choked out, "We will. Thank you."

Ty dropped Cory off at the high school, then headed for the baseball field in their new ride to log a few hours of batting practice. Cory took the shortcut through the cafeteria to his least favorite room in the school, the gymnasium. He didn't know how many people would be at the gym since this CPR/first aid class was just for the employees of Mott Enterprises. Between the three businesses, Harvey employed over two hundred people, so it could be anywhere from five to fifty. There was an eight-foot table set up on the far side of the gym next to a TV on a cart. Dummies were lined up on the floor, ready for chest compressions and rescue breathing. He was relieved to see it was a small group—just seven souls including himself. He recognized two from the dealership; the rest he didn't know, which meant they probably worked at the hardware store. He picked a seat at the end, wrote his name on a name tag, and stuck it to his shirt. The instructor, a short, thin guy wearing a dark blue LUSTER FIRE DEPARTMENT T-shirt handed him a class booklet and told him to take it home. Cory was looking at the big clock over the scoreboard, his mind elsewhere, when the one person he didn't expect to see walked out of the women's locker room. She spotted him right away, stopped, looked like she was going to turn right back around.

The instructor shouted, "Time to get started, Mott minions. We have a lot to cover and only three hours to do it."

She walked to the table, sat in the chair directly across from Cory. She already had a name tag on. The girl who'd avoided him at school and every other conceivable place for three months and had yet to say a single word to him smiled and said, "Hi, Cory."

He said, "Hi, Kayla."

She said, "Your tag is upside down."

Kayla paired up with Cory during the partner chest-compression practice, but their conversation was limited to commanding each other to call 9-1-1. She switched to a guy named Jackson for choking, tourniquet application, and splinting broken bones. Cory got nauseous as usual during the wound management section, and almost tossed his cookies when the instructor showed an actual picture of an open fracture where the bone punctured the skin. But he felt her brown eyes on him, and that helped him keep his cookies untossed.

When the class ended, Cory dashed to the men's room for a long-overdue visit. But when he returned, though most of the class was still there, Kayla was gone. *So we're back to avoiding mode,* he thought. Cory texted Ty that he was ready for a pickup, and headed for the door. On his way out, the instructor said, "Hey, Cory, you forgot your booklet. You need to fill out the back page and turn it in to your manager if you want credit." Cory grabbed it, stuffed it in his pocket, thanked him, and left.

Later that night, when they were both in bed, Ty turned off his light and said, "I stopped by the dojo before I picked you up."

"So . . . ?" Cory said, more interested in the shrimp creole recipe he was reading than what Ty had to say.

"Doug told me a guy called today wanting to know if Ty Bic trained there."

"Oh?" Cory said, significantly more interested than he was a second ago. "What did Doug tell him?"

"He said, 'Yes. But Ty's not here now,' and asked if the guy wanted to leave a message."

"Did he leave a message?"

"No. He hung up."

After a beat, "Did he offer Doug a free tow?"

"I didn't ask. But I'm thinking, yeah, he probably did."

"So how's that smoking-hot fastball working for you now?"

"Whatever." Ty rolled over on his side and faced the wall. "Sweet dreams, bro."

Cory waited for more but knew it wouldn't come. When Ty faced the wall, that meant talking time was done. He put down the cookbook, no longer interested in the right way to devein a shrimp. He considered filling out the back page of the CPR notebook but couldn't find the will to do that either. So he reached for the headphones and his laptop. Five minutes later he was facing certain death against a bilge hag on level six and had no time to worry about a phone call from some guy who may or may not be missing his pinky finger.

34

"The loo?" I say, struggling to not make a big deal of her finally using words. "That means the bathroom, right?"

"Yes," she whispers.

"Thanks for bringing it up. Now I have to go too."

She smiles.

"Number one or number two?"

She frowns, hold up three fingers.

"Shit," I say. Then, "Oops. Sorry. I didn't mean it that way. I meant like, oh shit, what do I do now?"

She whispers, "Please hurry."

I scan the space. Going outside—obviously not a choice. That means somewhere in here. But where? And how? Suddenly this hole in a hill feels even smaller. I spot the hammer and saw hanging on the wall behind the stove. "Can you hold it for three minutes?"

She shows me two fingers.

"Right."

I crawl to the stove, then stand and take down the hammer. I use the claw to pry loose two of the six-inch-wide floorboards, exposing the ground underneath. There are too many rocks to dig a trench. There's a board next to the stove that looks a little loose already. I slip the claw underneath it and easily lift the board. Then blink in disbelief. There's a green garbage bag sealed with duct tape.

I reach down and pull out it out, tear it open, and shake the contents onto the floor. There are at least a dozen ziplock freezer bags with stacks of money wrapped with rubber bands. I get my headlamp, crouch down, and peer underneath the floor. The joists run parallel to the front wall. The spaces between them are filled with garbage bags. I haul out another one, tear into it, and dump it out. More freezer bags, more money. I glance at Astrid. She's staring at me, her expression both pained and confused. I say, "Hang on another minute." Back to my discovery, I notice a couple freezer bags are smaller and do not contain stacked bills. I pick up one for a closer look, see a handful of clear crystals inside—and know instantly what that is.

Astrid groans. It's time to get back to the task at hand. I use the claw end of the hammer to dig a trench in the dirt. "There's your loo." I walk to Astrid and help her sit up. "What can I do?"

"Loo roll?" she says.

My mind is still reeling from the bags of cash. I'm too confused to translate.

"To wipe . . ." she says.

"Oops. My bad." I unzip a side pocket on my pack and realize the toilet paper is in Ty's pack. We could use one of my extra socks but how many times will that fix work? I don't have enough socks. I scan the space and settle on the only viable solution for this emergency. I unwrap and hand her a stack of twenties—the smallest denomination I could find. I say, "Only the best in Chateau de Stumptown." She smiles, more likely in relief than at my attempt at humor. I shove the bags of money aside to clear a path to the trench.

"What else can I do?"

She circles a finger in the air. That one I know. Turn around. Even though I'm worried about her weakened state and that she doesn't have the energy to squat over a six-inch-wide hole in the floor, I know better than to argue with her. I turn around and hum softly while Astrid does her business. When she's finished I help her back to her sleeping bag. She is shivering convulsively by the time I zip her in. My brain is screaming for answers about how this new development could impact our situation. Did Benny tell anyone else about Stumptown? That could change everything.

"Water and pills?" I ask.

She nods.

I give her three IBs instead of four because I'm starting to worry about the supply, and hold the bottle to her lips. "Drink what you need. I'll get more as soon as it's light." She takes two sips and stops. I take two sips as well, then cap the bottle. We have about one-third of a liter left. That should last us till morning.

She motions for me to come close.

I lean in.

"Why so much money?" she whispers. She's already on the downhill slide toward sleep.

"I don't know." *But I have an idea.*

"You're..." Her eyes close. "...rich."

No, Astrid. We're fucked.

LUSTER, OR.

35

I t was the morning after the CPR class, and Cory had the ski lodge and the Volvo all to himself. He had dropped Ty off in town at seven a.m. for an all-day karate tournament, and the Motts were at church, followed by a meeting with Lester Fitzroy, their overly enthusiastic Mott for Senate campaign manager. Cory's shift at Bravo started in two hours. He needed to keep his mind off yesterday's mystery call to the dojo, and the best way to do that was to cook. He found a recipe for a roasted-cauliflower-and-goat-cheese frittata at Finecooking.com, and had just put the cauliflower in the oven to brown, when his phone dinged with a text.

STELLAH DESHAY

> I have something for u. Meet
> at Drip n Sip at 11?

It was 10:09 right now. That meant she must have left Portland around eight a.m. It seemed odd that she didn't text before committing to that drive, but he didn't care. He was thrilled to see her and couldn't wait to share all the good things going on in their lives—with the exception of the dojo phone call. Cory had just enough time to roast the cauliflower, put the nicely browned bits in a plastic container, turn off the oven, clean the kitchen, and make sure Pavlov had water in his pail-size bowl, before he flew out the door with zero minutes to spare—and stopped. He ran back upstairs, grabbed the CPR booklet. He swore as he fired up the Volvo that he would fill out the back page before his shift started. Otherwise Rebecca, who treated all rules like the Ten Commandments, wouldn't let him clock in.

Cory found her in the Fit in the Drip 'n' Sip parking lot talking on her phone. He tapped her window. She hung up, climbed out, and gave him a big warm Stellah hug. After driving for three hours, she told him she didn't want to sit in a crowded, noisy café. She said, "While it's still nice, let's get our beverages and walk around that beautiful park with the pond and gazebo." Cory insisted on paying. She was reluctant at first, then shrugged and said, "I'd be honored."

Cory drove them to the park. Stellah was suitably impressed.

"This is a fine ride. It smells new."

"Harvey had it fixed up. It's ours to drive."

"You got all the insurance worked out?"

"That's what he said."

"Well, all right, then. And you're looking pretty sharp in that uniform."

Cory didn't want to wear the Bravo shirt, but he didn't think there would be time to change. "I'm not so sure I like the purple," he said. "Grease stains show up like a flag."

"And you kinda look like a big grape. But the money's good, right?"

"Yup. I started out as a busser. Now I'm the head grill cook."

"Well, good for you!"

"Two bucks above minimum."

"Excellent. You saving some?"

"Not as much as I should," Cory said, thinking about the new PlayStation he bought last week. "But it's more than I had a year ago."

"I hear that."

Cory parked the Volvo in the lot next to the entrance for the walking trail. It was a half-mile loop around a big pond. Near the water's edge a little girl and her father were surrounded by ducks feasting on bread they tossed from a brown paper bag. On the other side of the pond in a big grassy area, two shirtless guys were tossing a Frisbee. Cory and Stellah hit the trail, hot beverages in hand. Cory asked about the status of her soon-to-be ex.

Stellah said, "I bought him a week at husband refocusing camp."

"How'd that go?"

"Turns out he had a second asshole in his brain. Who knew? They removed it and he's been great since then. Best investment I ever made."

"So you're back together?"

"He's washing my bras as we speak. Can't fold for shit, though. I left a fitted sheet in the load. That'll keep him occupied for hours."

Cory laughed. It made him feel warm, despite the spring chill setting in as the sun inched closer to the hills. "How are your kids?" he asked, sorry that he'd forgotten their names. He knew there were two, one in diapers. Or maybe not in diapers anymore.

"We're all good," she said. "Thank you for asking. But that's enough about me. I didn't drive three hours to tell you about my world. It's spinning just fine." She took a long appreciative sip. "It's time to talk about your life. And I'm not talking the surface stuff. I want the good bits stuck down in the cracks. Then I have something to give you. But first—*damn!* This is outstanding coffee!" She bumped him with an elbow. "And there you are, drinking some kinda flowery tea shit when there's liquid gold to be had."

Cory thought about what she said, wanting the good bits down in the cracks. He decided to pry one loose. "My dad was a big-time coffee drinker," he said. "But his was Folgers out of a can. Ty and I alternated weeks cleaning the kitchen. I got mixed up one night and forgot to clean the counters. There was a half cup of coffee left by the sink. He'd put his cigarette out in it the night before. He made me drink it all, even the cigarette butt. I threw up. Then he made me clean up the puke with my toothbrush." He looked at his shoes, kept his eyes there, and said, "I never told anyone that. Not even Ty."

She took a beat. "Was that before or after your mother left?"

"After."

"Cory, I'm sorry. That's awful. And believe me, I've heard some awful stuff."

Cory thought, *Oh, I can go deeper than that.* "So anyway, the point is, that's why I drink tea." He felt his throat tightening, wasn't expecting that.

"Does this bother you?" she asked, and held out her cup. "Because I can toss it. It would hurt like hell, but—"

"Oh, no. I think coffee's awesome. I just can't bring myself to even try it." He forced a smile. "Besides, I hear tea is better for my skin."

They were at the quarter-mile mark, designated by a bronze statue of William H. Luster himself on a rearing horse. His hat needed a good hosing, though. Luster had a pigeon problem. After a short silence, Stellah said, "You ever do the grief counseling like I asked?"

"No."

"Why not? Tony said he got it lined up."

"He did. And I was all set to go. But I got a job and, well, Ty said Benny didn't deserve our grief."

"Well, that may be true. But grief is like a tick on a dog's ass. It just hides in the dark getting fatter and fatter until one day it pops and then there's a big ol' mess. It's best to pull it out before it takes root. Ty's gonna have to deal with it too someday."

"I doubt that."

Stellah sipped. "While we're on the subject, how is that brother of yours?"

"He did anger management. But only because he had to."

"He doing all right in school?"

"He's on the baseball team. And they asked him to play football in the fall. Friends, girls . . ." Cory shrugged. "Typical Ty."

Stellah's face clouded. "Any fights?"

"Nope. He knows how to find his quiet place now."

"So he's doing good?"

"Better than good."

"What about you? School? Friends?" She looked at him. "Girls, or ...?"

Cory noted the hesitation. It was subtle, a gentle, probing question that came without judgments or threats. Unlike Benny, whose words and actions left him bruised inside and out. "School's good. All A's, except PE. Friends—I have a couple at work, but most of mine are online. And girls?" He wanted to look at her, but chose his feet instead. "Let's just say I think I like tea more than coffee." It was as close as he could come to telling her the truth, and it still felt like a million miles away.

"Have you found another tea drinker?"

Cory managed to look at her this time. "I don't even know how to start."

Stellah smiled. "You just did."

Cory wanted to ask her *Why does it have to be so hard?* but was distracted by a yellow VW Bug driving into the lot. Even though there were plenty of spots, it parked next to the Volvo.

Stellah said, "So how's life at the ... what do you call it? The *ski lodge?*"

Kayla climbed out wearing that long black coat, hood up. She circled the Volvo, then cut across the grass toward the gazebo. "Life at the ski lodge is good," Cory said. "Charlene went to culinary school before she married Harvey. She's teaching me how to cook. We made asparagus risotto with toasted pine nuts and chicken sausage last week."

"Well, aren't you the little chef!"

"I do all right. In fact, I created a hamburger at Bravo called the Holy Aioli. It has jalapeño aioli, baby arugula, and caramelized onions sprinkled with sea salt. We sell more of those than the next two burgers on the menu combined."

"Sounds like you love your job."

"I do. I think...I think..."

"You think what?"

"I'd like to have my own restaurant someday." There. He said it. And it felt good.

"Well, here's to making that dream come true!" She held out her cup for a toast. He bumped her cup with his. She said, "How're the kids?"

"Justin and Chloe? They're a pain sometimes, especially Chloe's nosy friends. But mostly we get along. I'm tutoring her in math. She's always showing me pictures of dress designs she made up, and wants me to give her suggestions. Justin thinks Ty's the bomb because he teaches him karate moves and took over his chore of cleaning up the massive dog turds in the lawn. Ty hates the chore, but he loves that dog."

Kayla was at the gazebo. She stood at the rail, facing them, cupped a hand to her mouth. When she pulled her hand away it looked like she was exhaling smoke.

A gray-haired couple was sitting on a bench looking out at the pond. As Cory and Stellah passed the bench she stopped for a second to read the sign on the back:

THIS BENCH DONATED BY MOTT ENTERPRISES

The man was everywhere in this town, like fresh air, or pollen spores. Cory wasn't sure which, and that uncertainty was like a small rash that refused to go away. He glanced at Kayla. She was definitely watching them. Making it pretty obvious in fact.

"And how is the judge?" Stellah said.

"Former judge," Cory corrected. "He told us yesterday that he's running for the state senate."

Stellah raised an eyebrow. "Well, now, ain't that a twist in the plot?"

"Not really. Rumor is he's been planning it for a while. His campaign manager dropped off a truckload of campaign signs. They're piled up in the garage. Me and Ty have an appointment with him on Wednesday."

"About what?"

"I don't know. But he asked Charlene to buy us some suits and gave Ty fifty bucks to get a good haircut." Cory chucked. "You know what Ty did?"

"Oh, this should be good."

"He went to Walmart and bought twelve pounds of Swedish Fish. Then he cut his own hair with Charlene's craft scissors."

"That sounds like something Ty would do." They waited for a jogger to pass them; then she said, "What's Harvey like? I only met him that one time. He seemed very...formal to me."

"When he talks to me it feels like I'm a rookie lawyer in his courtroom and he's telling me what to do, how to behave. But he gave us jobs, and he fixed up the Volvo, and the people in town love him. So I'd say, yeah, other than being a judge, he's pretty cool."

"Is he a judge with Justin and Chloe?"

"Hmm... not as much. But he usually doesn't come home from work until they're getting ready for bed. We have family dinner night on Wednesdays. He always asks them to tell him a joke. If he laughs, then they get an extra fifteen minutes of TV. They worry about it all week."

"Does he ever laugh?"

"Every time."

Cory looked at Kayla. She tossed her cigarette. He decided to risk it and wave. She turned and headed for the parking lot.

"You keep looking at the gazebo," Stellah said, smiling. "Is that someone special?"

"Just someone I met at CPR class," Cory said. No point going into the former-babysitter thing. Or that she avoided him more than death itself—until yesterday.

"Do you mind if we walk to that gazebo?" Stellah asked. "I love these shoes, but they're not the best for walking."

They were three-quarters of the way around the pond, maybe five minutes from the car. He still had to drive Stellah back to the Drip 'n' Sip. Cory figured he had twenty minutes before his shift started. Plus, he had to fill out that CPR form. There was time if they walked fast.

"Sure," he said. "But I have to get back to work by twelve fifteen." That gave him fifteen minutes to fill out that stupid form.

When they arrived at the gazebo, Stellah sat on a wooden bench facing the pond and took off her shoes. Cory sat next to her, grateful to rest his legs. He could still smell the lingering scent of Kayla's cigarette. But it wasn't a cigarette. He knew the smell of weed from his days with Benny and Tirk. Stellah opened her purse and handed him a white envelope. The sides bulged out, like there was something big inside, almost too big to fit.

"It's from Detective Ostrander," she said.

Cory opened the envelope.

There was a folded piece of paper around a plastic pill bottle. The pill bottle had a printed label that read: BENJAMIN J. BIC—REMAINS. Inside the bottle Cory could see ashes, gray and powdery. He figured there was three, maybe four, tablespoons. The same amount of seasoning he used to make Bravo chili. He stared at the bottle for a few moments, felt his eyes going moist. He put the bottle on the bench, then read the message on the piece of paper.

In blue pen with big letters it asked, *Look familiar?*

Underneath the handwriting was a black-and-white picture of a hammer lying in some grass. There was a tag on it with writing too small for Cory to read. He recognized the yellow handle, worn down to the wood around the bottom where Benny liked to hold it. The same hammer he and Ty gave him for Father's Day when their mother lived with them. The same hammer Tirk took from their home.

Under the image was written *Murder weapon.*

Next to the hammer pic was a newspaper clipping taped to the page.

The header read: "Two Men, One Woman Executed in RV Meth Lab."

Cory thought about the previous tenants before they moved into the crack house. All Benny ever told them was it was two men and a woman. And they had a potbellied pig.

At the bottom of the page in big, blocky letters:

They know where you are. Keep your head down.

Cory's hands started shaking. They shook so much he couldn't return the paper to the envelope. He fought back tears. His stomach surged, threatened to empty right there on the gazebo floor.

Stellah said, "Let me do that." She folded the paper, put it in the envelope, then wrapped an arm around his shoulders, pulled him close. He felt all the bits come up at once. The open cracks turned into gaping fissures. Cory shuddered and fell apart.

Hot tears streamed off his cheeks and stained his shirt, the bench, the world around him. He struggled to breathe between deep gasps that hurt his ribs while Stellah held him close and whispered softly, "It's okay, sweetie. It's okay. This needs to happen. Let it out, let it out, let it out."

And that's exactly what he did.

Back at the Drip 'n' Sip, Cory apologized again for puking on her shoes.

"Not a problem," she said. "Now I have a reason to buy new ones. That's a win-win in my book."

"Sometimes...sometimes I throw up when I'm scared or nervous."

"You'll work that out. Just like you do everything else." Her phone dinged. She read the text and laughed. "That's my former ex-husband-to-be. He wants to know how to fold that damn sheet."

Cory smiled. "Thanks for this." He held up the envelope.

"You're welcome. And speaking of working things out, do you have a plan for your father's remains?"

Cory hadn't thought about it. His universe was still reeling from the hammer. "Not yet."

She took a moment to search his eyes, didn't seem to find what she wanted, and said, "Well, whatever Detective Ostrander wrote, I'm sure his intentions were good." She opened her door. "Take care and keep cooking. I plan on dining at your very own restaurant someday!" Stellah climbed into the Honda. Cory watched her back out and drive away.

On the way to Bravo, even though it meant he would be late, Cory spent a few minutes at the park to gather his thoughts and check all the appropriate boxes on the CPR form. By the time he arrived at Bravo his universe was back in relative order— except for the troubling questions about the picture and Detective Ostrander's note. When Rebecca frowned and handed him a spare uniform to replace the puke-stained shirt he was wearing, he smiled and handed her the completed form. It took him all of two minutes to get it done. He would have completed it in half that time if it weren't for the note that fell out when he turned to the back page:

231-0600. Call don't text. Kayla

It presented a whole new set of questions, which he would happily deal with later.

Rebecca said while he clocked in, "You're smiling pretty big for someone that's forty-eight seconds late."

"A friend just shook my universe like a snow globe. I'm smiling because I came up with the perfect fix."

"How did you do that?"

He thought about Stellah and her probing eyes. "I figured out what to do with the remains of Benjamin J. Bic."

36

I'm in our attic room in Luster, looking out the round window next to my bed at a full moon descending beyond the hills. But as it falls I'm consumed with a growing sense of unease. The moon is getting bigger, and it's moving way too fast. I realize as it fills the entire window with blinding white light that the moon isn't sinking—it is crashing into the Earth. The white is turning orange, then red. I turn to tell Ty good-bye, that this is the end—

A hand clamps over my mouth. I struggle against it, then remember where I am and open my eyes. Dim light filters in under the tarp. Both of the two-inch portholes are black. *That's strange.* I relax. Her hand slips away. There isn't enough light to see her, so I reach for the headlamp and switch it on. I get a startling glimpse of her sitting up, hair wet and plastered to her forehead, eyes wide and intensely alert. She yanks the headlamp off my head and stuffs it in her sleeping bag, plunging us into darkness and shadows.

I whisper, "What's wrong?"

Her lips brush my ear. "I heard something."

"Where?"

"Outside."

"You sure?"

"Yes."

"Maybe it was me. I was having a bad dream."

"It wasn't you. I heard breathing. And footsteps."

Shit. "What kind?"

Silence from her.

I don't know if she's listening for more sounds, or thinking about how to answer my question. I say, "Animal or human?"

"Shhhhhh!"

I listen.

The crack of light changes to dark, then back to light. A shadow darkens the entry and then passes. I hear a clicking—soft, muted. Realize it's her teeth as she shivers next to me. I focus on the tarp. Then I hear it too. *Outside.* Breathing. A heavy pant. I can't tell how far away, but close enough in my mind to be a threat. I left the hammer on the stove before I fell asleep, which means crawling over the garbage bags of drugs and money to reach it. That will make some noise, but I need a weapon. Something in my hand— and for a second I think about Tirk striking Benny and wonder if I could do the same. Then I think about Ty. And Astrid. And think, *Yeah, I could.*

I whisper, "The hammer's on the stove." My sleeping bag is zipped up. It's too tight for me to get out. I start to slowly pull down the zipper.

She grabs my arm. Nails dig through my shirt into my skin. Her lips hot against my ear whisper, "Don't!"

I freeze.

A beat.

The panting stops.

We wait.

And wait.

A minute passes. Then another.

Her hand relaxes, slides away.

I whisper, "I'm going to look outside."

She makes no move to stop me. I unzip, get the hammer, crawl to a porthole. It's blocked, which makes me suspicious. I move to the canvas flap, pull it back far enough to peer outside. A blast of cold air hits me, confirming my suspicion. Snow—again. An inch at least, and it's still falling. Big, fat flakes. I stick my head out a little farther, into the stump cavity. The snow is undisturbed around the stump. I move out a little more, risk exposing my head to whatever's lurking in the shadows. I can't stay like this for long, half in, half out. What little warmth we built up inside will seep away, and she needs every degree. I crawl out far enough to stand. Snow soaks into my wool socks, lands on my head and shoulders. I scan left to right, searching for tracks. The forest looks pristine to me. Maybe it was our collective imaginations hearing things that weren't there. Call it stir-crazy run amok. But I spot them on my second pass. Fresh lumps in the snow, farther away than I thought, down the slope about twenty feet. The spacing is right for tracks, but from this angle I can't tell if they're human. One thing for sure—they were made by something *human-size*, and it came close enough to hear us if Astrid hadn't heard it first. I scoot backward into the hole and go straight to the top of the stove and feel for the lighter. I spark a flame and light three candles. The soft glow helps to calm my nerves. I pause for a moment, trying to think of a way to break the news.

"Well?" she says. Her voice is more than a whisper. That's good.

"I saw tracks, but they were too far away to tell who or what made them."

She frowns. "It sounded pretty close to me."

I sit on my sleeping bag, look down at her. She's on her back, blue eyes focused on me. Her face glistens with a sheen of sweat, even though it can't be much above freezing in here. "I'm worried about your fever. May I touch your forehead?"

A beat. She nods.

I blow on my hands to warm them up, then lightly press down on her forehead. Just as I thought, she's hot. Not scorching, but getting there. Astrid reads the concern in my eyes.

She says, "Did I burn your hands?"

"Not quite. But you definitely have a fever."

"You didn't tell me it's snowing."

"How did you know?"

She reaches up, touches my shoulder. Her hand comes down with a few flakes of snow. They melt on her finger. This girl doesn't miss much. Actually, let me revise: *She doesn't miss anything.*

I say, "I need to look at your wound."

"I'd rather you didn't."

"I need to clean it. Put on a fresh bandage."

"We don't have enough water."

"I'll get more."

"How? There will be tracks."

"Let me worry about that."

"Can we eat snow?"

I shake my head. "The body uses water to create the energy to melt the snow. That will dehydrate you more. May I please see your arm?"

"Are you a doctor?"

"No. But I'm a proud graduate of the three-hour Luster Fire Department CPR and first aid class."

A beat. "Tell me something about you."

"Sorry. I'm not going to let you get away with that shameless attempt to change the subject. How about this? I'll tell you a story about me if you let me look at your arm."

"Your story isn't that good."

"Did you know you're shacked up with a felon?" Her eyes narrow in concern, like maybe I overshared. Then she cracks a smile. Even in her miserable state it is blindingly perfect. And then, for another brief flash—I feel like I've seen her before.

"I will let you see my arm. But promise me you won't cut it off. See, I've become rather attached to it. And there's something about you Yanks and hacking off limbs in the wilderness. It really must stop."

"I promise. Now bring out the beast."

She pulls her splinted arm out of the sleeping bag. I immediately know something is wrong. A thick vein runs up her arm and disappears into the sleeve of her shirt. It is dark purple and four times bigger than it should be, like a fat worm had burrowed under her skin and made its home in her upper arm. While I roll back the compression bandage she asks, "Why are you a felon?"

"We stole a car."

"Why did you steal a car?"

I slowly peel back the gauze, swallow a gasp. She winces.

"We were in a bad situation, and—" She tenses and grunts. Her eyes close, a tear leaks out. "Sorry. I'll be more careful." I want to cry and retch at the same time. The wound is red and puffy with spots of white—worse than I imagined.

"How does it look?" she asks.

"Are you sure I can't get the saw?"

"Only if I can use it on you first."

I dip a cotton ball in some water and dab at one of the white spots, thinking, *I don't know what the hell I'm doing*, and *This water isn't sterile. My hands aren't clean. I'm probably making it worse*. But I have to do something. "Anyway, we were in a bad situation. It was time to disappear. So we stole a car and headed for Stumptown."

"Then what?"

"We stopped for a deer in the road. Then we found a girl named Astrid in a trunk. And here we are." Saying *we* makes me think about Ty, and how that part of the *we* is gone and how I keep secretly hoping that he will stick his head through that flap and say, *Let's get the fuck out of Dodge*. But with every passing minute the degrees of separation from that hope become more and more distant. I fight back tears. It's a losing battle.

"I'm . . ." She stops what she was going to say and changes course. "You said your father found this place."

Wiping my eyes I say, "Years ago. I was still in diapers."

I've done enough damage here. I unwrap the last two gauze bandages, place them over the wound, then wind the compression bandage around it, hold it in place with a strip of tape.

"There," I say with the biggest fake smile I can muster. "All cleaned and good as new."

"You said you wouldn't lie to me."

"I'm not." Certain that she knows I am.

She takes a deep breath, coughs. "Pills and water, please."

"Sure. And drink what you need. I have a plan."

After she's finished and settled in, she says, "Tell me about Stumptown."

"What do you want to know?"

"You said your father found it. How did he find a place that is impossible to find?"

"That's an excellent question." I tell her about the arrow-shot elk, how Benny followed the blood trail to this hideout that was built by some mystery person for some mystery reason in the 1950s.

"How do you know it was the 1950s?"

"One of the soup cans has an expiration date of June 1956. And there's a *Playboy* magazine in this trunk with Marilyn Monroe, Miss December, 1953, on the cover."

"At least we have some reading material."

"When we're desperate." We both go silent, probably thinking the same thing: *If this isn't desperate, then what is?* I say, "Benny took us here for our birthday. That's when we named it Stumptown. He promised that we'd come back for a secret getaway, eat trout from the creek and live like robbers and kings."

"Did you do that?"

"No. He moved us to Portland the next day to start a tow truck business. He got . . . sidetracked."

"Does he know you're here?" she asks hopefully.

I smile. "Actually, he's in my pack. Would you like to meet him?"

Her eyebrows gather. "Uh . . . sure."

"Good. Don't go anywhere. I'll be right back." I put the bloody bandages in the toilet hole, doing my best to hide the carnage from her view, then reach into the front pocket of my pack and take out the plastic pill bottle and hand it to her. "Benny, meet Astrid What's-Her-Name. Astrid, meet Benny Bic."

There were lots of things she could have said, like *I'm so sorry* or *This is too weird* or *That's disgusting.* Instead she surprises me with "It's nice to meet you, Benny Bic. Why are you here with your son?"

"Give me the bottle. I'll show you."

She gives me the bottle. I crawl over the bags of money and drugs to the stove. "Welcome home, Dad. May you rest in peace." I open the bottle and dump his remains into the stove.

After a respectful silence, Astrid says, "But what if I want to light a fire in that stove?"

I say, "Considering how Benny died, I don't think that would bother him at all."

I pick up the empty water bottle and head for the door.

They agreed to meet at the south end of the soccer field at 3:45. But it started raining at noon and didn't let up. She walked up to him in the hall between fifth and sixth period, said, "Gazebo, three forty-five," and walked away.

He arrived first and walked out to the gazebo. The wood floor still had the splatter outline of Stellah's shoes when he yacked all over them. Kayla's VW showed up a couple minutes later. He watched her make her way across the wet grass, the hood of her black jacket pulled up over her head. She lowered her hood, sat beside him facing the pond. Other than the ducks huddled together, heads tucked under their wings, they were alone.

She said, "Someone didn't do their CPR homework."

He said, "Someone forgot."

"You do your compressions too hard."

"The dummy lived. That's all that matters."

"Maybe. But the trauma will scar it for life. It will have to retire from the CPR circuit and live a childless life full of loneliness and despair."

"Or," Cory said, "it could write a tell-all book called *CPR for Dummies*, sell a million copies, and move out of that Red Cross duffel bag into a mansion, get married, have dummy babies, and live happily ever after."

"You're still an optimist." She popped a stick of gum in her mouth. "That means you haven't been absorbed yet."

Cory wasn't sure he heard her right. "Do you mean adopted? Because we're just placed—"

"No. I don't mean *adopted*. I mean *absorbed*."

"I don't know what you're talking about."

"The Mott family doesn't just take you in. They absorb you. Then they spit you out."

"Still don't know what you're talking about."

"Has he taken you fishing?"

"Won't happen. I hate fishing. Stinky hands. Ugly vests. Worms..."

"He'll take you. Then you'll understand. But by that time it will be too late. Your fate is sealed, Cory Bic."

"I'll take my chances."

She stood and started walking on one of the two-by-four floorboards. Placed one foot in front of the other like a gymnast on a balance beam. "How are Chloe and Justin?"

"Chloe designed a prom dress for you."

"She's such a sweetie. Did you see it?"

"Yes. It's backless, lots of lace with a fun neckline. A classic."

"I'd like to see it. Will you bring it to me?"

That meant they'd meet again. "Sure."

Kayla reached the opposite side of the gazebo. She spun a half circle on one foot, arms framed in front of her ballerina-style, and walked toward him. Said with her eyes lasering into his, "But wait! There's a problem. Haven't you heard? You're not supposed to talk to me."

"Not officially. Is that why you've been avoiding me?"

"Officially, yes."

"Why?"

"I'm toxic. Like this pond when all the fish died."

"Why are you toxic?"

"I'm sure someone's told you by now. It's basically the first thing anyone says after welcome to fucking Luster."

"Nope. Definitely not the first thing I heard."

"What did you hear?"

"'That will be five dollars and sixteen cents. Do you want a bag?'"

"Then you're not listening, Cory Bic." She leaped forward off one foot, landed three feet away on the other foot. Stuck the landing dead center on the board.

Cory clapped. "That was very impressive. The gazebo judge gives it a five point nine."

"It's more impressive on a real beam."

"Are you a gymnast?"

"Was."

"What happened?"

After a beat, "I became unbalanced."

She sat next to him again. Eyes on the pond, she asked, "Who were you with in here?"

Cory was surprised she saw him. He thought she drove away. *Was she spying on me? And if yes, then why?* "She's a friend from Portland." Then, before she could squeeze in a follow-up: "I saw you smoking. Was it weed?"

"You have good eyes, Cory Bic."

"Not really. I'm just...familiar with the product."

"Want to know why I was here smoking weed watching you watch me?"

"Sure." He liked it when she asked the question he was going to ask her.

"It relaxes me. So I come here and smoke up before I have to do something I don't want to do."

"Is it helpful?"

"Usually."

It sure wasn't for Benny B.

She asked, "Want to know who taught me that trick?"

"Okay."

Her eyes shifted from the pond to him. "The future senator."

That answer set him back a second or two. Meanwhile, a dark two-door coupe pulled into the lot. Her eyes flicked away. She seemed to tense. Cory asked, "What was the thing you don't want to do?"

"Next question."

Of the fifty still in his head, Cory asked, "Why did you tell me not to text you?"

The coupe drove away. Kayla watched its taillights fade in the misting rain. She stood, walked to the stairs leading down to the grass, paused to stick her gum under the rail. Cory could see a mound of them, an inverted sugarless volcano. She turned and looked at him. "Before I go, tell me one true thing about you that no one else knows. You have this many seconds." She held up five fingers, then four.

He felt her watching him as he struggled to find an answer that didn't hurt. Cooking was his go-to secret, but he had already told that to Stellah. He could lie and make something up, but he didn't want to do that. He had this feeling that she would know and be disappointed. With one finger remaining he blurted out, "I'm scared! Every morning when I wake up. I'm always scared."

Kayla held his eyes for a few moments, her head tilted slightly as if assessing the value of each individual word. Then she smiled. "I like you, Cory Bic. You're not rude like your brother." She raised her hood and left.

Not rude like my brother?

What the hell?

STUMPTOWN

NOW

38

I need to spend as little time as possible outside and not make an obvious mess. Reaching a few feet beyond the stump, I scoop four handfuls of snow into the water bottle, then do my best to smooth out what I did. Not perfect, but hopefully good enough. I take one more scan of the area—see nothing other than the tracks that are starting to fill in. My right leg twitches. I want to run down to Anvil Rock because maybe we got our messages crossed and Ty is waiting for us there. I fight off that urge. He said give him two days, and this is day two. Which reminds me about the letter—the letter I don't want to read because of what it would mean. My entire body tenses. I want to scream into this falling snow that is trapping me here: *TY! WHERE THE FUCK ARE YOU?* But that would be stupid on too many levels. I whisper the words instead.

Then turn and head for the hole.

Astrid is on her back, eyes closed. I hope she's sleeping because I need some quiet time to work a few things out in my head. I slip the bottle of snow down to the bottom of my sleeping bag, then zip in and focus my eyes on the elephant in this room: ziplock bags filled with money and drugs.

How did it get here?

It has to be Benny. Ty said he was skimming. I had my doubts. Benny wasn't that ambitious or organized. He had grand ideas but never followed through, except when Tirk was involved. But what I'm seeing here suggests that Ty was right. It's the only explanation—unless Benny told someone else about Stumptown. If he did that, who would it be? And why? I decide that Benny treasured this "one in a million" secret too much to trust it to anyone other than me and Ty, and even when he told us, it was because he had to.

Astrid moans softly. I wait to see if she settles, and she does.

The next question on my greatest-hits list: How did Benny do it? He must have been sneaking it up here after we moved to Portland. It's possible it was up here when Benny introduced us to Stumptown, but there is meth in that load, and Benny didn't get into meth until after he met Tirk—at least that I knew of. Besides, I remember a conversation in the truck when Benny said, "Business is about to get a shitload better," but he wouldn't say what that shitload looked like.

Well, Benny, this sure looks like a shitload to me.

While Tweaker Teeth trashed Benny's bedroom and the kitchen, Tirk had asked all those questions about Benny and the shed and if he'd been letting anyone in. On the morning after Benny was killed, when Detective Ostrander grilled us about what we saw, then revealed that Benny was working with him as an informant, I figured there it was—that's why Tirk stopped by for a chat, and later why he hit Benny with the hammer and locked him in the shed. Ty had it right again: Benny was a snitch. But maybe it was something else that Tirk wanted.

And then there's the big question coming out of left field: Astrid.

Why was she in the trunk of a car? And why in this forest? On that night?

Astrid moans again, mumbles some words. She starts twisting and turning in her sleeping bag, like she's fighting off some unseen demon. I'm afraid she's going to hurt her arm, so I reach out and gently shake her shoulder. "Astrid, wake up. You're having a bad dream." Her eyes fly open. They are alive with that fresh-out-of-a-trunk-filled-with-gasoline look.

I say, "Hey, it's me. You're okay."

She sees me, blinks twice. "I thought...I thought you had left me."

"I was only gone a couple minutes."

"Where did you go?"

"Just outside. I brought you a treat." I reach into the depths of my sleeping bag and show her my creation.

She frowns. "A bottle of snow?"

"Oh, it's way more than just snow. It is delightfully seasoned with needle of pine, reindeer moss, and a hint of mud. It's a veritable trifecta of flavor and nutrition."

"But you said we can't eat snow."

"I did say that. But I had an idea thanks to you. If I put this bottle in my sleeping bag my body heat will melt the snow. Then we can drink it."

"Brilliant," she says. "But why thanks to me?"

"Because I was thinking that if your fever got too high, I could cool you off with snow. Which of course would melt and then we'd have water."

I return the bottle to the depths of my sleeping bag, then dig a granola bar out of my backpack and break it in half. I need her to answer some of those questions knocking around in my head, and there's no better time to have a conversation than over a good meal. "Let's have breakfast or lunch or whatever this is. And maybe you can tell me a story about you."

"What would you like to hear?"

"Everything."

Astrid says that when we showed up she didn't know why she was in the boot of a car, why she was covered in petrol, how her wrists and ankles got tied with plastic. She didn't know what her name was, or where she was from. She didn't know why she couldn't talk—just that when she opened her mouth it wouldn't happen. And she wasn't even sure she could trust us. All Astrid knew at that time was someone had done bad things to her, that same someone said, "I'll be back for you," and that to stay alive she had to get away. Astrid said the pieces started returning to her in a jumble when we woke and saw the deer. Something I had said triggered memories and they came at her like a flood.

Taking my last bite of the granola bar, I say, "If I may be so bold...what were those memories?"

"The first thing I remembered was a phone call. I had a mask over my eyes. A voice on the line said, 'Astrid, honey, is that you? Talk to me. Please.'"

"That's when you scratched your name in the snow?"

"Yes."

"Was it one of your parents?"

"I think so. My mum. I couldn't talk. He got mad. He called me a stupid bitch. He...he pushed me to the floor and kicked me."

I remember the bruises on her body when I pulled up the hoodie. That must be where they came from. I know this is hard for her, but I have to press on. "What else was in the flood?"

"It was all so random. There was a van that smelled like dog. A gun in my face. A needle stabbed into my leg. Floating..." She pauses, licks her lips. I hand her the water bottle. She sips, closes her eyes, and takes a breath. Like she's gearing up for something really bad. Although what I've heard so far is pretty grim already. "Since then it's been coming back to me in bits and pieces."

I pause. "Do you want to talk about those bits and pieces?"

Astrid's gaze shifts to the roof above her. Her silence makes me think she's ready for this conversation to end—but I'm wrong. She says, "We were chained to the floor."

"We?"

"There was another girl. Our ankles were chained to the same bolt. Like dogs. The floor was dirt, except for concrete around the bolt. The air smelled like onions."

"How long were you there?"

"I don't know. Days? Weeks? We slept on mats with a blanket. It wasn't enough. We huddled together to stay warm. She cried a lot."

"My God, Astrid. This is so awful." I see the pain deep in her eyes. "Is this too hard for you? Do you want me to stop asking questions?"

She shakes her head. "I need to do this. I'll let you know if it's time to stop."

After a beat I say, "Did you know the girl's name?"

"She spoke a different language. Russian, I think? I hardly understood anything she said. But I think her first name was Yana. I could never say her last name right."

"Where were you?"

"I don't know. It was always so dark. There were stairs going up."

I think about where she was, and what she must have thought when I showed her the stump and said, "Here we are!" No wonder she freaked. "Were you in a basement?"

"Maybe. The stairs would creak when he came down. We hated that sound."

I look at the money and drugs. Then I think about Benny and his world and Astrid and her world and I can't help but wonder if somehow these worlds collided in this place. But all I have are dots. I don't have the lines that connect them. I ask, "What did he look like? Was he big? Small? Did he have a beard?" I know it's a leap, but it's the only leap I've got. If it was Tirk or his minion, Tweaker Teeth, I'm rooting for the minion. Ty, even on his worst day, could take him down. But Tirk—I'm afraid if there were three Tys, that still wouldn't be enough.

"It was always dark. I never saw what he looked like. Whenever he took me upstairs he made me wear a hat over my eyes. He said if I took it off he would kill me." She starts to cry.

"What's wrong?" It's a stupid question. Because like, *what isn't wrong?*

"One time he took Yana upstairs. Usually it was pretty fast.

Never more than a few minutes. This time she didn't come back and didn't come back..." She takes a breath, wipes at the tears. "Then the door opened. He said, 'Listen up, buttercup. Here's what happens when you run.' He threw something down at me. A piece of clothing. It was wet. I could feel it slippery on my hands and face. Then he..." She takes a deep breath. "He turned on a torch. I was holding Yana's sweater. It was covered with blood."

I think about her scratching HE WILL KILL US in the snow. All the bruises on her legs and back.

"Astrid. I'm so sorry...."

She breaks down into deep, shuddering sobs. I don't know what to do. The horror of this and everything else overwhelms me. It's too much. Just too fucking much. I stroke her hair, cry with her. It goes on until we run out of energy and tears. We fade into a silence that is heavy and deep and suffocating. As the candles burn down and the flicker-light dims and the world spins without us beyond our little hole in the side of a hill, she says, "That's enough remembering for me. It's your turn."

"What do you want to know?"

"What was the bad situation you were running from?"

After her story, my sordid tale feels like a day in Disneyland.

I say, "I think we've had enough remembering for one day."

"No. You said you're a felon. I want to know why."

"All right." It's my turn to take a breath. "It all started on the best day of my life. Harvey took us fishing."

39

"**Y**ou talked to her?" Cory said. He and Ty were in the rock room, duffel bags by the door, at the ungodly hour of 5:35 a.m., when he'd brought up Kayla's name. They were waiting for Tony to pick them up for some mystery adventure he had yet to define. He was late as usual. But that was okay with Cory. Baseball games, martial arts tournaments, work, school, babysitting, and campaign obligations had conspired to keep them both busy.

He hadn't exchanged another word with Kayla since the gazebo, which was over two weeks ago. But she did smile at him in the hall, and he caught her looking at him yesterday during a school assembly. She signaled for him to call her. He did during his break at Bravo, but she didn't answer and her voice mail wasn't activated.

"Yeah, we talked," Ty said. "But I wouldn't call it a conversation."

"When? Where?"

"A month ago. At a party."

"A *month* ago?"

"Something like that."

"Why didn't you tell me?"

"I forgot."

"You *forgot?*"

"It didn't seem like that big a deal. Unlike when you forgot to tell me about Stellah's visit. It took you like, three whole days, to get around to remembering that *Oh, by the way, here's Benny's ashes and this picture from Detective Donut.*"

Cory stared at Ty. He kept that secret for three days because he was afraid that Ty would toss the ashes out the window. And he had other plans for that bottle.

Cory said, "What did you talk about?"

"I asked her if the rumor was true."

"What rumor?"

"That Mrs. M fired her when she came home early and caught the nanny smoking weed on the patio while the kids ate tuna sandwiches in the kitchen."

Cory compared what he just heard with the conversation he had with Kayla in the gazebo; she told him she "smoked up" to relax when she had to do something she didn't want to do. From what he could tell she liked Justin and Chloe, and the kids seemed to miss her too. Especially Chloe, who loved Kayla because she drew dresses with her instead of making her do her math homework. Cory didn't dismiss Ty's weed smoking rumor outright, but he was . . . skeptical. "Who told you?"

"I've heard variations from a couple people at work and school."

"What did Kayla say?"

"She said, 'Ask the judge.'"

"That's all?"

"No. Frankie J. dared me for ten bucks to ask her about the other rumor."

Frankie J. was Ty's catcher on the baseball team. They hung out constantly. It was widely known that the only thing bigger than Frankie J.'s ego was his mouth. "What was it?"

"Frankie heard from his girlfriend that Kayla got caught on the nanny cam making a sex video with Oliver." Oliver was the son of the mayor, who also happened to be a deacon at the church. "So I asked her if she got nanny-canned by the nanny cam."

"Why did you do that?"

"Frankie dared me." Ty smiled. "I had to."

"No, you didn't." Cory had issues with this version of Kayla. Plus, when Cory did an IP scan of the house he didn't pick up any wireless cameras. "What did she say?"

"She tossed her beer in my face, flipped me the bird, and left the party. But that's okay. I used Frankie's ten-spot to buy five pounds of Swedish Fish, so it's all good."

"I can't believe you did that." *Although actually I can.*

"She's a little strange, that one. Hot in an edgy kinda way. But too intense for me. Speaking of, word is you and her had a meet-up in the ol' gazebo. I've been meaning to ask how that went."

Cory found himself missing Portland. For a small town, Luster sure had a lot of eyeballs. "She didn't tell me much, other than we're not supposed to talk to her."

Tony's Jeep rolled into the driveway. As they picked up their duffel bags and walked out the door, Ty said, "Did you ask why?"

"No."

"Maybe we should ask Tony. He's an authority on all things Mott."

"No," Cory said, thinking about the secrecy Kayla used to reach out to him. There had to be a reason. And considering how tight Tony was with Harvey, asking him seemed like a bad idea. "Let's not."

Tony gunned the engine, rolled down a window, and yelled, "Chop, chop!"

They tossed their gear in the back and climbed into the Jeep.

"What's the big hurry?" Ty asked Tony.

"Harvey's waiting."

Tony hit the gas and they roared down the driveway.

"*Harvey?*" Ty said. "I thought he was in Eugene."

"He was. Now he's not."

"It's five a.m. You're dressed like a lumberjack. We've got our duffel bags and we're meeting *Harvey*? What's the freaking deal?"

Tony grinned. "Relax, guys. It's all freaking good."

Tony took them to a part of Luster Cory had never seen, and he thought he'd seen all there was to see. Tony braked, going from sixty to thirty in two seconds, took a screeching right onto a dark street, then aimed for a tall metal building with big doors and what looked like airplanes lined up out front. As they drew closer Cory spotted Harvey walking around one of those planes, checking under the wings. Tony pulled into a parking spot and looked at his watch. "Two minutes to spare. Am I the bomb or what?" He smiled at his bewildered passengers. "Welcome to Air Harvey. Don't forget to buckle up. You may experience some turbulence."

Cory tasted bile. He choked it down.

"You okay?" Tony gave him a probing look. "Seems like you're a little green around the gills."

"I've never been in a plane."

Tony laughed, opened his door. "If you're gonna pop that cherry, Harvey's the guy to do it."

"Harvey's the pilot?"

"It sure as hell ain't me."

"I didn't know he could fly."

Tony said as they approached a waving Harvey, duffel bags in hand, "Sometimes I wonder if his feet ever touch the ground."

Cory sat in the back next to Tony. Harvey had offered the copilot seat to whoever wanted it and Ty said, "Hell yeah!" Which was fine with Cory. Considering how his stomach had twisted into knots, he didn't want to throw up all over the controls and crash the plane.

The earphones helped keep the propeller noise down to a muted roar. After Harvey went through his preflight checklist, he inched the throttle forward. The plane rolled away from the hangar toward the runway. Cory listened to Harvey's chatter through the headset.

"Luster traffic Cirrus Four Niner Sierra Whiskey taxiing to runway one. Luster." The plane rotated ninety degrees and stopped, centered on the runway. "Luster traffic on runway one for a left downwind departure to the southeast. Luster." Harvey slowly pushed the throttle forward. The propeller screamed; the plane surged. Cory closed his eyes as his stomach threatened to revolt. He focused on breathing, wondered if his death would be mercifully fast or if he would feel the impact before being consumed in a ball of fire.

The plane accelerated, bumped, then untethered itself from the ground.

Ten seconds later the plane banked slightly to the left. Harvey said, "Seattle Center, Cirrus Four Niner Sierra Whiskey out of Luster climbing through seven thousand six hundred for eleven thousand five hundred requesting VFR flight following to Sunriver, Oregon."

Ty said over the headset, "Holy crap! This is awesome!"

Cory dared to open his eyes. The plane banked left and leveled as the lights of Luster faded to glowing specs. His stomach settled. A different, better thrill took over. He was *airborne*.

A female voice said over the headset, "Seattle Center Four Niner Sierra Whiskey squawk zero-six-five-one, maintain VFR."

While the little plane climbed smoothly through a cloudless sky, and an orange ball rose over snowcapped mountains in the distance, Harvey said, "Gentlemen, let's catch us some fish!"

Cory loved the view from on top of the world. Harvey pointed out all the volcanoes—Mount Hood, Mount Adams, Mount Bachelor dotted with skiers, Three Fingered Jack, the saw-toothed Broken Top—all of them shining and white and towering over the lesser but still impressive mountains around them. Harvey said, "Enjoy it, because you don't often see all the girls out like this, showing off their natural wonders." With the plane flying smooth and level, and with a window all his own, Cory managed to not think about dying long enough to eat the granola bar Tony offered him.

Forty minutes after taking off, Harvey was three hundred feet from the deck and lined up for the runway in Sunriver. Cory tensed for the landing, but barely felt it. Tony smiled, like *Here we are, business as usual.* Instead of parking the plane next to the hangar, Harvey taxied past a few giant homes, up to an even more giant home with a two-car-plus-one-plane garage. He pressed a button on a remote and the plane-size door opened. He shut down the engine and pulled the plane inside using a handheld tow bar. After they removed their gear from the plane, Harvey said to the boys,

"Welcome to Riverstone. I trust you will find the accommodations acceptable."

After a quick bathroom break, they entered the smaller garage that housed a white BMW SUV, a canoe, a kayak, and at least a dozen bikes of various sizes hanging on hooks next to a tall metal cabinet. Harvey unlocked the cabinet and hauled out the fly-fishing gear. They transferred poles, waders, nets, tackle boxes, and a giant Coleman cooler already filled with sandwiches, beer, and soda into the BMW. Then they headed off, yet again, for points unknown.

Harvey took them to a section of smooth-flowing water on the Lower Deschutes River, where the wide banks, low bushes, and thin trees were friendly to novice casters. After a thirty-minute lesson on the fundamentals of stroke, timing, and force applied, it became clear that Cory had found the one thing in the physical realm that he performed at a higher level than his brother. While Ty struggled to find a rhythm and hooked everything in sight *except* a fish, Cory shone. He fed out line and moved his hands smoothly from the ten o'clock to two o'clock positions while keeping the fly in constant motion. After three or four flicks of the rod he'd lay out that big green loop of line and the fly would float down to the current gentle like a leaf falling from a tree.

Forty-five minutes after touching a fly rod for the first time in his life, Cory landed an eighteen-inch rainbow on a pheasant-tail nymph with a barbless hook. Harvey, nearly thrilled beyond words, told him to wet his hands before touching the fish, keep them away from the gills, snapped a picture of the beaming Bic with his prize, then told him to release it so it could be caught another day. As the fish swam for deeper waters, Cory had an aching desire to email the picture to his father. It lasted three heartbeats, which was how long it took him to remember that Benny now resided in a brown pill bottle at the back of the top drawer in his nightstand and therefore would be unable to check his email account ever again.

When the fishing was done they lunched on tuna salad sandwiches and soda and beer from the cooler while Harvey told them stories about his childhood growing up poor in Spokane and how he used his talents to rise above it just like they would use their talents to rise above their unfortunate circumstances. Deer munched on grass in the meadow on the other side of the river and eagles circled on thermals up into a ridiculously blue sky and Portland felt a million miles away.

Just when Cory thought the day couldn't get better, it did. On the way back to Sunriver, with Tony behind the wheel, Harvey took a call on his cell. "Well," he growled, "what's the status?" After listening for a minute he brightened considerably and said, "So it's all arranged. Excellent. Dinner will be at Riverstone at six o'clock, then cigars and brandy after and we'll talk. We'll see you there." He ended the call, said to Tony, "That was Lester. They're all in. Who can you get to cater a dinner for nine tonight?"

Tony said, "That'll be tough. Maybe the Sunriver Lodge, but this is pretty late notice."

"These are heavy hitters. I need this to be perfect."

"Understood. Give me my phone. I'll call them now."

Harvey went silent for a minute, then said to Cory over his shoulder, "There's a decent grocery store in Sunriver village. If I give you the money to buy what you need, do you think you could reproduce your Holy Aioli burgers for my guests tonight?"

Cory wanted to open the window and scream, *YES! YES! YES!* He managed to say in a barely restrained voice, "Sure. I can do that. Would your guests like a salad as well?"

"What do you have in mind?"

"Charlene's charred romaine with the lemon-chive vinaigrette would pair quite nicely with the meat, plus I'm thinking a mushroom polenta in case there are vegetarians."

"And dessert?"

"A pear torte?"

"Excellent," Harvey said. "Do you need a cookbook?"

"Nope. I have them all in my head." *Plus two thousand more.*

Harvey said to Tony, "Sounds like you're off the hook. I found our caterer."

Tony said, "Cory, you're the bomb!"

Ty shot his brother a puzzled look, like *What planet are you from?* But a second later he smiled, leaned over to him and whispered, "My bro's a freaking rock star."

For the rest of the ride back to Sunriver, while Harvey discussed microbrews and politics with Tony, and Ty dozed with his earbuds in, Cory typed a shopping list into his phone. When that was done, he closed his eyes and considered this: Out of all the Harveys he knew, he liked River Harvey the best. That uncontested conclusion linked to another thought. He pictured Kayla in the gazebo balanced on a plank, asking him that odd question about being absorbed. Right now, in these soft leather seats with Vivaldi on the stereo, a night of cooking ahead of him, mountains rising up out of every window, he decided: *If this is what being absorbed feels like, sign me up.*

Dinner went off without a hitch. Well, almost without a hitch. Cory thought the polenta was a little dry, and the crème fraîche would have been a better topping for the torte instead of whipped cream, but there wasn't time to let it sit. Harvey's guests, two couples—one from Bend, the other from Portland, didn't seem too concerned. They ate everything he cooked, marveled at the hamburgers, and went away convinced that Harvey would make an excellent senator. They wrote checks to prove how convinced they were, and Lester declared the entire evening a success top to bottom.

With all the guests departed, Harvey said that he wanted to have a little talk with everyone before they retired for the night. They sat on deck chairs in sweaters and jackets arranged around a gas-fed fire pit, the night sky a blanket of stars above them, and the Deschutes River so close Cory could hear the current whisper as it surged restless against the banks. Occasionally a walker with a headlamp would pass on the walking trail thirty feet from where they sat. Cory wondered if they saw the glowing tip rise and fall from Harvey's cigar. After ten minutes of spotting satellites and naming constellations Harvey said, "There are matters to discuss, so let's get down to it." He nodded to Tony. "If you'll do the honors, please."

Tony pulled two sealed envelopes from his jacket pocket, gave one each to Cory and Ty. The envelopes were thin. Cory didn't think they contained more than a single sheet of paper.

"Before you open them," Harvey said, "I'd like to say how impressed I am with your progress. Steamer, that fastball of yours is turning into the talk of the town."

It was the first time Cory had heard Harvey reference Ty's baseball nickname. Even though "Steamer" was featured prominently on the sports page after every game, it felt strange to hear Harvey use it. He saw it as a sign, and hoped it wasn't a bad one.

"You've put the baseball team in contention to win the district title for the first time in how many years, Tony?"

"Ten. The drought is finally over."

Harvey waved his cigar at Ty in acknowledgment of his skill. "Keep this up and there will be a plaque with your name on it in the trophy case next to Tony's. And just like Tony, there will be scholarships in your future. And, Cory, what can I say? You've made a good restaurant even better. We are rated the number one hamburger establishment in Luster, beating Red Robin for the first time. I've had three requests for franchising—one of them tonight by our guests from Portland. They said your hamburger was—what was the word, Tony?"

"Transcendent."

"Yes, transcendent. That's the word," Harvey said. "I may take them up on the offer. Given your skills with math, and your ability to run a kitchen, I see a significant role for you on the management team. But let's save that discussion for another day."

Cory glowed with the praise. But secretly he hoped that day would never come. The kitchen of his dreams did not include flipping Harvey burgers for the rest of his life.

Harvey looked at Tony. "Do you have anything to add?"

Tony said, "I just think about the hand you guys were dealt, and how far you've come. You're amazing examples of how important the foster care system is, and how great it can be when good people such as yourselves are given half a chance to succeed."

Cory said, "Thank you."

Ty just nodded. It occurred to Cory that he might be bored.

Harvey said, "Now you may open your envelopes."

Cory briefly flashed back to the envelope from Stellah. The odds of the contents hitting him that hard were close to—but not quite—zero. Cory opened the envelope. It was a check. He had to hold it close to the fire pit to see. He blinked, then blinked again. There were too many zeroes. He counted four, preceded by a one. *Was that—*

Harvey answered for him. "That's ten thousand dollars, in case you can't see in this light." Cory looked at Ty. He was staring at the check, no doubt wearing the same stunned expression that Cory was sure he had plastered all over his own face. Harvey said, "But before you get too excited, notice the date."

Ty said, "Graduation day." Now he wasn't bored.

"That's right. If you meet two simple conditions that I'm about to share, then on the day you graduate I will contribute ten thousand dollars toward your continuing education. Call it the Harvey Mott Milestone Three Scholarship Award. Tony was the last beneficiary of this award."

Tony leaned forward, his expression more serious than Cory was accustomed to. He said, "I'm sure by now you've heard about what happened to me my senior year." Both boys nodded. Although several versions still circulated around town, the one most commonly heard was that eight years ago Tony and his best friend and teammate broke into a garage to steal some beer. DeShawn was shot in the back while running from the scene by homeowner Virgil Wiggins, father of three. DeShawn died with a six-pack of Budweiser in his right hand. Virgil Wiggins was still in prison. Tony got three weeks in juvie boot camp and six months' probation.

"What you don't know," Tony continued, his eyes on the flames, "is what happened after. My family fell apart. My dad stopped talking to me. My grades tanked. My mom couldn't deal with it and went into a depression and didn't leave the house for six months. Coach used to tell us that when you're in a hole, stop digging. Well, I dug me a great big black hole, but I kept flinging the dirt over my shoulder on the way to China. But Harvey..." Tony lifted his eyes from the fire to look at them straight on. "He gave me a job after boot camp. He offered to pay for my first year of school if I got my shit together. I managed to graduate, went to OSU, got a degree in education and a master's in social work so I could help kids like you not fuck up like I did. And here I am."

"Plus, you continue to work for me on the side," Harvey said.

"Yes," Tony said, and returned his eyes to the flames. "And I think I always will."

Harvey said, "I'm very proud of what Tony has done. What happened was tragic, and bad decisions were made by everyone involved. But people make mistakes and the challenge is to keep them from turning into roadblocks that limit...future opportunities. Before I list the two conditions, are there any questions?" Harvey ashed his cigar against the arm of his chair, stared at the glowing tip as if he'd created a work of art. In the wake of their silence, he said, "Condition one: You both must maintain at least a three-point-oh GPA until graduation. Cory, you're already there. Ty, with a little focus you will be. Condition two..." Harvey took a long puff on his cigar, blew out a slow stream of smoke. "I know about the rumors around town regarding the termination of a...valued employee. It was a painful time for us. This individual was very close to our family and the grounds for her termination are a private matter. Please respect our privacy by not pursuing a relationship with her. Normal civil interactions are fine and expected." He focused exclusively on Cory. "Just don't go for private rendezvous at a gazebo." The cigar tip glowed. "Does that work for you?"

Cory took a moment to think about Kayla's parting words: *I like you, Cory Bic.* Then he nodded. Harvey moved on to Ty. "And you?"

Ty said, "That's not a problem."

Harvey grinned. "Excellent! Now give me those checks." Cory and Ty returned the checks. He slipped them into his coat pocket and stood. "Gentlemen, I thank you for a fine and productive day. Great fishing, great food, great company. What else could a man ask for?" He tossed the stub of his cigar into the fire pit. "Air Harvey departs at six a.m. Sleep well."

Harvey left. Tony waited a moment, then said, "I don't know what happened at the Motts'. I know that Charlene was very upset, and whatever it was is still pretty much an open wound. They need time to heal—they all need time to heal. I've known Kayla since she was in middle school. I like her a lot. She's a special girl." He stood and gazed up at the sky. An owl hooted from somewhere across the river. "Harvey's running for senate, guys. It's...complicated." Then he turned and walked into the house.

As soon as the patio door was closed, Ty leaned in close to Cory and whispered, "How did Harvey know about you and Kayla?"

"I have no idea."

"Want to know what I'm thinking?"

"Sure."

Ty leaned back and smiled. "Ten thousand dollars buys a lot of Swedish Fish."

Cory watched the last of Harvey's cigar blacken and turn to ash.

"Yes, it does."

'm working on a theory. Rather than start at the fishing trip, I rewind all the way back to Portland. I tell her everything except a few of the gory details from Luster because, seriously, why pile my train wrecks on top of hers? By the time I get to the part about stealing the Volvo, I'm pretty sure she's down for the count. The last thing she said was "Tell me more about that Harvey chap." Her eyes closed and they haven't opened since. Enough time has passed between then and now for my toes to refreeze. I whisper, "Astrid? Are you awake?" She doesn't respond. I decide now is probably a good time to read Ty's letter and start to pull the envelope out of my pocket, when the girl who misses nothing whispers, "You think Benny did it?"

"Did what?"

"All this money."

"It makes the most sense." I put the envelope on top of the chest for later. "Tirk knew Benny was stealing from him and this is a killer place to stash it. But it's hundreds of miles from Portland. What I don't understand is how he got up here to do it."

She asks, "Who else knows about Stumptown?"

"Besides me and Ty? My guess is nobody. Benny's been dead for almost a year. If someone knew about it, this shit would be long gone. But I do know one thing: they're still looking for it."

A beat. "Can I have some pills and water?"

"Sure."

I don't know how long it's been since her last pills, but I give her three anyway. Death by ibuprofen is the least of her worries. I cap the water bottle after we both take careful sips. It's well under the quarter-liter mark now. That won't get her through the night, not with the way she's sweating. Hopefully the snow-in-the-bottle trick is working. My feet aren't cold anymore.

After Astrid settles in she says, "While you were talking about Benny and how this place was a great spot to hide his stash—I remembered something that might help."

"Like what?"

"It was my first night there. I woke up on the mat. It was dark. I didn't know where I was. Someone was crying. I had a heavy chain on my ankle. Then a torch turned on. He was sitting on the stairs watching us. There was a ski mask over his face. He aimed the light at Yana, then me. He said, 'Welcome to the warehouse. Checkout time is like, *never*.'"

The connection explodes like a bomb in my head.

She sees my stunned expression and asks, "Did that help?"

"Benny had this secret place he would disappear to on weekends. When he came back there would be pine needles in the truck. One time he came back with a really bad scratch under his eye. All he ever told me about the place was that Tirk had a side business and that's where he'd keep his spare parts. He called it the *warehouse*."

"Oh my God … your father … ?"

"Yeah. No shit. This recipe is starting to come together—and it stinks."

We both take a beat to process this latest revelation. But there's still another blank I need to fill. "I hate to ask you this—but... when this guy threw the bloody sweater down, you told me he said something about 'listening.' Can you tell me what he said again?"

Her eyes close. The silence becomes so complete I swear I can hear the snowflakes piling up outside. In a voice that screams with a pain I can't imagine, she whispers, *"Listen up, buttercup."*

And BAM! Another bomb goes off in my head.

42

Air Harvey was wheels down in Luster at 8:04 a.m., and that included ten minutes of waiting for a thundershower to pass before Harvey muttered, "I can fly around that," and took off. It looked to Cory like they were headed into the bowels of Mount Doom. But the little plane banked, shuddered up through some clouds, leveled off at eleven thousand feet, and cruised the rest of the way to Luster.

Harvey had some calls to make before church, so he headed for his office at the dealership. Tony dropped the boys off at the ski lodge, asked Ty if he wanted to shoot hoops later, which Ty did not. Then Tony left to do whatever Tony did on a Sunday, and the boys had a morning to kill before Ty went over to Frankie J.'s to watch baseball and Cory's noon-to-eight shift started at Bravo. As they walked in the front door, Charlene called out from the kitchen, "Cory, can you make breakfast for the kids? I need to get ready for church."

"Sure!" he said.

"Your special pancakes?" Ty asked.

"If there's enough yogurt."

And his phone rang. It was Kayla.

270

Cory stared at the face of his buzzing phone, not sure what to do. His finger hovered over the green button.

Ty said, "Milestone three, dude."

Cory sent the call to voice mail.

Ty said, "Not good enough. Give me the phone."

"I'll delete the message."

"You know you won't."

Cory hesitated.

"Give me the phone."

Charlene said, "Cory? Are you coming?"

"Be right there!" He handed his phone to Ty and hated himself for doing it.

Charlene breezed into the kitchen dressed for church and smiled at the four of them seated around the table finishing up the syrupy remainders of breakfast. Cory noticed that her hair was down instead of up, her lipstick was a muted shade of red, and her dress was new and a few inches closer to her ankles than was her usual style. He wondered how much of it was Lester, the perpetually frowning campaign manager, who believed optics were everything, and how much was Charlene just going for a new look on this sunny spring morning.

She said to Cory and Ty, "Did you have fun on your manly trip?"

"Cory caught a fish!" Justin said. "He showed me the picture! It was huge!"

"Oh really?" Charlene winked at Cory. "Can I see it?"

"Sure." Cory pulled up the picture and handed her the phone.

"Wow," she said. "That's a big fish. I'll bet Harvey was beside himself."

"He was," Cory said.

"What about you?" Charlene said, looking at Ty. "Did you catch anything?"

Chloe said, "Ty caught a tree."

Ty said, "And it was huge!"

And Cory's phone rang again.

Charlene's eyes narrowed at the screen; then she returned the phone to Cory, her lips a thin, tight line. It was Kayla. Again. He pushed a button to stop the ringing and buried it deep in his pocket.

"Sorry about that," Cory mumbled. He did his best to ignore the glare Ty shot his way.

Charlene forked the last bite of pancake from Justin's plate. "I heard your dinner was a great success. Thanks to you, Harvey managed to impress a very important donor."

"I made your charred romaine salad. It was a huge hit."

"Did Harvey smoke a victory cigar on the deck?"

"Yes," Cory said.

"I wish he would stop smoking those nasty things." Charlene shook her head sadly, and plated the fork. Then she leveled her eyes at Cory. "But some habits are just too hard to break."

Cory didn't answer. He didn't know what to say.

Charlene smiled. "Cory, your pancakes were delicious. The nutmeg is a wonderful touch!" She nodded to Justin and Chloe. "Thank Cory for breakfast. Then put away your dishes and let's go."

As soon as Charlene's SUV was headed down the driveway, Ty said, "Dude. You need to get that girl off your phone."

"*That girl?* Her name is Kayla."

"Her name should be *history.*"

Cory said nothing.

Ty shook his head. "What do you see in her anyway? I'm mean, seriously? She's not my type by a mile. And she's definitely not your type, so what's the deal?"

Cory had asked himself the same question on the flight back. He couldn't come up with anything definite. Just a feeling he had that something was broken and she was asking him for help. "She's a friend, that's all. I don't know what else to tell you."

"Well, that's one friendship you can do without. I've risked a lot sucking up to that rich asshole."

A red flag shot up in Cory's head. "What does that mean?"

This time Ty said nothing.

"*You've risked a lot?* Why did you say that? You have to have a reason."

"I've got ten thousand reasons. How about you?"

"This is about more than money."

After a beat, he said, "Don't fuck this up, *bro.*"

"I won't, *Steamer.*"

Ty shook his head and left.

Cory scrubbed the kitchen until it shone.

Then he went up to their attic room.

He thought about checking Kayla's message, had his finger over the button—but deleted it instead.

Then he deleted her contact.

Then he opened his laptop and pulled up the website for the

International Culinary School in Seattle. He knew exactly what he wanted to do with his ten grand.

Cory was in the Bravo kitchen showing a thoroughly bored Brian Castleman the right way to mince shallots when Rebecca walked up behind them and tapped Cory on the shoulder.

"How's our stock on condiments?"

"Fine," Cory said, wondering, *When did she ever care about condiments?*

"I think we need to check the inventory."

Cory knew what that meant. She had dirt to share, and since he was the unfortunate target this time, it almost certainly had something to do with him. He tossed his latex gloves in the trash and followed Rebecca into the supply closet.

She picked up the inventory clipboard but didn't look at it. "How many times are you going to show him how to cut those fancy onions?"

"They're shallots. And I'll show him until he gets it right."

"They stink."

"That's the price of using shallots."

Rebecca leaned in closer and spoke in a near whisper: "A couple of people stopped by looking for you yesterday."

"Yeah? Who were they?"

"One was Kayla. She ordered an aioli burger and was like, oh, by the way, have you seen Cory Bic? She was all casual about it, but I could tell she was like, *really wanting to know.*"

"What did you tell her?"

"I told her you and your brother went fishing with Harvey."

Cory thought about what Kayla said at the gazebo: *He'll take you. But by that time it will be too late. Your fate is sealed, Cory Bic.* That would explain all the phone calls—which he subsequently ignored. Cory said, "So I went fishing. What's the big deal about that?"

"I don't know. But I think it shook her up. She like, changed her order from the dining room to *takeout.* I mean, what's up with that?"

"I think you've been hanging around the fryer too long. All those grease fumes are scrambling your brain."

She hung up the clipboard, pretended to count the jars of relish. "You know the story about her and the Motts, right?"

"What story?"

Her eyes lit up like the Fourth of July. That's what happened when she had the opportunity to share some really big dirt. "OMG! Do you not know *anything?*"

"Please share."

Rebecca leaned in again, this time in a full whisper: "She got caught stealing meds from Mrs. Mott. Zoloft is what I heard. That's for like, *depression.*"

Cory's mind reeled from all the rumors why Kayla was no longer the nanny. It was hard to keep track. What was next? Something obviously happened, because Harvey put the hammer down on seeing her, and Charlene certainly wasn't a fan. As far as Cory could tell, the real reason was a mystery and that's how it would stay. But he couldn't just let this tale go uncontested. "I'm sorry. That doesn't sound like the Kayla I know."

"How well do you know her?"

"We saved a CPR dummy's life together."

Rebecca's eyes lit up again. "OMG. You're not . . . I mean . . . *you?* And *her?*" She shook her head like something cataclysmic had just reorganized her universe.

"What are you talking about?"

"No. It's just that I thought, you know . . . you and the onion slicer . . ."

"The *onion slicer?* Can you please talk in complete sentences? Preferably ones that make sense."

She smiled, headed for the door. "I think someone's been in the closet too long."

Cory followed her out, hot on her heels. His heart was pounding too hard to ask her what she meant. *And if she knows, who else knows?* Then she stopped and turned around. "Oh, and I almost forgot. The other person that stopped by? He was a sketchy dude that ordered a vanilla shake and asked about you just as we were closing. Tondi had like, just cleaned that machine."

Sketchy? That deserved a follow-up. "Why was he sketchy?"

"Leather pants, lots of chains. Beady eyes. And when he smiled, it looked like he'd been eating bark chips."

The thought hit Cory like a blow to the chest. He only knew one person that fit that description. He recovered enough to ask, "What did he want?"

"He wanted to know if you like, worked for this 'fine establishment.' I kid you not. That's what he said. *Fine establishment.* Ha! Like he'd know the difference? So anyway, I said yes, you did but you were like, fishing in the wilderness somewhere. So he gave me this." She dug a piece of paper out of her jeans pocket and gave it to him.

Cory stared at the business card. He recognized the cheesy T&B Towing logo. Except the *B* was crossed out with pen.

She said, "He wrote a message on the back."

Cory flipped the card over.

My boss wants a chat with Ty.

Cory pocketed the card. He felt like he'd swallowed sand.

Brian called from the takeout counter, "Hey, Cory! It's getting close to one. Shouldn't we heat up the fryer?"

He was too nauseous to think about grease right now. Meanwhile Rebecca was still talking. She said something about her name. "I'm sorry," Cory said. "My head was somewhere else. What did you just say?"

Rebecca sighed impatiently. "I said he called me *buttercup*. As in 'What's up, buttercup?'" She pointed to her name tag. "So tell your brown-toothed friend he needs to learn how to read. Or next time he'll be wearing that shake on his face."

43

"I'm pretty sure I know the man that killed Yana."

Astrid was on the verge of sleep. Her eyes snap into focus with this revelation.

"Who was it?"

"A big-time meth head. We called him Tweaker Teeth. He worked for Benny's business partner. A guy named Tirk."

"How do you know it was this . . . Tweaker Teeth?"

"He showed up at my job in Luster and said the same thing to my boss. 'What's up, buttercup?'"

"Why was he there?"

"Looking for me. But I really think Tirk was looking for Ty. Tweaker Teeth was just there to deliver the message. He left a business card."

"Why did he leave it for you and not Ty?"

"Ty would have ripped up the card, then beat the shit out of Tweaker Teeth."

"Did you give the card to Ty?"

"I did. He ripped it up, then beat the shit out of me."

She laughs. Under normal circumstances I think I would look forward to that sound. This time it bubbles and rattles around in her chest, then sends her into a coughing spasm. When it's finally over she asks for a sip of water, which I give her and make a mental note to check the bottle in my bag. She settles and asks, "Do you know why Tirk was looking for Ty?"

"The people of your country sure ask a lot of questions."

"My other choice is sleeping. When I sleep I have dreams. The pain is better than the dreams."

I nod in understanding. Benny wasn't a good influence on my dreams either. "I don't know why Tirk was looking for Ty. I asked him the same question that night. He said, 'Tirk's a piece of shit. I'm not scared of him and you shouldn't be either.' Then he ripped up the card."

"What do you think?"

"I think Tirk is a scary MF and dangerous as hell and he wanted something from Ty. It was all related to Benny's death in some way. That's the puzzle piece I haven't figured out yet."

She seems to have run out of questions. Either she's reloading, or more likely giving in to sleep. Meanwhile, I do a mental replay of Ty's last words to me before he disappeared into the canyon to save our asses: "Read the damn letter." There had to be a reason why he wrote it, and a bigger reason why he waited until then—a time when we might not see each other again—to give it to me. I reach for the letter on top of the chest and say, "Maybe there are some answers in here." I hold the letter in my hand, but I can't open it. I glance at Astrid. She definitely is not asleep.

"What's wrong?" she asks.

"I don't want to do it."

"Why not?"

"I'm afraid if I open this envelope, it means…" I take a breath. "It means I'm giving up on him. And I'm not ready to do that." I'm also afraid of the secrets that are locked inside, secrets that might send me spinning to very dark places. We can't afford that. I need to keep my shit together.

"You're not giving up on him," she says. "You're just doing what he asked you to do."

"My father's ashes were delivered to me in an envelope. That didn't turn out so well."

"Would you like me to do it?"

"Says the girl with a broken arm." I shake my head. "Thanks, but I need to get over my fear of envelopes." I force a smile, peel the flap open, and pull out the single sheet of paper. It's covered with Ty's handwriting. I have to read it twice because the lighting in here sucks and my tears keep falling on the paper and blurring the ink.

Dear Cor

Benny was murdered and I saw it all.

If you're reading this letter that means I was too chickenshit to tell you. Or something happened to me and I couldn't do it. I should have told you the next day, and I almost did at the coffee shop. I should have told you a million times later. But I didn't, so bad on me. After you read this letter maybe you will understand why.

Tirk and his soulless minion Tweaker Teeth showed up that night. Benny was in the shed cooking meth and you were drugged up with painkillers and asleep. When I came out of the house Tweaker Teeth was loading the motorcycle into Tirk's truck. I didn't give a shit about the bike. Good fucking riddance! But Benny came out screaming like a lunatic at Tweaker Teeth. While they went at it, Tirk walked out of the garage and gave Benny's skull a whack with a hammer. He went down like a rock. Then Tirk and Tweaker Teeth hauled Benny into the shed. They saw me on the porch and just walked on by. A minute later they came out of the shed. Tweeker Teeth asked Tirk what to do with me because I was a witness. Tirk told me to lock the shed. I said no. He pulled a gun and said do it or I'll kill you then your brother, then put you all in the shed and have a little family barbecue. I figured Benny was already dead, so I locked it. Tirk told Tweaker Teeth to take a picture with his phone. Then he looked right at me with those dead eyes of his and said you're a part of this now. We go down, you go down. Tweaker Teeth winked and said BOOM. They drove away with the ninja. Smoke was coming under the door by then. I swear I didn't know they had set the shed on fire before I locked it. But I knew it would explode any second. Instead of trying to bust into the shed to get Benny, I ran into the house to get you.

They murdered Benny. I didn't warn him. I didn't stop them. I was so pissed at what Benny did to you. For never letting you be who you are. For hitting Mom. For moving us into a crack house and bringing Tirk into our lives. All his lies and constant bullshit had to stop, bro. So yeah, I just stood on the porch and let it happen. But truth be told, if they didn't kill him that night, I would have. Like Benny used to say, "Kill or be killed. It's the only rule that matters."

Feel free to share this letter with Detective Donut. Give my regards to Stellah.

Peace out, Ty

I refold the letter, stuff it in my pocket. I might read it again later. If there is a later.

"Did it help?" she asks.

I guess she was reloading. "It cleared up a few things."

"Do you know why Tweaker Teeth was here?"

"No. But I know he killed Benny. With some help."

Her eyes narrow on me. "Are you okay?"

"Yes."

"You don't look it."

"Neither do you." I see by the way she flinches that my words hurt. I wish I could take them back. But I'm too shaken up to give it another thought. Let's just add it to the list of stupid shit I said. I'm sure by the time this is over it will be a very long list.

After a beat she says, "What are you thinking?"

I'm thinking I finally understand what Ty did and why he did it. And maybe even why he wasn't afraid of Tirk: *You're a part of this now.* All this time I thought there was some outside chance that he killed Benny and didn't think I could handle the truth. I just wish he would have told me sooner so that I could have told him that it's okay. I would have told him *Thank you for saving my life* and *It's not your fault that Benny got mixed up with drugs and killers.* Instead I say to her, "I'm thinking that if there were a competition for the most messed-up family in the world, my little clan would be a contender for the top prize."

After a beat she says, "I can't remember anything about my family. Except that my mother's name is Deanna. Maybe my family is more messed up than yours."

"Sorry, but that award is all mine."

"Is there anything I can do to help?"

I stare at her, lying there with an infected broken arm. With a fever I can't stop. We probably don't have enough water to keep her alive through the night. Or enough pills to reduce her pain. We have to leave tomorrow, with or without Ty. That means a five-mile hike out of here with a killer hunting us and hundreds of miles to drive to the nearest hospital—in a stolen car that doesn't work. And she's asking how she can help me? *Something needs to change with this picture.*

But first there's a question I just have to ask. If I don't it will haunt me through the night.

"Do you know why Tweaker Teeth put you in the trunk?"

She closes her eyes, then opens them. "I just remembered something. Was Tirk missing half a finger?"

How could she know that? A chill sweeps through me. She had never said anything about there being two people at the warehouse. Up to this point it was all Tweaker Teeth. *Shit.* "Yes."

"Someone different put the plastic around my wrists and ankles. Someone bigger. When he touched my hands I felt the stump. He's the one that carried me out to the car and put me in the boot."

"Okay. But that doesn't mean he was the driver."

"There's more. I remember it clearly now."

I don't like where this is headed.

"Tweaker Teeth started yelling at Tirk. He said something about a 'payday.' Tirk told him to shut the fuck up. Tweaker Teeth yelled, 'You can't do this to me.'" She looks me hard in the eyes. "I . . . I think Tirk killed Tweaker Teeth."

"Why?"

"I heard two loud bangs."

"Then what?" I ask, but not really wanting to hear what comes next.

"Tweaker Teeth shut the fuck up."

LUSTER, OR.

FIVE MONTHS AGO

44

Early polling data just after Harvey launched his campaign showed him trailing his Republican rival in District 30 by twenty points. By mid-May he narrowed the gap to fifteen. One poll out of Portland put him on the cusp of single digits. Of the four individuals with their hats in that ring, Harvey was considered the most likely to win the nomination. The keystone of his campaign was his record as a job creator, and the co-op he started at Mott's Lumber and Landscaping was the cherry on top of his political sundae. The lowest wage in that store was four dollars over minimum and the business continued to prosper. That appealed to Democrats and Independents and he was beginning to build a coalition of voters, helping to fuel his rapid ascent in popularity.

After the fishing trip Cory and Ty returned to their Luster lives. The visit from Tweaker Teeth was ignored and seemed to pass without repercussions. Ty continued his success on the mound, and pitched seven shutout innings to record his twelfth win and send the Luster Raptors to the district finals. They lost 4–3 thanks to a walk-off homer in the thirteenth inning. Ty's grades dipped to a 2.8 after a couple of missed assignments in algebra and a devastating surprise quiz on Oliver Cromwell. But Cory helped Ty recover, and the 3.0 was looking solid heading into June.

Meanwhile Cory settled into his own groove. Since he'd completed his PE requirements he no longer had that anchor on his GPA. His 3.9 placed him among the top ten students in his class. With physics almost out of the way, he set an attainable goal of a 4.0 for his senior year. His three vices—late-night gaming, Dr Pepper, and the chocolate-chip cookies from Safeway, which he consumed by the bag—kept his weight hovering near the two-forty mark. Ty, with his relentless martial arts training and a new passion for parkour, tipped the scales at a ripped one-seventy-five. Cory confided in Charlene one night that he thought his lack of friends was due to his weight. She said true friends wouldn't care about that, but recommended he start with some light exercise, like walking.

Cory resorted to daily walks around the park and the pounds started dropping, although not as fast as he would have liked. On two occasions he saw Kayla smoking weed in the gazebo. It was always from a distance and he never approached her. After those three calls from her on the day he returned from Sunriver, she stopped trying to contact him. Two weeks later he found an envelope slipped into his locker at school. The neatly handwritten card inside read: *You're officially absorbed. Congratulations. It was nice knowing you.* He almost called her that night because her number was committed to memory and he couldn't sleep and for once he didn't feel like gaming. Then he reminded himself that he deleted her contact for a reason—or, as Ty liked to remind him, *ten thousand* reasons.

As June approached and the semester was almost over, Cory noticed that Kayla was ditching classes more than normal, and heard from the rumor mill that she was seen in tears leaving her boyfriend Oliver's car. Rebecca, always a reliable resource for unreliable Luster gossip, cornered him once in the storage closet again with news that Kayla had been discussed at a Mott, Inc. managers meeting because she was written up for using a profanity in front of a customer. That customer happened to be Kayla's boyfriend's father, who also happened to be: oh, by the way, *the freaking mayor*!

The Cory-Kayla firewall Cory built and diligently maintained was the only dark spot on his otherwise brightening horizon. He visited the International Culinary Arts School website every night. He built an Excel spreadsheet with first-year costs calculated down to the penny. Financial-aid applications were filled out and submitted. With that money, plus Harvey's milestone-three tuition incentive plan and whatever he'd saved from Bravo, that dream was within reach. As much as he wanted to reach out to her, Kayla would be, as Harvey might put it, an impediment to that opportunity.

Three days shy of school letting out for the summer, Ty picked Cory up at work. He was unusually silent during the drive to the ski lodge. Cory figured something happened at work, or at school, or with his latest girlfriend, or at the dojo, or any of the million other things he had going on in his life. Cory didn't ask because, honestly, he didn't want to have yet another reminder about how big Ty's world was compared to his. Charlene was making fried chicken for family night. He had a final to study for and a tutoring session with Chloe; then he'd submerge himself in a sneak peek of the latest release of *Assassin's Creed* by Ubisoft. That was the size of Cory's world and he didn't see it changing anytime soon.

But instead of walking into the house, Ty said, "Let's take Pavlov for a walk."

Cory could smell the chicken frying. Ty never asked him to come with on his walks with Pavlov. "Sure," he said.

With Pavlov on the leash, it always looked to him like they were walking a small horse. They walked in silence to the end of the driveway, turned right onto the path through trees that Harvey used for his run. Then Ty said, "Something strange happened at work today."

"Okay."

"So cars come into the dealership different ways. Trade-ins, trailers, dealer swaps. Sometimes they hire someone to deliver them after an auction. There's a process they go through before we see them in the detail shop. We're like the last stop before they get a sticker and are put on the lot. So I've been thinking about buying a car—"

"You want to buy a car?"

"I knew you'd ask that question. I'm telling you this important thing, and you go off on me wanting a car of my own."

"What's wrong with the Volvo?"

"Dude, it's like, a soccer-mom car."

"Still not seeing your point."

"Can we save this battle for another day?"

"All right. Finish. But just to be clear, that ten grand is not for a car."

Ty yanked hard on Pavlov's leash, pulled his nose out of a bush. They moved down the path. "Anyway. I'd been scoping out the deliveries, watching for what I want, and the perfect little Civic is delivered by one of those auction dudes. Two doors, black, tinted windows. Sweet. They parked it in the back lot. I'm about to take a look—and Tony scoops me. He grabs the keys and drives it away."

"Wow. That's pretty dramatic. A long-time employee test-drives a car. Did you call SWAT?"

"Just shut it, okay?" Pavlov stopped, raised a leg. Ty said, "I'm thinking what's up with that? Tony's taking a car out before it goes through the process. He only works a couple hours a week, and he's not a salesperson—in fact I don't even know what the hell he does. So I ask Miranda about it, and she says it's just something Tony does from time to time. He always signs it out. No big deal, and Harvey gave his okay. 'So why do you care?' she wants to know. I say, 'Forget I asked,' and went about my business."

Pavlov moved on. Cory thought the bush looked like it was hit by a firehose.

Ty said, "Well, as luck would have it, the Civic shows up in my detail station the next day. I've got my trusty crevice tool out and am working between the door and the front passenger seat—and see this." Ty pulled something shiny out of his pocket, gave it to Cory.

It was a necklace. Cory knew it looked familiar, but couldn't quite place it. A thin silver chain with a small angular cross for a pendant. The clasp was still intact.

"Flip it over," Ty said.

Cory looked at the back of the pendant. Squinted, saw *KS♥OT* etched in the silver. Then he remembered where he saw the necklace. Kayla wore it at the CPR class. It dangled from her neck when she was doing chest compressions. She had to tuck it into her T-shirt, but it kept falling out, interrupting her rhythm. In fact he made a joke about it: *And the coroner's report said death by pendant.* The *OT* must have been Oliver Tice.

"It's Kayla's," Ty said.

"I know. How do you know?"

"She had it on at that party. She kept twisting it when we talked."

They walked in silence for a few paces. Cory didn't feel as hungry as he did when they started their walk. "So this strange thing that happened at work is really about you wondering how Kayla's necklace got into the car that Tony was driving?"

"Yup."

Cory flashed back to his conversation with Kayla, when she told him why she was in the gazebo smoking weed: *It relaxes me. So I come here and smoke up before I have to do something I don't want to do.* Dots started to form. He just needed to connect them.

"When did Tony take the Civic?"

"Yesterday, around five."

"Can you get the sign-out logs from Miranda?"

"Way ahead of you, bro." Ty pulled three folded sheets of paper from his back pocket. They had entries from the past three months. "I copied them when she was on her break. And no one takes more breaks than her."

Cory scanned the entries. Ty had highlighted all the dates with Tony's initials. There were four, dating back to January 7. The most recent was yesterday. Cory was looking for something about three weeks ago that would correlate with when he was walking in the park and saw Kayla in the gazebo. And there it was, five up from the bottom:

May 10 | 5:00pm OUT | 5:35pm IN.

The dots connected. He handed the sheets back to Ty. "You think Tony's taking cars from the lot and using them to hook up with Kayla?"

"That's right. But why?"

"I don't know. But there has to be a good explanation."

"Like what?"

"Maybe he was counseling her."

"Right. And she takes off her necklace for that?"

"All right. Maybe he found her necklace at the park and was going to give it to her, borrowed a car from the lot instead of driving his own car, and then lost it in that car just before he gave her the necklace." Cory knew that wasn't the answer either, but he had to say something while his brain tried to come up with a better explanation.

"Wow," Ty said, his eyes wide with mock admiration. "And I thought you were going to say that he was slipping her the old wicked weasel. Of course he just *randomly* found her necklace, *randomly* checked out the car on the same day you were *randomly* in the park, and then *randomly* lost the necklace, which I just happened to *randomly* find—on the passenger side of the car. Of course that's what happened! You're such a freaking genius!"

Stalling for time, Cory said, "Wicked weasel? Where'd you hear that one?"

"I was watching cartoons with Justin."

Cory suppressed a smile, thinking that whatever truth Ty had uncovered here, it would not be funny. He looked at the necklace again, felt a seed of anger rising that he hadn't felt since Portland, since that night when Benny showed them the motorcycle and sent their world spinning. He took a breath and pushed it down. Cory showed the necklace to Ty. "Can I hang on to this?"

"Sure. Are you going to give it to Harvey?"

"No. That would make it worse."

"Kayla?"

"No. I think it was there for a reason."

"*Tony?*"

"No. That would just be stupid."

"Then what the fuck, Cor?"

Pavlov hunched his back and dropped a steamer. Cory thought the timing was perfect.

"It's time for an op."

LUSTER, OR.

45

In the great before, as in before Benny hurt his back jumping off the forklift he drove for eight hours a day, five days a week for seventeen years; before he stole pills from his friends' bathrooms between bouts of downing beer and whiskey like it was holy water; before their mother wrote that note on the refrigerator; before Benny carried a grudge against life in general because it conspired against him at every opportunity; and especially before Tirk and all the shit he brought into their lives—Cory and Ty used to play a game in their backyard. They draped painting tarps over lawn chairs to make an FOB (Forward Operating Base) and sent each other on Operations of Doom. Every op had to have a name. This time around, Cory picked Operation Majula, after the central town-hub in *Dark Souls II*, which was everything and nothing like Luster.

They knew patience and vigilance would be key to a successful op because Tony didn't sign out cars very often, and when he did it happened fast. A successful op also needed a camera with a decent lens, so he bought a Panasonic with a 30x digital zoom.

They looked for patterns to help anticipate when it might happen; the only consistencies they saw were that Tony was never gone for more than an hour, and all four sign-outs since January were two-door coupes bought at auction, had tinted windows, and were dark, either black or gray. Ty asked Miranda if she'd share the list of cars bought at auction, and she was always ready and willing to exchange favors with him. When Ty saw a monsoon-gray Audi TT Quattro, 55k miles, six-speed manual with tinted windows was arriving from Boise on Wednesday, he told Cory to be ready for a text.

Cory was ready. The car arrived; the text didn't. But it did the following day when Cory was at Bravo flipping burgers.

TY

> Operation Majula is
> a GO!

Luckily it was a little after four in the afternoon, so they weren't slammed with orders. Cory asked Brian to cover the grill, then asked Rebecca if he could borrow her car (Tony would recognize the Volvo) to buy some allergy meds at Walmart, because otherwise he'd have to wait for Ty and by then it might be too late.

Rebecca asked, "Too late for what?"

Cory said, "You'll know when the blood starts coming out of my ears."

She gave him the keys.

He shouldered his daypack and blew out the door.

• ● ●

Phase One was to establish recon at Woodland Park in the southeast lot, farthest away from the gazebo and sheltered by trees. He would wait there to see if Kayla showed up, then watch for a gray Audi TT. All events transpired as expected—except one. Kayla didn't get into the Audi. It did a slow pass through the lot, then headed due east on Constitution Ave. Cory had to make a split-second decision. Stay with Kayla to see what she did, or follow the Audi. He followed the Audi.

Cory caught up to the car at a red light and followed it east into a residential neighborhood named Fairview Heights with modest one- and two-story homes. He maintained a distance that he hoped wasn't conspicuous, yet close enough to not lose track of the car. He turned off the Hollywood gossip channel Rebecca was listening to so he could concentrate. The Audi made a right, then left, then turned in to a cul-de-sac and drove up a driveway. Tony lived in a third-floor condo with a view of the golf course, so this wasn't his place. One of two garage doors opened, and the Audi drove inside. The door closed. Cory parked a half block away behind a red pickup and texted Ty:

CORY

At a residence in Fairview
Heights. TT in garage.
Will hang for 15min.

TY

Roger that.

Three minutes later the door opened and the TT backed out. Cory hoped Tony wouldn't head toward him, because if he did he'd have to duck below the dash, then pull a Uey, allowing Tony to disappear in this maze of streets. Luckily the Audi headed west. Cory waited for a Subaru wagon to pass, then pulled out behind it.

Tony's route took them away from downtown Luster, toward an older part of town on a quiet tree-lined street. One side featured run-down homes needing new roofs and paint jobs. The other side had a sports complex with two baseball diamonds, a soccer field, and four tennis courts. The entire facility was closed pending construction of a new aquatic center. The tennis courts didn't have nets, and weeds grew up through cracks in the asphalt. The baseball diamonds had tumbleweeds piled up ten feet high against the backstops. Tony slipped into a spot next to a hedge, nose in, facing the tennis courts. The brake lights went off. Cory pulled up to the curb fifty yards away on the opposite side of the street. He noticed that the Mott's Lot license plate was gone. It had been replaced by a regular Oregon license plate. Tony must have switched it in the garage. *What's up with that?* He dialed up max zoom and snapped three pictures of the car. A silver-haired woman was two houses down, cutting back roses in the front yard. He snapped a picture of her just for something to do, then looked for Kayla's yellow Bug. Couldn't find it. *Maybe this whole thing is a bust.* He texted Ty:

CORY

> At future site of Aqua
> Park. No KS.

TY

> How long can you wait?

> 15min

> K.

One minute later, he saw her walking across the parking lot toward the Audi.

> K spotted! Approaching TT.

Even though she was wearing a gray sweatshirt with a hood pulled up and sunglasses covering half her face, he was certain it was her. He recognized her gait, balanced and straight like she was crossing a beam. Cory searched for her car. It had to be here somewhere. Then he saw a splash of yellow—it was parked on the other side of the big sign with a picture of the future water park. Cory opened his daypack, took out the camera, and snapped pictures of Kayla as she walked up to the TT, opened the passenger door, got in. He also snapped a picture of the bogus license plate. Then he sat back, eyes on the TT, and pondered his next step.

According to Phase Three of their plan, he would leave the scene undetected. Phase Four would involve confronting Tony with the pictures, give him a chance to explain, and if it wasn't good enough to ease the worst of their fears, then threaten to take the evidence to Harvey (or CPS) unless he stopped. But as the minutes ticked by, Cory grew increasingly uncomfortable with Phases Three and Four. There were too many holes, too much deniability for Tony. Without physical proof, Tony could say he and Kayla were doing Carpool Karaoke—instead of, as Ty would say, "slipping her the old wicked weasel." With those tinted windows it was impossible to get the evidence he needed to truly help Kayla, assuming she did want his help.

With four minutes remaining before he had to return to Bravo, Cory reminded himself that Kayla was the important person in all this. She told him flat out that she didn't want to do whatever it was she was doing. Then he remembered Tony's words on the deck that night in Sunriver: *I like her a lot. She's a special girl.* Those words had sounded so genuine then. Thanks to the necklace in his pocket, the entire context had changed. He felt that seed of anger expanding in his gut. Cory had hoped it died with Benny in the fire. But it was there and flowering and this time he couldn't make it stop.

Cory opened the door, walked across the street, camera in hand. Since he couldn't see through the tinted glass, he approached the

Audi from the east, using the hedge as a shield. There was a small gap between the hedge and the tennis fence. He thumbed the mode setting to where he wanted it, then squeezed through the gap, camera held up, and aimed at the windshield.

His heart stopped.

It wasn't Tony.

The melted-snow-in-the-water-bottle idea is a bust. The melting part worked okay. But apparently the snow-to-water ratio is like ten-to-one because a nearly full bottle of snow, mixed with dirt and pine needles, reduced down to an inch of brown, sludge-like liquid. I offer to filter it through one of my socks but Astrid passes.

"How about the soup?" she asks, nodding to the cans on the shelf. "You could even warm it up over the candles."

"I've already thought about that. First, I don't have anything to open them other than the hammer, and we'd lose most of it. And even if I did manage to open a can, we shouldn't eat it."

"Why not?"

"I know a few things about cooking—and high-acid foods, like tomato soup, will last up to two years. Those cans date back to the 1950s. They're not worth the effort."

A silence descends as we both consider our narrowing options. A few hours ago, there were only two: wait for Ty, or go. Looking at the shape she's in and the resources we have, waiting is off the table. And on top of that, if Ty was going to show up, he would have done it by now. So we have to leave. The question is, how soon? We're down to just a few swallows of water. I'll drink the sludge. She can have the good stuff. But that won't be enough to get her down that slope to the creek. The ground will be too slippery for me to carry her. To make that journey she'll need more water than what we have left. I need to refill the bottles. Period.

I crawl to the door, lift the flap, and peer out beyond the stump. The snow has turned to rain—I'm liking that development. Unfortunately there is still too much snow remaining for me to go without leaving tracks. I wasted the day talking and sleeping. I should have left sooner. I return to my bag, mentally kicking myself for being so stupid.

She says, "He's still looking for us."

"Maybe. Or he could be long gone."

Astrid responds with a squinty-eyed glare. Then says, "Cory, I'm sick."

"I know. I'm sorry."

"I don't want to die in here." She glances at the stove. "There are too many dead people in here already."

I smile. "We'll leave soon. But no way you'd make it down to the creek without more water. It's getting dark, and using the headlamp would be risky. Soooo...I can either leave now or wait until the morning."

"I'd rather you didn't leave now."

"Then morning it is. First thing."

"Okay."

"We should get some sleep. Tomorrow will be a long day."

I snuff out all but one candle. There's about an inch left, so it probably won't last the night. I doubt we'll get much sleep anyway, but I keep the headlamp handy just in case. I worm my way down into my bag, seeking warmth, then turn and face her. She is looking at me. I reach out and brush her hair aside, which is really a move designed to touch her forehead. I frown, thinking about the infection raging inside of her.

She says, "You think I'm hot?" and bats her eyes.

"Like, *obviously.*"

A beat. "Thank you."

"For what?"

"For being who you are."

My body starts to shake. It could be the cold seeping in, but I know it's not. I think about Benny behind me in the stove, about his pathetic hoard of money and how that worked out for him. Just once, I wanted to look into his eyes and see something other than an unending tide of disgust. That I was somehow less than human and undeserving of what little love he had to give. My eyes start watering because this girl I hardly know, who may not survive the night *because of me*, knows me better than he ever did. Even in this small dark hole I am free to feel good about my place in the world. She waits patiently while I pull myself together. I smile and say, "The people of your country say very nice things. I must visit sometime."

"They would welcome you."

A few moments pass. The candle dims.

She says, "Tell me a bedtime story."

"What would you like to hear?"

"The one about the boys that steal a car."

"I told you that one already. It's not that interesting."

"I suspect you skipped the good parts."

I think back to where the shit really hit the fan.

"Did I mention that I bought a camera?"

Harvey was behind the wheel, eyes closed, a thin smile on his lips.

Kayla was in a bra, doing something down there with her left hand. She saw Cory and screamed. Harvey opened his eyes, saw Cory, and struggled with his pants while Kayla pulled on her hoodie, flung the door open, tumbled out of the car, and ran away. The entire scene lasted twenty seconds tops. Despite the disturbing images burned into his brain, Cory managed to keep the camera up and clicking through it all. He lowered the camera to chest-high, took a quick glance across the street at the woman. She wasn't working on her roses anymore. She was watching them.

Harvey's window slid down halfway. He hissed, "Give me the camera!"

In the background Cory saw Kayla's car leave the lot. He raised the camera, moved to the window, and aimed it at Harvey. His hair was askew, his tanned face red with rage. He said, "You fucking idiot!" The door clicked, started to open. A city maintenance truck pulled into the lot, parked fifty yards away in front of the construction sign. The TT door closed, but the window stayed down. "C'mon, Cory," Harvey said in a softer tone. "Let's be reasonable here. You made your point. Give me the camera. Please."

Cory discovered that even though he couldn't talk, his legs could move. He turned and ran across the parking lot, all the way to Rebecca's car. By the time he was safely inside with the door closed, the TT was screeching out of the lot. Cory struggled to put the keys in the ignition. The car started. He tried to put it in gear, but couldn't do it.

And then he spewed sweet potato fries all over Rebecca's white vinyl seat.

48

I t was a process Cory knew too well. He stopped at a carwash to clean up the mess, then bought a pair of pants and a shirt at Walmart. It gave him time to think and gather his nerves, but it was time he didn't have. He dreaded finding out what the repercussions of what had just happened would be, and he imagined they were already set in motion. That was probably why Ty had texted three times, and phoned once. All Cory gave him was a three-word text in all caps: *IT WASN'T TONY.*

To which Ty replied with three letters.

TY

WTF!!!!!

Cory arrived at Bravo twenty-two minutes late and had an excuse lined up for Rebecca. That proved to be wasted mental effort because Harvey's white Lexus was parked in his reserved spot, three spaces from the door. When Cory walked in, Rebecca nodded gravely toward her office and said, "He's waiting for you. Whatever stirred his coffee, make it quick. The drive-through is slammed." He handed her the car keys to her Ford Escort. As he walked past her she wrinkled her nose.

Cory said, "I bought you an air freshener."

She headed for the exit.

Harvey was behind Rebecca's cluttered desk, glasses on, studying a spreadsheet. He put the sheet down, smiled at Cory, walked up, and put his arm around his shoulder as if he were greeting a long-lost brother. Cory knew what Harvey knew—Mott Enterprises had security cameras in all the offices. He wasn't sure if they had audio. Odds were that Harvey would not spare that expense.

"Someone's been busy," Harvey said, giving his shoulder a little squeeze.

"I could say the same thing about you," Cory said.

Harvey's arm dropped. The smile stayed but lost some of its wattage. He pointed to Cory's backpack. "Is your camera in there?"

"Yes."

"How long have you been interested in photography?"

"It's a recent investment."

"I see. Is it a hobby, or is it a passion?"

"I'm still in the information-gathering stages."

Harvey nodded, seemed to study Cory in a new light. Cory backed away, walked to Rebecca's office window and looked out. She had a view of the front counter and the main dining room. Tables were starting to fill.

Harvey said, "Speaking of passions, do you know the origin of the Bravo Burgers name?"

"No. It wasn't in the employee manual."

"I had three older sisters. The youngest died five years ago. A brain tumor. When we were kids our family had a Christmas tradition. The four of us would team up to perform one Christmas carol of our choosing for our father while our mother played the piano. We continued to do that until I graduated from law school. After every performance, no matter how bad, our father would always clap his hands and say, 'Bravo! Bravo!' So every time I see that sign over the door, I think about that memory."

Cory didn't know what to say. Other than that he wished he had just one memory like that.

Harvey said, "But back to the subject of your hobbies and passions. There's a key distinction between the two. Hobbies come and go. But passions, they consume you. And they can be very, very expensive." Harvey chuckled to himself. "For example. I bought a nine-foot bamboo rod last week from a dealer in Brazil. I won't bore you with the details, but let's just say I paid more for that rod than that hostess will earn in an entire year. And you know what the sad thing is?"

Cory shook his head.

"That rod will never have the pleasure of flexing its tip under the weight of a fighting fish."

"That is sad," Cory said, thinking that this man valued an old fishing rod more than his employees.

Harvey turned from the window, leveled his eyes at Cory. "Here's what you need to know about passions. They use valuable resources that might be better served on more … worthy pursuits."

Cory hesitated. Rebecca waved to them from the counter, then shook a menu at them.

Harvey said, "I think she needs her office. Let's continue this conversation on the deck."

"Okay."

They walked through the dining room. Harvey stopped to chat up a couple of customers at their tables; then they exited via a patio door into the outside dining area. It was a little windy and the sun was barely a blush of orange as it sank below the horizon. Harvey headed for a table in the far corner by the fireplace, but he didn't sit. They were alone and unwatched.

Harvey said, "Before we dig into this situation, I would like to apologize for my outburst. You caught me with …" He paused as if searching for the perfect word. Cory thought he was going to say *my pants down.* But Harvey said, "Without the benefit of *context.*" And then with surprising force, he said, "My initial response to your stunningly deceitful action was unprofessional. Are we clear on that point?"

Stunningly deceitful? Cory said, "Yes."

"Now let's cut through the bullshit, shall we? What you did, after everything that we have done for you and your brother since we welcomed you into our home, is a heartbreaking disappointment. I gave you a job, a phone, a computer. Let you drive one of our cars! Then you do this? You betrayed our trust, *my* trust." Harvey sighed heavily, shook his head.

Cory thought, *What about Kayla and Charlene's trust that you broke?*

Harvey said, "But that history can't be revised, so here we are. I'm assuming Ty is involved?"

Cory considered saying no. He doubted Harvey would believe him. "Yes."

"Have you shared the pictures with him?"

"No."

"Have you shared the pictures with anyone?"

"No."

"Have you copied the pictures?"

"No."

"Good. Then containment is possible." Harvey smiled. "We can rebuild those bridges of trust."

Cory thought, *What happened to cutting through the bullshit?*

Harvey said, "What you saw, or you think you saw, will not happen again." He extended one manicured finger. "That is my first promise to you. Now on to the second." He raised a second finger; this one displayed his wedding ring. "I'm aware that you've been researching a culinary school in Seattle."

"How did you—"

"Don't worry. I haven't been snooping through your email. You told Charlene and she told me. We think that's great. You have genuine talent. And it promises a much, may I say, *brighter future* than your misguided interest in photography." Harvey's eyes narrowed as he stepped closer to Cory. "If you give me that camera right now, I will fund your first year at the culinary school. In fact, you can keep the camera. All I want is the memory card. Plus, I will still honor the ten-thousand-dollar commitment I made in Sunriver, assuming you continue to meet the conditions per the agreement." Harvey reached out with his right hand, palm up.

Cory backed away a step, almost tripped over the leg of a chair. He was trapped by a wall. There was no exit, except through Harvey.

"If that offer doesn't appeal to you, there is a different path. As a judge I have access to channels of justice that are not available to the public at large. Case in point, I researched Ty's violent history in Portland. What he did to that unfortunate youth, a Francisco Alvarez, I believe, was clearly first-degree assault with a deadly weapon. The prosecuting attorney asked the judge, a personal friend of mine, to remand him to criminal court so Ty could be prosecuted as an adult. I saw the pictures, and a jury will too. He'd be looking at five to fifteen years in a state prison. But the trial didn't happen. A certain individual with suspected ties to unrestrained *acts of violence* stepped in and suddenly the victim realized that he provoked Ty, and POOF! The charges were dropped. But don't think that double jeopardy applies. The case never went to trial and the statute of limitations has not expired." Harvey scratched his head, as if trying to remember another detail. Then he smiled. "Ah, yes. Let's not forget about the matter of your father's untimely death. The murder weapon has been found, but there were no witnesses to date other than Ty. Combine that with his history of assault and the evidence is very compelling. All it would take is one call from me to the right person and your brother's future prospects as a pitcher would narrow considerably. Of course, that path is not my preference."

Cory didn't know how much of that was true and how much was a bluff. He remembered a conversation between Benny and Tirk about the possibility of Ty being charged as an adult, so Harvey obviously knew enough to be dangerous. Cory glanced at the door. Where was Rebecca when he needed her?

Harvey said, "My patience is not a bottomless well."

Cory glanced down at his hands, then risked a direct look in Harvey's eyes. "You're really done with Kayla?"

"It's over. I give you my word."

"And you won't hold any of my actions against her?"

His voice softened. "I wouldn't do that to her." For once he sounded sincere.

Cory slipped off his backpack, removed the camera. Harvey reached for it. Cory pulled it away.

"Don't fuck with me," Harvey said.

Cory felt the man was one second from taking the camera by force. He said, "Ty can't make the three point oh. I need that to go away."

After a beat, "If I set the bar at two point five, is that low enough?"

"Okay." Cory had problems opening the side compartment on the camera because his fingers were too sweaty. He needed several tries to pull the memory card out of the slot. But finally, Cory dropped the card in Harvey's outstretched hand. Harvey slipped it into his pants pocket. Then he said, "I'm sorry this happened.

I truly am. We all make mistakes. You did the right thing here."

Harvey left.

Cory watched the door close behind him.

Then he collapsed into a chair and cried.

49

Ty picked up Cory after he finished his shift at Bravo. Before heading for the ski lodge, Ty wanted Cory to show him the exact route he used to follow the TT. They drove past the house where Harvey and Tony made the switch. Then he parked in the same spot that Harvey used when Cory showed up like a paparazzo from hell and ruined his little party.

They sat on the hood of the Volvo, facing the empty tennis courts. Ty asked Cory to review the conversation at Bravo, particularly the one on the patio. Cory covered everything except the part where Harvey threatened to revisit Ty's fight in Portland.

Ty asked, "You really didn't copy the pictures?"

"Not a one."

"So we live at the ski lodge till we graduate? Then collect our twenty grand and leave?"

"On the first bus out of town."

"We've survived worse."

"No doubt."

Ty studied his brother's face. "So why am I not believing you?"

"I'm worried about Kayla. What he did to her is wrong. No, I can do better than that. It was sick."

"You said he was finished with her."

"There's more to this story."

"Of course there's more. But he promised it was over. You did a good thing. End of story."

Ty jumped off the hood. He flung a rock at the construction sign. It clanged off the metal, ricocheted into the street.

Cory said, "You didn't see what I saw."

"And that's a good thing. Otherwise the judge would be wheezing through a tube right now."

Cory thought that might have been the truest thing he'd heard all day. He pulled Kayla's necklace out of his pocket. Watched it shine under the glow of the streetlamp.

Ty asked, "What are you going to do with that?"

"What I should have done in the first place."

"And that would be...?"

"Give it back."

50

Her scream pierces my sleep and sends my heart racing a mile a minute.

I say, "Astrid, it's okay. You're all right. You had a nightmare." I don't know that for sure. The space is completely dark.

What happened to the candle?

"Someone is in here!" she hisses.

"What?" I grope blindly for the headlamp.

"He's . . . he's at my feet!"

She struggles. I hear her kicking, grunting. Then another sound. *Scratching?* And a foreign smell. Earthy, wet. My fingers wrap around the strap to the headlamp. I fumble for the button and push.

The beam hits the roof, slides down to the door, then across to two yellow-green eyes framing a narrow snout, brown fur, four legs. The animal stands only two feet from the bottom of Astrid's sleeping bag, tail down, eyes locked on me. Its ears press back against its head, and the lips curl up, exposing sharp white fangs. A snarl rumbles from its chest. Without moving my eyes from those teeth, I grope behind me for the hammer. Just as I squeeze the wooden shaft and swing it around, the animal turns, slinks through the flap, and is gone.

Astrid and I stare at each other, the vapor clouds of our breath joining in the beam of the headlamp. She is sitting up, her splinted arm exposed above the bag. "Was that a wolf?" she gasps between breaths.

"That was a coyote. Wolves are bigger."

"It smells the death on me."

"That's not it. A coyote had died in here. It was behind the stove. I hauled it out yesterday before you woke up. This must be their den."

"Will it come back?"

"Probably not. I think we scared it as much as it scared us."

Her body sags. She leans back. I hold up the top of the sleeping bag while she tucks her bad arm inside. Then I light three candles, mad at myself for only lighting one before. The only reason that coyote came inside is because there wasn't any light.

"More pills, please." Her words barely rise above the sound of the candle flames.

"Is the pain bad?"

She nods. "The pills probably don't help. But I pretend they do."

I open the bottle, shake out four, put them in her open hand. "That leaves four for the hike out. You can finish the water. I'll be getting more soon."

"What about you?"

"I'll have the sludge."

She drains the bottle.

I lie down beside her. We stare up at the roof, at the chicken mesh and plastic holding back the dirt. I'm too wired to sleep. She's in too much pain. It feels like dawn is just around the corner. I hope so because neither one of us can take much more of this.

She says, "Are you sure about this?"

"Hell yeah," I say with a lot more confidence than I feel. "It's just a walk in the park."

"He has a gun. And an ice ax."

"We have a hammer. And a saw."

She doesn't smile. "Wake me before you leave."

It sounds like her last breath.

51

After he left five increasingly desperate messages on her phone, Kayla returned Cory's calls the following morning with a terse message: "Flat Top. Six fifteen a.m. You're late, I'm gone."

Flat Top was the biggest of three hills on the outskirts of town. There was a hiking trail with switchbacks that took an hour to climb if you didn't rest, or a road up the back side offering a three-minute drive, which was what Cory took. Tony had brought them up there on their third day in Luster to give them a bird's-eye view of their new home, to hear as much of their story as they were willing to tell, and to let them know that they got the mother of all lottery picks with the Motts. "Treat them well," he said, "and they will do the same for you tenfold."

There was a small parking lot at the summit, a cell tower, two concrete picnic tables with a view of Luster, and trail signs indicating a path that led to the south side of the mountain. Cory saw the yellow VW first, then spotted Kayla sitting on top of a picnic table gazing out at the town below. It was always windy up here and today was windier than normal. It flung her black hair back in waves and made the cell tower hum. No one else was up here.

Cory sat next to Kayla and handed her the necklace. She smiled at him, which made him feel like he had finally done the right thing. Then she stood up, pulled her arm back, and launched that piece of jewelry into the wind. He watched it disappear over the lip and into the bushes somewhere below.

Cory said, "Now, that's a first. Is this a tradition in Luster that I don't know about?"

She sat, took a sip from her water bottle, then spoke slowly while they looked out at a sleepy town on the cusp of dawn. "He makes me wear my hair in a ponytail. No braids, never down. He sets his phone alarm for eight minutes and puts it on the dash. He checks my phone and deletes the text he sent me. Then he tells me to take my top off. Never my bra, which must be black. I don't take off anything else. He never touches me. Sometimes he doesn't even look at me. Most of the time we just talk. He asks about my mother and her disease and school and last time even about you. But sometimes we do more than talk. Sometimes he'd ask me to do what Donna did. He told me I can say no, but I know I can't. Sometimes he takes pictures with his phone. Once after I finished he cried. When his alarm goes off I leave."

Cory sat in the space of her silence, felt the crushing weight of it as she peeled the label off her water bottle and dropped pieces that spiraled down like snowflakes into the dirt.

He wanted to know what she did, and who this Donna was, but decided to save that for later. A more pressing question was lined up and ready to go. "How long have you been doing this thing with Harvey?"

"This *thing*? It's abuse. Don't be a dick, Cory Bic."

He blinked at the heat of her sudden fury. "I'm sorry. I didn't mean—"

"The answer is this *thing* has been going on too long." She stood and said, "I'm tired of this fucking view. Let's change it."

Cory followed her down a short graveled trail that led to the south-facing side of Flat Top. As they rounded a bend he saw an ocean of windmills with shimmering white blades rotating slowly in the light of an emerging sun. The closest one was maybe a mile away, but they still looked huge. There was a wooden bench covered with graffiti that looked out over the view. Instead of sitting there, Kayla climbed down through some bushes and around a small outcropping to a rocky ledge big enough for two people to sit on if they dangled their legs over the lip. It was quiet here, sheltered from the wind and the world. Cory got the sense that Kayla had been here many times. Unlike a few minutes ago, she looked peaceful. She pulled a joint out of her pocket and lit it. She inhaled deeply, offered him a hit.

He declined and said, "All that stuff you talked about with Harvey. Why do you do it?"

"It's not what *I do*. It's what *he does*. It's not *stuff*. It's *abuse*. Get your terms right."

Cory felt his face turn crimson as the sting of her words sank in.

"I'm sorry. What I meant is why...I mean, what is..." He couldn't finish the sentence.

She said, "You mean why am I giving the future senator hand jobs in the front seat of black sports cars?"

"Okay. Let's go with that."

"My mother came down with a neurological disorder two years ago. It started in her extremities and her face but now it's everywhere. Her muscles get all knotted and feel like they're on fire. Sometimes she goes fetal and is like that for hours. At first they thought it was central pain syndrome. One night the pain was so bad she was medevacked to Portland. A specialist there thinks it may be something else, but we've heard that before. Anyway, I had to cancel babysitting at the Motts' that night. The next day Harvey called me into his office at the hardware store. He said he heard my mother was medevacked and wanted to know what happened. I told him everything. That my mother was sick, that my father was unemployed and we didn't have any insurance. That he was selling the house, we'd go bankrupt and move in with his brother in Bellingham to be closer to Seattle. Harvey said not to worry, he'd take care of everything. But I had to keep it between us."

"Did you?"

"Yes." She exhaled a cloud, looked at him. "Until now."

"You left that necklace on purpose."

"You're quick, Cory Bic."

"How did you know Ty would find it?"

"The guy with the bad mustache in the detail shop—he used to be my gymnastics coach. I asked him to make sure that Ty got the Civic coupe."

"You assumed Ty would know who it belongs to and give it to me."

"Yes."

"I'm not even going to try to explain how many ways your plan could have failed."

"Karmic forces are at play," she said. "Never underestimate them."

"So I guess this means you wanted me to see you with Harvey."

"Yes. But I didn't want you to show up with a fucking *zoom lens*. Speaking of which, where are the pictures?"

"Harvey has them."

"All of them?"

"Do you mean did I make copies? That answer is no."

Kayla studied him for a moment, looked like she was going to respond, then turned to face the windmills. He watched her take a hit off the joint. After the exhale he asked, "Why me? Why am I the chosen one?"

"I needed to tell someone I could trust. Someone that wouldn't run to Harvey. After you put all that energy into saving a rubber torso, I decided you had trustworthy potential. So I asked you a question at the gazebo." She took another hit. "I liked your answer."

"Which answer? As I recall you asked a lot of questions."

"I asked you to tell me one true thing about yourself. You said you wake up scared every morning. I figured we had a lot in common. So I anointed you."

Cory nodded. While he could understand the logic, there were still gaps in her story. "What about your parents? You had to tell them something after Harvey started paying the bills."

"I told them that Harvey called a guy that called a guy and got Mom on the company insurance. All she had to pay was a twenty-five-hundred-dollar deductible and POOF, the bills were gone. They think he's a hero, just like the rest of this ignorant town." Kayla looked at Cory and shrugged. "Like it or not, I consulted with the karma gods and they pointed at you."

"Then I show up with a fucking zoom lens. Definitely not my finest hour." Cory shook his head at the memory.

Kayla nodded. "I had a long talk with the gods after that. They were not pleased."

"So what now? Am I hopelessly absorbed?"

"You have that enzymie smell about you. But I'm here, so that means there is still hope." She showed him what was left of the joint. "Do you know how I get this excellent weed?"

"No. Other than you said the future senator was involved."

"He buys all my mother's medical marijuana. He says it's for her pain. I figured if it works for her pain, then it should work for mine."

They locked eyes for a moment. Cory saw the hurt in there, deep and raw and unsettling. He ached to help but didn't know how other than to listen to her story. "Speaking of weed," he said, "I heard a rumor that your babysitting services were terminated because Charlene caught you smoking a joint on the deck while the kids, so the story goes, were in the kitchen eating tuna sandwiches."

Kayla laughed. He wondered if it was his delivery, or the marijuana. "Those kids hate fish. They don't even eat those cheesy goldfish crackers. So the tuna sandwich rumor is obviously *fake news*. What *really* happened is the future senator and the future senator's wife had an epic fight. I couldn't hear most of what they said but I did hear my name a few times. And some crying. The next day was Thanksgiving. She met me at the door and said that my services were no longer needed—ever. She gave me a check for five thousand dollars and asked me not to talk to anyone about why they were letting me go. I asked her why she was doing this. She said, *You know why,* and slammed the door. As if it was *my fault*! Then you showed up the next day."

Cory remembered their arrival. "I saw you in the window that night. Why were you there?"

"I had a few personal items to pick up. Plus, I wanted a good look at the replacement nannies before they got absorbed." She checked the time on her phone. "This place will be crawling with runners soon. We'd better go."

"Wait. I have one last question. You said that when you're in the car with Harvey, sometimes he would tell you to do what Donna did. Who is Donna and what did she do?"

Kayla looked at him. There was no sign of the marijuana now. The pain had morphed into something hard, something with an edge. He steeled himself for a stinging rebuke.

Instead she whispered, "This is where it gets really sick, Cory Bic."

"I can handle it."

"He had a black Mustang in high school. Donna was his girlfriend. They were on the debate team together. She would meet him in the Mustang before a competition. He'd pull it out and she'd jerk him off. He said it helped him clear his mind so he could debate better." Kayla stubbed out the joint, crumbled the remainder, and sent it flaking off into the wind. "It must have worked. They won the national championships."

"Why does he set a timer for eight minutes?"

"Why do you think?"

"I don't even want to guess."

"Obviously you're not up on competition protocols. That's how long a debate lasts."

Cory shook his head at the sickness of it all. She stood and he joined her. They watched the sea of turbines spinning white under a risen sun. Clouds had gathered to the east. It looked like rain was on the way. She said, "Thank you for listening to my story of woe."

"You're welcome."

Kayla turned and headed for the trail. Cory took one last look at those storm clouds, then followed her off the ledge.

STUMPTOWN

NOW

52

I sit up for the tenth time since the coyote left. The gray light of dawn finally leaks in under the tarp. I crawl out of my sleeping bag and peer out a porthole window. The forest is wet but I don't see any signs of falling snow or rain. It's time to go.

I put on my cargo pants, my boots, my coat. Then I pick up the water bottles, gag down the sludge, and almost puke. She asked me to wake her before I go, but I think she needs the sleep more than she needs to say good-bye to me. I head for the door.

Her voice behind me whispers, "Hey. I asked you to wake me."

I stop and turn. "Busted."

"Forgiven. How long will you be gone?"

"About an hour."

"Are you taking a weapon?"

"Like what?"

"The hammer?"

I think about the supreme irony of me using a hammer to defend myself from Tirk. "No. I'm going to leave it here with you. If someone comes in that door and it isn't me, pound his head like a rusty nail."

"What if it's Ty?"

I hadn't even considered that possibility. How could my brother be more alive to her than he is to me? If I answer that question now the pain will consume me. All I say is, "You'd better miss."

"I'm going to worry. What shall I do while you're gone?"

"Read the *Playboy* magazine in the chest. Then you can entertain me with fun facts about Marilyn Monroe while we hike out of here."

She smiles faintly. "I'd like that."

I raise the flap and crawl out of the stump.

53

"**S**o this whole deal is about that twisted fuck living out some old *high school fantasy?*" Ty slammed a fist into the heavy bag. The impact echoed inside the gym.

"Yup."

Ty started to bob and weave as he ducked imaginary punches. He spoke between jabs. "I know she's got a few screws loose, but seriously, dude? Why does she do it?" He unleashed a flurry of left-right-left-right punches, his hands taped and his sweat-soaked T-shirt clinging to his torso. Cory stood on the other side of the heavy bag, leaned into it. He felt the shuddering impact of each blow and was grateful that he had thirteen inches of sand-filled canvas between him and Ty's fists. When his brother finally stopped and toweled off the sweat, Cory scanned the gym. A man was bench-pressing a huge amount of weight with a woman in a sports bra spotting him. Luckily they were on the other side of the gym and the ambient rock music playing on the sound system was loud enough to keep them from listening in. They would not be a problem. Ty on the other hand—he was getting riled up. That could be trouble. Cory had to play this just right.

Ty asked, "Why didn't she just stop?"

Cory heard the tension in his voice. Benny mode was around the corner. The jabs were increasing in force. He had to be careful with the next dose of information.

"Her mother is sick and Harvey is paying the bills. If she says no, then the Harvey money train stops."

Ty switched from jabs to punches. "Why doesn't she go public? Just sink his sick ass."

"He checks her phone and deletes all the texts. He said it would be her word against his. No one would believe her, and he'd sue them for libel. With the legal bills on top of the medical bills—it would be too much for their family. She said just the guilt of knowing what she had done would kill her mother."

Ty stopped punching. He stared at Cory for a moment, then ripped the tape off his hands. His eyes filled with suppressed rage. "And this asshole wants to be a senator! I'm gonna kill that lying two-faced motherfucker. End of story."

This was the moment Cory was waiting for. He had to pull Ty back from the edge. "Hold on a minute. I need you to stay calm. Don't go all Benny mode on me."

"Too late." Ty picked up his gym bag and towel. "Let's go."

"Where?"

"The ski lodge, the dealership. Wherever the fuck that snake is hiding."

"Not until you calm down."

"This is calm. I'm saving angry for later."

Cory pointed to the heavy bag. "Tell you what. We'll go, but first

I want you to show me what you're going to do him." He stood behind the bag, leaned into it.

Ty smiled. "Good thing you weigh a lot."

He unloaded on the bag with a fury of punches, side and front kicks. Then he launched himself into the air and executed a perfect 360-degree roundhouse strike. The impact sent Cory reeling backward. Ty wiped his face with the towel, left behind a streak of red on his jaw. Cory noticed that his bare knuckles were raw and bloodied, and the bag had a dark wet stain.

Cory said, "Whatever that was, I have a better way."

"Not possible. Where's the car?"

"Shower first. Better make it a cold one. Then we'll talk."

Cory explained his plan in the Volvo on their way to the ski lodge. He finished just as Ty turned in to the driveway. He stopped halfway up, left the lights on and the engine idling. Cory could see the house through the trees, heard Pavlov barking at the door.

Ty said, "I'm impressed. It could actually work."

"It's going to take some patience." Cory was relieved. He expected more of a fight, since twenty minutes ago Ty was out for blood.

"You're okay with stealing the Volvo?"

"I don't think he'll press charges. Not with what we know."

"When do we leave?"

"Three months from now. We need to store up provisions, get our ducks lined up. And I need to lose thirty pounds. No way I could hike the blood trail that many times. Especially with a pack."

"Give me a specific date. Something I can look forward to."

"October 20."

"It'll be cold by then."

"Stumptown has a stove. We can handle it. The question is, can you handle three more months at the ski lodge?"

Ty thought for a moment. "That might be a problem. But, hell, if you can, I can."

Cory hated to ask this question. But he had to. It was the only big problem with his plan. "What about Tirk?"

"I can handle him."

He studied his brother for a moment. Ty sounded confident, but there was something in the way that he avoided Cory's eyes that left him less than convinced. "Are you sure?"

"Dude! I got it covered. Trust me. Now back to the plan." This time Ty found Cory's eyes and stayed there. "People will get hurt your way, you know. People who have been very good to us."

Cory winced. This was another flaw, but he didn't see a way around it. "I'll do my best to limit the damage."

"My way is cleaner. Only one person gets hurt."

Cory resisted telling him about Portland and Harvey's threat. Ty's solution wasn't as clean as he thought. "We need to do this right. If you hurt him, he'll just bounce back."

"Dead people don't bounce."

"Point taken. But you have to stop talking like that."

"Hey, I'm jus' sayin'. . . ."

The front porch light turned on. Three seconds later Chloe's face appeared in the living room window, no doubt looking for them. Cory remembered he promised to help her figure out a new fashion app after dinner. He said, "Harvey uses his power to create weaknesses; then he exploits them. He's a predator. A wolf in sheep's clothing. We're going to expose him for what he is. That's how we take him down."

"That's all true. But you gave Harvey the evidence. We don't have any pictures of what happened. And he's got Kayla too scared to tell her story."

Cory smiled. He'd been waiting all night for this moment. "I didn't give him everything."

"What else is there?"

"Harvey asked for all the *pictures*. He didn't ask for the video."

Ty blinked. "You shot video?"

"Twelve seconds of pure Harvey highlights."

"But how . . . ?"

"I uploaded the video file to my iCloud account, then deleted it from the card. I snapped some stills while the video was recording, and I left those behind. When he sees the content, he won't suspect that anything is missing."

Ty said, "My bro the badass ninja chef. This is genius."

"So you're good with my way?"

"Oh, way more than good. You got a name for this op?"

Cory had already given this question a lot of thought. He wanted something symbolic, something that reminded him of an empire crashing to the ground. "Operation Rome Burning," he said.

"Well, here's to Operation Rome Burning." They bumped fists.

Ty drove up to the house.

Harvey opened the front door as they climbed out of the car. He looked at them for a moment, then smiled as wide as the day they first arrived. "You're just in time. Dinner is on the table. I hope you're hungry!"

54

My first move after exiting the stump is to check the immediate area to see how bad the damage is from our struggle two days ago. There are still some snow patches and a few have recognizable prints. It looks natural enough to be missed by most people unless you look closely. And even then, the stump gives nothing away. I walk down to the remains of the tracks from yesterday's visitor. There is enough snow left to see part of a boot heel. It looks like they are headed south, maybe toward the creek.

I make a quick perimeter check of the hill, looking for more tracks, but don't see any except something with hooves, then take off at a jog heading southwest for my first landmark, the bent tree. The morning air is colder than I expected, plus there's a little wind to add some bite. Unfortunately it isn't cold enough to freeze the ground like it was on the way up. That would have been nice—fewer prints. As I run I calculate how long this mission should take. Once I reach the ridge it's ten minutes down to the creek. Two minutes to fill the bottles, a twenty-minute climb to the ridge, and fifteen minutes to Stumptown. I told Astrid I would be back in an hour. It should be less if I'm lucky.

The hike to the ridge is easy, although I have to cross several patches of snow and post-holed twice past my ankles. I locate the crooked-finger tree without any problem even though Gooseneck Mountain is covered in thick gray clouds. I stop for a quick look back toward Stumptown. I see a few of my tracks, but not enough to be obvious.

Once I hit the ridge I try to keep my descent as close as I can to the route we took on the way up. Meanwhile I do visual sweeps of the slope below, constantly searching for signs of movement in the shadows. Unfortunately there is more snow here and lots of deadfall to work around. It's impossible to descend without leaving a trail. I stop and listen every twenty yards. The forest is silent except for the wind, which seems to be picking up, and not much farther down, I can hear the whisper of Tanum Creek. It's a little louder, restless. Must be the recent rain. I run past the rock where Astrid and I woke to see the deer—then hit the brakes and turn around. I thought I saw a speck of something that looked out of place. And there it is, a cigarette butt. I scan for more tracks but all I see are a couple of ours. Maybe an elk hunter stopped at this rock for a smoke a long time ago. Cigarette butts take years to biodegrade. So I keep moving. It's five minutes to the creek from here. On the way down I slip in the mud. The water bottles bang against each other. The sound echoes in the cold air.

The last twenty feet down to the creek are steep and slick thanks to the rain and snow. I do a slow 360, looking for anything out of place, any movement that might be a threat. All good. I make my way carefully down to Tanum Creek. The water is cold and clear.

I wash my hands and face. I drink nearly a full liter of creek water before I top off the bottles and head back up to Stumptown.

As I'm reaching for a root to pull myself up over the bank, I hear a sharp SNAP a few degrees to my right, maybe thirty feet away. I freeze, then slowly lower myself to the dirt. I stay that way for a minute, listening for more sounds. All I hear is the burbling creek. I count to twenty, raise my head up over the bank. I'm hoping to see a deer like I did two days ago. It could have been a branch breaking under the weight of snow. Or a rock falling. I will my nerves to settle. Whatever or whoever made that sound, I'm not seeing it. I have to decide now—climb up the hill, or stay here. But Astrid is in bad shape. She needs water now.

I scramble up the slope, water bottles in each frozen hand. I hit the ridge with my lungs on fire, find the tree, then angle toward Stumptown. I stop suddenly twice and turn to look behind me. Again, I think I hear something, but another frozen minute of standing perfectly still reveals nothing.

Just when I pass the hill and head for the stump, I sense movement off to my left. I spin in time to see the arm of a black jacket slip behind a tree. He's fifty feet from where I stand. No way I can make it to Stumptown. There's only one choice now—keep walking past the stump and hope he follows me. With my heart pounding in my ears, I walk past the stump toward another rise. For a second I remember feeling this same way in almost this same spot when Ty and I believed Benny was going to shoot us in the back. When I'm a hundred feet beyond the stump, I risk a glance over my shoulder to see if he's following me. A man in a black coat and black knit hat is standing fifteen feet from the stump, looking at the ground. He's smaller than Tirk, and he's holding a gun. He bends down, picks up something small and white. It's the iPhone. *Shit!* He looks in the general direction of the stump. Then he looks at me, raises his gun, and smiles.

LUSTER, OR.

TWO MONTHS AGO

55

Cory divided Operation Rome Burning into three phases. Phase One was planning and preparation. Phase Two was the escape. Phase Three was living off the grid. Phase One had three components: gear and supplies, technology and tactics, strength and stamina. Between himself and Ty they scraped together $2,200. The first thing Cory did was reserve a ten-by-ten storage space and pay for three months in advance in cash. Then he listed all the things they needed to put in that storage room, and they started to buy their supplies a little bit a time, here and there. Never enough to catch the attention of a town with too many prying eyes. Their goal was to stay off the radar before they went off the grid.

On the technology and tactics front, Cory needed an insurance plan in case the video wasn't convincing enough. He remembered seeing Kayla exit Harvey's office on the day they arrived, so he thought she might have a key, and she did. He borrowed it, made a copy, and snuck in while Harvey was out of town. Ty wanted to mess with some of the fly rods, maybe break one or two, just tiny little cracks, but Cory nixed that idea. He planted two motion-activated mini spy cam video recorders, one on the bookshelf and the other in the planter behind Harvey's desk. Harvey's secret phone that he used late at night was an old Samsung with the pattern-style password. Between the two cameras Cory was able to analyze Harvey's hand motion frame by frame and determine the pattern. It took him all of five tries, but he figured it out—the pattern was a "hook," of course. Then Cory hacked his phone and cloned it by using a SIM duplicator. He built a Squarespace website, uploaded the video plus the hacked texts and image files. He subscribed to MailChimp and scheduled an email blast for noon on October 20. The blast contained a letter of introduction and a website link for three media outlets: the local NBC news affiliate in Luster, the *Oregonian*, and CNN. He cropped out all of Kayla except her hand. That was the best he could do to protect her identity. He hoped that catching Harvey in a car with another woman, plus the pictures Harvey had on his phone, would be enough to sink him. Anticipating that this operation would have collateral damage, one of them being Kayla's mother's medical expenses, Cory created a GoFundMe campaign that would launch the day they left. The goal was $250,000.

The gear and supplies started to accumulate in the storage room. They bought their backpacks on different weeks, Cory's at Walmart, Ty's at Mel's Outdoor Store. The following month they bought a first aid kit, cook stove, sleeping bags, and foam pads. Ty insisted on buying a Petzl ice tool. He thought they were totally badass and might come in handy since Cory, despite Ty's determined efforts, would not allow them to acquire a gun. Too much risk, not enough reward. For food, they bought small amounts of canned and dried foods at separate grocery stores, and kept buying until they had enough to fill the back of the Volvo. By the time

September rolled around, Cory calculated they had enough food to last them through the winter, particularly if Cory caught fish in Tanum Creek and Ty managed to kill a deer with a spear, which was all he talked about for a solid month.

Cory also started running. At first he couldn't run to the end of the driveway and back. He slowly increased his distance to a quarter mile, a half mile; then, as his weight continued to drop, he added running trails to increase agility and strength. He sold his PlayStation on Craigslist, deleted his Battlenet account, swore off hamburgers, pizza, soda, and even Chloe's double-chocolate fudge brownies. Meanwhile he discovered interesting ways to cook kale, spinach, and lentils. Rebecca was the first to comment on his weight loss and asked him, "Who's the special guy...I mean, girl...I mean, *whatever?*" Charlene noticed the following week and insisted on a shopping spree because all his clothes were saggy. She wouldn't take no for an answer. They spent a fun afternoon together and hit all the expensive spots, purchasing clothes that were way outside Cory's budget. She loved his new look, and declared at lunch over their salads that his inner heartthrob was showing. Cory felt guilty about allowing her to spend all that money on clothes he would never wear—until she explained that it was Harvey's money. Then he tried on and liked everything she hung over the dressing room door, secretly whispering, *"Thank you, asshole,"* every time Harvey's credit card flashed.

Ty did his part too, by avoiding prolonged exposure to Harvey. Ten minutes at dinner was about all he could handle. He signed up for summer two-a-day workouts as if he intended to play football in the fall. Coach told him it looked like he would be a starting DB, as long as he kept his bad ankle taped, and didn't let that mean streak of his get in the way of his instincts and talent. Ty didn't get into any fights until their second home game on October 11. He was chop-blocked by an offensive tackle on the side with his weak ankle. That hit resulted in a thirty-yard touchdown reception. On their next possession Ty upended the guy in front of the opposing team's bench, even though the play had already been whistled dead. Ty was ejected from the game. He limped off the field, then turned in his uniform that night.

On the morning of October 17, seventy-two hours before Operation Rome Burning entered Phase Two, Cory was stretching in the driveway for his morning run. Harvey walked out the door dressed in his running tights.

"Trail or road?" he asked.

"Trail," Cory said.

"Perfect. Let's go."

Cory hesitated. Harvey was usually done with his run by now. Cory had never run with Harvey, and he was pretty sure he didn't want to start now. On the one hand, he was leaving in three days, so why not? On the other hand, he was leaving in three days, so why risk it?

"What's wrong?" Harvey said. "Afraid you can't keep up with a forty-eight-year-old retired judge with a pacemaker?"

"No. I have a class in an hour and I can't afford to be waiting around for you."

Harvey grinned. "Well, I know you know CPR, so I'm in good hands."

They ran to the end of the driveway and turned right onto a

well-worn path through the trees. It was wide enough for two side-by-side runners, but not by much. Cory fell in behind Harvey, who waved his arm and said, "Get up here with me."

Cory picked up his pace and matched Harvey, stride for stride.

Harvey asked, "How much weight have you lost?"

"Thirty pounds."

"When did you start?"

Cory thought he should be careful here. Vague was better than specific. "Mid-July."

"Ten pounds a month. That's impressive."

Cory concentrated on the path. Now would not be a good time to sprain a knee.

Harvey said, "Justin told me you sold your PlayStation."

"Yeah."

They rounded a short bend, then followed the trail down into a gully. This was where it followed a dried-up creek and got tricky with lots of rocks.

Harvey said, "No more late-night gaming?"

"There are better ways to use my time."

The path climbed out of the gully, angled steeply up to a ridge with a split-rail fence at the top that marked the neighbor's property line. It was hard work and Cory's lungs were burning, but this part was his payoff. The neighbors raised llamas, and when they were in the pasture he would stop and talk to them. They always seemed interested in what he had to say. They were out this morning, and his favorite, the white one with the black ear, was waiting for him by the fence. But Harvey pressed on with his questions. Cory preferred the llama.

Harvey said, "Three months ago this activity would've killed you."

"*Thinking* about this activity would have killed me."

The path swung away from the fence, took a short hundred-foot pitch down to the road. Cory was relieved to be off the dirt and onto solid pavement. From here it was less than a quarter mile to the driveway.

Harvey accelerated. He looked over his shoulder, saw that Cory was struggling.

"Keep up," he said. "Always finish strong."

Cory stayed with him, but when they reached the driveway he nearly collapsed. He bent over, gasped for breath. It felt like his lungs had shrunk to the size of walnuts. Harvey stretched beside him, waited for him to recover. When Cory could breathe again they walked up the driveway toward the house.

Harvey said, "You think I haven't noticed, but I have."

"Noticed what?"

"You're different."

"Different how?"

"Ty's basically the same. But you were drifting. Now you seem more . . . directed."

Cory focused on the door. Twenty more steps.

Harvey said, "In my experience, people don't change unless there's a reason. What's your reason?"

Not what. Who.

"I was tired of being overweight." Then, "Actually I wasn't tired of *being overweight*. I was tired of people *seeing* me as fat."

Harvey laughed. "After thirty years of fishing, I know when I'm playing the fish, and when the fish is playing me."

Cory didn't know how to respond, so he didn't.

Ten feet from the porch, Harvey stopped and said, "It occurs to me that I asked all the questions. Do you have any for me?"

Cory thought for a moment. Yeah, there was one. He decided what the hell.

"Why did you do it?"

Harvey looked at him. In that instant Cory saw it there, the wolf, in those eyes behind the gray. He wondered if that's what Kayla saw when she was in the car with him.

Harvey said, "Do what?"

"Be foster parents."

The gray eyes softened from hardened steel to liquid mercury. The wolf faded. "Fostering was Charlene's idea. She wanted to do something positive with the good fortune we have. She thought it set a good example for the kids, to help the less fortunate and welcome them into our family. I thought the idea had merit and flew it past Lester. He thought the optics were good."

The optics were good? So it was political. "But why us?"

"That's a little more complicated." Harvey put his arm around Cory's shoulder, whispered in his ear. "I knew your father."

His words stopped Cory cold.

Harvey smiled. "I was filling in for a judge in Jefferson County for a month. While I was there a man was brought up on possession charges for a small amount of cocaine. During the arraignment an attractive woman walked into my courtroom with one of those strollers for twins. I have a vivid image of her in my mind because she sat down, exposed a breast, and started feeding her babies. In my courtroom! Unfortunately for her, she was married to one Benjamin Bic. I lectured him on the evils of drugs, that he had two infant sons and a wife. It was all standard stuff. Since it was a Class C felony and he was a nonviolent first-time offender, in exchange for a guilty plea I sentenced him to three months in a drug treatment facility and mandatory drug testing for one year. When I saw the Bic name come up as twin siblings looking for a foster care family, I had to say yes. If not for your mother and her brazen stunt, I would have written your father off as another loser destined for a lifetime of incarceration, sent him to jail, and forgotten the name completely."

Cory wondered how differently life would have turned out for those twins if their mother had fed them in the hall instead of the courtroom that day. "So the reason we're here is my mother's boobs?"

"That may answer your question, but it doesn't answer mine."

"What is your question?"

Harvey smiled and opened the door. "What I want to know is, why are you *still* here?"

56

Tweaker Teeth says, "Where is she?"

I could run but I won't get far. If he kills me then I can't help Astrid. She's dying twenty feet away from where he is now. She won't make it out of here without me. So I stand there while Tweaker Teeth points the gun at me, hoping he needs me alive more than he needs me dead. I say, "She took off."

"Yeah? Then why're you still here?"

"Looking for my phone."

"That's two lies you told me. Wanna try for strike three? But before you answer you need to know that I am not in the fuckin' mood."

I say nothing. His right eye is nearly swollen shut. It could be the car wreck. *Or,* I think as my stomach clenches, *it could be Ty.*

He says, "If she's gone then why two water bottles?"

This is an easy one thanks to the first aid class. "I'm a diabetic. I need a lot of water."

Tweaker Teeth shakes his head. I don't think that answer works for him. He turns the gun sideways a little. "Right. And I'm a runway model. You know what I think?"

I shake my head.

"Benny talked a lot when he was high. An' he was one of the highest flyers that ever lived. One night he went on and on about a magic stump in the woods that was gonna solve all his problems. Meanwhile I got Tirk on my ass sayin' that Benny skimmed at least two hundred grand from the business. So I'm thinking: Here I am in the woods with one of the Bic boys and guess where I find his phone? Not ten feet from a stump in the fuckin' woods. So I'll give you one more chance to speak the truth. Don't be stupid like your brother. Where'd he hide it?"

What did he do to Ty? I have to swallow that thought for now. He wants the money. I focus on that. "Benny showed us a map once, but it burned in the fire. It was thirty feet from a stump buried in garbage bags next to a big boulder." I point to a boulder. "I'm pretty sure that's where the money is."

"How do you know this is the right stump?"

"He took us up here once. He told us about an elk he shot and followed the blood trail to this spot. We figured this had to be the place."

Tweaker Teeth looks at the stump. Takes a beat. Then he closes the distance between us and walks behind me. "I think you're full of shit." He presses the gun into the center of my back, nudges me toward the stump. "Time to start digging."

This can't happen. My mind races for an answer. "He called it Coyote Rock."

"What?"

"He killed a coyote and used it to mark the spot."

"There's a dead coyote behind that rock?"

"Yes."

"If you're lying, then this is over here and now."

I lead him to the opposite side of the boulder.

He looks down and says, "Looks like we got us a treasure hunt."

57

The Motts left for church just like they did every Sunday. Cory and Ty went with them occasionally, but not recently, and especially not today. As soon as they turned out of the driveway, Phase Two was launched. They made their beds, put their clothes in the laundry hamper. Everything they needed to wear on this trip was already in their backpacks in the storage room, loaded and ready to go. Cory grabbed the thank-you cards he and Ty had written to Charlene and the kids, then took one last look around to make sure they didn't miss anything while Ty gave Pavlov a goodbye belly rub. They left the ski lodge with a full tank of gas at 9:33 a.m., three minutes behind schedule.

The next stop was the Drip 'n' Sip, where Cory accessed the Wi-Fi with his laptop. He made sure all the files were uploaded, the MailChimp email blast was still scheduled, the GoFundMe campaign was ready to launch, and the website was functional. There were zero visitors on the counter. That would change starting at noon tomorrow. When he finished, Cory walked behind the store to the dumpster, made sure no one was looking, then pulled the hard drive and tossed the laptop in with the garbage.

Meanwhile Ty walked down to the mailbox on the corner and slipped in the thank-you cards. They would be delivered on Tuesday or Wednesday, latest. Cory and Ty met up at the Volvo and left for the next stop, the storage rental facility. They loaded up the back of the Volvo with the food and camping gear, then closed the door, locked it, and left.

Cory checked his phone. 10:05 a.m. Five minutes late.

Their last stop before departing Luster was the gazebo. Ty parked the Volvo in front of a big white boulder with the inscription: PARK FACILITIES MAINTAINED THANKS TO GENEROUS DONATIONS BY MOTT ENTERPRISES, INC. Ty leaned back against the Volvo and watched his brother walk out to the gazebo and tape an envelope under the bench. An email would arrive in Kayla's in-box tomorrow and tell her where to look. Then Cory walked to the duck pond and tossed in the hard drive. There was a couple walking their dog that saw him do it. He didn't care.

On the way back to the Volvo, Cory felt so light his feet barely touched the ground. He hadn't felt this free since…since… basically his entire life. He walked up to Ty, they hugged, then separated.

Ty said, "How are you doing?"

"Good. Real good."

Cory checked his phone. 10:17. He wanted to be leaving Luster city limits at 10:15. They were behind, but still inside the margin of error. He probably should've just drilled the hard drive and not bothered with the symbolism of tossing it in the pond, which was also built and paid for by Harvey. But the envelope, that he absolutely had to do. It was worth the time, whatever it cost. Cory said, "Let's shut down the phones."

They turned off location services, turned off the phones, then placed them in a foil-lined cooler. Cory didn't want the phones pinging any cell towers on the way there. Once they reached their destination, around eight tonight, it wouldn't be a problem. He checked the coverages last night. There wasn't a cell tower within fifty miles of where they were going.

Per the plan, Cory would drive the first three-hour leg; then Ty would drive the mountain roads at night. Just as they opened their doors, they heard a horn, then a loud screeching of tires. Tony's Jeep swung into the lot and parked directly behind them. They couldn't back out. They couldn't drive forward.

He climbed out of the Jeep. "Hey, guys. What's up?"

Ty said, "Move your car. We have places to go."

Tony walked to the Volvo and peered through the windows.

Cory said, "Why are you here?"

Tony returned to the Jeep, leaned back against the driver's door like he had nothing better to do, frowned, and scratched his head. "So Harvey called from church. He never calls from church. A Rotary pal just told him that you rented a storage space for three months, and it expires tomorrow. He asked me to find you and call the second I make contact. I was on my way to the house, and guess who I spot at the park? In a Volvo loaded with groceries and a freaking ice ax. So now it's my turn." Tony popped a stick of gum in his mouth. "Why are you here?"

"Just let us go," Cory said, acutely aware that they were now outside the margin of error. "We know what we're doing."

"Really? So this plan of yours includes car theft? Because I'm pretty sure Harvey didn't approve whatever adventure you're planning."

Ty took a menacing step toward Tony. Cory grabbed his arm. Ty shook it off.

Tony said, "I was going to let you explain, but on second thought, I did promise Harvey I would call the second I make contact." He tapped his phone while keeping a wary eye on Ty. Tony held the phone to his ear. "I'm at the park. Call me." Then, to the boys, "You've got about sixty seconds. Speak."

Cory wasn't sure what he'd say, or if he'd find the voice to say it. All he knew was that he'd buried his emotions deep, under layers that piled up year after year. Down where light died and bones turned to ash. But he felt it stirring, the hurt and disappointment rising up and then it was there, ready to explode from his broken soul and it was all he could do to stop from screaming through the pain. He said through clenched teeth, "We're tired of all the lies and bullshit."

"What lies and bullshit?"

"These people we're supposed to look up to and respect. We're supposed to trust them. Believe in them. Be like them. And then they feed us more lies and bullshit. We're done, Tony. Let us go."

"What people? Give me specifics."

"We know about you and Harvey and the secret cars."

After a beat, "What cars?"

"I followed you in the Audi TT to a house in Hillview Heights. You switched cars with Harvey. Then I followed Harvey."

Tony stared.

Cory felt tears coming. This time, he held them back. "Do you know who he was meeting?"

"No."

"You never asked?"

"No."

"Why not?"

"He...he looked the other way for me. I looked the other way for him."

"Big mistake." Cory looked at Ty. Ty nodded. "He was meeting Kayla."

Tony shook his head. "No. No, you're wrong. He said he was meeting an old friend from high school."

Ty snorted. "We have video, dude. It's over."

Tony looked at Ty, then Cory.

Cory said, "You let it happen. You're supposed to be protecting kids from predators like him."

"I didn't..." Tony closed his eyes and took several deep breaths, his chin tucked into his chest.

"We're checking out of the ski lodge. And we're taking Harvey's car. But we're leaving a little something behind. It probably won't go over very well. Harvey isn't a fan of surprises."

Tony head snapped up, his eyes wide in alarm. "What did you do?"

"You'll find out. Tomorrow."

Tony's phone rang.

Ty said, "Leave it."

Tony muttered, "Sorry, guys. I gotta do this." He took a breath, tapped the face, pressed the phone to his ear. "Hey. I'm still at the park.... Yeah, I found them." He listened, then with his eyes on Cory and Ty, "No, it's all good. Cory's at the Drip 'n' Sip. He said Ty's at the gym.... I don't know why they aren't answering the phones.... Yeah, you can relax. They're okay.... You're welcome. Sure, I'll stop by for lunch. We need to talk." Tony ended the call, pocketed his phone. Ty started to speak. Tony held up his hand. "Not a word." Then to Cory, "You sure about this? Car theft is a big deal. He won't let it rest."

"I don't care."

"Wherever you're going, I hope it's better than here. And for what it's worth, I'm sorry. I let you down. I let Kayla down. You all deserved better." Tony got into his Jeep. He started the engine, rolled down his window. "You may think you're off the hook with the judge, but you're not. Catch and release, guys. That's what he does." Tony drove away.

They climbed into the Volvo. Cory wasn't sure he could drive, wasn't sure his stomach would settle. But it did the second he saw the WELCOME TO LUSTER sign shrink to a dot in his rearview mirror.

Ty said, "You okay?"

"Absolutely."

"Then it's you an' me, dude." Ty grinned, pushed play on the CD player and cranked up the volume. With the Mountain Goats singing their getaway song, "Palmcorder Yajna," he screamed over the music, "Let's go live like robbers and kings!"

Cory accelerated to fifty-five, but not a mile more. He calculated the rate/time/distance to their destination and figured as long as there were no more delays, they'd be all right. The last thing he wanted to do is give the karma gods one more reason to mess with what was turning out to be a pretty awesome day.

58

Tweaker Teeth hands me the ice ax, then stands behind me. I stare at the spike end. There's dried blood. *Ty's blood.* He says, "Like I told you, your brother got stupid. Start digging."

I sink the blade into the rotting carcass and drag it a few feet away. Then I pick a spot next to the boulder and slam the blade into the soft dirt, imagining it's Tweaker Teeth's skull. As I pry loose the first clump of dirt I say, "Did my brother do that to your eye?"

"He landed a couple solid hits. But I jabbed him good in the shoulder. That took him down a few notches. I hit him again and he fell into the canyon. It was a fifty-foot drop at least. The water sounded like a runaway train. Ty's a good fighter, but he sure as hell can't fly."

I take a quick glance over my shoulder. He's about twelve feet away, leaning back against a tree, his gun pointed at my back.

He says, "You turn around again an' I'll put a bullet in your head."

I keep digging, thinking that if each blow moves me backward a few inches at a time I may get close enough for one desperate swing before he shoots me.

He says, "She tell you anything about our operation?"

"She didn't talk."

Silence. Then: "That was definitely a problem."

"So tell me about your operation."

"What would you like to know?"

His tone is friendly, like we're chatting over coffee. Before today I'll bet he hasn't said ten words to me. *He's planning something.* "How did Benny get involved?" I slam the blade down. Back up another inch.

"It was your old man's idea. At least the warehouse part."

"How's that?"

"The meth market was getting flooded with dealers, any yahoo with a beaker and Bunsen burner was setting up shop, cutting into our profit margins. Tirk decided it was time to whatcha call it? Di-versify. So a pimp at the titty bar told him the sex trafficking business did something like a hundred billion a year and he had buyers lined up in Mexico and LA. Tirk's eyes lit up like fireworks on the Fourth of Ju-ly!"

"So where does Benny come in?" I back up another inch.

"We needed a place to store the inventory. Someplace without nosy neighbors because this inventory had a tendency to be a little loud, you know what I'm sayin?" Cory hacked his way through a root. "Your old man found a cabin up here way the fuck off the beaten path and Tirk bought it with a suitcase fulla cash. We acquired our first asset and checked her into the warehouse. Sold her three days later to the buyer from Mex-i-co an' we were off to the races! Hey, you better dig a little deeper or we'll never find this damn treasure." He pauses. I dig down into a clump of wet dirt, and wonder if this is it. This is when he pulls the trigger. But he keeps talking. "So like, Benny and I took turns watching the inventory while Tirk handled the business side. I liked it up here with all the trees an' owls an' shit, but it got lonely. Benny shot coyotes. I found other ways to occupy my time. Had to sample the inventory, make sure it was trained properly." He laughs behind me. "That job had a very good benefits package, you know what I'm sayin'?"

Down goes the blade. I back up another inch. Resist the urge to look over my shoulder. I ask, "Where's Tirk?"

"We had a falling-out with the buyer from Mexico. Seems he wasn't placing the proper value on our commodity. That's when Tirk had me reach out to Ty with a business opportunity. When your dipshit brother turned him down, I knew Tirk was ready to go in a different direction."

I freeze midblow. "Ty turned what down?"

"He didn't tell you about that?"

"No."

"You just keep digging. Find that buried treasure. I'll fill in the blanks."

It takes a huge effort on my part not to look at Stumptown, even for a second. I try not to think about Astrid and what she must be going through. Hopefully she's sleeping. I focus on the hole—a hole that's starting to get disturbingly big.

I back up another inch.

He says, "After the Benny barbecue you guys disappeared for a bit. Then Ty's name shows up on the web. Turns out he can throw a decent fastball. I believe he was called the Steamer, or some shit like that. We traced you to Luster, took a little road trip. Tirk liked the setup you had. That was a big fucking upgrade, I tell you what! A mansion in the woods, an aer-o-plane, a judge with political aspirations. An' best of all, he had a little girl—Chelsea, I believe? Cute as a damn button!"

I clench my teeth. "Chloe."

"Right. Chloe. Anyway, Tirk figured with the kind of bank Harvey was pulling in, she'd be worth a mil, maybe a mil-five. We had the infrastructure in place. So he thought why not shake the ransom tree, see if it bears fruit? I mean, it had to be easier than dealing with the psycho machete man from Meh-he-co, right?"

I bite my tongue so hard I taste blood.

He says, "But that beast-dog was a problem. Like something out of the fucking Stone Age. We needed someone on the inside. Tirk told Ty if he helped line that up, then Benny's debt would be forgiven an' he'd tear up the shit we had on him. But if he didn't join the team, then he'd come after both of you—and still snatch the girl. We thought he was on board, then something happened and he told Tirk to go fuck hisself."

"When was that?"

"Late spring. Tirk sent me there to have a personal chat with Ty, make sure he was still on our team. But that hot register girl at the burger place with the hooties out to here? She said you guys were on a fishing trip." I slam the blade so hard it sinks down to the shaft. Ty had this going on and he never told me. *How could he do that?*

Tweaker Teeth says, "A couple weeks after that Ty called and told Tirk the deal was off, except not in those same words. So we were about to put our own plans in motion and settle up with you guys—an' of course a deer steps in the road at the wrong damn time. Imagine my surprise when I find Ty in that Volvo! Talk about a mind fuck. That's one for the record books! Then you idiots run off with my payday, and whooee! We're off to the races all over again!"

"Your payday? What about Tirk?" The cut on my hand from the accident has reopened. My blood is slicking the shaft, making it hard to dig. That's okay. *This can't go on much longer.* At some point he's going to stop talking. I back up another inch.

"I had a little complication with one of the guests. She tried to check out early, which is strictly against hotel policy. That reduced our inventory by fifty percent. Then me an' Tirk had differing opinions on how to deal with—what's her name? I don't recall."

"Her—" I stop myself just in time. "Her voice doesn't work. She didn't say."

He laughs. "April, Ashton, something like that. I'm so bad with names. Anyway, Tirk put her in the trunk and I was pretty sure at that point it was either him or me. I got proactive on his ass."

I remember Astrid telling me about the gunshots. "You killed him?"

"More or less. Actually more *than* less."

I can't believe he's telling me everything. There has to be a reason. I slam the blade down. It clangs against a rock.

He says, "That don't sound like treasure to me."

"It's here somewhere." I've moved back almost five feet. That might be close enough.

He says, "How tall are you?"

His tone is different, like our conversation is about to end. It takes all my will not to turn around. "I'm six feet."

"Good. Then I'd say that hole is big enough."

I stop digging. Sweat drips from my forehead, runs into my eyes.

He says, "Did you actually think I believed your horseshit story about the money being behind this rock? You don't get to be the last man standing by being stupid." His voice is close. I grip the shaft of the ice ax, hope that it doesn't slip. He hisses, "I know the money's in the stump."

I raise the ice ax, start my spin. A blinding pain expands into the back of my head. It staggers me. I drop to my knees, then the ground. The ice ax slips from my hand. He kicks me in the ribs twice. Then the side of my head. My mouth is full of dirt. I can't breathe. I try to get up to my knees. *Where is the ice ax? Maybe if I can—*

He kicks me again. Ribs break. I fall flat. Pain explodes in my chest.

I hear a click.

I wait for the bullet. Think about Astrid, hope she isn't looking out the porthole. A few seconds pass. He says, "I want you to see this. Me, little ol' Tweaker Teeth as you assholes call me, walkin' off with your daddy's treasure. Then I'll be back for you. An' don't worry. I won't let this hole go to waste."

Footsteps walking away.

I can't draw a decent breath. I rise to my knees. Tweaker Teeth is at the stump. He bends down, peers inside. "Well, look what we have here! A little cave!" His head disappears inside. I crawl forward. Blood streams from my face. I try to stand but the pain sends me down. A voice from inside says, "Time's up, buttercup."

Then a gunshot.

And silence.

I struggle to my feet, wait for the wave of pain, and move past it. Ten agonizing steps and I'm at the door to Stumptown. I fall to my knees. There's a soft sound inside. A familiar sound.

Is that crying?

I pull back the flap, peer into the flickering light of a single candle.

Astrid is pointing a handgun at the door. She sees me and lowers it.

Tweaker Teeth is facedown, the back of his head an open mess. Next to him is the *Playboy* magazine. His blood pools on the cover.

The gun slides from Astrid's fingers. I recognize the handle. Pearl and bronze.

Outside I hear the barking of dogs. *Are they looking for us?*

I ask, "Are you okay?"

She nods.

"Where was the gun?"

She points to the old wooden chest.

"In there?"

She nods. Then in a whisper, "Marilyn was hiding it."

59

C ory stood next to his brother on a makeshift stage in the cavernous lobby of the Marriott in downtown Portland. He was able to stand on his own, although not for long. The bandages around his ribs made it difficult for him to be upright and breathe at the same time. He hoped this press conference would be shorter than the five minutes promised to them. Being up here was easier for Ty. He was in a wheelchair and would be until the metal pins in his shattered right femur and hip could start to bear weight. The current estimate was four to six weeks. Both boys looked like they had survived a bomb blast. Cory's upper lip was split down the middle and held together with stitches. His right eye still had some swelling nine days after the impact from a boot. Ty had butterfly bandages on his forehead, cheek, and chin, but at least he could smile without pain, and not eat his food through a straw. They appeared uncomfortable in their new clothes and fresh haircuts courtesy of the hotel salon.

To Cory's right was a podium with a microphone. Assembled in front of them were reporters from various media outlets ranging from local and statewide TV and news channels, to heavy lifters like CNN, Fox, the *New York Times*, and the BBC. Behind them was a theater-size screen with a slideshow of images that displayed where the Volvo was found, a topo map of the spot where Ty directed the SWAT team, breathtaking aerial shots of Tanum Creek Canyon, the sixty-foot waterfall where Ty fell, and the pool with the swing tree where he was found by a fly-fisherman, floating under the Tanum Creek Bridge.

Cory searched the crowd for the one face he wanted to see. She wasn't there yet, but had promised him yesterday that she wouldn't miss it for the world. At eleven o'clock on the nose, a heavyset man in a blue suit, sweating under the lights, walked onto the stage and growled into the microphone:

"Good morning, everyone. Thank you for being here. I'm Detective William Ostrander with the Portland PD. Before we begin, I need to make it clear that these boys are still in the recovery stage of this ordeal. They will not be available for questions afterward, so don't even try. You can make arrangements to speak with them separately with their agent. Her contact information is on the press briefing you received. Also know that this is an ongoing investigation so the details I can share this morning are very limited. Now I will read a brief statement, then take questions.

"On October tenth at 11:07 p.m. local time Astrid Loftman was abducted in the parking garage at the Biskhoft Hotel in Seattle. Surveillance footage helped us trace the plates to a stolen vehicle found in Kirkland. That's where we suspect they switched vehicles to a silver Ford Taurus. It was found on October twenty-eighth in a ravine off a forest service road fifteen miles north of the Tanum

Creek Bridge. We had resources in the area when Ty made contact and told us where to go. The bloodhounds did the rest. Now for your questions."

Voices rang out again.

Ostrander pointed to a face in the crowd. "You with the green coat."

"How many girls were recovered from the cabin?"

"We found one girl inside who had been abducted from a shopping mall in Boise. Her name was Abigail Weston, sixteen. We also found a female Russian national with multiple stab wounds a short distance from the cabin. Her last known location was her uncle's home in Portland three months prior. One more question."

"Can Ty tell us how he got to the bridge?"

"I'm sorry, but as I stated earlier, there will be no—"

Ty coughed, motioned to Ostrander for the microphone. He gave it to him and muttered, "The shorter the better."

Ty said, "I jumped the bad guy. We had a scuffle. I fell off a cliff and landed on a rock. I crawled into the creek. A fishing guy found me under the bridge. That's pretty much all—"

Cory snagged the microphone from Ty. "My brother survived a twelve-mile death canyon with a shattered hip, a fractured leg, and a stab wound in his shoulder. He's a badass ninja warrior stud!" He and Ty bumped fists. The reporters laughed and snapped pictures.

Ostrander took the microphone and returned to the podium. "I'll take one more question; then the Loftmans would like to say a few words." There was a clamor of hands. Ostrander picked a woman standing next to a man holding a CNN camera.

"Why was Astrid in the trunk?"

Detective Ostrander glanced at another officer standing close but not on the stage. The officer nodded. Cory wondered if Astrid was watching this press conference from her room. He'd visited her in the hospital two days ago and she'd been mostly out of it.

"Ransom negotiations had broken down. Based on information provided by the victims, we suspect there was a disagreement between the captors. They may have been moving her to a new location, or there may have been a more... sinister intent. We can only speculate since both of the perpetrators are deceased. That's all the questions now. I'm turning this over to Mr. and Mrs. Loftman."

Cory felt Ty's hand brush his pant leg. He glanced down. Ty flashed a smile. *Here comes the good part.* Cory returned his gaze to the audience. His search for her face came up empty. *Maybe she won't make it after all.*

Detective Ostrander was replaced by a man and a woman. They shook hands with Cory and Ty. Cory had already met Astrid's father. He was tall, thin, and very formal. But her mother—Cory saw Astrid's resemblance right away. And that's why he remembered her. He had seen her on the cover of one of Chloe's fashion magazines. She was striking with wavy blond hair, the same high cheekbones, intense brown eyes, and a perfect, wide smile. Mr. Loftman stepped up to the microphone and spoke with the same accent that Cory heard whispered inside the confines of Stumptown.

"Good morning. I am Reginald Loftman, and this is my wife, Deanna. I shall make this brief because I promised Cory and Ty that we would keep it to five minutes. We want to personally thank them for their bravery and self-sacrifice. Thanks to their efforts our lovely daughter, Astrid, was returned to us. She is in the hospital now and wishes she could be here. The doctors assure us that the infection is under control. She will recover fully and can return home as early as next week. I will take one question, then turn the microphone over to Deanna."

A man in the crowd shouted, "Why was Astrid in Seattle and why was she in the parking garage at that time?"

"Astrid was in Seattle for her two-year checkup at a speech therapy clinic specializing in children suffering from trauma-induced mutism. The trauma resulted from a visit with her grandmother in Nice, France. She saw her run over by a truck and killed during the terrorist attack. Astrid stopped talking three days later. After a year of consulting with local therapists, we sent her to a clinic in Seattle and they helped. She…" Cory heard Reginald's voice breaking, and he felt a tightening of his own throat. "Astrid was back to normal when she returned with her mother for a final checkup. She forgot the charger for her phone and went down to the car to retrieve it. They must have been waiting for her." He wiped his eyes, then changed places with his wife.

Deanna said, "I get the easy part. It is my great honor to give these checks to Cory and Ty for their share of the reward."

She handed them each an envelope. They already knew the amount. It exceeded Harvey's milestone three by a factor of ten. Cory glanced at Ty's face. His smile was so wide he was afraid it might pop the stitches on his face. Through the corner of his eye he saw someone walk through the lobby door. It was her. And he was happy to see that she wasn't alone. He smiled despite the pain.

Cory and Ty held up the checks while the cameras clicked and the flashes flashed. Some people shouted questions, but Detective Ostrander stepped in and shut it down. The Loftmans thanked them again and said they had an open invitation to the UK anytime. Deanna hugged them and said she owed them a debt she could never repay. As Ty began to speak to them, Cory limped off the stage and made his way through the last of the reporters to where Stellah stood waiting with Kayla. Stellah threatened to give him a big Stellah hug, but Cory asked for a rain check. She laughed and said, "Now with money like that, I expect to see a fine dining establishment opening with your name over the door. I thought up one myself, Cory's Kitchen. What do you think?"

Cory said, "I was thinking more along the lines of an ice-cream parlor. I'd call it Bic's Licks."

Stellah waved her hand. "You'd better not. You're too good a cook to be selling some damn ice cream. Although I do like ice cream." Then she smiled at Cory and Kayla. "Well, I see you two have some catching up to do. I'm gonna visit that coffee cart. See if there's anything worth my dime."

They watched her bulldoze through the crowd. Then Cory said, "I didn't think I'd see you again."

"That feeling was mutual."

"What happened?"

"I got your email, then read the letter you stuck under the bench in the gazebo."

"I almost didn't leave it."

"I'm glad you did. I made a solemn vow to say your name in vain every day for the rest of my life. That letter changed everything."

Cory took a moment to consider the hidden truth of those words.

If he hadn't detoured to hide the letter, then Tony wouldn't have trapped them at the park. If not for that twenty-minute delay, Tweaker Teeth would have hit the deer after they passed. Astrid would be dead and this press conference would never have happened. As Benny would say, *Fate'll screw you like a pine board unless you screw it first*. Cory asked Kayla, "What was your favorite part?"

"Where you wrote that you hoped that when this is all over I'll be able to find my balance again."

"And . . . ?"

"I'm not ready for the beam yet, but the future looks good."

Cory smiled. Her answer was more than he deserved to hope for. "How are things in Luster Land?"

"The future senator decided that being a senator wasn't in his future."

"Karmic forces at play?"

"Ignore them at your peril."

"What about Charlene?"

"She hired a divorce attorney out of Bend, formerly from LA. Rebecca told me that she was the lawyer for Steven Spielberg's third wife. Harvey will be lucky to keep his pacemaker."

"Ouch. Well, I'm happy for Charlene." He was sad for Chloe and Justin, but they'd be better off in the end. "And how are you?"

"For a while I was feeling worse than your face looks."

Cory took the hit and expected more.

"That video did a lot of damage. But I thank you for keeping me out of it."

"It had to stop."

After a beat, she said, "I know."

"I saw the GoFundMe campaign just passed one hundred and thirty thousand dollars."

"That was pretty slick, Cory Bic." She steps a little closer, looks him in the eyes. "So now that this is all behind you, do you still wake up scared every day? You've got five seconds."

He only needed two. "No. Aside from the broken ribs, I wake up feeling pretty darn good."

Ty rolled up to them, grinned wide at Kayla. "Hey, Cor. Our ride's here. Can you believe it's a freakin' limo!"

They laughed. Cory's eyes watered. The stitches in his lip didn't like to be stretched.

Kayla gave Cory a careful hug, kissed him on the cheek. "Send me a text when you open your restaurant."

"So I can text you now?"

She flashed him a parting wink. "It's a brand-new day in Luster Land."

At last, Ty and Cory headed for the doors.

Ty said, "Does this restaurant of yours even have a name?"

Cory smiled at the inside joke. He had asked Benny the same question when he told them about the tow truck business. Cory responded with the same answer Benny gave them. "Yeah. It's a real classic." They exited the lobby. A tuxedoed driver opened the door to a shining black SUV limo. Cory said, "I was thinking of something catchy and fun, but with a dash of intrigue."

"Cory's Clam Shack?"

"Nah. How about Robbers and Kings?"

Ty laughed. It was big and loud and echoed against the concrete and glass. Cory helped him out of the wheelchair and into the leathery cavern. There was plenty of room for his leg. While the driver stowed Ty's wheelchair, Cory opened a small refrigerator built into the center console. He handed Ty a Mountain Dew and took a Diet Pepsi for himself. They popped the tops, then clanked their cans in a toast.

The driver sat behind the wheel, closed the door, and the engine purred to life. "Where to, gentlemen?"

Cory paused for a beat to savor this moment, then said, "Providence Medical Center. A girl with a broken arm wants us to sign her cast."

ACKNOWLEDGMENTS

While so many people contributed to the writing of this book, I want to thank the following friends and colleagues for their expertise and thoughtful comments: Dean Olin, Marti Carl, Ryan Vogt, Mike Pickett, Kevin Sergeant, Don Donais, Pat Ferrell, my wife, Teresa, and the best reader I know, my son Michael. I cannot overstate the importance of my talented editor, Hannah Allaman, whose patience, vision, and deep understanding of my characters helped me take this book to where it needed to go. And my profound appreciation for Doug Stewart and Chris George, who encourage me, beyond all reason, to keep writing.

In memoriam:
To Jared Peterson